The Prayers of Agnes Sparrow

Library of Congress Cataloging-in-Publication Data

Moccero, Joyce Magnin.
 The prayers of Agnes Sparrow / Joyce Magnin.
   p. cm.
 ISBN 978-1-4267-0164-1 (pbk. : alk. paper)
 I. Title.
 PS3601.L447P73 2009
 813'.6--dc22

                            2009014854

Printed in the United States of America
1 2 3 4 5 6 7 8 9 10 / 14 13 12 11 10 09

THE PRAYERS OF AGNES SPARROW

by

Joyce Magnin

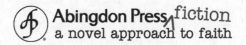

Abingdon Press fiction
a novel approach to faith

For my sister, Barbara

Acknowledgments

This book could not have been written without the love and support of:

Pam Halter, my dear friend who kept listening and reading from the very first word.

The Writeen Crue: Pam, Tim, Dawn, Candy, Dale, Rosemarie, Winnie, Floss, Brenda, and especially Nancy Rue, who got it where it needed to be.

Lisa Samson who helped me find the heart of the story.

Marlene Bagnull. She never let me quit.

Thank you also to my family for understanding when "Mommy is working!"

Thank you to my wonderful editor, Barbara Scott, who taught me much along the way.

A special thank you to Jean Shanahan and Phoebe Wagner who came through when I really needed them.

And last, but never least, thank you to my mom, Flossie, who showed me that life does not always have to be taken so seriously and that perfect pie is possible.

1

Even a blind squirrel finds a nut once in a while.
—*Ruth Knickerbocker*

If you get off the Pennsylvania Turnpike at the Jack Frost Ski Resort exit, turn left, and travel twenty-two and one quarter miles, you'll see a sign that reads: Bright's Pond, Home of the World's Largest Blueberry Pie.

While it is true that in 1961 Mabel Sewicky and the Society of Angelic Philanthropy, which did secret charitable acts, baked the biggest blueberry pie ever in Pennsylvania, most folks will tell you that the sign should read: Bright's Pond, Home of Agnes Sparrow.

October 12, 1965. That was the day my sister, Agnes Sparrow, made an incredible decision that changed history in our otherwise sleepy little mountain town and made her sign-worthy.

"I just can't do it anymore, Griselda. I just can't."

That's what Agnes said to me right before she flopped down on our red, velvet sofa. "It ain't worth it to go outside anymore. It's just too much trouble for you—" she took a deep breath and sighed it out "—and heartache for me."

Agnes's weight had tipped a half pound over six hundred, and she decided that getting around was too painful and too much of a town spectacle. After all, it generally took two strong men to help me get Agnes from our porch to my truck and then about fifteen minutes to get her as comfy as possible in the back with pillows and blankets. People often gathered to watch like the circus had come to town, including children who snickered and called her names like "pig" or "lard butt." Some taunted that if Agnes fell into the Grand Canyon she'd get stuck. It was devastating, although when I look back on it, I think the insults bothered me more than they did Agnes.

Her hips, which were wider than a refrigerator, spread out over the sofa leaving only enough room for Arthur, our marmalade cat, to snuggle next to her. "I think I'll stay right here inside for the remainder of the days God has set aside for me." She slumped back, closed her eyes, and then took a hard breath. It wiggled like Jell-O through her body. I held my breath for a second, afraid that Agnes's heart had given out since she looked so pale and sweaty.

But it didn't.

Agnes was always fat and always the subject of ridicule. But I never saw her get angry over it and I only saw her cry once—in church during Holy Communion.

She was fourteen. I was eleven. We always sat together, not because I wanted to sit with her, but because our father made us. He was usually somewhere else in the church fulfilling his elder's responsibilities while our mother helped in the nursery. She always volunteered for nursery duty. I think it was because my mother never really had a deep conviction about Jesus one way or the other. Sitting in the pews made her nervous and she hated the way Pastor Spahr would yell at us about our sins, which, if you asked me, my mother never committed and so she felt unduly criticized.

Getting saddled with "fat Agnes" every Sunday wasn't easy because it made me as much a target of ridicule as her. Ridicule by proximity. Agnes had to sit on a folding lawn chair in the aisle because she was too big to slip into the pew. And since she blocked the aisle we had to sit in the last row.

Our father served Communion, a duty he took much too seriously. The poor man looked like a walking cadaver in his dark suit, white shirt, and striped tie as he moved stiffly down the aisle passing the trays back and forth with the other serious men. But the look fit him, what with Daddy being the town's only funeral director and owner of the Sparrow Funeral Home where we lived.

On that day, the day Agnes cried, Daddy passed us the tray with his customary deadpan look. I took my piece of cracker and held it in my palm. Agnes took hers and we waited for the signal to eat, supposedly mulling over the joy of our salvation and our absolute unworthiness. Once the entire congregation, which wasn't large, had been served, Pastor Spahr took an unbroken cracker, held it out toward the congregation, and said, "Take. Eat, for this is my body broken for you." Then he snapped the cracker. I always winced at that part because it made me think about broken Jesus bones getting passed around on a silver platter.

I swallowed and glanced at Agnes. She was crying as she chewed the cracker—her fat, round face with the tiny mouth chewing and chewing while tears streamed down her heavy, pink cheeks, her eyes squinted shut as though she was trying to swallow a Ping-Pong ball. Even while the elders served the juice, she couldn't swallow the cracker for the tears. It was such an overwhelmingly sad sight that I couldn't finish the ritual myself and left my tiny cup of purple juice, full, on the pew. I ran out of the church and crouched behind a large boulder at the edge of the parking lot, jammed my finger down my throat and threw up the cracker I had just swallowed. I swore to Jesus right then and there that I would never let him or anyone hurt my sister again.

Which is probably why I took the whole Agnes Sparrow sign issue to heart. I knew if the town went through with their plan it would bring nothing but embarrassment to Agnes. I imagined multitudes pulling off the turnpike aimed for Jack Frost and winding up in Bright's Pond looking for her. They'd surely think it was her tremendous girth that made her a tourist attraction.

But it wasn't. It was the miracles.

At least that's what folks called them. All manner of amazements happened when Agnes took to her bed and started praying. It made everyone think Agnes had somehow opened a pipeline to heaven and because of that she deserved a sign— a sign that would only give people the wrong idea.

You see, when my sister prayed, things happened; but Agnes never counted any answer to prayer, yes or no, a miracle. "I just do what I do," she said, "and then it's up to the Almighty's discretion."

The so-called Bright's Pond miracles included three healings—an ulcer and two incidents of cancer—four incidents of lost objects being located miles from where they should have been, an occurrence of glass shattering, and one exorcism, although no one called it that because no one really believed Jack Cooper was possessed—simply crazy. Agnes prayed and he stopped running around town all naked and chasing dogs. Pastor Spahr hired him the next day as the church janitor. He did a good job keeping the church clean, except every once in a while someone reported seeing him howling at the moon. When questioned about it, Pastor Spahr said, "Yeah, but the toilets are clean."

Pastor Rankin Spahr was a solid preacher man. Strong, firm. He never wavered from his beliefs no matter how rotten he made you feel. He retired on August 1, 1968, at the ripe old age of eighty-eight and young Milton Speedwell took his place.

Milton and his wife, Darcy, were fresh from the big city, if you can call Scranton a big city. I suppose he was all of twenty-nine when he came to us. Darcy was a mite younger. She claimed to be twenty-five but if you saw her back then, you'd agree she was barely eighteen.

Milton eventually became enamored with Agnes just like the rest of the town and often sent people to her for prayer and counsel.

But it wasn't until 1972 when Studebaker Kowalski, the recipient of miracle number two—the cancer healing—that Agnes's notoriety took front seat to practically everything in town. Studebaker had a petition drawn up, citing all the miracles along with a dozen or more miscellaneous wonders that had occurred throughout the years.

"Heck, the Vatican only requires three miracles to make a saint," he said. "Agnes did seven. Count 'em, seven."

Just about everyone in town—except Agnes, Milton Speedwell, a cranky old curmudgeon named Eugene Shrapnel, and me—added their signatures to the petition making it the most-signed document ever in Bright's Pond. Studebaker planned to present it to Boris Lender, First Selectman, at the January town meeting.

Town meetings started at around 7:15 once Dot Handy arrived with her steno pad. She took the minutes in short-hand, typed them up at home on her IBM Selectric, punched three holes in the sheet of paper, and secured it in a large blue binder that she kept under lock and key like she was safe-keeping the secret formula for Pepsi Cola.

That evening I settled Agnes in for the night and made sure she had her TV remote, prayer book, and pens. You see, Agnes began writing down all of the town's requests when it became so overwhelming she started mixing up the prayers.

"It's all become prayer stew," she said. "I can't keep nothing straight. I was praying for Stella Hughes's gallbladder when all the time it was Nate Kincaid's gallbladder I should have asked a favor for."

Nate ended up with Stella's prize-winning pumpkin and had to have his gallbladder removed anyway. Stella had apparently entered the same contest as Nate and asked Agnes for God's blessing on her pumpkin. Stella forgave Agnes for the oversight, and Nate agreed to share the blue ribbon with her. But, as Agnes said, God blessed her blunder because Nate and Stella got married six months later. They've been raising prize-winning pumpkins ever since.

After the pumpkin debacle, Agnes wrote down all the requests in spiral notebooks. She color-coded the names and petitions, reserving black ink for the most severe cases, red for less dire but still serious needs (marriage troubles and minor illnesses like warts and bunions) and blue ink for the folks with smaller troubles like broken fuel pumps and ornery kids—that sort of thing.

"I got to get going now, Agnes," I told her a few minutes before seven. "The meeting's about to start and I don't want to be late."

"Could you fetch me a drink of juice and maybe a couple tuna sandwiches before you go? And how about a couple of those cherry Danishes left over from last Sunday?"

"I'll be late, Agnes, and you already had your dinner."

"It won't take but a minute, Griselda, please."

I spread tuna salad onto white bread and poured a glass of golden apple juice into a tall tumbler with strawberry vines.

I was standing at the kitchen sink rinsing my fingers when I heard rain start—hesitant at first. It was the kind of rain that started with large, heavy drops and only a hint of ice in them but would soon turn to all snow. Most of the time foul weather meant a smaller crowd for town meetings, but with the Agnes Sparrow sign debate on the agenda I doubted the weather could keep folks away.

"I better go," I said. "I want a seat in front on account of the sign situation."

"Phooey," Agnes said. "I told you I don't want a sign with my name on it. I don't want the glory."

"I know." I took a deep breath and blew it out. "I told you I'd take care of it."

Agnes took another bite of her sandwich and turned on the TV while I buttoned my coat and slipped into yellow galoshes. I was just about to step outside when Agnes spoke up. Her high voice made her sound like a little girl.

"The Lord just gave me an idea," she said, swallowing. "Tell that town council of ours that the sign should read, Bright's Pond. *Soli Deo Gloria*. That's Latin. It means—"

"I know what it means. I'll be back as soon as I can."

That was when all the trouble started. And I don't just mean over the silly sign. I thought the town's enthusiasm to advertise Agnes's prayers got something loosed in the heavens and trouble came to Bright's Pond after that—trouble no one could have ever imagined.

2

I always enjoyed the short walk to the town hall. The rain had turned to snow by the time I rounded Hector Street and laid a thin, white veneer on the pavement and streets. Dog prints dotted the walkways. Probably Ivy Slocum's mutt. That dog wandered the streets like a hobo begging for handouts and fathered more litters than Bayer had aspirin. I watched the snow come down in the glow of a street lamp, multisized flakes that fell at an angle. They had an otherworldly look and for a second I could have been on any planet watching it snow by the light of the moon. I can't tell you how many times I wished I could have left Bright's Pond to visit the sights and wonders I knew existed beyond the brown-purple-green mountains I sailed my dreams over every single day. A dog bark brought me back to earth.

Bright's Pond was pretty much your average small town. Most of the businesses were located on Stump Road, including a small drinking establishment called Personal's Pub. It was run by a man named Personal Best—that's right, Personal Best. He was the last of nine children born to Haddie and Zachary Best. Haddie had said, "When that boy popped out

I knew I just did my personal best. So that's what we named him." Down on Hector Street there was a movie theater called The Crown. Movies came late to Bright's Pond, so by the time we got them they had already been and went in the big towns. Cooper P. Stern ran the projector for years and years until he died—died right there, loading the second reel of *The Guns of Navarrone*. After that anybody who could figure out the machinery ran the movies.

The Bright's Pond Chapel of Faith and Grace, the town hall, and the library were all located on Filbert. I worked at the library even though I never went to college. I taught myself the Dewey Decimal System, which by the way, was not easy. But now you toss the name of any book my way and I can tell you what number it is and on which shelf you'd find it. I spent my days behind the circulation desk or hidden in the stacks replacing borrowed books. It was a good job that kept me busy for the most part. But to be honest, other than the school children and a few regulars, not many folks in town frequented the library. Sad thing. Every September I tried to get a rally of sorts going for books, trying my best to get people eager to read. But it mostly fell on deaf ears, and if I wrote out ten new library cards a year it was a bumper crop.

Anyway, the only business on Filbert Street was The Full Moon Café. Mabel Sewickey's son Zebulon owned it and was the chief cook and bottle washer, as they say. Cora Nebbish, a seventy-two-year-old sprite of a woman with platinum hair and petite features flitted around as waitress and hostess. She did a fine job. She kept all the orders straight and still collected pinches from the good old boys off the turnpike who parked their rigs at the town limit and walked to the café.

Zeb served a heck of a burger, but the menu favorite was the fried baloney sandwich—a half-inch slice of round boloney served on a hamburger bun with any condiment you desired from Tabasco to chili, even applesauce. Most folks ordered the Full Moon pie for dessert—a thick slice of Zeb's homemade lemon meringue pie that resembled a full moon the way it sat in the glass carousel before getting sliced.

Every full moon folks gathered at the café. Zeb served free pie and coffee to the first fifteen folks in line. He always sent a pie to Agnes, ever since she prayed and Zeb's second mortgage on the place went through without a hitch and then he won the state lottery and paid it off in no time.

The town hall was located right next door to the Full Moon, which was convenient for the council members who gathered there at least once a day for coffee.

On my way to the town meeting a brisk, freezing wind swirled around me. I hiked up my collar and hurried to the town hall. I met Ivy on the steps.

"Evening, Griselda. How's Agnes?"

Ivy was a middle-aged widow with long blonde hair and exceptionally large breasts that she tried to keep hidden under oversized sweatshirts. Agnes prayed for a breast reduction for her but no volunteer surgeon ever stepped forward. Ivy never held it against her.

"Lord wanted me to have a big bosom," Ivy said, but often lamented the fact of never having had babies to suckle. "Seems a waste."

"Agnes is fine, Ivy. How are you?"

"I'm doing okay, you know, well as can be expected. Tell Agnes I'll be coming by in a day or so. Got some things to discuss."

"I'll be sure to tell her."

My foot landed on the top step and the thought hit me that just once I'd like someone to ask how I was doing. But it was always Agnes on their minds.

The building was packed to the gills by the time I got there. Studebaker Kowalski was up front. He held tightly to the petition, already in deep conversation with Boris Lender. It might have been my mood, but Studebaker looked like a cheap TV evangelist. He wore a maroon polyester leisure suit with white stitching around the wide lapels, pockets, and seams. His shoes matched his white belt, and I swore I could smell his Brut aftershave across the room. Studebaker and I made eye contact, and he waved the pages at me. I motioned back, feigned a smile, and then turned my attention to Edie Tompkins.

"Well, hello there, Griselda. So this is Agnes's big night." She pushed her persimmon red lips into a smile. "Uh, no pun intended."

My eyebrows arched like a gothic cathedral. That woman made my blood boil. Edie was a nosy neighbor. She stood about six feet tall, which meant she towered over me by half a foot. She wore her frizzy hair piled on top of her square head, adding nine inches to her tallness, and was partial to flowered dresses straight out of 1953. Edie was married to Bill Tompkins, the automobile mechanic and member of the council as president of the commerce association. Bill was a good egg and, I was hoping, the one member who would understand Agnes's situation.

I hung my coat on the last available hook and made my way through the crowd gathered around the refreshment table laden with all types of snacky finger food. Town meetings, and just about every occasion in Bright's Pond, called for refreshments. I think it might have been in the charter. Ivy plopped down a plate of brownies, but I managed to snag the last piece of Bill Tompkins's fudge. He was not only an excellent mechanic but made the best fudge in the universe, a recipe I understood required him to stir for hours. Every two years his extended family gathered at Bright's Pond for their "Family Fudge-Off." They tried to out-fudge one another and unseat Bill as king, but he won every year. Boris and Studebaker judged the contest.

Edie offered me a cup of coffee to which I added a table-spoon or so of half and half. The coffee was another reason to attend town meetings. There was just something about it percolating in that big, silver urn that gave it a special taste that not only warmed your hands on a cold night but also warmed a spot in your soul.

"Here you go, Griselda," Janeen Sturgis said. She handed me a paper plate stacked with treats and covered with two or three paper napkins. "For Agnes. I sure hope the sign is approved. I'd be so proud to be from her town." Her eyes lit up when she smiled. "We're all so proud."

I took a deep breath. "Thank you, Janeen." I put the plate on the table and made a mental note to pick it up on my way out. Agnes loved Bill's fudge and Cora Nebbish's lemon squares, although I hated bringing her plates of treats like they were some kind of offering. Janeen tilted her head and looked at me the way a dog does when he can't understand what you're saying. I guess she expected me to get all excited about the stupid sign.

What really scared me though was what her husband said next. "Yeah, maybe we'll rename the town. You know, call it Agnesville." He chuckled. But I knew he was serious.

Janeen slipped her arm in his. "That's wonderful, dear, Agnesville." She chortled.

I would have shushed them, but they had taken their seats and I supposed it was too late to make a difference. The idea of Agnesville had just been released to the universe. I watched it escape out the door as Eugene Shrapnel walked in.

Eugene was as mean-spirited and dyspeptic as they come, always complaining and shouting about one thing or other. He was a little more manageable when Edith, his poor, skinny wife, was alive. Eugene hated Agnes—called her a sorceress and thought she was "in league with the devil." He stood maybe five-feet, eight-inches tall and walked hunched over: claimed he took mortar fire in the back at the Battle of the Bulge. I think he withered from his own nastiness.

Eugene wore dark clothes, suits mostly, and a weird little felt hat with a feather stuck in the band. His raspy voice seemed to come from some tight, tiny spot in his throat. But his worst feature and the one that garnered the most attention was his nose, a bulbous, lumpy thing that resembled a chunk of cauliflower with bright red and purple veins running through it. Most folks accepted the fact that it was impossible to talk to Eugene without staring at his nose. To top it off he smelled like wet wool and Lysol.

"Good evening, Miss Sparrow."

"Hello, Eugene."

"I hope you aren't thinking that this . . . this sign disgrace will actually come to pass."

I popped a lemon square into my mouth and chewed, staring at his nose without saying a word.

Eugene harrumphed his way to a seat—the last one, in the last row, closest to the exit. Fortunately, I found a seat up front. Unfortunately, it was directly behind Studebaker. He turned around, sending a waft of cologne around the room. I sneezed.

"Bless you," he said. "You still have time to sign it." He shoved the petition under my nose.

"I already told you. Agnes doesn't want a sign."

"She's just being humble, that's all. Once she sees her name in giant block letters, she'll be glad we did it."

I shook my head. "No, she wouldn't, Stu."

He ignored my comment and said, "I'm gonna ask the council to commission Filby Pruett to make a statue."

My heart raced. "Please, Stu, you can't be serious. A statue? Of Agnes? Fat Agnes?"

Boris banged his gavel. "Let's come to order," he shouted. "Order." He said it five times before the crowd finally quieted down.

Boris was a lawyer and a pretty fair man. No one ever complained about him or the way he ran the town meetings. He managed to get a few people out of scrapes with the law including the Tompkins's boy Nelson, who was arrested for driving through a cornfield while intoxicated. Farmer Higgins claimed he lost about three thousand bucks, but when the damage was assessed it tuned out to be more like three hundred. Nelson slopped the farmer's pigs for a month to make up for the loss.

Boris wore gray suits with red ties and had a penchant for cheap cigars. His teeth had turned a most disagreeable shade of yellow from the habit, and when he smiled they looked like rows of rotting corn niblets.

Dot Handy had her pad and pencil fired up with two extras perched behind each ear and one stuck in her hair bun. She nodded to Boris, and the meeting began. After the Pledge of Allegiance and the approval of the previous month's minutes Boris called for new business. I could see Studebaker was primed to present his petition. His legs twitched like a schoolboy's. But before that there were a few other issues to discuss, including the need for a new stop sign at the corner of Ninth and Hector. The hiring of a crossing guard to replace the retiring Sam Gaston was approved. Dot Handy took the job.

"I'll take good care of your children," she said and sat down.

The chair reluctantly recognized Eugene Shrapnel, who tapped his cane on the floor.

"You got to do somethin' about that mangy beast that's been tramping around town going on four years now," he whined.

He was talking about Ivy's pooch. He made the same speech every meeting.

"That hideous hound keeps doing his smelly business in my rose garden."

Boris shook his head. "We told you, Eugene, put a fence around your roses." He turned his attention to Ivy. "And you keep that dog on a leash."

"A leash?" Ivy took a breath. "I just couldn't."

"Then you got to fence him," said Bill Tompkins from the committee. "It's the only way. You can't let him loose all the time, Ivy."

Boris banged his gavel. "I could get a court order, Ivy. Just save us all the trouble and keep your dog off the streets."

"I'll poison that stinking mutt," Eugene said.

Ivy choked on her cider. "Do and I'll poison you, you bloated old windbag."

Boris brought the meeting to order before it went any further awry.

"Go see the police chief, Eugene. Get an order for the fence."

The chief of police was new to Bright's Pond that year. She might have been all of twenty-five years old. Her name was Mildred Blessing, and for most of the men in town she was exactly that. Even in uniform it was easy to see that Mildred had truly been blessed in a Jane Russell sort of way—beauty, breasts, feminine brawn. She was one of my regulars at the library, checking out hard-boiled detective stories and psychological thrillers. Mildred hoped for a real crime in Bright's Pond, but the most she got was dog poop and drunken teenagers.

An hour later we finally got to the real reason there was a record turnout for the meeting on such a snowy night. Studebaker Kowalski stood up.

"Mr. Chairman, members of the council, distinguished people of Bright's Pond." Stu turned around and nodded to the crowd. "I move that a vote be taken to have our town sign changed to read: Welcome to Bright's Pond, Home of Agnes Sparrow."

Spontaneous applause broke out and Boris pounded his gavel several times to bring the meeting back to order.

"Okay, okay, calm down. Now, I know we're all proud of our Agnes Sparrow but I am obliged to ask if any one would like to present an argument."

I swear I felt every single eyeball in the building lock on to me. My heart raced. I was never very good at public speaking. My hands went sweaty, and a chill wiggled down my back. But I shook it off and raised my hand.

Boris pointed his gavel at me. "The chair recognizes Griselda Sparrow."

"My sister doesn't want a sign with her name or her picture on it, so I move we table this petition. And she most certainly does not want a statue."

I couldn't believe the ruckus that broke out. I thought for sure an avalanche started rolling down Jack Frost it was so loud. Boris let the shouting go on for a few minutes during which time I heard more than a few people tell me that I was being selfish, that Agnes was famous and deserved the sign.

"Why, she's done more good than anyone for this town," Janeen Sturgis said. "Without her prayers Frank and I would have . . . well we wouldn't be together, I'll tell you that."

"That's right," Studebaker shouted. "I'd be dead by now." He turned to me. "Dead."

"Abomination," Eugene shouted. "This is an evil generation. They seek a sign; and there shall be no sign given it, but the sign of Jonah, the prophet."

"But Agnes doesn't want the sign," I said as loudly as I could over the din.

"Abomination," Eugene said.

Ivy Slocum shimmied to her feet. "Oh, hush up, you miserable, old man."

"You'll see," Eugene said. "You'll all see her for what she really is. One day . . . one day the sky will fall, mark my words."

Boris pounded his gavel. "That's enough, Eugene. You said your piece; now sit down and be quiet."

Eugene pointed his cane toward the door and left the hall.

"I move for a vote," Stu shouted.

Boris banged his hammer one more time.

"You can't call for a vote, Studebaker. Now sit down and be patient."

I raised my hand.

"You got something else to say, Griselda?" Bill Tompkins asked.

"Yes." I managed a smile even though I knew nothing short of the Rapture would change their minds. "Agnes said she isn't against you changing the sign but she wants it to say Bright's Pond, *Soli Deo Gloria.*"

A hush, peppered with several words of amusement or confusion, fell over the crowd like a heavy, wet blanket.

"What in jumpin' blue heck does that mean?" someone shouted.

"Sounds like some witch's spell," said another.

"Witches? We don't want no witches in our town."

"Maybe Eugene is right," shouted another, "if she's talkin' in spells, maybe it's a curse."

"It means," I said as loudly as I could, "to God alone the glory."

"I don't get it," Studebaker said.

"You saying we don't believe in God?" shouted Frank Sturgis, Janeen's husband.

"Of course not," I said. "Agnes doesn't want the glory. It isn't hers to have."

Another three minutes of ruckus broke out as folks spewed nonsense about me not thinking they believed in God and bringing witchcraft to Bright's Pond. The whole thing gave me a headache. Feeling outnumbered I sat down.

Bill Tompkins asked to address the council.

"Maybe we should honor Agnes's wishes," he said looking directly at me.

"Witches?" said Jasper York who was hard of hearing but would never admit to it. "What's with all the witches?"

"Wishes, Jasper," I said leaning into him. "Agnes's wishes."

Jasper rested on his three-footed walking cane. "Oh, in that case, I guess it's all right with me."

But Bill's endorsement of Agnes's desires did little good as I only heard a few voices ring out in agreement with us.

Finally, after Boris regained control, I again urged we table the petition, but a vote was taken in spite of my protest.

3

Agnes and I still lived at the Sparrow Funeral Home. Our parents died in a train wreck when I was seventeen and Agnes had just turned twenty-one. A few days after the funeral, while we were staying with our Aunt Lidy, Boris Lender, Pastor Spahr, and some of the others helped sell off our father's mortuary equipment and dispose of what they could. The women in town did their best to take the funeral parlor look out of our home by recovering chairs and replacing drapes. But, no matter, it still looked like a funeral home and smelled like it at times, especially during high humidity when odors from the embalming room seeped through the floorboards.

It was a large Queen Anne Victorian built in 1891, which meant we had miles of coursers and gingerbread, two turrets, and a wide wraparound porch with three hundred and fifty-one spindles. I counted them when I was seven. The entryway was two wide, dark green doors that opened out to accommodate a coffin. On hot summer days, guests arriving for a viewing would often sit on the porch, where my mother served sweet iced tea and cookies while they discussed the deceased and waited their turn to pay their respects. There wasn't any air-conditioning or even a fan inside. My father said a fan oscillating in the corner would have been undignified and could have mussed ladies' hair.

A bronze sparrow perched on a twig with one leaf served as our doorbell. You turned it and chimes sounded all over the house. We always stopped what we were doing, whether it was mid-stride on the steps or buttoning a shirt, because the chime generally meant there had been a death in town. Now the chime most likely meant that someone with a prayer need had come looking for Agnes.

I stood at the door, shivering against the frosty air and touching the cold little sparrow. I wondered how to tell Agnes about the meeting.

She was still wide-awake when I went inside. I stamped the snow that had been falling all night off my boots and hung my coat on the rack. I shivered. Agnes had managed to change into a sleeveless baby blue nightgown while I was gone. The cold never seemed to bother her as much as me. She claimed it was because she had so much insulation.

"It's cold in here," I said. I nudged the thermostat past seventy.

Arthur greeted me and wrapped his body around my legs with a loud purr. I reached down and picked him up. He was a former stray that used to come by the library. I started feeding him there, but one day decided to take him home.

"I prayed for the meeting," Agnes said from her bed. We had moved her bed to the first floor, the old viewing room, because Agnes could no longer climb stairs. She was in a good spot, able to look out a large window and watch the comings and goings of Bright's Pond. We still called it the viewing room.

She not only prayed for the people who made a point to come by and ask for Agnes to deliver their requests to the

Almighty but also for anyone who walked past the house. Most of the time she knew the folks who went up and down our block, but every so often a stranger would wander by, usually a visitor from out of town. She prayed for him or her too.

"Did you tell them?" she called.

I dropped Arthur and sat on the sofa.

"Yes, I told them, but they passed the petition anyway."

"How could they? I don't want a sign with my name on it. It ain't right, Griselda. They don't know what they're doing." I saw a shudder rattle through her body. She took a labored breath as her cheeks turned red. "I told you to keep them from letting this happen." Agnes reached for her jar of M&M's.

"A few people were in agreement with me and you, but we were outnumbered, if you can count Eugene as people."

"So, I got no say." She popped a few of the bright candies into her mouth.

I yawned and rubbed my right eye. "They mean well, Agnes. Most of them think you're just being humble and once you see the sign—"

"No. You don't understand." She took a deep, rattly breath.

"Understand? Understand what?"

Agnes popped more M&Ms. "Look. It's just that, well, it'll attract attention, Griselda."

"It sure will. Folks will be coming here looking for you and asking for all sorts of miracles, you know."

A vision of pilgrims lined up outside—some in wheelchairs, some on crutches, and some carrying children in their arms—flashed in front of me. For a second I saw our yard blanketed in burning candles, flowers, and other gifts for Fat Saint Agnes.

"That's the ticket," I said. I threw my arms around my sister, "They never thought about the crowds that will come, crowds with all manner of illnesses and broken bones and troubles we can't even think of making their way to see you. I should have told them that. I should—"

"Oh, Griselda. Do you think that'll do it?"

"I bet it will. Why would they want all those people clogging up the town?"

"You go see Boris Lender first thing tomorrow." Agnes's face and neck turned bright red, revealing tiny, white blotches on her skin. "Tell him what you said. I am certainly not a holy icon." Then she closed her eyes. "Far from it."

I thought a moment and caught myself biting my lower lip. "If it doesn't, you could always stop praying."

Agnes glared at me with her tiny eyes—the only part of her that didn't grow larger as her body did. They were like two tiny, blue bulbs set in a round, pink face.

"Stop praying?" She used her littlest, little-girl voice. "I could never do that. The people . . . what about the people? I have to pray, Griselda."

I hated to see Agnes so upset. She rarely let her emotions get the best of her, but when she did I would kiss her cheek and smile into her eyes and let her know I would be with her, no matter what.

I kissed her cheek. Agnes had a smell about her. For the most part, I had grown used to it. The only way I can describe it is that it reminded me of old marinara sauce. Tiredness had settled into my muscles even though it was only a little past nine-thirty. She grabbed my hand.

"I'll keep praying for every soul the Lord puts on my heart or walks past my window and I'll keep praying they forget about that silly old sign." She labored a breath. "It's all about timing, Griselda. The fullness of time."

Agnes's words swirled in my over-tired brain. God's timing always seemed out of sync with my own.

"Think I'll make a cup of tea. Get you one, Agnes?"

"Sounds good." Arthur curled up on Agnes's huge belly like it was a comfy bed.

I started into the kitchen when I remembered. "Shoot." I turned around. "Your lemon squares. I forgot your lemon squares and fudge. I had a plate of treats for you, and I left them there."

"Oh, gee, I was looking forward to Cora's lemon squares. But bring me something, maybe that peach pie. I still have some fudge from Frank's last visit."

Agnes and I ate peach pie and drank tea while we watched the rest of *Ironside* and half of *The Dean Martin Show*. Then I hauled the trash cans out to the curb and went to bed.

Morning came—chilly and silent. I looked out my bedroom window. The snow that had started falling the evening before had continued all night, leaving at least seven inches on the ground. Bright's Pond was Christmas-card pretty in her snowy best, particularly while it was untouched. The snow drifted in the night and piled mounds of it against the backyard shed and clumped it around the wrought-iron lawn furniture and tree trunks. There was something pure and sacred about snow that had been blown about by a cold wind.

We had a large yard that reached all the way back to Bright's Pond. My father enjoyed fishing there whenever he could. Sometimes he would catch a trout as long as his arm or a heavy striped bass that my mother would fry over an open fire outside, but mostly he snagged carp and tossed them back in.

I loved to watch him fish. He had a small, green boat that he paddled out to the middle of the water where he would cast his line and wait, demonstrating more patience for the fish than he ever did for me or Agnes or even our mother. Some of my best memories of my father are fishing memories—collecting gargantuan night crawlers with him after a rain, watching as he untangled hooks from his net and tied tiny shots of lead onto his line. Fishing was all the Holy Communion my father ever needed, although he always took the sacrament the first Sunday of every month; but fishing, fishing was when he felt closest to God.

He used to say that preparing a body for burial was religious, but he could always hear God's voice a little clearer, a little louder, on the pond.

I breathed deeply and closed my eyes for a second and sailed a silent, shaky prayer that God would grant us a good day and that the sign situation would get resolved. I prayed that Boris would understand, even though I knew Agnes had probably already prayed. The odd thing about living with an apparent miracle worker was the way it diminished my own prayers.

Agnes was eager to get to the bathroom. Our father had a powder room for funeral guests installed off the back of the viewing room. It has since gone through some major reconstruction, including the addition of wide pocket doors and a reinforced toilet and toilet seat. Most of the time Agnes could make the short trip on her own, but in the mornings she often complained of feeling stiffer than an ironing board and she got winded easily.

"Hurry, Griselda," she said. "I got to go something fierce. Been holding it in for over an hour."

"You should have called me."

"I didn't want to disturb you."

I helped Agnes off her bed and twisted some of the material of her nightgown into a handle and led Agnes to the bathroom. Then I waited and counted to eighty-seven after I heard the toilet flush because that's how long it took Agnes to adjust herself.

"How 'bout if you take me to the couch this morning?" she asked. "I need to get off that mattress."

"For a bit. I still need to open the library even though the weather will probably keep folks away until past noon. So I'll need to get you back in bed before I leave."

"The plows came down an hour ago. Woke me up with all that scraping and grinding."

"I think I'll walk today. Don't feel much like digging out the truck. Sun's supposed to come out and warm it up a little . . . melt some of it."

"Coffee sounds good," Agnes said. She dug herself into the sofa.

"I'll put a pot on and fix us some oatmeal."

"And a Danish. I love those cherry buns."

A few minutes later the smell of brewing coffee filled the house. That morning it reminded me of our mother. She always had coffee on, all day long, just in case.

"You never know when someone will come by in need of Daddy's services," she used to say. "Quite often they appreciate a cup of coffee, especially if they're coming from a long night at Greenbrier."

Greenbrier was the nursing home not far from Bright's Pond. I often thought that one day Agnes would end up as a patient there when her breathing became too difficult and she needed constant oxygen, or when her heart would start to wear itself out. Doctor Flaherty said the day was coming. He did his best a few years ago to find a way for Agnes to lose all that weight, but nothing helped. No diet or exercise routine seemed to put a dent in the situation. I think Agnes liked her fatness, in spite of the pain it caused her.

I stirred the oatmeal, and then I fed Arthur. He mewled a few times and circled my ankles in appreciation. He sauntered to the back door, arched his back, yawned, and telepathically ordered me to open the back door.

"Not today, old man. The snow's deeper than you. You'll just have to stay inside."

Agnes and I ate our breakfast as we always did, watching the morning news and jabbering about the day.

"Ivy Slocum said she'd be coming by," I said.

"Her bursitis must be acting up."

"And I'll go see Boris around lunch time. Figure he'll be at the Full Moon then."

"I hope they stop this silliness. Can't I get a lawyer or something?"

"Boris is the best lawyer in town."

"Maybe we can make them wait until I'm dead and buried."

"I'm sure Boris knows all the legal ins and outs. Let's try the other thing first, you know, about the crowds?"

"Been thinking about that. Those men will probably just say it's good for business. Put Bright's Pond on the map, or some such nonsense."

I felt the wind blow right out of my sails. I hadn't thought of that. I saw dollar signs light up above their mostly bald heads.

"Well, it isn't right," I said. "If a woman doesn't want a sign, she shouldn't be forced to have a sign—no matter how much revenue it brings in."

Agnes kept eating her oatmeal that I had topped with brown sugar and raisins. I poured her a second cup of coffee to which she added cream. The skin that hung from her arms looked like freshly risen bread dough. It jiggled as she stirred, the spoon nearly lost in her fat hand. She tapped the side of the cup and took a breath. I could hear the wheeze in her chest clear over from where I sat across from her.

"Maybe I should get the doc to take a listen," I said.

"I'm fine. Nothing he can or will do."

"Don't let me leave without making sure you have a full inhaler."

"Worrywart."

"I'm not a worrywart, but someone has to look after you, Agnes."

"I got the good Lord looking after me."

I helped Agnes get settled in bed.

"Don't forget to open the curtains, Griselda. And would you hand me my notebook and pens?"

It was the same routine every morning. "I know, Agnes."

"Don't get snippy, Griselda. I was just asking."

"I'm not getting snippy. But do you really think I would forget to open the curtains and get you your notebook? Only been doing it every morning for how many years now?"

"There was that one time," she whined. "I sat here in the dark all day."

"You could have turned on a lamp."

I handed her a green spiral notebook. "Add anyone new, or still praying for the same people?"

"I pray for them all, Griselda. You know that. Some prayers just take a little longer asking time. I don't give up on noooooobody." She pulled the word "no" like it was a piece of gum and somehow that made her commitment to the people all the more ironclad.

"But Agnes—"

"No buts, Griselda. I have my work to do. The Lord's work. The work he gave me."

Agnes traced a cross with her fat, sausage index finger over the book's cover. "All these folks in here depend on me."

I pulled the cord and opened the heavy green drapes that had been hanging in our window for more than a decade. They had faded at the top and looked something like the bad side of a watermelon. The sky was the color of an aluminum pot with a copper bottom as the sun rose. High, stringy clouds made their way across the eastern sky like pieces of torn lace caught on the wind.

"Look at all that snow," I said. "Must be seven inches out there."

Agnes handed me her breakfast tray. "Six inches. I heard the weather repor—"

She tried to adjust her legs, and I saw the pain shoot from her toes to her eyes. I had gotten used to Agnes's pained expressions but could do precious little to alleviate the cause. Most of the time all I did was stand by and watch until she was able to arrange her massive body into a configuration that resembled comfortable—an ordeal that often left her breathless and reaching for her oxygen mask.

"Help me." She patted her left leg. "See if you can get this leg to bend."

I pushed up on her shin and heard her knee crack like it always did.

"Now, scratch behind there just a bit, will you, Griselda?"

My fingers sank into the thick folds of skin. I winced as a wave of nausea rippled through my body when I felt her sweat. "I got to go, Agnes." I wiped my fingers on my jeans.

"Don't go saying I shouldn't be praying." She smiled at her rhyme. "You just remember who it was that prayed for Studebaker Kowalski and Jack Cooper and they got healed. Griselda, you remember that?"

"Yes, Agnes, I remember. You prayed and Jack stopped running around town all naked and chasing dogs. Your prayers made him sane."

I grabbed my boots and sat on the sofa. "You might not have any visitations this morning. Folks will probably wait until after it melts a little."

"That's fine, Griselda. I got plenty in my books to—" She stopped talking.

"What is it?" I asked. "You okay?"

"Who is that?"

"Who?"

"Outside, rooting around in our trash cans."

I looked out the window and saw a strange man I had never seen in town. He was wearing a heavy, dark-blue pea coat and a woolen cap over his ears.

"Never saw him before. Must be some drifter." I pushed my glasses up on my nose.

"Don't get many of them." Agnes craned her neck to get a better look. "He looks sad."

How she could tell that I didn't know. "Well, if that sign goes up and word gets out about you, there'll be plenty of drifters."

"I'll pray for him."

"Suit yourself. Now I really got to get going and open the library."

I pulled on a boot and felt my foot sink into something soft and squishy.

"Mouse." I sighed. "Arthur left me another gift."

"He loves you."

I pulled it out by the tail. Arthur's gifts have included mice, moles, birds, and one time a pheasant's claw. I kept it on the mantle.

I buttoned my coat and wrapped a long yellow and green scarf I knitted myself around my neck and pulled a red cap onto my head and headed out. The stranger was still standing near our cans. He flicked a cigarette butt into the street.

"Hi," he said as I walked closer.

All of my instincts said to ignore him. "Hello." I ignored the instincts instead.

"Can you spare a quarter for a cup of Joe?"

I reached into my pocket and happened to find a few coins.

"There's a café on Filbert."

"Much obliged." He looked at me through tired, yet piercing eyes. "I was looking for Agnes Sparrow. Do you know her?"

4

Now you might think I'm going to say something like I thought I got hit by a Mack truck when he mentioned Agnes, but I didn't. As far as I can recollect, it's a bit of a blur. I stood there for a good ten or eleven seconds staring at him like he had just sprouted petunias out the top of his head. It didn't immediately register that this stranger could have known my sister.

I had to think fast and, in the time it takes to blink, I filtered through all the permutations of possible answers. My first thought was to lie and say no and then hurry away. But that wouldn't have made him go away. Surely someone in town would tell him.

"Agnes? How do you know Agnes?"

The stranger replaced the lid on my trash can. "I heard she performs miracles." He said it like he was talking about any old subject.

My heart raced, and I smashed my glasses into the bridge of my nose, as was my habit when I felt uncomfortable. My sister's reputation was spreading.

"How did you hear about Agnes? You're not from Bright's Pond, are you?"

He shoved his bare hands under his armpits. "No. I . . . I heard some folks talking down at the Piggy Wiggly Market, you know the big one in Shoops." He tried to suppress a shiver. If looks meant anything, he didn't look all that sinister. He was tall with what I thought must be either extremely short hair or a bald head. I couldn't see a stray strand sneaking out of his cap anywhere. He had a long, ski-slope nose and a strong chin with two or three days worth of stubble.

My curiosity heightened. Agnes's renown had spread beyond the borders of Bright's Pond. "Yeah, I know the one."

"Well, anyway—" the stranger pulled another cigarette butt from his coat pocket "—got a match?"

"No."

He smiled like maybe he didn't believe me. "No bother. I'll save it for later."

My patience had run out. "Look, I need to get to work."

"Please. I need to see her."

"Agnes isn't taking visitors today. Maybe you should head into Shoop's Borough. I think they have a Salvation Army there. You can get a bed and a meal."

He smirked and spit tobacco-stained spit on the white snow. "That's where I come from. Terrible place. Roaches as big as my index finger." He raised one finger and wiggled it slightly. "Rather wander the streets than go back."

"Suit yourself." I stepped onto the plowed street.

"Wait a second . . . please." He took a few steps toward me. "I really need to see her."

I turned around and waved. "Sorry, I can't help you."

"But ain't this the old Sparrow Funeral Home?"

I stopped. My heart leapt into my throat, and I took a few steps back toward him.

"How would you know that?"

He found a match in another pocket and lit his cigarette by striking the tip with his thumbnail. He blew the gray smoke past my head.

"I heard the folks at the market, remember? One of them said he thought it was weird that Agnes still lived at the funeral home, and you got to admit, this house sure looks like it's had more than a few bodies lying around. Creepy old place."

I had lost the battle. "Okay, listen. Just leave my sister alone this morning. You can come back tonight—after supper. I'll see if she'll talk to you then. Agnes isn't a sideshow freak for people to gawk at, and she isn't a vending machine handing out miracles to every drifter who happens by."

"I got nothing but respect for her, Ma'am. Nothing but respect if the stories I heard are true. It's just that I'm in need of some powerful prayers—powerful prayers." He started to bounce up and down to shake off the cold. "When I heard those men talking about her I knew I had to see her. I knew that God Almighty put me in that market at that time and He sent me to find her, to find your sister, to claim my miracle."

I took a breath for him, sighed it out, and watched it turn to smoke and blow away. The very thing I was fighting had already begun.

"Come back tonight. After six."

"Thank you, Ma'am. Thank you very much. I'll just go on down to that diner you mentioned and get me a cup of hot coffee. A man could use a cup of hot coffee after walking so far."

"Fine. It's about three blocks that way." I pointed toward the town hall. "You can't miss it. There's a big full moon hanging over it."

I crossed the street but kept turning to make sure he didn't head for the house. Agnes would let him in for sure. She never turned anyone away.

That morning my walk to the library was tinged with worry. I didn't like the notion of people coming from out of town to see Agnes.

I loved the library. I always did, ever since I learned to read. My mother would take me every Saturday to pick out a new book. I fell in love with stories like other kids fell for sports or ballet. I could get lost inside a story and dream and consider the possibilities.

The building itself was unique for a library—a converted old Victorian, older than the funeral home, with miles of gingerbread, arches, and porches that created interesting spaces for reading and dreaming. In 1952 the owner of the house, Thomas Quincy Adams, donated it to the town. Many of the books belonged to him, including a first-edition collection of the poems of Emily Dickinson that I kept under glass.

During the winter months and well into the first couple of weeks of spring I left a snow shovel outside the library doors. If it accumulated more than six or seven inches, I could usually count on one of the boys in town to shovel the walk and steps for me. But not that morning. I had to clear a path myself.

Once inside I went about my usual morning routine, turning on lights, raising the thermostat, checking in books returned the previous day, and answering mail. I kept a coffee pot in the kitchen and always had a pot percolating throughout the day.

By noon I had completed all my tasks. Not a single patron stopped by, so I decided to head on over to the Full Moon and see if I could catch up with Boris. He always had lunch there along with Studebaker, and I was chomping at the notion to quell the whole sign issue that morning if I could.

I hung a little cross-stitched "closed for lunch" sign on the door just as Officer Blessing stepped out from behind a large rhododendron.

"Anything the matter, Mildred?" I asked, more out of politeness than interest. I had learned a long time ago that it was best to keep to myself and not ask too many questions.

"That mangy perpetrator is on the lam. I saw him heading this way."

Once I connected the dots I understood that Mildred was talking about Ivy's dog.

"You'll never catch him." I laughed.

She didn't appreciate the chuckle. "I have a warrant for his arrest if you see him."

"You'd be better off staking out Ivy's house. He goes home eventually."

"Thanks."

I started down the path and turned around. "Oh, by the way, Mildred, a new Raymond Chandler came in this morning."

"I'll be sure to check it out," Mildred said, still poking around some suspicious-looking shrubbery.

Of all the places in Bright's Pond the one I loved the best, besides the library, was The Full Moon Café. The original structure was built in 1938 and resembled a stainless steel railway dining car. I remember the grand opening like it was yesterday. Agnes was eight and I was only five, but I know I spent most of the evening perched on my daddy's shoulders while a Dixieland band played and Pastor Spahr prayed a blessing.

It's gone through lots of changes, including the name. For most of its life it was known as the Bright's Pond Diner. But when Zeb Sewickey purchased it in 1969 he changed it to The Full Moon Café and hung a large neon moon over the roof. Folks came out for that too. It was quite a production with a crane and three men guiding the moon into position. Edie Tomkins's mother, Idabelle, took it upon herself to treat us with her rendition of *Fly Me to the Moon* as the men bolted it into place. Zeb's moon swayed a little in the high winds that day, but the installation went well, and people clapped once the last bolt was in place. Pastor Speedwell never came out to pray a blessing over the name change, and Zeb always felt slighted. But he never said anything to anyone but me.

The inside was pretty much what you'd expect, with a long counter and vinyl upholstered stools that turn all the way around like an amusement ride. I used to think they were bolted to the floor to keep folks from walking off with one, but my mother said it had more to do with safety and stability. Agnes could never understand why anyone would want to spin while they ate.

Booths upholstered with the same blood-red vinyl sat in a row across from the counter, and large round lights illuminated the place. But I have to admit that what I liked the most was the aroma that wafted around the room on currents of warm diner air. I guess there isn't anything like the bouquet of grilled hamburgers, baloney, and coffee mixed with occasional cigarette smoke and perfume. The café had a smell all its own, and I often wished I could bottle it and bring it home to Agnes. She missed so much. I couldn't have stood being imprisoned like her in my own home. But Agnes managed to take it all in stride and never complained or let on that she would like to step out into the sunshine or the snow. Truth is, I doubt Agnes could even have gotten through the door of the Full Moon anymore, and I know the tables would never have accommodated her.

Boris and Studebaker sat at a table looking over what I could only imagine were plans for the sign. Studebaker, long since retired from the coal mines, moved to Bright's Pond in 1967 from Carbon County. Stu was truly one of the more generous people in town. He tithed regularly from his meager pension and Social Security, although word had it that Stu had stock holdings that might have qualified him to be a millionaire. That was only speculation that came out during the time of his illness. Then he started giving away money right and left to everyone in town and every charity that plucked his heartstrings.

Boris, as always, wore one of his lawyer suits and sucked a cigar while they talked and pointed to things on the papers.

I sidled over to their table. "Afternoon."

They stood politely. "Griselda," said Stu, "did you tell Agnes about the sign?"

"I sure did and I got to tell you, she—"

"Sit," interrupted Boris. "Excuse us for being rude."

I sat next to Boris, but before I could finish my thought Zeb was standing over me with a pot of coffee.

"Thanks, and bring me a grilled cheese, please." My stomach rumbled.

"Sure thing, Grizzy."

I hated it when he called me that. But, Zeb seemed to get a kick out of it. We graduated high school together—class of 1950. He was a good-looking fellow—always wore a white tee shirt and blue jeans. Zeb had asked me out a couple of times but we never seemed to make it. Something always came up with Agnes and I got stuck at home.

"I'll bet she was thrilled to the tips of her toes," said Studebaker.

I reached for the cream. "Actually, she wasn't."

Boris snuffed his cigar into a glass ashtray with an image of a boar's head in the middle. "What are you saying?"

"I told you last night. Agnes doesn't care for the whole sign thing."

"Pish," said Studebaker. "She's just being shy or something."

I looked at the pages on the table.

"Are these the plans?"

Boris smiled at me. "Studebaker here had another great idea. He thought instead of painting Agnes's picture up on the sign—"

"I already told her," said Stu. "I told her about the statue."

My first instinct was to laugh again, but the horror of the idea was just too terrible.

"I told you, Stu, you can't do this. If she doesn't want a sign, what makes you think she'll okay a statue."

Studebaker stared out the window. "Look, Griselda, she saved my life and I want the whole world to know it."

"She didn't save your life, Stu. God saw fit to do that."

"But Agnes asked for the miracle. She put her hands on my head and prayed that the Holy Spirit would come down and take my cancer away. She prayed for a whole five minutes, and all of a sudden I got a warm tingling feeling like a gazillion ants were crawling all over my body and I knew, Griselda, I knew my cancer was gone."

"But, Stu—"

"She prayed. It was her prayer. It wouldn't have happened without her."

Zeb put my sandwich in front of me and refilled my cup. "You gonna be wanting dessert?"

"Not today, Zeb."

"Fine. But I'll wrap up a nice piece of pie for Agnes, and one for you." He winked.

Studebaker peered out the window again, and I thought I saw a tear roll down his cheek. He swiped it away.

"She saved my life, Griselda."

I sighed and popped a chip in my mouth. I could not even imagine how remarkable it must be to have had your life spared, to be on the cusp of death and then given a new life, a second chance—just like that.

Boris bit the corner of his baloney sandwich. "I'm afraid you're outnumbered. Everybody in town feels the way Stu does. And we thought we'd install the statue near the town hall, not out on the highway."

"But she doesn't want the sign and I'm certain a statue is just gonna make—" I stopped talking and bit my sandwich. These two had already turned Agnes into a minor deity. I signaled Zeb for a glass of water.

I enjoyed the comforting feeling I got from the warm grilled cheese Zeb always served with a cup of cream of tomato soup.

"Where's Cora?" I asked when he put the glass on the table.

"Oh, she went to see the Doc."

"Nothing serious, I hope."

"No, just her blood pressure check. You know, old folk stuff."

I finished my lunch with Boris and Stu. We said nothing more about the sign or the statue.

It started to flurry as I walked back to the library. Snow on snow. I watched people still clearing their sidewalks and driveways. Even Eugene was digging out his old Rambler and cursing up a storm.

"Afternoon, Eugene." I waved and smiled.

He shook his shovel at me. "Abomination. That sister of yours is an abomination."

I kicked a clump of snow out of the way. The sun had started to melt the white stuff, and I watched little streams flowing toward the storm sewers. For a second I had a fantasy of Eugene being swept away. But I supposed that wasn't very Christian-like. Agnes would never think such a thing.

Ivy Slocum sat out on her porch looking about as exhausted as I had ever seen her. She leaned on her shovel. She wore one of those hats with fur-lined earflaps and a parka that she bought at the Army/Navy store.

"Why don't you get one of the men to shovel, Ivy," I called. "I'm sure Fred Haskell will be glad to help."

Fred lived next door to Ivy. He was the town plumber and another good egg. I think Fred was one of those people who would truly take the coat off his back to help you. He often accepted blueberry pies and potato bleenies as payment for a plumbing job.

One winter, a blizzard came up the coast and knocked out all the power. Fred went door-to-door making certain that everyone's furnace pilot light was on and that people were at least getting heat.

"He was already here, but got called out on an emergency," Ivy puffed. "Edie Tompkins's toilet overflowed and started coming through the dining room ceiling."

I waved. "Go get a piece of pie or something. The snow will wait."

"Planning on it."

By the time I got back to the library it was nearly two o'clock. The drifter from the morning sat on the steps with his arm around Ivy Slocum's dog. She never did bother to give him a name. That mutt took one look at me and hightailed it off the porch. I swear he knew there was a warrant out for his arrest.

"Afternoon," said the stranger. He rose to his feet. "That there is a fine dog."

"He's a scoundrel."

I unlocked the door and the drifter followed me inside.

"Never was much of a reader," he said. "Just never got the knack."

"Too bad."

I sat behind the circulation desk and pretended I had something to do by flipping through a box of library card records.

"My name is Hezekiah," he said. "Hezekiah Branch."

"Hezekiah—he was a—"

"A king of Israel." Hezekiah pulled himself up to his full height and straightened his shoulders when he said it. Then he slumped. "Not me though. I ain't king of nothing, you know."

No, I didn't know, but from his tone and the fact that he was picking through my trash earlier, I imagined that Hezekiah had a well full of troubles that brought him to Bright's Pond. "Hezekiah was one of Judah's finest kings," I said. "You should be honored."

He put his head down. "I know. Someone told me the Holy Bible says he was approved by God."

"That's right."

Hezekiah wandered a few feet away from me. "Mind if I just plant myself here for a spell? It's cold on the street. Feels like it barely made it above freezing."

"Suit yourself. I'll be here until three."

"Then I can walk back home with you?"

That was the last thing I wanted. "Maybe you could go on down to the café and wait there until six, then come over to the house."

He nodded and as he disappeared behind a row of books, I couldn't help but feel sadness for this displaced king.

"I'll be leaving now," I called to Hezekiah around three o'clock. I waited a moment but heard no response. "Hezekiah," I called louder. "I need to lock up the library."

He poked his head out from around the shelves. "Okay." He rubbed his eyes like he had just woke up. Probably did.

I locked the door and walked down the path with Hezekiah. "I'm sorry, but I'd rather walk alone. You can find the café, right?"

"Oh, for sure. I'll see you at six o'clock, then."

"Right. Six o'clock."

Hezekiah sprinted off toward Second Street, and I lagged behind a few seconds. The truth was I didn't want anyone to see us together.

5

"Who shoveled the walk?" I called as I entered the house.

"Fred Haskell did it after he finished up at the Tompkins," Agnes said.

"Remind me to give that man a hug." I hung up my coat and took my boots off in the tiled entryway. Arthur was asleep near the small radiator, but he woke as I walked past and shot me a disagreeable look.

"Excuse me all the way to jumpin' blue heck."

"He's been in a surly mood all day," Agnes said.

I went to her bedside. She looked comfortable enough and had managed to make herself a lunch. The remnants were left for me to clean up. The M&M jar was open on the table.

"Ivy came by. Prayed for her bursitis. Then Fred stopped by."

"Fred? That's unusual."

"Sure is. He's worried about his boy, Clive."

"The little guy?"

"He's only six but he's having trouble in school. Gets bullied on account of he has that lisp."

"That's terrible. But if anyone can understand about bullies it would be—"

"I prayed the Good Lord would reach down and give that child his proper s's."

"Good for you. Now I need to go get changed and make some supper." Agnes always interrupted when the conversation even brushed by being about her.

"I'll be here," she said. "I was thinking some of that rare roast beef and mashed potatoes tonight."

"Okay."

I didn't want to tell her about Hezekiah right off.

Arthur followed me upstairs where I was certain to find another bloodied mouse in my room. I didn't think there was any way to stop the behavior. He was wild when he came to me, and you just can't get the predator out of an animal that has it in his genes. I was right. I carried another dead body to the window and tossed it out. No matter how many times I fed the little creatures to the crows, I always felt a twinge of remorse and guilt.

I changed while Arthur cleaned himself in the hallway. It felt good to slip into a pair of sweats and warm socks.

"How about a nice fire?" I called to Arthur. "Think I'll get one going before I make supper."

Fortunately, I had loaded plenty of wood onto the back porch before the heavy snow fell. It was good, well-seasoned hardwoods—oak and poplar and some long-burning cherry from a tree that fell in a storm a while back.

In no time I had a crackling fire going. I poked at it and let the warmth reach my face. Our house, like most Victorians, had multiple fireplaces; we had four. The one in the viewing room was large and worked fine. For some reason the others didn't draw as well and I needed to schedule a sweep to come out. But it was one of those things I never seemed to get around to doing.

"That's nice," said Agnes. "Thank you."

I sat on the sofa. "It is nice. Fire." It spirited me away sometimes. I could get lost in the dancing flames.

I asked Agnes to turn down the television. "Remember that drifter this morning?"

"Yeah, why? He left hours ago. Never came back."

I was glad to hear that. "He came by the library today. Says he needs prayer and wants to see you. In fact he came to Bright's Pond looking for you."

"Oh. Well, tell him to come by."

"I did. He'll be here around six. But, Agnes, I have to say it worries me. We don't know this man."

"God knows him."

"That's true. But I think you should tread easy, you know."

Agnes popped a few candies. "I'm hungry."

"I'll get supper."

"Hold on," she said. "How did he hear about me?"

"He heard some people talking about you down at the Piggly Wiggly in Shoops."

"No kidding?" She looked toward the ceiling. "I didn't know folks down there knew me."

"I know, Agnes, I was afraid of something like this happening and with this whole sign thing—"

Agnes closed her eyes a few seconds. "I'll still see him. He must need help if he came this far. God must of sent him to me."

"Says he needs powerful praying. Wants to claim his miracle."

By five I had supper ready. Arthur was desperate to get outside, so I set him free and brought Agnes her meal. Oh, how I longed to sit at a table and eat a meal surrounded by family. But that wasn't in the cards, and I set Agnes's food on a tray and carried it out to her, the way I did every meal.

"Looks good, Griselda, but don't forget the salt and pepper and maybe some more butter on my mashed and a couple slices of bread."

I sucked in air. "Okay. I'll get it."

Our daily bread was down to the last two slices. And I mean daily. I went through a loaf a day, keeping Agnes full. Doctor Flaherty said her body required a lot of calories, even though I honestly don't believe Agnes realized how much she ate in a day.

"Apple butter," she called. "Slather on some of that apple butter Cora brought over."

I did and grabbed the salt, pepper, and butter and headed for the living room just as the doorbell chimed. I stopped in my tracks for a second. It couldn't be him. It wasn't six o'clock.

"You gonna get that?" she said.

I placed the condiments and Agnes's apple butter bread on her table. "I'll get it. But if it's Hezekiah, I'm sending him away until six."

"Who?"

"The drifter. The guy poking around in the trash this morning."

"Oh, don't do that. Maybe we should feed him. Probably hungry, poor soul."

It was him on the porch looking like a lost traveler, which I suppose he was.

"Hezekiah. It's only five-fifteen. I told you six."

"Please, ma'am, I'm just so desperate to meet Agnes."

"I'm sorry, but we're in the middle of supper. Come back at six."

"Invite him in," Agnes called.

Hezekiah smiled. "I'd be much obliged. I'll just stand in the doorway until she's ready to see me."

"No, no, you don't have to do that."

"Are you hungry?" Agnes asked.

Hezekiah had sidled up next to Agnes before I could say Piggly Wiggly. I offered to take his coat and hat but he refused. "Still warming up," he said. I watched his red cheeks turn white when he saw Agnes. I suppose nobody at the Piggly Wiggly mentioned her weight. "Uhm, hel . . . hello. I'm Hezekiah." Then he pulled himself up to his full height. "That roast beef sure smells delicious. Can't tell you the last time I tasted real, honest-to-goodness mashed potatoes. They had some watered-down, dehydrated slop at the mission in Shoops. Tasted more like wallpaper paste."

"I'll get you a plate," I said even though every cell in my body seethed. I watched Hezekiah look Agnes up and down like she was a sideshow freak—something I hadn't experienced in a while. He tried to hide it and did manage to contain his amazement and smile at Agnes in a way that didn't drip of remorse or embarrassment. Even though Agnes was, for all intents and purposes, a freak to most people. They didn't know her inside like I did.

I sliced beef and plopped mashed potatoes on a plate, added a pile of peas, and poured brown gravy over it, but before I could lift the plate off the table, Hezekiah was standing next to me. He had removed his coat and hat. His hair was cut so short it was more like peach fuzz. "I'll help you," he said.

"She too much for you?"

He looked away, out the kitchen window. "N . . . no, not really. I just never been that close to someone so . . . so. . ."

"Huge?"

He looked at his feet like most people did when they were ashamed. "I'm sorry."

"Thank you. That's your plate, and I'll get you some juice or—"

"Milk, if you got it."

Hezekiah carried his food into the viewing room, and I prepared my own plate.

I had just joined them, thinking that this drifter seemed a mite too polite, when he said, "Pardon me, Ma'am but could I please wash up? The street is a grimy place to be living."

"Oh, certainly," Agnes said. "There's a bathroom right over there behind those pocket doors."

Hezekiah excused himself, and I placed a forkful of mashed potatoes in my mouth when I heard, "Oh my sweet Je—"

Agnes laughed. "He must have noticed the toilet seat."

The drifter returned to the viewing room, wiping his hands on his shirt.

"Never seen such a large . . . commode?" Agnes asked.

"N-n-no, Ma'am, I never did."

"It's called the Big Flo," I said. "Our friend Fred Haskell designed and built it for Agnes. He's got a patent pending down in Washington, DC."

"That's right," Agnes said. "I consider it my own doublewide miracle."

I watched Hezekiah try to hide his laughter in his glass of milk but he couldn't hold on and spit milk halfway across the room. "Sorry," he said wiping his mouth.

"Don't worry," Agnes said. "It's good to get it out of the way."

Hezekiah ate fast, shoveling in large mouthfuls. He asked for seconds and then thirds. He and Agnes finished off the roast and all the potatoes and peas.

"Thank you," he said, "that was the finest meal I've had in . . . in . . . well, let's say a long time."

"You're welcome, Hezekiah," Agnes said. "Griselda is an excellent cook."

"Could open a restaurant."

I served the pie Zeb had given me for dessert.

When we finished, Hezekiah carried our plates into the kitchen, and a few minutes later I heard water running. I went to investigate and found Hezekiah washing our dishes. He looked funny standing at the sink with a pink apron tied around his waist.

"You don't have to do that," I said.

"Yes, I do, Ma'am. I always pay my check in one way or another."

Arthur mewled at the door.

"My cat," I said. "Arthur."

"Arthur?"

I chuckled. "He was named after a great king too."

Hezekiah cracked a smile that exposed straight teeth and a dimple on his left cheek.

Arthur sauntered inside and wrapped himself around my legs. I put the kettle on to boil for tea and placed cups and saucers on the table.

A short while later, after Hezekiah adjusted the fire and carried more logs into the room, the conversation finally turned to Hezekiah's prayer needs.

"Griselda told me you were in need of prayer," said Agnes.

Hezekiah looked down and rubbed his hands together. "Yes, yes I am. Some powerful prayers."

"Tell me why," Agnes said. "What exactly do you need me to pray for?"

Hezekiah took a breath. And when he did his strong chest expanded like a bellows. He brushed the top of his head. "Lice. Stinking lice."

"Lice?" said Agnes. "You askin' me to pray for lice?"

"No. no. I had them, that's all. Miserable vermin crawled and laid eggs all over my head. I had to shave my hair off to get rid of them. That's why it's so short. Before the infestation I had grown my hair down to here." He pointed to a place on his shoulder. "Had me a nice ponytail."

Agnes and I locked eyes, both of us grateful, I'm sure, that God waited until after the lice plague to bring him to her.

"Well, if it ain't lice then—" said Agnes.

"A person doesn't have to say the words out loud, do they? Can't you just pray some mumbo jumbo about God being able to read minds and stuff?" He folded his arms across his chest.

Agnes took a minute to adjust herself. I asked Hezekiah to push up on her knee while I straightened her pillows.

"First of all, Hezekiah, it isn't mumbo jumbo, and if that's what you believe then maybe now's not the best time to pray," Agnes said.

Hezekiah's eyes grew wide like a startled deer's. "Oh, no, ma'am, I didn't mean that; I didn't mean it was mumbo jumbo, like it was silly. I just don't know much about proper prayer talk."

Agnes and I exchanged looks and then smiles.

"I guess it will be all right," Agnes said. "God knows what you mean."

"Just tell the good Lord that I need him to help me to . . . to . . . " He pushed his fists into the sides of his head like a terrible headache had taken hold all of a sudden. "Please, I'm begging you, Agnes, pray for me."

Agnes prayed for a full three minutes, asking God to grant Hezekiah all manner of mercies from his health to his financial situation to helping him find a job. But Hezekiah didn't react to any of the requests in a way that would have clued us in to his real need—the one thing, if it were one thing—that he had locked inside himself. Sometimes it happened that way. Sometimes folks came to Agnes asking for prayer about a particular matter when all the time there was something else, something darker, something more serious that needed God's attention.

That's how is happened for Studebaker. He came to Agnes asking for prayer about his aching back and a nagging cough when all the time he knew he had lung cancer and was dying.

"Amen." Agnes finished her prayer, but Hezekiah remained with his head bent for a several more seconds, so we all sat in silence until he finally spoke.

"Thank you, Agnes. But I didn't feel nothing. I mean, ain't I supposed to feel a tingling or something? Ain't that God's way of letting you know you got a miracle?"

Agnes reached out, and Hezekiah took her hand. He laid his head on her arm. "Maybe I just don't deserve a miracle. Maybe I'm a hopeless case."

"Now you stop that talk, this instant," said Agnes in such a way that Hezekiah's head snapped to attention. "There is no such thing as hopeless cases where God is concerned. Some miracles take a little longer than others. This might be the kind that takes repeating."

Agnes grabbed her well-worn King James and thumbed through the pages. "See here, this is a story about Samuel's mother. She prayed for years before she got her miracle."

"Years?" said Hezekiah. "I don't have years. I need it now. I needed it a long time ago."

Agnes closed her Bible and began to pray again. This time she raised her voice and even asked God to bind any devils that might be chasing after Hezekiah. He crossed his arms tight against his chest when she said those words.

"In the name of Jesus, we pray for these things," Agnes finished.

Hezekiah lifted his head. "Nothing," he said. "I still got nothing."

I watched him slowly ball both hands into tight fists. He rubbed them into his eyes. "You're my only hope, Miss Sparrow."

I put my hand on his shoulder. "Hezekiah, give it a little time. You'll get your miracle." The second those words left my mouth I felt my stomach sink. I had never promised anyone a miracle before that evening.

Agnes patted my hand to silence me.

"Listen," she said looking at Hezekiah, "why don't you stay in town. I'm sure Vidalia Whitaker will give you a room."

"But I got no money."

"That doesn't matter. You can work around here. Do some odd jobs and such. I'll pay you—not a lot, mind you—but enough to help out. Maybe you can get another job in town."

I stood straight up. "Agnes, what are you saying? Shouldn't we . . . discuss this first?"

"I'm sorry," Hezekiah said. "I didn't mean to start a family squabble."

"Phooey." Agnes blew out air that smacked of beef gravy. "Don't let my sister bother you."

Hezekiah stood and rubbed his head. "I can't thank you enough. And . . . and I suppose I'm willing to wait as long as I have to for God to grant me my miracle."

6

Agnes reached out her thick arm to the bedside table and picked up the phone. "I'll call Vidalia right now and let her know you'll be coming to see her tonight."

Hezekiah stood at Agnes's side with his hands folded like a child's in prayer against his chest and his chin bent downward. When Agnes started talking he sneaked a peek at me. I smiled politely.

"Vidalia," Agnes said into the phone. "I got a favor to ask." Agnes spoke for only a couple of minutes, but I could tell from her tone that Vidalia agreed to give Hezekiah a room. He caught on also and practically beamed at her as she spoke. I stood back and watched, fighting my feelings of apprehension. Agnes placed the receiver on its cradle, winced, and tried to grab her knee.

"Cramp," she said, "another cramp."

She needed to adjust herself, and Hezekiah wasn't shy about helping. He pulled the offending leg out as straight as it would go.

"Better?" he asked.

"Thank you, Hezekiah. Yes, much better. Sometimes I get myself into the oddest, tangled up predicaments."

He patted her arm. "I'm glad I could help."

"Well, you go on down to Vidalia's and get settled. She's expecting you. Griselda will point the way."

Hezekiah shook Agnes's hand, and then he grabbed mine and pumped it up and down with vigor. "Thank you, thank you both. I knew the Almighty God led me here. I knew it."

Agnes raised her hands and said, "Praise Jesus."

I walked Hezekiah to the door and told him how to find Vidalia's house. "Just look for the wreath on the front door. Vidalia always has a welcome wreath."

"I guess I'll be seeing you in the morning," he said with a sigh. "I'm excited to get to work for you and Agnes."

"Not too early, Hezekiah. Make it around nine."

Vidalia Whitaker was one of my favorite people in town, and I had no doubt that she would take generous care of him. Vidalia was a small lady with enormous grace and compassion. She rarely complained, never attended town meetings, went to church every Sunday, and, as far as I knew, only went to Agnes once for prayer. And then, it wasn't for herself, but for a family member who lived on the other side of the country. I doubt if Studebaker even asked her to sign the petition for the Agnes Sparrow sign. I'm certain he knew she would have no part of the spectacle. I could have heard her reply, sweet, gentle, but to the point. "Now you know I am not going to sign that piece of paper," she would have said. "Now get on back to the café or somewhere and stop this foolishness."

Vidalia was one of my regulars at the library. I think she might have been the smartest woman I ever met. I always thought it a shame she never went to college. It was easy for me to picture her teaching history at a university.

But college wasn't in the cards for Vidalia. "It was hard enough for a black woman to finish high school," she told me once over tea and sugar cookies. "And colleges didn't take many colored folk back then either."

So, Vidalia self-educated herself, reading everything she could get her hands on that pertained to American history. The teachers at the high school even considered her an expert on the Civil War, and every year, when the subject was taught, students lined up, waiting to pick her brain for facts to include in their essays.

She spoke with a slight Southern accent, having been born in Georgia. She could tell stories about the War Between the States like an actress on a stage and breathe life into history that excited the children. I only asked her once about why she moved to Bright's Pond. She smiled at my question a moment, patted my hand, and said, "Griselda, there are some stones better left unturned."

I never asked her again. It wasn't important. What really mattered was the way Vidalia and her husband Drayton dovetailed into our community in the early sixties. While the rest of the world burned down cities and marched for racial equality, Bright's Pond had managed to put it into practice. Drayton passed on just a few years after they moved to town and left her to raise their daughter alone. She married and moved away. Although she offered, Vidalia said she would never leave Bright's Pond. She turned her home into a boarding house, often giving a room to visiting relatives and on rare occasions perfect strangers.

And so she did for Hezekiah. She gave him the room in the front—a large, sunny bedroom with flowered wallpaper and its own bathroom. She only charged him ten dollars a week, but always left a list of chores for him on Saturday morning.

By Groundhog Day Hezekiah had shoveled our walk ten times, patched the roof well enough to stop the occasional waterfall in one of the upstairs bedrooms, replaced the pipes under three sinks, and told Agnes that when spring came he would build us a new garage. I guessed he planned on putting down roots in Bright's Pond.

Every Groundhog Day folks gathered at the Full Moon to watch the early morning festivities at Gobbler's Knob in western Pennsylvania. Zeb brought in a small TV and sat it on the counter and we all gathered around waiting for the official groundhog decree to be read.

It was my father's favorite holiday, believe it or not. "Six more weeks to spring: just about halfway through," he'd say whether good old Punxsutawney Phil saw his shadow or not. I only remember Phil not seeing his shadow maybe one or two times. But in the mountains you can rest assured that winter would have her icy claws dug deep for at least another six and probably eight weeks no matter what Phil predicted. The spring thaw was important to my father because some winters were so cold and the ground so hard, bodies had to be kept until spring before the cemetery could bury them. Some years they were stacked three or four high in a garage at the cemetery. Imagine that, having to wait weeks before you could bury your loved one, knowing he or she was stacked like cordwood in a garage all the while.

Hezekiah joined us that year at the café. At first he didn't understand what all the hoopla was about. I was standing near the counter with Vidalia and Ruth Knickerbocker when Hezekiah pushed his way through the crowd to take a seat at the counter like he was some kind of dignitary invited for the occasion. Ruth was one of my best friends even though she was more than a decade older than me. We enjoyed each other's company and she often made me smile when it was the last thing I wanted to do.

"What's the occasion?" Hezekiah asked.

"Groundhog Day," Ruth said. "We always come out to watch Phil."

"Phil?" Hezekiah twisted on the stool.

"Happy Groundhog Day, Hez," Zeb said as he wiped the counter in front of him. "Coffee?"

"Sure thing. But what's the big deal? Why's everybody here?"

"You might say it's a tradition in town." Zeb grabbed the pot and poured. "Spring is mighty important to these folks."

I watched Hezekiah contain what I interpreted as a smirk.

Zeb had taken a liking to Hezekiah from the first day he met him. It was about three or four days after he started working for Agnes and me. He had just finished replacing a pipe under the kitchen sink, and Agnes said he looked like a man who could use a piece of pie.

"Why don't you take him on down to the café," she said, "and introduce him around?"

I did. I took Hezekiah on down to the Full Moon, and at first Zeb thought he recognized him—thought maybe they went to summer camp together, but that wasn't the case. Hezekiah had one of those faces that reminded many people of a loved one far or near. The two men took a shine to one another.

"Oh, I remember about Phil now. I never knew folks took it so serious. It's just an old wives' tale." He looked around at the disgruntled faces of those who overheard. "But it's nice to get together now, ain't it."

"That reminds me," said Ruth. She pulled my elbow and led me away from the counter and an offending waft of cigarette smoke. "The church potluck is next Friday night," she whispered. You might have thought she was telling a government secret.

"Oh, that's right. Well, I'll make some scalloped potatoes and maybe a ham."

Vidalia took my other elbow. "I'll mix up a mess of something special."

"No, that's not it," Ruth said. "There's always plenty of food. I was wondering if anyone bothered to tell Hezekiah. He hasn't come to church since he got here and—"

"Do you want me to invite him?" I asked.

"Well, you or Agnes. Don't you think Agnes should do it? I say that because Hezekiah doesn't seem the church-going type and all, and we'd hate to have him think we were twisting his arm, you know?"

Vidalia shot me a crooked smile. "I'll leave you two to chat, but I'll come by the library later."

I winked at her. "I'll be there around ten or so this morning."

"Oh, that's fine. I got to get to the market and the post office. My grandbaby, Jackson, has a birthday coming up and I got a package to send. So I'll see y'all later."

"Aren't you going to stay and wait for Phil?"

"No, I just came in for a cup of coffee this morning. Believe it or not, I ran out. That Hezekiah drinks coffee like it's water."

Vidalia pulled a knit hat over her ears and went out into the overcast day. The weatherman called for more snow, and from the looks of the clouds I figured it would be arriving soon. Snow had a funny way of creeping over the mountains. It would start out with a slow moving rack of gray clouds, and just when you thought the clouds had passed over, the flakes would start.

"So how about if you ask Agnes to ask him," Ruth said.

"Sure. I'll tell her this morning. Hezekiah will be by, I'm sure, to do some work."

"Oh, that will be just fine." She turned around and looked in Hezekiah's direction. "I'd ask him myself, but, well, that wouldn't be proper since we only just met."

"I'll take care of it, Ruth."

"Fine. I'll see you at the potluck then. Oh, and scalloped potatoes will do fine, just fine."

The potlucks at Bright's Pond Chapel had a reputation for getting a bit . . . well, a bit rowdy—rowdy for a small Pocono Mountains town, and I guessed that was why Ruth thought it might make Hezekiah nervous. Pastor Speedwell would often stand up to say "just a few words" and before you knew it, he was off and running, spouting hellfire and damnation as we polished off the cherry cobbler. The Pastor Speedwell who attended church functions was different from the pastor we saw in the pulpit on Sunday. At church functions, Pastor had an easier time letting his hair down. He spoke more from his heart than his notes.

"You know," Ruth said, "Hezekiah is such a quiet man and still a stranger. We wouldn't want to give him the wrong impression."

Before I could speak, Zeb turned up the TV as loud as it went. "Here comes Phil," he said.

All ears turned toward the TV as the official groundhog handler, who wore a top hat and tails, pulled Phil from his stump. A few seconds later the president of the Groundhog Inner Circle read Phil's prediction. "Six more weeks of winter, there will be."

A series of mock groans of disappointment rang out.

I took hold of Ruth's hand. "You know what? Just ask him yourself," I said. "We don't need Agnes to do everything.

There's nothing indecent about you asking him. I'm sure he'll be delighted to come."

Ruth seemed pleased and maybe a trifle too excited but she was entitled. It had been a long time since anyone new came to church. Ruth was the official membership coordinator, a duty she discharged with great seriousness. Getting Hezekiah to join the church would be quite a feather in her cap.

Studebaker moved toward me as the crowd started to thin out.

"Griselda, I'm glad you're here. I have something to tell Agnes. Think I could stop by this morning, or does she have other visitations?"

"I'm not certain, Stu. I left without asking her if she had any appointments this morning." The protective side of me emerged. "Is there a message I could give her? I'm heading back to the house for a little while. I could save you the bother."

Studebaker's eyes widened. He moved close to me, and I could smell coffee on his breath—that nutty, leftover odor. "It's no bother, Griselda. I'll just follow you back. That way you both can hear my news."

"What news, Stu? Don't tell me the sign is finished already."

"Almost. But I want to talk to her about the statue."

My stomach tightened. "You still going through with that cockamamie idea?"

"It's not cockamamie. I got Filby Pruett all signed up to get started. He'll need to take some pictures—"

Hezekiah interrupted us. He had a way of appearing and disappearing. He looked good. His hair was growing back, he was clean-shaven, and I thought Vidalia's home cooking was responsible for the sparkle in his eyes. "Are you going back to the house?" he asked.

"Yes."

"Great. Mind if I grab a ride? It's really cold out there."

I'm sure the temperature was still below freezing, but that wasn't unusual for early February. "Sure, Hezekiah, I'll give you a lift."

"I'll meet you there," Stu said. "Agnes won't mind me barging in on her."

My old Ford pick-up complained, but she started and we were back at the house in a few minutes. Stu pulled up behind us in his baby blue Caddy.

"I'll go on in and see what Agnes has planned for me today," Hezekiah said.

He walked ahead of me while I waited for Stu to catch up. Hezekiah was inside the house before Stu and I even took three steps. Hezekiah told me he didn't like the frosty mountain air.

"He's a nice guy, ain't he," Stu said.

"Hezekiah? Yeah, he's a good egg, I suppose."

I opened the door and nearly fell over Hezekiah who was standing in the entryway.

"Shh," he said. "I think she's praying."

I took a few steps into the house and listened. Sure enough, Agnes was deep in prayer for someone. I heard a cough, and I could tell it wasn't Agnes.

"She's in there with someone," I whispered. "We should just wait until she's finished."

The three of us stood like statues.

"You can come in now," Agnes called after a minute or so.

She was with Cora Nebbish from the café. Zeb had told me she went to see Doc Flaherty, but she said it was just a check-up—nothing serious. That morning, though, she looked a little thinner.

"Everything all right, Cora?" I asked.

"Oh, it is now," she said. "I saw the doctor the other day, and well, he was a little concerned." Cora smiled in that way that people did when a smile was the last thing they wanted to muster.

"More than concerned," Agnes said. She popped some M&Ms. "Tell them, Cora. It's all right."

Cora looked at Agnes and sighed. She placed her palms on her knees and leaned a trifle forward in the rocking chair. "Ah, it's nothing, really. That old curmudgeon had the nerve to tell me my heart is giving out. He said that's why I've been getting out of breath and feeling so dogged tired of late."

"Oh, Cora. I am sorry."

"Nothing to be sorry about, Griselda," Cora said. She took a breath.

Studebaker touched her shoulder. "You come to the right doctor now."

I watched him and Agnes exchange a glance that tightened my stomach.

Hezekiah stood uncharacteristically quiet.

"That's right." Cora's voice was tinged with excitement and nervousness. "Agnes prayed for me."

I took a breath and looked at Agnes's expression. "The good Lord will make your heart like new," she said.

"Agnes."

She put her finger to her lips and shushed me.

Stu helped Cora with her coat. She slipped a red scarf around her neck. "I best be getting to the café." She puffed a little.

"Maybe it would be a good idea to take the day off. Zeb can handle things."

"Oh, no, he can't, he'll get the decaf mixed up with the regular and all sorts of things will go wrong." Cora said. "I never missed a day of work, and I am not about to start now. I can't give in to what the doctor told me."

Stu followed her to the door as Hezekiah plopped on the sofa. He stared at Agnes for a moment, and I thought I could read his mind. I knew he was wondering why Cora believed she got her miracle and he was still waiting on his.

"It will come," Agnes said. She knew too. "I told you that some miracles take longer. Remember I showed you in the Scriptures where Jesus said that some demons require much prayer and fasting."

"I remember, but it's been going on three weeks."

"Three weeks is but a blink of an eye in heaven."

"You think I ought to start fasting?"

"Maybe. But ask the good Lord about it first."

Agnes grabbed her breakfast plate from the bedside table. There was still a slice of toast and half an orange left.

"I don't know," Hezekiah said, "that's why I come to you. The good Lord and I ain't been on speaking terms for a dog's age now."

"Then that's why you got to start talking to him," Agnes said. "Maybe he's just waiting until you do. Maybe God's waiting to hear the words come out of your mouth, not mine."

"Maybe you should just get about your chores, Hezekiah," I said.

"I guess that would be the sensible thing to do."

Agnes rubbed her knee.

"I'll get some liniment for you," I said, "and I thought Hezekiah might start in the basement this week. It really needs some cleaning out."

"The attic might be the better place," said Agnes. "I'd love for him to go through all those Christmas decorations and Mama's old things."

"Nah, the basement," I said. I patted Agnes's knee. "He can get to the attic next."

I turned my attention to Hezekiah. "There are some boxes in the garage. You'll need to pack things away—books and such. But make sure you mark the boxes clearly, please. You'll find a marker in the junk drawer in the kitchen."

"You might come across some of our father's equipment that never got sold, and there's stacks of papers and magazines down there," said Agnes.

"You mean like funeral stuff?"

"Sure, embalming tools and what not," I said. "We got rid of a lot of it over the years, but you might come across a few strange items."

Hezekiah hunched his shoulders. "Creepy."

"Not really." Agnes laughed. "If you find anything you aren't sure of, just drop it in a box and Griselda will go through it another time." She sucked in a breath. "And probably old rags. Lots of rags with stains and such. Just toss them out to be burned. You can build a fire in the backyard."

"Yes, Ma'am."

Studebaker returned. "Agnes, you know who Filby Pruett is?"

Agnes twisted her mouth. "Filby Pruett. I remember him. Scrawny fellow. Wore tortoiseshell glasses. Said he came to town to paint in peace and quiet."

"That's him. He bought the old Bradley house on Hector Street," Stu said.

"Never came to me for prayer, though." Agnes pushed her head into her pillow.

"You should see what he did to that house, Agnes," I said. "He painted it all kinds of wonderful colors—yellow, salmon, blue, even turquoise trim. He hung some pretty strange wind chimes and put odd-looking statues out front. One of them is a giant cement turtle with a rabbit in its mouth."

Studebaker patted Agnes's hand. "That's what I came to tell you. Boris and I hired him to make a statue of you, Agnes. We'll put it right in front of the town hall."

Agnes choked on a piece of buttered toast. "Sta . . . statue?"

She barely got the word out, and all I could do was stand there and let out the laughter that had come into my belly in one loud snort. "It sounds even sillier today, Studebaker."

"There is nothing silly about this idea," he said. "What with Agnes stuck in the house all the time, it would be like . . . well, it would be like she was outside, enjoying the fresh air and sunshine. It's a way for her to be with us." He patted Agnes's hand. "It's like you'll be right there with us at our meetings and town events."

"Impossible," Agnes said. "I don't want a sign and I certainly don't want a statue of me out there for all the world to see. Ridiculous. Just ridiculous."

"But, Agnes. You're our hero. Every town has a hero, like Daniel Boone or Winslow Pickett. And they have portraits and statues."

"Winslow Pickett was a true hero," Agnes said. "I'm just a fat woman who prays." She took a breath and rubbed her stomach. "Just a fat woman who prays."

Winslow Pickett was famous in Kulp City, where Studebaker was born, for single-handedly capturing seventy-two Nazis. His statue stands in the center of Kulp City on the spot where he got off the train to a crowd of grateful citizens and a fifty-piece band playing something by Sousa on September 26, 1948. Every child in the mountain region studies about him in the third grade.

A red glow like the blush of a pomegranate crept into Agnes's face.

"Think about it, Agnes," Studebaker pleaded. "Everyone thinks it's a swell idea. Just imagine the comfort it would bring to the town. Folks will get to see you everyday."

"Yeah, and the next thing you know, they'll be laying flowers at her feet and people will travel miles and miles to gaze upon the stone face of Agnes Sparrow." I had heard about enough at that point and was about to usher Studebaker out when Hezekiah appeared in the subtle, silent manner in which he was accustomed.

"Sure is a mess down there," he said. "It'll take me days to get it cleaned and organized and—" He stopped talking and looked at the three of us like we had broccoli growing out of our ears. "Sorry, looks like I might have barged in on something."

"Nothing important," I said, thankful for the interruption.

Studebaker made a noise. "Don't say that, Griselda. It's very important." Then he pulled his hat over his ears and patted Agnes's hand. "Just think about it, dear. It would mean a lot to the town . . . your town, Agnes, to all the people you've helped. Don't you see, you'd be doing it for them."

Stu leaned down and kissed Agnes's fat, red cheek. "I'll see my own way out."

Hezekiah stood at the end of Agnes's bed and reached out his open hand. "I found these odd looking things in the basement. You got a whole box full of them. Look like some kind of weird screws."

"Eye caps." She laughed. "They hold the deceased's eyes closed. Wouldn't want them popping open during the viewing. That would scare the bejeebers out of a few mourners, don't you think?"

Hezekiah went white. "Makes me happy my daddy worked in the sewers. Least that's what my Mama said he did. I never knew for sure since my old man run—" He stopped talking and pocketed the eye caps. "So what's the hubbub with old Studebaker?"

"Oh, he's talking about having that artist fellow make a statue of Agnes and put in front of the town hall."

"No kidding," he said. "That's a little silly, don't you think?"

Agnes took a hard, raspy breath. "More than silly. Plain ridiculous."

Hezekiah reached his hands into his back pockets and looked out the window a second. "But you know, Agnes, you are the most important citizen here in Bright's Pond. Don't all towns have statues of their most important citizens?"

"But this is different." I wanted to pull Hezekiah away and give him a piece of my mind, but I knew that would upset Agnes.

"I'm not so important," Agnes said in a whisper, "far from it, in fact." She closed her eyes and settled back on her pillows. "How about a bowl of soup? Chicken noodle if you got it, Griselda, and a piece of that Full Moon pie."

"I could use a slice of that pie myself," Hezekiah said following me into the kitchen. "Nothing like lemon meringue to take your mind off of eye caps and statues."

He stood by the cellar door. "I noticed you got a major problem brewing down there. Think you better take a look."

My brows wrinkled. "Problem? What are you talking about?"

Hezekiah started down the steps. "Come on, and I'll show you."

"I'll just be a minute," I called to Agnes. "Hezekiah wants to show me something in the basement."

"Near as I can figure," he said, "it's under Agnes's bathroom."

"What is?"

"That." Hezekiah craned his neck back and pointed to the cellar ceiling which was not much more than large wide boards and pipes and electric lines. "She's sagging quite a bit. Probably from years and years of all that weight up there. It's a wonder her toilet ain't crashed through by now."

I looked where Hezekiah pointed and noticed the sag right away. "It's dangerous then?"

Hezekiah let go a chuckle. "You might say that, Griselda. That poor old floor has been supporting a lot of weight for a lot of years."

"Oh, my. I'm so glad you discovered it."

"And there's a crack along one of the joists."

"Joists?"

"This thick beam here."

I sighed deeply. "Okay, what can we do?"

"I'll need help; probably Studebaker and Fred Haskell will volunteer. We'll have to set lolly jacks and maybe sister them joists to make them hold better."

"Sister?"

"That's right. Add extra wood to each side of the beam for support."

I smiled at the quaint and appropriate term.

7

I sat in my truck with the engine running for a full hour that afternoon listening to the Rassie Harper talk radio show. If I parked Old Bess on top of Hector Street, facing west with the windshield wipers going, I could tune in to WQRT out of Jack Frost. Never did figure out what the wipers had to do with the price of jellybeans in Japan, but for some odd reason the talk station came in louder when I had them on low.

While Rassie spouted on about Vietnam and President Nixon and how much he hated both of them, all I could think about was a huge billboard with my sister's fat face lighting up the road to Bright's Pond and a giant stone statue in front of the town hall. The thought gave me the willies.

I never gave a lick for politics and had actually tuned in to catch Vera Krug's *Neighborly News* in which she delighted the audience with local news, gossip, and calendar events. She always had something to say about Bright's Pond, and ever since Hezekiah blew into town, I was skittish about word of Agnes and the miracles filtering downstream. So I listened as often as I could.

"A rare bolt of snow lightning struck the Miller's Oak tree igniting a barn fire that turned into a three-alarmer quicker than Jake Miller's cows make it back for milking." That was Vera's lead-off story for the day. I relaxed then, after fearing that news of Agnes would have taken precedence over the Miller's Barn.

"'Course them sad, old gals got no barn for the night," Vera said in her best editorial voice. I heard Rassie snicker in the background and say something like, "It's udderly ridiculous."

I listened to the rest of her five-minute daily news spot. Then I dropped the truck into gear and started down the hill in time to hear Vera advertise the potluck at the church before I lost the signal. Bright's Pond had once again found its way onto the airwaves, thanks, I was certain, to Ruth Knickerbocker, who was Vera's sister-in-law and regularly provided news, which made it hard to believe she never said anything at all to Vera about Agnes. And I had no intention of inquiring for fear I'd plant an idea in her brain. I chose to believe that God had closed her mouth on the issue.

By then it was nearly two-thirty. I decided to open the library, even though given the nasty weather, library patrons would be few. Truth is, the library was my city of refuge, and I generally enjoyed it even when I was there all by my lonesome.

Vidalia's lovely house was on the way, and even though she told me she had errands that morning, I stopped outside a minute or two hoping she would come to the door or spy me out one of the large windows. The library might offer me solitude, but I was certain Vidalia Whitaker would offer me sticky buns and coffee.

I looked up at Hezekiah's room. Tangy, orange curtains hung in the window frames like two large, Halloween eyes. I had been in that room before, many years ago. Vidalia's daughter Winifred and I spent hours there listening to the

Beatles and talking about boys and God and periods, swearing that we would never let a boy, "do that to us." She apparently changed her mind and got married right out of high school, moved to Detroit, and increased the world's population by six. They didn't start having those babies right away, even though Winifred wanted them. The Lord just didn't bless her until she turned twenty-seven and then she couldn't seem to stop. Lonely, I sat in my truck. I missed my friend and wished her mother would come out on the porch and invite me inside like the bygone days.

"Hello, Griselda."

I rolled down the truck window and waved at Vidalia, who stood in the doorway.

"Come on up," she called. "I just put on a fresh pot, and I got some sticky buns warming in the oven."

I clomped up the newly shoveled porch steps and went inside.

"Now unwrap yourself from all that winter garb," Vidalia said. "Let me take a good look at you. Too much commotion down at Zeb's this morning to really see you, you know what I mean?"

Vidalia often added, "You know what I mean?" after her sentences. It wasn't that she thought folks seriously didn't understand her. It was a way of making an emphasis.

"I look the same now as I did this morning."

"Maybe not. You look a bit peaked."

I hung my coat and hat and scarf on the oak hall tree, left my sopping boots near a hot radiator that hissed a little, and followed Vidalia into the kitchen. Her house was similar to the others in the area—a large Queen Anne with lots of wood, charm, and drafts.

"Let me just get the sticky buns out of the oven," she said. "It's a good morning for them."

The nutty, brown aroma of cinnamon, butter, and walnuts wafted around the room and wrapped me like a warm blanket.

"I suppose I am feeling a little . . . down. It's all this sign talk."

"Um, I can understand that." She placed china cups and saucers rimmed with tiny pink roses on the table. "But like my Drayton always said, 'You can't fight city hall.'"

"I keep trying, but it seems the louder I scream the more hardheaded Studebaker and Boris get."

"Men."

Vidalia sat down and slathered butter onto a sticky bun. It melted and dripped down the sides onto the plate. A raisin fell and landed in the tiny butter pool. She plucked it up and ate it. "Go on, Griselda. Put some butter on that bun."

I ripped off a corner of the square roll and noticed she had given me the middle piece—the only one that was soft on all four sides. "Now they're talking about having a statue built by that Filby Pruett," I said with my mouth full. I didn't even really know Filby all that well but just the thought of him chiseling and hammering out a graven image of Agnes turned my stomach against him.

"Mercy me." Vidalia clicked her tongue and shook her head while pouring coffee into her cup. "I can't believe it."

"You can believe it. I just don't know what I'm going to do."

Vidalia added a splash of half and half to her coffee, stirred, and then tapped her spoon against the rim of the cup. She took a sip and held it in her mouth for a second. "What you're gonna do?" She clicked her tongue. "My, my, my, Griselda. Ever think that maybe this isn't your problem?"

"Not my problem? But, Vidalia, Agnes has no one else looking after her, not really, not in the way she needs."

"I hear that, darlin', I'm just saying you got to let it rest in God's hands sometimes while you carve out your own life, you know what I mean?"

"No time. Agnes needs me. It's not like she can go romping down to the town hall and make her case. I just hoped folks would understand and—"

She grazed my hand with a light touch. "Griselda, Agnes is in the hollow of God's palm. He isn't gonna drop her."

I finished my sticky bun. "God must have some huge hands."

Vidalia's words stuck in my brain that week, and I pondered them from time to time as I went about my routine. Every time I brought Agnes a meal or sat down to play Scrabble I considered her words. What was my life without Agnes? And how could she fight city hall without me?

By Friday I still wasn't able to shake Vidalia's words from my brain, but I hunkered down to business as usual, accepting what was as things that couldn't be changed.

Old Man Winter decided to tease us and allow a warm front over the mountains. By warm I mean the temperature had risen to nearly forty degrees. I opened my bedroom window and filled my lungs with the sharp, cool air. Spring was on its way, and soon I would be searching for the first yellow or purple crocus to poke its head through the snow.

Even though it was only seven in the morning, Hezekiah was already hard at work, chopping firewood in the backyard. I stood at the window and watched him sling the axe far over his head and bring it down neatly and cleanly, splitting the wood. It made a nice sound, an honest but hollow sound that echoed around the yard—the slow heartbeat of a lonely man. Hezekiah never told me, and, as far as I knew, Agnes either, what it was that put him on the streets, and for some reason or another, that morning, it no longer mattered. Like Vidalia said about her Drayton, "some stones are better left unturned."

I carried Arthur down the steps and tossed him out the front door. "And don't bring me any prizes today."

"That cat will never stop his killing ways," called Agnes. "It's in his blood."

I helped Agnes sit up. She coughed and sputtered more than usual that morning. "You all right?" I patted her back.

"Fine." She coughed.

"I'll open a window. It's a little warmer this morning. You could use some oxygen in here."

Agnes took another labored breath. "Bacon and eggs would be good today."

It was that kind of morning, the kind of morning when the smell of bacon frying and coffee percolating made everything else seem right and good.

Hezekiah clomped into the kitchen carrying an armload of freshly chopped oak and setting down snowy footprints. "Morning, Griselda."

"Good morning. A fire might not be the best idea today. Agnes is having trouble breathing, and that'll just make it harder."

"Oh, sure. I'll stack this on the back porch then."

"Are you hungry?" I laid six more slices of bacon in the pan anticipating his answer.

"I could do with a bite."

"How'd you like your eggs?"

"Scrambled is good."

That was good. I had intended on scrambling them anyway.

Agnes preferred three eggs and a slice of toast for each one. She could eat bacon like a lumberjack and cherry Danish until the cows came home. Every once in a while I got the feeling there was a little unspoken competition going on between Agnes and Hezekiah, and more often than not, Agnes out ate him.

We finished breakfast and Agnes began to pray, asking the Lord for good health for me and Hezekiah and for a good day all around town.

"And Lord," she said, "thank you for the warmth of your blessed sunshine today. Amen."

I dropped plates in the sink, put away the food, and made certain Agnes had enough tuna salad for lunch. She liked it with a bag of Fritos, chocolate chip cookies, and milk. Hezekiah had started getting her lunch for her, which meant I didn't have to leave the library all day if I didn't want too.

Arthur mewled at the back door. Hezekiah let him in.

"There you are. Hungry?" I asked. He slid through my legs.

"Okay, okay."

I slopped food into his bowl and changed his water.

"Sometimes I think that cat is your best friend," Hezekiah said. He stood at the kitchen doorway. I wasn't about to agree with him or tell him that I often preferred Arthur's company to that of any human.

"Not really. He's just a stray that came knocking one day, looking for a handout."

Hezekiah lowered his eyes. "Well, I can say this much for us strays . . . we're nothing if not loyal."

I pulled a loaf of wheat bread from the breadbox and plopped it on the table. "She might not like tuna on wheat, but I don't want to go to the store this morning."

"I'll go." He smiled. "Us strays know how to be thankful."

"Good. Now I better get to work. Keep going in the basement and—"

"Yes, ma'am, I got it covered."

"I was going to say . . . and that drip under the kitchen sink isn't getting any better."

I put on my coat and scarf and sat on the couch to pull on my boots.

"You walking today?" Agnes asked. Her voice was raspy.

"No, I'll take the truck, and you make sure you take your medicine."

"Worrywart."

"Just do it. Got any visitations today?"

"I told Cora to stop by, and goodness me, there might be more folks." She looked toward the window. "Open the curtains, Griselda, so I can see, and don't forget my pens and notebook."

I sucked in air and opened the drapes. The sun reflected off the snow and glinted through the glass. Flurries fell and rode the air currents like tiny ladies with parasols. Ice crystals gleamed like diamonds in the yard.

"It's like living inside a snow globe," said Agnes.

8

I had just finished the morning mail at the library and picked up a publisher's catalog when Hezekiah bolted through the door.

"It's Agnes!" he hollered. "You better come."

I dropped the magazine and caught my breath. "What happened?"

"I . . . I don't know. She just all of a sudden started having a terrible time breathing." Hezekiah huffed and puffed like dogs chased him all the way to the library. But I suppose the first time seeing Agnes in distress would cause anyone to tremble and run.

"Asthma. It's her asthma. Did you call the doc?"

"Sure did, Griselda. He just got there when I came to get you."

I pulled on my coat, and we headed for my truck. "She'll be all right, Hezekiah. This happens every now and again. The doctor will take care of it."

Thankfully, Old Bess started up without complaint, and Hezekiah and I were back at the house in less than five minutes. I saw Doc's Dodge Dart parked on the lawn. He had a way of taking emergency license when it came to parking, saying, "Sometimes a few seconds can make the difference between life or the big house."

Doctor Samuel Flaherty was a small, middle-aged man who wore perfectly round glasses on his not so perfectly round face. He was pretty much bald except for two tufts of gray hair above each ear. His wife and nurse, Grace, left him a few years back. She ran off with a drug salesman from Binghamton. Doc never bothered to hire or marry a new one.

"Doc," I called the second my feet landed inside our house. "Is she all right?"

"I got here in plenty of time, Griselda."

I sloughed off my coat and went to my sister. Her face was redder than an Empire apple, and the elastic bands of the breathing machine sank into her cheeks. I'd seen this before, but Hezekiah looked in shock. I suppose a fat woman with tiny frightened eyes, breathing into an oxygen mask, could shock a person.

"She'll need the nebulizer twice a day for a week," Doc said. "Don't let her tell you otherwise."

I looked at Agnes and smiled like I always did at those times. The little machine buzzed like a mosquito on the table next to her. I patted her hand and pushed stray hairs away from her sweaty face. She was breathing pretty steady now. Agnes hated the nebulizer even though it was probably the one thing in the room that did more to keep her alive than any other. Talking was still too strenuous, so her eyes did the pleading.

I shook my head. "A few more minutes, Agnes. Then you can take it off."

Hezekiah stood on her other side and held her hand. "That's right, Agnes, a few more minutes."

"Do you know what triggered it this time?" I asked Doc.

"Not yet. I didn't have time to ask questions. I sure am glad Hezekiah was here though." Doc stuck the ends of his stethoscope into his ears and listened to Agnes's chest.

"It's a wonder I can hear anything through all this gall darn blubber, Agnes," he said. Doc was the only person in Bright's Pond who could talk to Agnes with such honesty.

I patted Agnes's shoulder. "You always get through these episodes, so hang in there a little longer and let the medicine do its work."

Agnes nodded and closed her eyes.

"Fifteen more minutes," Doc said. Then he called me aside.

"I'm going to give you another prescription. I think your sister has been getting herself all worked up lately, and like I told you both, Griselda, stress can trigger this kind of attack."

"It's that blasted sign and now they're talking about a statue. I don't know what else is bothering her but she's seemed a trifle out of sorts these days."

I looked over and saw Agnes shaking her head. She popped the clear, plastic mask off her face. "It has nothing to do with that silly old sign—" She wheezed and took a second to catch her breath. "I don't give a hang about it anymore. Let them do what they want. It was the pickles."

"Pickles?" I said. "Agnes, you know you can't eat pickles. What in tarnation made you eat pickles?"

She snatched the mask from her mouth and nose. "I . . . I wanted a . . . a pickle." Even with her breath getting caught somewhere between her bronchial tubes and her lips she was vehement.

Doc replaced the mask and it instantly fogged up as Agnes breathed in the medicine. "I said fifteen minutes. And I

83

warned you about food triggers. Of all things Agnes, you've got to be mindful of the foods you eat."

She talked through the mask. "It was one gherkin, Doc. One."

"One gherkin will kill you, Agnes. Imagine that on your headstone. Here lies Agnes Sparrow, who died from eating a pickle."

"Hezekiah," I said, "I don't expect you to know everything that can set off my sister like that but in the future . . . no pickles."

"I'm sorry, Griselda."

"It's not your fault, but I think I better make a list of the things Agnes can't have."

I walked the doctor to the door. "Thank you, Doc. I'll keep a closer eye on her."

"Get that script filled. It's a mild sedative. Use it today and maybe tomorrow. She should rest now, so no more visitors."

After Doc left I went to check on Agnes. Hezekiah was still standing over her and holding her hand. Agnes breathed dutifully—in and out, in and out as the nebulizer machine chugged.

"Ten more minutes, Agnes," Hezekiah said looking at his watch.

"The doctor wants Agnes to have this medicine," I said, "so I'll go on down to the drug store and have it filled. Just turn the machine off—" but before I finished my sentence Agnes ripped the mask off.

"I hate that thing," she said. "Now turn it off will you, Hezekiah?" She was breathing easier. "And I don't want no more medicines. What's that fool giving me now?" She puffed.

"A mild sedative. It's important that you rest for a day or so: no visitations, Agnes, and put that mask back on. You want to die?"

Hezekiah rubbed the back of her hand, and then he brushed some damp, stray hairs out of her face. "Please, Agnes. It's just ten minutes."

Agnes smiled at him in a way that reminded me of the way she smiled at our father.

I left the two of them with Agnes breathing in the life-saving medicine and Hezekiah standing over her like she was Cleopatra on her barge. I half expected to come home and find him fanning her.

Not my problem? How could Vidalia even think such a thing? Agnes was more my problem than any one else's. I handed her prescription to Bob Smith, the pharmacist. Fresh from pharmacy school, he was a recent Bright's Pond acquisition and a nice enough fellow, but a lot of people looked at him with suspicion on account of his being so young. They sometimes treated him like a child and would ask him to check, double check and even triple check the pills he handed out. And with a name like Bob Smith, it just made him all the more suspect, especially since Bob knew some folks most private medical conditions. He knew who took tranquilizers and who got pain medication.

"Will you wait for it?"

"If that's okay. The doc said she needed it right away."

"About ten minutes."

I walked away from the counter, wondering why in the world it took so long to drop a few little pills into a bottle and type up a nametag.

An hour later, Agnes had nearly recovered from her crisis. Doc Flaherty told me he would have hospitalized any other patient with her symptoms, but moving her would have been more traumatic. When I told Agnes, she countered with, "I probably get better quicker at home anyway. Hospitals only make you sicker; bacteria factories, that's what they are." Although I couldn't dismiss her opinion, I lived with the concern that one day home remedies were not going to cut it.

Hezekiah spent the rest of the day and clear through the next week working in the basement. Every once in a while he wandered up the steps holding one suspicious looking instrument or other. Some of my father's equipment was pretty gruesome looking and would have turned even the strongest of stomachs.

I managed to keep Agnes visitor-free until Friday morning, when Cora came by with Studebaker.

"I'm sorry, Griselda," Cora said, "I heard you were keeping folks away this week, but I—"

"It's okay, Cora, you come on in."

Studebaker helped her with her coat and hat. She left her unbuckled boots on and padded into the viewing room. She wore the same, thin, flowered dress she had worn every time I'd seen her.

"Cora's feeling kind of poorly," Stu whispered.

My heart sank.

Cora sat in the rocker near Agnes. Studebaker and I hung back and let them talk. Within minutes Agnes was deep in prayer, so I walked into the kitchen and put on a pot of coffee.

Afterwards, I offered Cora a cup of tea, but she declined and explained that she wanted to get home.

"I won't be making it to the potluck," she said. "First one I've missed in forty-five years."

Stu helped her down the porch steps and into his car. I lingered as they drove away.

Our potluck dinners always started around six o'clock, which was late for some of the parishioners. Most folks in Bright's Pond had finished supper by five-thirty, especially in the winter months. But they made an exception once a month and staved off their appetites for an hour or so to accommodate the men who didn't make it home from work until then.

The Bright's Pond Chapel of Faith and Grace sat like an old mother hen right across the street from the Sparrow Funeral Home. Back when it was still a funeral home it was especially convenient for moving the casket over to the church for services—if that's what the family wanted. Agnes had a good view of the comings and goings from her bed and often reported to me who she had seen entering the church on an off-day, that being any day but Sunday or Wednesday evening when the men gathered for their weekly prayer meeting. I never could understand why no women were allowed at those meetings, and I harbored an image of the men sitting in a circle on metal folding chairs with their Bibles on their laps discussing the latest football game instead of praying. But what did I know?

Our Daddy went every single Wednesday and always came back happier than when he left, which at one time led our mother to believe there was some hanky-panky going on and that Daddy wasn't really praying or talking sports. But he managed to allay her fears.

"Now you know you're my little puddle duck. Trust me, honey. I'm not doing anything but praying." Then he'd kiss her and her left leg would lift slightly off the ground as he pulled her close.

The church building, constructed around 1900 from gray, Pennsylvania fieldstone dug from nearby quarries and hauled on sledges by horses, had always been a place of worship. It still had the original bell hanging in the tower, although the bell, which at one time called people to worship or signal a death in the town, was no longer used.

I left for the church a few minutes past six.

"I'll bring you back some food and goodies," I told Agnes.

"It's the one thing I miss more than anything else," she said.

The potlucks and most every other occasion were held in the fellowship hall, a large rectangular room with coat racks lining one side and chairs and tables set out in a way that made for the best traffic flow. The potluck committee, chaired by Vidalia Whitaker and Ruth Knickerbocker, assembled three long tables side by side and served the food buffet style.

Now you can think what you want but there are few things in life that can stack up against a church potluck. A person could derive sustenance from the aromas alone.

Vidalia set a casserole of steaming macaroni and cheese on the table between the scalloped potatoes and a ham. "You were able to come, Griselda, I was afraid you wouldn't. I heard about Agnes."

Funny how your eyes close sometimes and a small sigh escapes your heart without you even making the conscious decision to do it. "She's fine now, but I'll probably leave early."

"Oh, she'll be all right. And you're just across the street." As usual, Vidalia was right. For these occasions Pastor Speedwell had the phone company install a telephone in the kitchen, and we always kept the ring on its loudest, just for Agnes's sake.

Vidalia turned the ham. "That's better. Now everyone can see those pretty pineapples and cherries all shiny in that brown-sugar glaze."

"It's a nice ham," Ruth said. She padded up beside us, carrying a Full Moon pie in each hand. "How's your sister, dear?"

"Fine, Ruth. Doc said she needs to rest this week, and then she'll be back to her usual self."

"I'm glad to hear it. Zeb brought four pies, but I think we should just set out two at a time. They go so fast. I'll leave the other two in the kitchen."

The noise level in the room increased as more and more folks dribbled in, some carrying armfuls of food and others armfuls of children. Clay Gilmore dropped a basket of rolls on the table.

"Thank you, Mr. Gilmore," Ruth said.

He tipped his hat.

By six-forty every seat was taken and folks looked half-starved as we waited for Pastor Speedwell to arrive. Food wasn't served until Pastor prayed.

Sheila Spiney sat down at the piano and started playing *That Old Rugged Cross*, and pretty soon everyone was singing, singing and swaying. Just as we belted out the last stanza, Pastor and his wife entered through the back door, followed by their four boys, Matthew, Mark, Luke, and John. You can make your own observation on that one.

Darcy and the boys took their usual seats, and Pastor stood with his Bible tucked under his arm. He was a nice enough fellow, tall and lanky as a Slim Jim with curly black hair, high cheekbones, and a way of talking that hovered somewhere near hellfire and brimstone. But he was never able to whip the congregation into the Holy Spirit frenzy I think he dreamed about.

I was still standing with Ruth and Vidalia when he started to pray. He went through the usual routine, thanking God for the blessings of living in a country free from war but careful to ask for special mercies of safety for the two young men Bright's Pond sent to Viet Nam, at which point their mothers began to cry.

He thanked the Lord for the meal we were about to eat and the many hands "that so lovingly prepared it" and was winding up to put his Amen on the end when Cora Nebbish bounced into the room like a cheerleader. A collective gasp rose through the congregation as she stood in the middle of the room.

"Hello, Sister Cora," Pastor said. "Are you all right?"

"I thought she was on her deathbed," I heard Janeen Sturgis say.

Cora took a few steps closer to Pastor but not without laying a hand on every shoulder she could reach. "I've been healed. I've been healed," she said with each touch. "Agnes prayed and I got healed. My heart never felt stronger—never ticked stronger."

Doc Flaherty, who always carried his medical bag, went to her. "Now, now, Cora, you got to take it easy."

"Not anymore. Agnes healed me. Praise God for Agnes."

That was when Hezekiah showed up wearing a brand new suit and a smile about as wide as Montana. "It's true. Cora was just with Agnes and Agnes prayed and all of a sudden, Cora took a deep, long breath and started to cry, saying she felt the touch of God all warm and tingly."

"Just like me," Studebaker said. "Did it feel like a zillion fire ants were crawling all over your insides, Cora?"

"Sure did, Studebaker, like a zillion fire ants. Hallelujah!"

Doc pulled out his stethoscope and made Cora sit down. Pastor Speedwell put his hand on her shoulder.

"It's true," he said, "I can feel the energy pulsing through our dear, dear sister."

"I'll be the judge of that," Doc said.

The congregation quieted down, so quiet I could hear the steam rising off the casseroles.

"It's true," Doc said pulling the stethoscope from his ears. "Cora, your heart is beating like a twenty-year-old girl's."

Tears started to flow down Vidalia's cheeks, and Ruth was so overcome she dashed into the kitchen crying, "It's a miracle. It's a miracle. Agnes did another miracle."

Cora rose and took Pastor Speedwell's hand. "She did it, Pastor. Agnes saved my life."

Studebaker joined Cora and kissed her cheek. "Another miracle."

And, I thought, more ammunition to fire at the sign/statue debate. Then, in the blink of an eye, the sound of pots and pans crashing to the floor turned everyone's attention from Cora.

"Oh, my sweet Lord," Ruth screamed from the kitchen. "Oh, my gracious Lord in Heaven."

All heads turned to the clatter. Me and Hezekiah and Vidalia rushed for the kitchen. I thought Ruth Knickerbocker had keeled over, taking half the kitchen with her. But we were stopped in our tracks as Ruth, who I will admit was glowing, appeared in the doorway.

Ruth walked slowly to the center of the room carrying a Full Moon pie. "It's . . . it's Jesus. It's Jesus himself come to put his blessing on Cora's healing."

"What are you talking about, Sister Ruth?" Pastor said.

"The pie! Just look at this pie. It's got Jesus's face right on it and . . . and he's smiling . . . I . . . I think."

"Now, hold on there, Ruth," Pastor said, "we can't go saying—" He looked at the pie. "Holy cow and jumpin' Jehosephat!" He smacked himself in the forehead. I averted my eyes in time to see Darcy cup her hands over her youngest boy's ears while the other three sat with mouths open wide. They weren't accustomed to hearing such obscenities spew from their father's mouth.

"It does look like Jesus," Pastor said.

The people gathered in a circle around Ruth and Cora and Pastor. Hezekiah and I stayed back.

"It's not everyday Jesus comes to call," Hezekiah said.

"It's a pie, Hezekiah, just a pie. Ruth and all the others are just seeing what they want to see."

Apparently, the golden dewdrops on the meringue had arranged themselves in a pattern that if you looked at it just right you could see the face of Jesus.

"A miracle," Ruth said. "We've been blessed with two miracles tonight."

Cora, even though her heart was beating like a child's again was still seventy-two and needed a little help to stand. She looked long and hard at the pie. Sheila played *Amazing Grace*, pianissimo, and the second Cora nodded and declared, "It's Jesus," everyone started to sing and sway as the music swelled. There was weeping in the fellowship hall that evening, weeping and singing, weeping and singing.

Zeb walked out from a corner and took a long, hard look at the pie and put his arm around Cora, "Imagine that, Jesus showing up in one of my pies. I didn't see it when I pulled it out of the oven."

"The Good Lord honored you, Zeb," Cora said.

Zeb reached down and kissed Cora's cheek. "Seems appropriate, seeing how you're my waitress."

When the singing stopped, Ruth held the pie toward Cora. "I think Cora should get the first piece. It is her miracle, after all."

Ruth walked past Hezekiah and me and I caught a glimpse of the pie. I don't know. All I saw were oddly spaced lemon meringue dewdrops. Although, just as Ruth passed by and the fluorescent light of the fellowship hall hit the pie at a different angle, I thought I might have seen a nose.

I glanced at Hezekiah who had craned his neck around me to see. His smile had disappeared, and he slinked away. It had been a while since I had seen him looking so dejected. Where was his miracle?

8

Now as you might expect, the Jesus pie created quite a stir in Bright's Pond, and nobody ever did get around to cutting it, much less serving and eating it.

Ruth brought it into the kitchen after the excitement died down but returned to the dining area in a fluster of emotion.

"I can't do it. I just can't cut into it. There's just something wrong about the whole notion of eating Jesus pie."

Pastor Speedwell draped one of his long arms around Ruth's shoulder. "It's fine, Sister Ruth, ain't nobody here who could blame you. Fact is I couldn't eat that pie either."

A mighty applause broke out, and the pie was set aside and later placed in the refrigerator until someone could figure out the proper way to dispose of it . . . or preserve it.

Pastor finally got around to asking a blessing on the meal, even though everyone thought it had already been blessed. I sat with Hezekiah and Vidalia, when she wasn't running all around catering to the needs of the congregation.

"Such is the duty of the potluck committee," she said after Janeen complained that the second macaroni and cheese hadn't been brought from the kitchen.

Ruth and Cora sat with the Speedwells, and the two women never glowed as brightly as they chewed their roast beef and potatoes.

"I can see why folks would never want to leave Bright's Pond," Hezekiah said.

"You stay as long as you like," Vidalia said. "I got no plans for your room."

Hezekiah smiled and loosened his tie. "I wasn't certain how to dress for a church potluck. But seeing how Jesus showed up and all, I'm glad I bought this suit."

"You look very nice," I said. And he did. That evening Hezekiah was a far cry from the bedraggled man I found rooting through our trash. His color was better, and he had put on some weight that was especially evident in his face. He looked more like a man and less like an outcast.

After dessert was served and the tables cleared, Pastor Speedwell stood up.

"I was going to tell you people the story of Daniel in the lion's den, but after what happened in this room tonight I feel it just ain't the right story."

Cora and Ruth both beamed when Pastor put his hands on their shoulders.

"We got Agnes to thank," he said. "Let us rejoice and thank God Almighty for the prayers of Agnes Sparrow."

Five minutes later people were on their feet singing and rejoicing as Pastor told how Jesus had seen fit to enter our midst that evening.

"It is a sign—a sign, brothers and sisters—that Jesus has found favor with Bright's Pond: favor through Sister Agnes, favor through Cora and Zeb and Ruth."

He balled his hand into a fist and pounded the table, causing the dishes and glasses to rattle. "If God is for us, who,

I say who, can be against us? Or better yet, I say . . . what? What can be against us? Not cancer."

"Hallelujah," shouted Janeen Sturgis.

"Amen," said Studebaker.

Pastor smiled and looked around the room. "Not heart trouble or ulcers. Not even a hangnail is lost from the healing touch of God Almighty through the praying lips of Sister Agnes Sparrow."

Another round of applause rose up, and people shouted their hallelujahs. Cora cried as Ruth held her hand. Pastor went on like that for the better part of an hour until the folks with little children dribbled out and the older folks started to fall asleep.

He claimed every miracle, every lost object, every saved marriage, every soothed bunion and arthritic hip in town. Finally, by 9:30 he wrapped it up, and Janeen shouted one final hallelujah with her hands raised over her head as she danced a little jig.

The pie, by the way, sat in the church refrigerator for the better part of two weeks until Jack Cooper finally had enough of it. I was on my way home from food shopping when I saw him sitting on the church steps with the pie on his knees.

"Watcha doing?" I hollered across the street.

"I just don't know what to do with it." He stood up and stretched the pie toward me. "You wanna care for this Jesus pie?"

"It's not Jesus pie, Jack. It's lemon meringue."

"But this sure does look like his face, Griselda. I can't see tossing it in the trash . . . and even Pastor said he saw him."

Crows chattered and squawked in the trees above the church. "How about if you feed it to the birds."

Jack looked up into the branches and then gently sat the pie on the snowy, church lawn.

"Maybe the birds will fly it back to Jesus," Jack said.

Within seconds a flock of crows gathered around the pie like chubby women at a basement bargain bin, each taking a bite and flying toward heaven until all that was left was the silver pie tin glinting in the afternoon sun.

Agnes wasn't so impressed about the Jesus pie, although she didn't entirely dismiss it. I wasn't even going to tell her but I couldn't help myself.

"Some of them folks have quite the imagination," she said. "Jesus showing up in lemon meringue."

"I know, I didn't really see it myself but just about everyone else did. Got real excited about it, Agnes."

"I suspect seeing Jesus in any shape or form could be exciting." She took a deep breath and reached for a candy bar—a Mounds that Stella Hughes left her earlier that day.

"You ever see Jesus?" I asked.

Agnes ripped open the Mounds and took a big bite that she chewed and chewed like she was stalling for time.

"You saying you did?"

"Not sure, Griselda. I don't want to make it sound like I saw him, flesh and blood, walking down the street or knotted up in a tree trunk like some have. More like an experience deep inside. But that was a long time ago."

"Like getting saved?"

Agnes pushed the rest of the chocolate into her mouth. "Different, but yeah, kind of like that."

Cora went back to work after Doc insisted she spend three days in the hospital where she said she was poked and prodded with every medical instrument known to the modern world, or worse, she had said, the medieval world. Two internists and a cardiologist who had come from Wilkes-Barre to see if what he heard was true, declared Cora as sound as a bell and released her.

I caught up with her at the Full Moon the day after Jack fed the Jesus pie to the crows. She stood behind the counter holding a pot of decaf and chatting with a couple of truck drivers.

"The look on that pointy-headed specialist's face was priceless," she said. "He couldn't believe it and told me there must have been something wrong with the first set of tests."

One of the truck drivers, a short, stocky man, bit into his baloney sandwich while the other stared at Cora. "Maybe he's right, Cora. Maybe those earlier tests were all hogwash, a medical mix-up. I hear it happens all the time. Hospitals are always removing kidneys by accident, so maybe—"

"I won't hear that talk," Cora said, "It weren't no mistake. Jesus healed me—healed me and then he showed up at our potluck in one of Zeb's pies just to prove it."

With that the first driver choked and the second paid the check, and they left without another word.

Cora spied me sitting at a booth listening to the whole conversation. She cleaned up the counter and then headed my way. "Can you believe that, Griselda? They practically called me a liar."

"Don't fret about it Cora, they just don't get it. People get scared at the thought of miracles and images of Jesus showing up in pie when they're not accustomed to it. You understand."

Actually, I was glad the truck drivers didn't stick around to ask more questions, and worse, ask to see Agnes.

Cora poured me a cup of regular coffee and dropped several tiny containers of half and half on the table. "You're right, Griselda, those good old boys don't know Agnes."

Zeb called Cora away before I had a chance to order a grilled cheese.

"Oh, I'm sorry, Griselda, I'll be right back. Let me go see what he wants."

Stu walked in and noticed me right off.

"Griselda," he called with a wave. He hung his jacket on the pole at my booth. "I'm glad you're here. I got great news."

I swallowed coffee. "What is it, Stu?"

He sat across from me and smiled like a dog going for a car ride. "The sign is finished. Just got to be shipped from Scranton and then we can set it up out on the interstate. But first we're planning an unveiling at the town hall."

My heart skipped a beat. "You know how I feel about this, Stu. I wish you'd stop yakking at me about it."

"I'm gonna stop by and tell Agnes just as soon as Boris and I wrap up some business."

"I have to go back to the library, but—"

"Don't matter, Griselda, you don't need to be there. I just want to tell Agnes . . . and Hezekiah, I guess, if he's there."

"He's supposed to be working in the basement."

I don't think he heard me because his attention was diverted when Boris walked in.

"Well, you take care, Griselda," Stu said. "I'll just go sit with Boris."

That was fine with me. Cora brought me a grilled cheese and tomato soup. "Zeb said for you to bring home a pie to Agnes. I already put it in a box up at the cash register."

I dipped a corner of my sandwich into my soup and smiled at Boris. Stu pointed me out to him. They were all smiles that day, no doubt discussing the sign and their plans to unveil it to the town.

Zeb came out from the kitchen and slid into the other seat at my booth. "Hey, Grizzy, what's new?"

"Not much, Zeb. You know, same old stuff. Except Stu tells me the sign is all finished and—"

"I know. They're planning some celebration at the next town meeting."

I shook my head and chewed.

Zeb looked around the diner a few seconds and then looked me in the eyes. "Say, Griselda, I've been thinking. The Daisy Daze dance is coming up in June, and I know it's a ways off, but I was wondering if you'd be my date."

To say his question came as a surprise would certainly be an understatement. Not that it was the first time Zeb ever asked me out on a date. It had just been so long and I thought he'd lost interest seeing as how all my free time was spent caring for Agnes.

I wiped my lips with a paper napkin I pulled from the silver table dispenser. "Well, I don't know, Zeb. I—"

"I know you have to consider Agnes, but I was thinking maybe with Hezekiah around, he could, you know, babysit. Not all night mind you, but for a little while, and then you and me could check in on her from time to time."

The nervousness inside Zeb's belly was obvious. He always rambled and talked fast when the butterflies started fluttering.

"It might work out—"

But before I could finish my thought, Zeb jumped up and grabbed my hand. "Thank you, Griselda. I knew you would, and you'll even have enough time now to choose a pretty dress and all."

He caught his faux pas. "Not that you need me telling you that."

"It's okay, Zeb."

He smiled and his eyes twinkled in the bright diner lights. "I better go flip some baloney."

I had trouble getting the rest of my grilled cheese down and pushed the plate away. Cora offered to refill my coffee.

"Zeb said to tell you that lunch is on him today." She winked. "And don't forget Agnes's pie."

I took the pie home instead of going to the library. I wanted to tell Agnes about the sign before Studebaker got there.

Agnes was with Mildred Blessing of all people. As long as she's been in town, Mildred had never stopped in for prayer. But I probably should have known there would be a surge in visitations after Cora's healing.

I stood in the entryway for a minute. I always felt uncomfortable walking in on a prayer session and just as uncomfortable standing around with nothing to do while Agnes prayed. Arthur sauntered near, and I picked him up and held his warm body to my cheek.

"How long has she been here?" I whispered.

"Come on in, Griselda," called Agnes. "Mildred and I are finished."

Agnes had managed to move herself to the couch. That was generally a sign she was feeling good, her breathing easier.

"I'm glad to see you out of bed," I said.

"Mildred and I were just chatting about how she came to join the police force—fascinating story."

"Oh, you must tell me about it someday."

"Not so fascinating," said Mildred. "It was after my father was killed by a hoodlum on the streets for fifty bucks that I dedicated my life to crime fighting."

"Oh, kind of like Batman," I said.

Mildred wrinkled her forehead and glared. "I suppose but Batman wasn't a cop."

"No, a crime fighter." I looked at Agnes and watched her roll her eyes. "He dedicated his life to fighting the bad guys after his mother and father were killed by thugs."

"Oh, okay, sure," said Mildred. "Well, we've been bumping gums long enough. I better get back to my patrol. I've got to crack down on the folks not obeying the parking laws in this town. It's just a sin the way some people ignore the law. And Eugene called in another complaint about Ivy's dog."

I nodded. "You'll never catch that mutt."

Mildred zipped her heavy uniform coat and plopped a fur-lined hat with earflaps on her head. "Thank you, Agnes, I think I'm feeling better already."

"Cramps," said Agnes after the door slammed shut. "The girl's got some nasty cramps."

I took a breath while Agnes popped M&Ms into her mouth. "I'm a mite hungry. Got any of that ziti left?" she asked.

"Sure, but I need to tell you something first."

"Shoot."

"I ran into Stu down at the café. The sign is finished and on its way from Scranton."

Agnes closed her eyes and sighed. "Oh, dear. Nothing is gonna stop those fools."

"I'm afraid not. He's on his way here to tell you."

"Think I have time for a sandwich first?"

"Sandwich. I thought you wanted ziti."

"I do."

I no sooner had the ziti warming in the oven and a tuna on white bread ready when the doorbell rang. Thinking it was Stu and maybe even Boris, I took my good old time getting to the door, only it wasn't them. It was Filby Pruett standing there with a 35mm camera slung around his neck. He wore a straw Panama hat, a gray wool overcoat with fur around the collar and sleeves, and a mood ring the size of a quarter. It was cobalt blue.

"Forgive the intrusion, Miss Sparrow. I know I should have called first, but I wanted to catch Agnes in, well, an unrehearsed pose if you catch my drift."

"Mr. Pruett." I offered my hand. "I don't think we've ever really met."

"No, no, I suppose not."

Artists. Loners. Antisocial is more like it. He had a weak grip. I hated that.

"Agnes was just about to eat her lunch—"

He pulled a fancy pocket watch from his coat pocket. "It's nearly 2:30."

"She has two, Mr. Pruett."

"Oh, may I come in anyway? It might provide some good shots. I only need a few . . . really."

"Who's that?" called Agnes, "I don't recognize the voice."

"The artist. Filby Pruett."

"Oh, dear me, Studebaker said he was gonna be sending him by, and I am not ready."

"It's better that way." Filby, a short man, reached his head around me. "I just need a few candid shots."

Then he looked at me. "I won't be long, Miss Sparrow, just a few. I can't do the statue without them."

"Let him come in," said Agnes.

I stood to the side and let Filby pass. "Nice house. Fabulous house." He had no trouble finding Agnes and like most folks seeing her for the first time, he stood stock-still a few seconds and caught his breath.

"It's a pleasure to meet you, Mr. Pruett," said Agnes. She reached her hand out.

Filby took it for all of a second and then wiped his palm on his pants. "Call me Filby, and I just need a few shots. Need to determine the best pose."

I was standing behind him, and he stepped on my foot when he backed away, no doubt assaulted by the smell. Most folks don't expect it, but getting close to Agnes was sometimes a challenge.

"I'll just go get your lunch," I said.

Agnes smiled, and Filby took a shot.

I headed back to the kitchen to get her baked ziti from the oven. Arthur showed up with a bloody mole in his mouth.

"Now where did you find that?"

"The basement," said Hezekiah. He had just entered the kitchen holding an old book—looked like one of my father's old texts. He placed it on the kitchen table. "I saw that artist fellow walking up the pavement and thought it best to hide out. I don't cotton to his kind."

"Kind?"

"You know, all artsy fartsy. Girlie."

I shook my head. "Oh, I see. Well, you don't know for sure that he's homosexual. Being an artist doesn't make it so."

"You ever look at him?" Hezekiah laughed and snorted air out his nose. "That silly hat and the way he sashayed all fancy up the walk."

Hezekiah put his hand on his hip and wiggled around the room.

Arthur dropped the mole at my feet. "Thank you. Just what I wanted . . . another bloody carcass." Only the mole was still alive. Arthur watched it wiggle and writhe, and then he batted it with a cupped paw across the kitchen. "You don't have to be that cruel."

Hezekiah grabbed the mole from the floor and tossed it and Arthur out the back door. "Murder is in his soul."

104

"He's just following his instincts. I suppose if he came to me when he was still a kitten he'd be a different sort of cat."

"Not always. Some cats are just born that way. God's design."

Hezekiah touched the heavy, hardback book. "You want I should toss all these books? I don't know who in their right mind would want to keep them." He rubbed his nose. "I was flipping through them down there—grizzly stuff. I think if most folks knew what was gonna happen to their bodies after they died they'd never get born in the first place."

"Not exactly easy reading." I opened the cover and saw my father's signature scrawled across the flyleaf. *August T. Sparrow.* I barely touched the name with my fingertips, but in that tiny trace of time a flood of emotion wriggled through my body like an electric current from a wire and I saw my father standing at the kitchen sink plucking a pheasant.

I snapped the book closed. "Keep the books."

"One more Agnes." I heard Filby's voice.

"No, that's enough, Mr. Pruett. How 'bout if I pray for you." Agnes had enough of camera flashes going off in her face.

"I better get in there," I told Hezekiah.

Hezekiah stood with his back against the sink. "I'll stay here till he's gone."

Fine with me.

"So, Filby. All finished?" I said.

"I suppose I got enough to get started. I may need some more. I mean there's just so much of her . . . to carve."

Agnes laughed. "It's all right, Mr. Pruett. I know I'm fat."

Filby feigned a smile and took one final snapshot. "I think I might just use the couch too. That might be nice: a statue of Agnes sitting on the couch. What do you think?"

Agnes sucked in air. "Whatever you like, Mr. Pruett. Now how can I pray?"

"You can pray that he crawls out of that den of sin he's been crouching in all these years. A den of sexual sin and immorality." Hezekiah could no longer contain his true feelings.

"Well," said Filby, "if that ain't the pot calling the kettle black, I don't know what is. You coming to our town and weaseling your way into the affections of the people. What is on your agenda, Mr. Branch?"

"At least I'm a man—all man."

The argument could have gone on, but Agnes put a quick end to it.

"Hezekiah, you got no right to judge people. And Mr. Pruett, I think it would be good if you left now."

"I was trying to. Good day, ladies."

Filby plopped his Panama on his head and left in a huff.

Hezekiah laughed in a way I had never heard him laugh before. It sent a chill down my back.

"I finished the south side of the basement," he said after a moment. "Think I'll get started in that little room near the furnace. It's black as coal in there, but I saw some boxes and maybe even a raccoon when I shined a light inside."

"That room can just stay as is," said Agnes. "Maybe you could start on the north side."

I took a second and tried to remember what was in that little room. All I could see in my in my mind were boxes piled against a wall.

"Agnes has a good idea, Hezekiah," I said. "I'd like to get the clothes out of there. Most of them belonged to my parents. The ladies who helped us after they died kept them thinking me and Agnes might use them but . . ."

"I understand, Griselda. I'll start tomorrow. If you wouldn't mind I'd like to knock off a little early today."

"Of course, Hezekiah." Agnes smiled.

Hezekiah wasted no more of his or our time and bolted out the front door like he was late for an appointment.

"Where do you suppose he's going in such a rush?" I asked.

"Can't say, but Janeen Sturgis was here earlier, and she said she heard that Olivia Janicki and he have been seen together."

I swallowed. "Really, but she's—"

"I know, I know," Agnes said. "She's not so . . . wholesome."

"Nice way to put it."

9

Studebaker showed up ten minutes after Hezekiah left.

"Good news, Agnes," he said. "Your sign is all finished and on its way from Scranton. Be here the day after tomorrow."

Agnes continued chewing her ziti. She looked at me as if looking at Stu would open up floodgates that hadn't been opened in years.

"I told you, Stu," I said. "Agnes isn't interested in the sign."

She swallowed and adjusted herself. Her left leg was bent up toward her chest and her thigh was a thick lava bed of extra skin. Agnes peered out the window for more than a minute before she turned her head to Stu.

"It's all right, Studebaker. Whatever you all need to do is fine with me."

Her words about knocked me off my feet.

"But, Agnes that's not—"

She put her hand up. "I'm not fighting the will of the people anymore, Griselda. In the end, what does it matter anyway? It's just a sign."

I can't say for sure what happened in that long minute that Agnes looked out the window, but something changed her mind.

Studebaker lit up like a Christmas tree. "Agnes, thank you! Thank you. This means a lot to the people, especially Cora right now. She's been skipping around town like a teenager."

"God bless her," said Agnes. She turned to me. "I'm only here to pray."

Stu pulled the rocking chair close to Agnes. "I was just at the diner, and me and Boris got to talking about the unveiling."

"Unveiling?" Agnes looked at me when she said it.

"Of the sign," Stu said. "We got it all planned for next month's town meeting. "It might be too big to get into the building, but we figure folks won't mind standing outside for it. Boris is lining up the Dixieland band to come out and maybe even the VFW will do something."

It made my toes curl up. I wanted to run, but it was like watching a car accident. I couldn't turn away.

"Did you hear that, Griselda?" Agnes said. "They're gonna get a Dixieland band."

"And maybe a barbershop quartet," Stu said.

If I didn't smile, I would have cried.

"The only thing missing will be you, Agnes." Stu bent down and kissed her cheek. "But we'll have Dabs Lemon take lots of shots. He's gonna write it up for the paper, Agnes. Front page news, I'm sure."

The sign arrived that Thursday on the back of a long flatbed truck with the name Scranton Sign Company in gold letters on the side of the cab. Stu and Boris went on out to the turnpike and escorted the driver into town with their horn blasting and flashers flashing all the way. Stu borrowed Mildred's cop light and stuck it on the top of his station wagon. I was surprised the Dixieland band wasn't there or at least a barbershop quartet to sing *When the Saints Go Marching In*.

I was standing in the viewing room waiting for Agnes to finish her asthma treatment when I saw the truck carrying the sign moving ever so slowly down the street.

Folks popped out of their houses. Small kids lined the street and waved. The driver tooted his horn once and Agnes flipped the nebulizer mask off her face.

"What in tarnation—"

"A truck horn, Agnes. A big truck horn. Looks like your sign made it up the mountain."

"Let me see."

"Too late, it's down the hill now."

I replaced the mask on Agnes and patted her arm. "About lunchtime. I'll bring you some pot roast."

Agnes and I finished out the day sorting through our parents' clothes, a task we had avoided for years. Hezekiah brought them up from the basement and piled them on the red velvet couch. It wasn't so tough handling their things, especially when we made the decision to keep none of it. I did catch a whiff of my father's Aqua Velva every so often and had to swipe a few tears. Agnes never flinched, although I sensed she might have been looking for something in particular the way she rifled through the piles I placed on her bed.

All I kept was one of my father's striped ties. I put it with his fishing rod and tackle box. And I found a string of pearls tucked into the pocket of my mother's Sunday coat.

"They're the real McCoy," said Agnes. "I remember when Daddy gave them to her—their tenth anniversary."

I didn't remember the occasion. I left the pearls on Agnes's bedside table, thinking she deserved something pretty even though the strand would never fit around her neck.

Hezekiah helped me bag them up the next day and used my truck to haul the sacks to the Salvation Army—the very one in Shoops he used to frequent.

"Seems a good thing to do after all the soup I ate there," he said when I handed him the key.

The welcome sign sat under a plastic tarp on a trailer out in front of the town hall until the unveiling. Seeing as how it got dark at six o'clock and the meetings didn't start until after seven usually, lights were brought in for the occasion. Boris asked some of the men to park their cars and shine their headlights on it.

I was at the library the day of the unveiling when I heard the Dixieland band marching down the street playing *Stars and Stripes Forever*. It was around three o'clock; I suppose they had to practice and get in proper formation.

Vidalia was checking out a book.

"What is that?" she asked.

"The band for the meeting tonight. Stu and Boris are unveiling the welcome sign."

"And they hired a band for that?"

"And a barbershop quartet or at least the VFW might be there to . . . I don't know, to salute it or something."

"Well, if that don't beat all."

I made it home around four and found Agnes praying with Hezekiah again. As far as anyone knew, he still hadn't received his miracle. And, as far as I knew, no one had any idea what his request was all about anyway. Usually, I stayed in the foyer until I heard the "Amen," but that day I didn't. I ignored them both and went straight upstairs.

March blew into town on the back of a fierce lion that year. The wind whipped around outside, and I thought it was a pretty terrible day to unveil anything. Arthur mewled on the windowsill. He was watching the crows high in the tree-tops. It always amazed me how they clung to the tippiest top branches as they swayed. I scratched his ears.

"What a day this has turned out to be, huh, Artie."

Most early March days in the mountains were windy and cold, but that day was especially raw and blustery. Tears filled my eyes as I watched outside. A small tempest of leaves swirled over the lawn like the small tempest of worries swirling in my brain. I hated the sign, and I hated that I was going to the unveiling, but how could I not go?

Vidalia would have said to stay home if I wanted, but my thoughts turned to Agnes. She would want me there, if for no other reason than to bring the attention back to God. But that day I didn't see how God could have anything to do with that sign or Bright's Pond.

The front door slammed shut as it was prone to do in a high wind. Hezekiah must have left for the day, although I was certain he would be at the unveiling. Hezekiah had become as devoted a follower of Agnes as anyone who had lived in Bright's Pond their whole lives.

I changed into jeans and a sweatshirt, pulled my hair in a ponytail, and slipped into sneakers—a favorite pair that had remained mole and mouse-free.

"Thank you, Arthur, for not leaving me a prize today."

I plucked him from the sill in time to see a pheasant explode out of the woods in a whirlwind of rust and gold and purple and leaves.

Agnes and I ate a quiet supper together. I expected her to say a few things—at least about the sign—but she didn't.

"Guess you better go," she said in-between mouthfuls of spaghetti. "They'll be expecting you."

"How come you're not so upset about it anymore, Agnes? It's like you . . . well . . . like it's all okay now all of a sudden."

"Okay about what, Griselda?"

"Oh, don't be that way. You know perfectly well about what."

She rolled a meatball around her plate with her fork. "It wasn't helping being upset. Letting them have their sign is just another way to—" she took a labored breath "—to take care of them."

After supper I cleaned up the plates and left them in a sink of soapy water. I put food away and brought Agnes a large piece of pie, and then I decided I still had time to drop a load of laundry in the washer. Laundry seemed endless at our house—endless. I often stepped over piles in the viewing room as Agnes would change and leave her clothes wherever they fell. Sometimes, Hezekiah would carry the clothes into the laundry room, but he never washed them and that was fine with me. I didn't like the idea of him handling my sister's clothes like that, particularly her underwear.

Once the washer was full and the plates soaking and Agnes situated in front of the TV with pie and M&Ms, I headed down the street. The wind had quieted with the sunset. A crowd had already gathered inside the Full Moon for dinner or coffee before the meeting.

Zeb spied me the second my foot landed inside. A wide smile lit up his face. "Griselda," he called, "come sit at the counter."

He poured my coffee and tried to talk to me, but the place was so busy he couldn't finish a sentence. I signaled him that it was okay, drank my coffee, and headed outside.

The Dixieland band—a group of seven men—had assembled on the lawn. They wore red coats with shiny silver buttons and hats made of leather and cloth. The tuba player stood next to his instrument that sat on a chair. He didn't look very happy.

The headlights from a dozen cars illuminated the tarp that kept the sign under wraps. Studebaker was standing near it like he was guarding Fort Knox.

"What are you doing, Stu?" I asked.

"A couple of boys were by here earlier," he said. "They tried to lift the tarp, so I'm keeping my eye on it."

"You're a good man, Stu. True to your cause."

I caught up with Ruth Knickerbocker in the crowd filing into the town hall.

"Everyone is so excited," she said. "It's like static electricity in the air."

"Sure is."

"I imagine Agnes is awful excited," said Ruth. She took off her hat and coat.

"Oh, excited isn't the word for it."

Just then, the reporter Dabs Lemon stopped me.

"You're the sister," he said.

I sucked freezing air into my lungs. "Yes, I'm Agnes's sister if that's what you mean."

"Can I ask a few questions?"

Did I have a choice?

I motioned for him to follow me into the building. There were no treats or coffee that night as Zeb agreed to stay open past eight. Everyone had gotten their fill at the café anyway.

"First, I need to tell you that I don't believe in all that miracle stuff and prayer nonsense, so don't go thinking you're gonna sell me your religion."

I snorted a small laugh. "Then why are you here, Mr. Lemon?"

"The story. It's a mighty fine human-interest story. And . . . my boss sent me."

"So how can I help you? Agnes is the one who prays."

"I know. I've gotten the history from Studebaker Kowalski, but I want to know the real Agnes," he said. "Tell me about the real girl . . . woman." He poised his pencil on a small, yellow legal pad like I was about to solve the riddle of the Sphinx.

"I don't understand, Mr. Lemon. What are you asking?"

"Well, you live with her. You care for her. What's it really like for a seven-hundred-pound woman to be a hero, a hero that can't leave her house, can't even enjoy her one night of recognition? How fat is she anyway? I mean I can't picture seven-hundred pounds of anything let alone a woman."

"Agnes doesn't consider herself a hero."

Janeen Sturgis grabbed his elbow. "Oh, she is so a hero, a true hero. Let me tell you how her prayers helped me."

She pulled him far enough away that I didn't have to listen.

Vidalia sidled up next to me. "Let's sit together."

"I'm surprised to see you here."

"Like I said, Griselda, I couldn't let you come alone."

I squeezed her hand. "I guess we should find a seat."

Within minutes the room was jam-packed and Boris was upfront with Stu. Boris had settled down the room and was just about to bring the meeting to order when Eugene Shrapnel nearly stumbled through the door.

"Oh, ye den of vipers," he shouted.

Ivy Slocum was first to her feet. I could see from the look on her face she was not about to take any grief from Eugene that night.

"Shut your mouth, now, Eugene Shrapnel. You got no business here."

"That's right," shouted Bill Sturgis. "Just get on home with yourself."

"One day," Eugene said with a finger raised above his head, "one day you'll regret your actions."

He stamped his cane on the floor but was quickly ushered out by Nate Kincaid, who never said much, but was big enough that words weren't necessary.

Vidalia took my hand in hers and leaned close. "I am so sorry, baby girl."

Boris pounded his gavel.

Many of the formalities of the usual town meeting were dispatched with haste since everyone was anxious to get to the unveiling. Dot Handy scribbled notes so fast I thought I saw sparks. Boris turned the meeting over to Studebaker.

He wore a crisp, brown suit with a herringbone pattern and a yellow and white polka dot tie.

"Looks like he pulled his burial suit out of moth balls," I whispered to Vidalia.

Stu cleared his throat. "I don't have to tell you why we're here." Applause drowned his words. "But I will anyway."

More applause and a whistle.

Stu took five minutes to explain all about the sign and Agnes and the miracles, including the Jesus pie. He even thanked Jack Cooper for having the good sense not to toss the thing in the trash. A collective amen filtered through the crowd as Stu explained that the pie was fed to the birds.

I found out later that he suspended the tin from a string and tied it on a branch of the willow tree out back of the church. Zeb said he didn't want it—said he couldn't see baking another pie in it—so now it shines in the sunlight like an ornament.

"And now," Stu said, "without further ado—" He chuckled a second. "I've been wanting to say that my whole life. Without further ado, I suggest we all head outside for the unveiling."

The second the doors opened the band started playing *When the Saints Come Marching In*. The crowd assembled around the sign. Vidalia and I managed to work our way closer to the diner and joined Zeb who stood in the cold with only a white apron over his clothes.

"Pretty exciting, huh, Grizzy," he said.

A drumroll drifted through the cold air, and Stu climbed onto the trailer and unknotted the rope that held down the tarp. The tarp dropped. Cheers and applause went up as the headlights shown like moons in the starry night.

Stu stood next to the sign like a proud fisherman as Dabs snapped a few shots. Then Stu turned his attention to the large blue sign with gold lettering and flowery embellishments.

"Welcome to Bright's Pond," he read. "Home of Agnes Sparrow."

"Sparrow?" shouted a voice from the crowd, followed by other exclamations. "You better look again, Studebaker. That sign don't say Sparrow."

Stu shushed the band that had started playing the *Stars and Stripes Forever.*

"It says Swallow," Bill Tompkins shouted. "They got the wrong dang bird. Ain't no swallows in town, only Sparrows."

Zeb, Vidalia, and I moved as close to the sign as we could. Studebaker looked at the sign with a face that showed every emotion known to the human race. Every couple of seconds it would contort into something different and turn redder. Steam rose off his neck.

Boris leaped onto the trailer. "Swallow. It says Swallow, Studebaker. The name is wrong."

"I can see that now," he said. "You don't got to bring it to my attention."

"Didn't you bother to look at it before tonight? The sign's been sitting out here the better part of two weeks. And in all that time you never bothered to look under that tarp?"

"Yeah," said Bill Tompkins, "how come you never checked the sign? This is your fault, Studebaker."

"Now hold on," said Stu. "It ain't my fault. It's the sign company's."

I believe it was then that the band started playing a terrible, but still distinguishable, rendition of *Nearer My God To Thee,* as Studebaker was about to go down with his sign.

"We aren't paying for no wrong sign," said Fred Haskell.

"Of course not," said Stu. "I'll call them first thing in the morning. We'll get this fixed."

Zeb snickered and put his arms around mine and Vidalia's shoulders. "That's too bad. Poor Stu. I shouldn't laugh."

Plenty of laughter came from other directions that night, including a small pack of teenagers who lurked near the town hall steps. I saw one of them form a snowball and was just about to let loose when Mildred grabbed his arm. Good old Mildred Blessing—always on the lookout for troublemakers.

"Well, at least this mistake will spare Agnes for a few more weeks," I said.

Vidalia held my hand and squeezed. "It ain't just a mistake. Never really is, Griselda. You know what I mean?"

Folks drifted away after they filed past the sign like mourners paying their last respects. Janeen and Frank Sturgis lingered a moment. "It's only three letters," said Janeen, "and it is a bird; at least they got that right."

Frank reached up and shook Stu's hand, "I've got to give you some credit, pal, when you screw up, you really screw up."

Stu dropped Frank's hand like a hot rivet. "I told them Sparrow. S-P-A-R-R-O-W. It's not my fault."

"I can't watch this no more," said Vidalia. "It's just too painful to see that man so humiliated."

"Yeah," said Zeb, "I better get back to the café. Cora's probably going nuts in there with orders. You coming, Grizzy?"

"Nah, I better get home and tell Agnes what happened."

"Come on," said Vidalia. "I'll walk with you as far as my house."

We walked a full block before it came to me. "I didn't see Hezekiah all night. Thought for sure he'd be here."

"He ran off with that Olivia Janicki again," said Vidalia with a tiny tinge of venom. "Been seeing a lot of that . . . that . . . woman."

"I heard, but I didn't know it was a regular thing."

Vidalia folded her arms against a cold wind that whipped up.

"I ran into Doc at the market the other day, and he said he saw them coming out of Personal's Pub hand in hand."

"He told Agnes he wasn't a drinking man," I said.

"Maybe not, but that Olivia, well, you heard the tales."

Vidalia brushed by a rhododendron that was growing too far out onto the sidewalk. "You don't suppose they could of found each other, and maybe this is all part of God's plan for them?"

"You mean like two lost souls brought together by destiny and now that they found each other they'll settle down, start a family, and live happily ever after?"

"Something like that."

I chewed on it a second as we made the turn onto Vidalia's street. "Sorry, but I can't imagine Olivia having a soul."

We stood outside Vidalia's house a minute, and she asked me inside for cake, but I had to hurry back to Agnes. I wanted to tell her what happened before anyone else could get to her.

"Look for me tomorrow," said Vidalia, "I'll stop by the library."

10

I found Agnes asleep with the television on and half a ham sandwich in her hand. She woke when I removed it.

"That you, Griselda?"

"Sure, Agnes. Just got home."

She straightened herself the best she could. "I must have dozed off." She tried to twist her shoulders but that was never easy for her.

"I didn't mean to wake you."

"How did it go?" she said in a sleepy, little girl voice. "The people get their sign?"

I twisted the lid onto her M&Ms jar and helped organize her blankets.

"Not exactly."

"What do you mean?"

I pulled her left leg as straight as I could. "You're gonna get sores in the folds of your skin again, Agnes, if you don't keep that leg straight. I'll put some ointment in there."

"You're stalling. What happened?"

"The sign company messed up—spelled your name wrong."

"What? Really?"

"Yep. Instead of Agnes Sparrow, it said Agnes Swallow. S-W-A-L-L-O-W. You should have seen poor Stu. You'd a thought he had his pants pulled down and his heart ripped out at the same time. I thought he might cry." I pulled Agnes's notebook out from under her pillow. "It was quite a sight with the band playing and all. You might want to add him to your latest prayer list."

"Now ain't that a shame." Agnes said. "I'm sorry, I don't mean to sound sarcastic. It's just that—"

"I know. It's hard not to laugh, but I felt bad for him, too, especially when Boris started yelling at him."

"Oh, that is a crying shame. So what are they gonna do?"

"Send it back to be fixed. Everyone was pretty upset."

Arthur strolled past, and I picked him up and sat on the edge of the bed.

I grabbed a large tube of A&D Ointment from the bedside table and slathered some of the oily goo in between the folds of heavy and, in places, discolored skin on Agnes's thighs. I think she might have put on another fifty pounds in the last five years.

"It's late," I said when I finished. "And since you were already asleep when I came in, I think we should just call it a night."

"I'm not done talking," Agnes said. "Was Hezekiah there?"

"Didn't see him. Which surprised me. I thought for sure he would be. But then I heard he's been seeing a lot of that Olivia Janicki, and it was suggested they might have . . . had other plans."

"Now, that goads me. I had a feeling he might have found a girlfriend the way he's been leaving early lately—but Olivia Janicki? Suppose he knows she's got a reputation a mile long."

"I hate to say this, Agnes, but I don't think he cares about that."

The next morning around ten, I parked my truck on top of Hector Street and tuned into Rassie Harper before heading to the library. I waited for Vera Krug's *Neighborly News.* I wanted to hear if Ruth had gotten to her about the sign fiasco. As much as I hated to admit it, it did make good news.

A thick, blotchy rain started to fall, and even with the truck heat going full blast, I felt shivery. Ivy's dog sprinted across the street with what looked like a steak in his mouth. Ever so often he'd go by Personal's and snag a meal from the trash. It only made Personal angry because that dog never cleaned up the mess he left in the alley. Ivy, of course, blamed Personal for not feeding the dog out the front door like Sylvia did at the bakery.

"Here she is, ladies and gentlemen," said Rassie, "that winsome woman of the airwaves with all your small town news—Vera Krug."

"Thank you, Rassie. And I hope your wife is feeling better. For those of you who don't know, she's been down with the flu. Anyway, I got some juicy news today, folks, so turn up your radios, and you might want to grab another cup of coffee. Go on, now, I'll wait."

And she did. There was a full sixty seconds of dead air before Rassie hollered. "Vera, you can't do that."

"I'm sorry, Rassie. Just wanted to make sure all the people were ready for my lead-off story."

"I'm sure they are, dear."

Vera cleared her throat. "This first story might be hard for some of you to, hm, swallow—especially all you folks up in Bright's Pond." She laughed right out loud over the airwaves.

I sucked all the oxygen out of the truck cab.

"Seems there was an unveiling of the new Bright's Pond welcome sign last night, and well, wait till you hear this folks. They got the wrong dang bird, as Bill Tompkins said during the ceremony. The sign was supposed to read, Welcome to Bright's Pond, Home of Agnes Sparrow, but the sign company wrote Agnes Swallow—S-W-A-L-L-O-W."

I heard Rassie Harper spit coffee.

Vera shushed him. "That's right, ladies and gentlemen, you heard it corrr-ectly," she said. "The sign company wrote swallow, and don't that beat all, especially considering how that Agnes likes to *swallow*." She laughed liked a hyena. "Oh, Johnny Carson could do ten minutes on it."

"Agnes Sparrow?" Rassie cut in, "Ain't she that fat woman who's supposed to do miracles? I hear she's so fat she can't leave her house."

"That's right," said Vera, "but I don't believe that nonsense about the miracles. That's why I never reported on her before. My sister-in-law, Ruth, keeps telling me stories, but I found them all too hard to . . . SWALLOW." She laughed again like the Wicked Witch of the West.

My heart sank, not so much because of the news, but because of the way they made fun of Agnes. Nothing ever changed; even grown-ups were heartless.

When I arrived at the library I found the Society of Angelic Philanthropy waiting outside like a flock of quails. I had forgotten they were coming; they met once a month or so to plan their latest charity.

"I'm sorry," I said. "I plum forgot about you, ladies."

"Oh, that's all right, Griselda," said Tohilda Best, Personal's wife. The thing is Personal didn't know about Tohilda's membership in the society and would probably split a gut if he found out she gave a portion of his profits to help the less fortunate.

Tohilda came from a backwoods family. She and Personal met during deer season, not that backwoods folks paid any attention to Pennsylvania's hunting rules and regulations. Personal had said that the minute he saw her field dress a six-point buck, he knew she was the one for him.

The Society ladies set up in the periodicals section because there were tables and they could spread out notes and maps— some of them hand drawn by mountain folk. I usually kept the library door locked while they met because they were, after all, a secret society. But I remembered Vidalia would be dropping by so I warned Tohilda.

"Oh, that's okay," she said. "We can trust Vidalia."

I put on coffee and went about my business until Tohilda and Sylvia approached me.

"Excuse us, Griselda," said Tohilda, "but we were wondering if we could ask you a question."

"Shoot."

"It's about that Hezekiah fella. We were thinking about putting him on our list to receive shoes and socks. What do you think?"

"I think that would be fine—mighty fine. I think he spent all his money on that suit he wore to the potluck and didn't have money left over for shoes."

"I saw," said Sylvia. "He was wearing those awful clodhopper boots. Looked like they were a size too small at least, and the leather's been chewed through by rats. He wasn't wearing any socks at all."

I hadn't noticed. But it was decided right then to provide Hezekiah Branch with a new pair of shoes and socks to go with them.

True to her word, Vidalia showed up an hour later to return three books and check out six more. The S.O.A.P. finished up their meeting as I stamped Vidalia's books. They always cleaned up the area and left silently like it was some sacred part of their meetings.

"So do you know who they're blessing this month?" Vidalia asked.

"Hezekiah for one. Asked if he could use some shoes and socks."

Vidalia laughed. "I'll say. I told that boy to buy some socks, but he claimed he never wore them—made his feet sweat."

"Looks like he'll be getting some now."

Vidalia looked around the empty library. "Sure is quiet in here. How long you staying open?"

"I'll be here until dinner. It's term paper time. Some of the high school kids will show up later."

Vidalia smiled. "Send them my way if you think I can help."

"Always do."

I walked Vidalia to the door. "So what time did Hezekiah get home last night?" I asked.

"It wasn't until a quarter to three. I got to have a talk with him. If he's gonna start keeping those hours he'll have to find another place to live."

"You don't mean that."

Vidalia pursed her lips. "I know. I'm just worried about the boy. I'm just so glad Agnes keeps him busy all day."

"I'll say. He's been working in that basement for days. I haven't been down there. But if the amount of trash he's burned in the backyard means anything, it should be clean as a bowling alley by now."

Vidalia thought a moment. "It ain't that I begrudge Hezekiah his time out. I know a man needs certain things, but I just wish he'd steer clear of that hussy, speaking of trash, you know what I mean."

Vidalia had no sooner left than I heard a knock on the library door. Nobody ever knocked unless it was locked. I opened the door and found Ruth Knickerbocker standing there with a plate of lemon squares and two baskets of fried chicken.

"Griselda, I come to apologize to Agnes."

"Agnes? Apologize for what?"

"For yakking to my sister-in-law about that whole sign thing and for telling that blabbermouth about Agnes in the first place. I'm afraid—" She took a breath. "I'm afraid I might of started something, because Vera called me this morning and said I could expect a call from Rassie Harper about having me and Agnes on the show by something she called remote. I think it was remote."

"Slow down, Vera." I pulled her into the library.

"Remote," she said. "I never heard of such a thing. Sounds like something straight out of Jules Verne."

"First of all, Agnes won't go on any radio show, and secondly, why does he want you too?"

"That was Vera's idea. She said it would be fun for me, and she made Rassie agree."

I invited Ruth behind the checkout counter and poured her a cup of coffee.

"Oh thank you, dear, but I couldn't drink any more coffee. I'm as nervous as a butterfly—flitting here, flitting there, standing outside in the cold like an idiot. Do you think Agnes will be mad at me? You think she can reverse miracles? I mean I'd hate to get that terrible bleeding ulcer back on account of me blabbing to Vera." She placed the food on the counter. "That chicken is probably cold as ice now. I was standing outside waiting for those society ladies and Vidalia to leave."

"I'm sure it's fine, Ruth. Your chicken is real good, hot or cold."

"Thank you, dear. But let's stick to the problem."

"There is no problem. You just tell Vera to tell Rassie that you and Agnes will not appear on his radio show."

"You mean he can't force us to do it?"

"Of course not, Ruth! It's a radio show, not jury duty."

"Well, that despicable Rassie Harper is always going on about Richard Nixon. So I was afraid maybe he had some pull, you know, and could make us be there—like it was court."

God bless her soul. "I'm sorry you got so worked up, and the next time I see Vera I'll have something to say to her."

"I can't stand her myself, you know," said Ruth. "She's just got this odd power over me and makes me say things I don't mean. I only told her about Agnes because I was hoping it would turn her to Jesus, but she always laughed at me."

"Then why did you tell her about the sign?"

Ruth started to cry. She wiped her eyes and blew her nose into a pretty blue hanky with lace trim she pulled from her shirtsleeve. "I don't know, Griselda. I don't know why I went and spread that news. It's like the devil got to me."

"I'd say you were just being human. And to tell the truth, it is kind of funny—Agnes Swallow, imagine that."

We laughed and Ruth started to relax. "Think I'll have that coffee now."

"And another thing, Ruth. Agnes really can't make you grow another ulcer."

"Are you sure? Seems to me if a person can pray for an ulcer to go away, she can pray for one to come back."

In some strange way, it made sense. People were always thinking of miracles in terms of really, really good things happening. Why couldn't an ulcer or cancer or any other affliction be just as miraculous if it served God's purpose?

"She won't, Ruth. Agnes won't ask God to give you another ulcer."

"That's what I was worried about."

"I know. Now you go on home and forget all about Rassie Harper and Vera."

"Okay, I will. And please give that food to Agnes, will you, Griselda?"

"Sure."

Actually, I fed it all to the high school kids later that day.

I took the slow way home that evening and drove past Personal's in time to see Hezekiah opening the pub door for Olivia Janicki.

Olivia blew into town about four years ago on the back of a Harley-Davidson with her arms wrapped around the waist of a Hell's Angel. He was the biggest man I had ever seen in my entire life. They rumbled up to the café that Friday night and when they walked through the door you would of thought Marilyn Monroe had seen fit to visit Bright's Pond.

Every head in the place turned and craned to get a better view of the buxom blonde and her friend. Or he could have been a bodyguard for all we knew. She wore a pair of leather pants that looked painted on, and when she took off her leather jacket, well, if you've ever seen those cartoons where the character's eyes bug out, you get the picture. That went for the women as well as the men, except the men had a hard time averting their gaze no matter how loudly their wives clicked their tongues.

The woman's breasts filled out her baby blue sweater and made her tiny waist all the smaller. She and her friend sat at the booth behind the one I shared with Vidalia without making much eye contact with anyone. It looked like they'd been arguing. Anyway, Cora rushed right over, seeing as how they were new customers, and I was pretty certain Cora wanted to make a good impression for the Full Moon. She treated all newcomers with preference.

Vidalia grabbed my hand across the table. "Look what the wind blew in."

"I'll say. They must be lost, looking for Jack Frost or something."

"Did you notice his jacket? It says Hell's Angels on it. What do you suppose that means?"

I craned my neck, and sure enough there it was blazoned across his back in big, red, embroidered letters—HELL'S ANGELS. Underneath that was a creepy image of a skull with wings. And below that it read, PHILADELPHIA, although the PH and A were hard to see.

"I've heard about them—a motorcycle gang. They have chapters all over the country."

Vidalia leaned closer. "Suppose they're here to make trouble?"

I didn't think so, especially when I heard him order a bowl of vegetable soup and a Coke and she asked for a cheese-burger and Tab.

"You from Philadelphia?" asked Cora as she scribbled their order.

"Uh, huh," he grunted.

The woman seemed more personable. "That's right, honey. Philly." Then I watched her pull gum out of her mouth and, I was pretty certain, she stuck it under the table.

"I'll be right back with your food," said Cora, "and you might want to save room for a piece of Full Moon pie. It's famous here."

The man laughed a deep, booming laugh. "Full Moon pie. I had me a big, old piece of full moon pie just yesterday."

Cora looked like she'd been zapped with a paralyzing ray. It took her a second, but then she got the stranger's meaning and hurried away.

"Shut up, Gizzard," said the woman, "You are so ignorant."

"I hope they leave soon," Vidalia whispered.

I shushed her, and we sat there like common gossips sipping coffee, eating pie, and listening in on their conversation. As it turned out I was correct; they had been fighting. He was mad because she gave him wrong directions, and she was mad because he never appreciated her.

About forty minutes later, Gizzard went to the bathroom and never returned. I heard the motorcycle start up and rumble away. The woman ran to the door and hollered. "Gizzard, you S.O.B., I'll kill ya for this."

The woman turned around to a sea of wondering eyes and open mouths, including Vidalia's and mine. She sat down and poked at her pie.

"You all right?" Vidalia asked her.

"That scum rode off and left me," the woman said.

"He'll be back, won't he?"

"Gizzard? Nah, he's gone for good."

Vidalia squeezed into the booth, and I joined her. "What will you do?" I asked.

"Don't know. Don't suppose you got a hotel in this stupid, little town?"

Vidalia looked at me, and I knew exactly what she was thinking.

"I don't know if that's a good idea," I said.

Vidalia reached out her hand to the woman. "My name is Vidalia Whitaker, and I run a boarding house of sorts down the street. You're welcome to take a room."

The woman reached into her pocket and pulled out three, one-hundred dollar bills. "Ain't got much money."

"You got enough and more to stay," Vidalia said.

"I'm Griselda Sparrow." I shook her hand. "You'll be fine at Vidalia's until you can figure things out. You got family in Philadelphia that can come get you?"

She laughed and jabbed her fork into the middle of her pie. "Nah, I got no people." She looked out the window. "Not even Gizzard wants me, and believe me, it ain't like he was some catch, the miserable, no-good, cheatin', bas—"

"You been together long?" Vidalia asked.

"One whole month." She pulled herself up like that was something to be proud of and poofed her already high hair.

"Come on," said Vidalia, "I'll take you home."

Three days later, Olivia started taking orders at Personal's. About two months after that, Vidalia threw her out and she took a two-room apartment on top of Zack's Feed and Grain Store.

Now four years later it seemed she had poked her fork into Hezekiah's heart and twisted it around the prongs. I parked the truck outside of the pub and waited a few minutes, thinking that maybe Olivia was working that night and Hezekiah would come out soon. When he didn't show I was filled with the oddest sensation that I can only describe as . . . jealousy.

11

Sunday morning arrived chilly, but with the promise of sunshine. Clouds that had been hanging over Bright's Pond for days disappeared and left behind a clear blue sky.

I stood at my window and watched as robins fresh from Florida perched and sang in the dogwood trees. I made a mental note to hang suet cakes and fill the birdhouses with seed. The snow line had receded, and blotches of ground and grass appeared like little tufts of hair on an otherwise bald head.

"Spring is coming." I picked up Arthur. "Won't be long now, boy, and you'll be out cattin' all night." I snuggled him close to my cheek. "Just like Hezekiah."

Agnes coughed. "Griselda," she called, "you up?"

"Guess I better get down there and fix her some breakfast."

Arthur mewled his agreement. He was hungry too.

"I'll be down soon. Got to get dressed first."

Sometimes I grew weary of feeding hungry bellies that never got full. But I pushed that feeling inside to save it for another day. Right then I had to make breakfast and get off to church. Sunday worship had become more of an obligation, an opportunity to see people I ordinarily don't see during the week, than something deep and spiritual. I felt closer to God at the library or strolling through the backwoods looking for teaberries and wild mushrooms than I did sitting on a hard pew.

I opened my closet door and stood there like an idiot scanning the contents and knowing full well there was nothing new or attractive inside—just the same old clothes I'd worn for years. Although the sun promised to shine bright today, I knew I'd be more comfortable in jeans and a sweater than a dress. I only owned two. Vidalia had given them to me after her daughter moved away—both leftover and discarded things with flowers and lace around the collar and sleeves— one purple, the other blue like a robin's egg. It didn't really matter. Not everyone dressed up for church, although there were a few diehards who thought a woman entering God's house in pants was akin to murder.

"Griselda," Agnes called. "I got to get to the bathroom."

I pulled a brush through my hair, took a final look in the mirror, shrugged, and headed downstairs.

"Took you long enough this morning," Agnes said. "My bladder's about to burst."

"I'm sorry. I overslept a tad and wanted to get dressed for church."

I pulled Agnes up by the shoulders and slipped her fat feet into slippers that used to be soft and pink but were now gray with crushed heels. She clambered to her feet like an elephant, and I led her down the hall.

"You seem so stiff this morning. You feeling all right?"

"A storm is brewing. I can always feel it in my knees, like bone on bone."

She finished in the bathroom and opened the door. I grabbed a handle of nightgown and led her back to bed. "You sure it's gonna rain? The clouds are gone and the sun is shining."

"Don't matter. There's a storm brewing out there. You'll see."

Agnes dropped onto the couch with a huge thud, and the sides of the red velvet sofa lifted off the floor. For a second it looked like the sofa might have grimaced.

"What do you want to eat this morning?"

"I was thinking some sausage and eggs with toast and jelly and some of them home fries you made the other day would be good."

"All right. You just sit and I'll get to it."

"Turn the television on, please. It's just about time for Sheila Makefield."

Sheila Makefield was Agnes's current favorite television preacher. She sometimes listened to the PTL Club, but she couldn't stand that woman who wore too much makeup and cried all the time.

"I just don't see how you can say you're so close to Jesus and do all that crying," Agnes had said. "But I do like it when they sing."

Sometimes a few of her visitors would leave money on the bedside table, and Agnes would put it in an envelope marked "charitable giving." When she had saved enough she'd have me deposit it and write out a check, sometimes for as much two hundred dollars, and send it to the PTL Club.

When we were girls, Agnes would hurry home from church and turn on the TV, blaring out Kathryn Kuhlman. Agnes thought Kathryn was the best thing since M&Ms and watched her religiously.

"She's got that way of talking at me, you know, like it goes right through my skin and bones and muscles and makes me feel all scared inside, but a good scared."

This morning, I put on a pan of sausage to fry and scrambled six eggs in a bowl with a splash of milk.

"Maybe you could toss some of that cheddar cheese on the eggs," Agnes called.

I fed Arthur while the sausage fried and washed a sink full of dishes.

Agnes enjoyed her breakfast while Sheila Makefield sang and preached and hollered about forgiveness and righteousness. I slathered butter and jelly on her toast and wondered why God made a world full of unrighteous people to begin with. He had to know we'd all fall short.

"Now, I got to go, Agnes. Take your pills, and I'll get the nebulizer ready." I gathered up her dishes.

"I don't need that today. My lungs feel good, Griselda, real good."

"I think you should continue the treatment. That's why your lungs feel good, Agnes. You don't want to spoil that."

"Bring me another cup of coffee before you go."

After Agnes was satisfied, I headed across the street. I spied Vidalia at church and squeezed in next to her on the pew. Thin, red velvet cushions used to soften the hard wood, but over the years they had become so worn and tattered we had to toss out most of them. Some of the pews still had them, and they were usually the first to fill, especially on a cold morning. There was talk of replacing the cushions, but it seemed every time Ruth Knickerbocker made plans to buy the velvet she needed to make new ones, a toilet needed replacement or a tree fell in the back. Necessity always won out over comfort and aesthetics.

"Morning, Griselda," Vidalia said. "It's a fine, sunny morning."

"It sure is, Vidalia, and about time. I thought the sun had forgotten about us."

"Now, now, Miss Sparrow, the sun will always come back." She smiled.

Vidalia looked real nice in a crisp, navy dress with white trim and a white belt to match. She wore a little navy hat with a dainty veil that covered her eyes and nose. She slipped her white gloves off and stuffed them into her purse and tucked it next to her on the pew. I never carried a purse. Never knew what I needed to put in one that I couldn't carry in a pocket.

The sanctuary filled up as the clock neared ten. I had hoped to avoid conversation about the sign that morning, but I should have known it would be impossible. Janeen Sturgis took a seat behind me and tapped my shoulder.

"How's Agnes? Is she terribly upset about the sign having the wrong name on it?"

"Not particularly, Janeen. She's okay."

"Well, I for one am just appalled. Appalled that such an error could have happened in the first place. That Studebaker Kowal—"

"Now don't go blaming Stu. It wasn't his fault. I'm sure he gave the right name to the company."

"But he should of checked," said Ruth who had just slid into my peripheral view. She motioned for Vidalia and me to inch down a bit so she could fit.

Edie and Bill Tompkins sat in front of us. Edie turned around and smiled, letting a whiff of coffee breath into the air that mixed with her Jean Nate' and made my nose itch. "You tell Agnes not to worry. We'll get the sign fixed and it'll be out there on the turnpike in no time, telling all the world that Bright's Pond has a prime citizen to be proud of."

I could hear Vidalia's thoughts, and they pretty much matched my own. Fortunately, Sylvia started the prelude before Boris, who had just spied me, could climb over people's feet to get to me. He signaled something, some weird semaphore with his bulletin.

"I think he wants you to meet him after the sermon," Vidalia said.

Pastor Speedwell, dressed in his three-piece, black suit, followed by Fred Haskell and Frank Sturgis, entered from the side door onto the platform. Fred stood at the podium while the other men sat in the fancy chairs with high backs and crimson velvet cushions. They always seemed to get their cushions refreshed.

"Let us sing together hymn number 134, *Come Thou Fount of Every Blessing*," Fred said and nodded to Sylvia, who started playing while we all scrambled to find the page and get to our feet. The congregation was not up to its usual voice that morning, and the singing sounded a lot like a bunch of drowning cats. I suppose every church has that one voice, though—that one off-key, clunker voice that is so much louder than the rest. The tin ear in our congregation was Eugene Shrapnel, although no one ever told him not to sing. That wouldn't be right, not even when it came to someone as surly and silly as him. My mother told me it ain't the quality of the singing that counts because all God hears is angels singing and their beautiful voices drifting through the gates of heaven.

After that hymn plus two more, Frank replaced Fred at the podium and began the congregational reading of the Scripture—Romans, chapter thirteen. He read a verse and then the people read one and then he read one and so on until Fred finished up with a resounding recitation of verse

14: "But put ye on the Lord Jesus Christ, and make no provision for the flesh, to fulfill the lusts thereof." He emphasized the word *lusts* like it had special meaning for someone in the crowd.

I think it worked because as the offering was taken, I noticed someone had placed two white dice into the basket.

"Has to be Nate Kincaid," Vidalia whispered.

She was most likely correct. Just about everyone in town knew Nate had frequented a floating crap game down in Shoops. I imagine it was hard for him to give up his dice. Stella had her arm around him and was patting his shoulder.

Pastor Speedwell took his place at the podium and cleared his throat about six times before he spoke his first word. He nodded to his wife and children and then looked out over his flock. He raised his Bible over his head and launched into a sermon so full of hellfire and brimstone it made Ruth cry.

"Why does a flamingo stand on one foot?" he called out. Then he waited a second, letting the peculiar question float around the room. "I'll tell you why! Because if he lifted the other leg he'd fall down . . . flat." Pastor slapped the podium with his free hand, and it shook for a good minute. A couple of mothers pulled their startled children close.

No one knew whether it was a good idea to laugh because Pastor was so serious. "And some of you—" he said and pointed the Good Book at us, "don't even got a leg, not one leg to stand on. You hear what I am saying to you?"

Poor Nate rested his head on Stella's shoulder.

Pastor went on like that for the better part of an hour, and then he wound down. He nodded to Sylvia and gestured for all of us to stand.

"Hymn number 72," he said. *"Are You Washed in the Blood?"*

We all remained standing while he raised both hands out over the congregation and said a benediction.

"And now may the Lord bless thee, and keep thee. The Lord make his face to shine upon thee, and be gracious unto thee. The Lord lift up his countenance upon thee, and give thee peace."

The benediction was always my favorite part of any sermon, and probably the reason I went to church—not to get yelled at about my sins but to have the pastor pray a blessing over me in the way I had always imagined Jesus would.

Vidalia and I escaped into the sunshine after shaking Pastor Speedwell's sweaty hand and before Boris Lender caught up. "I never got a chance to talk to you after the other night," he puffed. "I am so sorry about the mistake. That Studebaker—"

"It wasn't his fault," I said, "and I wish people would stop making it so."

Boris took a step back. "I just wanted you to know it'll be fixed and back in town in about two weeks."

"That's nice, Boris. Now I better get home to Agnes. She always expects the bulletin."

"You tell her I said hello, Griselda, will you do that for me?"

"Sure, Boris."

The air was warmer as Vidalia and I walked across the street. "I didn't see Stu," she said.

"I know. I haven't seen hide nor hair of him since—"

"I do hope he's all right. I hate to think of him sitting all alone in his house feeling poorly about that stupid sign."

"Well, if I know Studebaker, he's probably down in Scranton making certain they do it right this time."

Vidalia laughed. "You know, I bet you're right. I bet he followed them back and is standing over them like a drill sergeant."

"And speaking of no shows, I didn't see Hezekiah, either." He had been attending church kind of regularly—if you can call two weeks in a row regular.

"Never came home last night," Vidalia said. "Probably stayed the night at Olivia's."

My heart skipped a beat. I hated the way talk of Hezekiah had started to affect me. It was out of my control, but for some reason just the thought of him produced strange feelings inside—feelings I wanted to have for Zeb but couldn't muster.

Vidalia grabbed my arm. "Where'd you go? I lost you there for a second or two."

I pushed my glasses up on my nose. "I'm sorry, Vi, it's just that . . . well, lately . . . oh, I don't know . . ." I didn't want to tell her what was really on my mind. "I was just thinking about Agnes. I better get inside and give her the bulletin and fix her lunch."

Vidalia looked into my eyes. "Uh, huh, you do that. And let me just tell you, Griselda, you better think twice before you allow yourself to get hung up on Hezekiah."

"I'm not hung up on him." I took a breath. "I better get inside."

Agnes was still watching television. Her face was red like she had suffered an asthma attack while I was gone. She held on to her emergency inhaler.

"Did you take your treatment?" I handed her the bulletin.

"I'm okay, Griselda, just a little coughing fit. It might have been the spices in the sausage."

"Well, I think you should take a treatment just to be safe. You'll feel better and, and so will I, Agnes."

I changed clothes, tossed in a load of laundry—whites with plenty of Clorox. For lunch I made Agnes her usual tuna sandwiches and soup with Fritos and milk. My stomach was a little upset so I opted out of lunch and continued separating laundry. The phone rang. It was Vidalia.

"Griselda," Vidalia said, "did you know anything about the Pearly Gates Singers coming to town?"

"Pearly Gates Singers? No, I never heard a word about it. When did that happen?"

"I just ran into Ruth at the market—had to pick up coffee and bread—and she told me."

"How did Ruth know?"

"Well, you're about to find out. She's heading to your house."

I hung up and turned my attention to Agnes, who was swallowing the last of her sandwiches. "Did you know about the Pearly Gates Singers coming to town?"

She choked and spit her last bite onto her plate. "What? When? I never heard a word."

"Vidalia said Ruth Knickerbocker told her and is coming over here to tell us."

Agnes let out a little whoop and holler.

"Imagine that, Griselda, the Pearly Gates—here . . . in Bright's Pond."

The doorbell chimed.

"That must be Ruth," I said. Sure enough I opened the door and there was Ruth looking like she had just snagged the last of the Full Moon pie.

I grabbed her hand. "Come on inside and tell me about it. Vidalia just called."

"Ah, I told her not to, but news like this is hard to keep down, I suppose."

Ruth said hello to Agnes from the entryway. She took my hand. "Can we talk in the kitchen," she whispered.

"I suppose, but why so secretive?"

"Just don't want Agnes to hear."

I shot Agnes a quizzical look; she shot one back and waved me on, knowing full well I'd tell her anyway. Ruth and I sat at the kitchen table with coffee and pie.

"How did this come about?" I asked. "The Pearly Gates only go to big towns like Scranton and Philadelphia."

"Rassie Harper arranged it. I let on that I was gonna do his show by that remote thing. You know . . . me and Agnes, right here in the viewing room, if he could get the Pearly Gates Singers to come."

"But you said you didn't want to go on the radio."

"I ain't. Rassie and Vera don't know I ain't gonna do it. By the time I tell them, everyone will be expecting the Pearly Gates Singers, and Rassie wouldn't dare cancel and make a lot of people unhappy, especially after the Pearly Gates get it on their schedule and all. They'll expect to be paid, you know." She sipped coffee and swallowed hard. "I went right directly home from church instead of stopping out anywhere, like I usually do, and the phone was ringing off the wall when I got inside. It was Rassie Harper telling me he arranged for them to come and now I had to get Agnes." She slapped the table and laughed.

"Why, Ruth Knickerbocker, you're positively sly."

"Like Lucy Ricardo. I just had to give them the what for after the way they laughed at Agnes."

I couldn't help myself and I started to laugh like I hadn't laughed in a long time. "We got to tell Agnes," I said. "She'll get a kick out of it."

"Does she know what happened on the show Wednesday?"

"No, but that's all right. She'll be good-natured about it."

"You don't suppose there's a chance she'll want to go on the radio show, do you?"

I swallowed the last drop of my Maxwell House. "That's just silly talk. Agnes won't go on Rassie's show."

Ruth finished her pie while I went out back and found Arthur. He was up one of the dogwoods, trying to grab a robin.

"You come down from there, you mean old varmint." I tossed a stone past his head. He leapt to the ground and ran into the house.

"Maybe it would be better if you told her," said Ruth as we walked to the viewing room.

Agnes didn't have quite the reaction I expected. No, sir, she didn't. Ruth slid out of the rocker and onto her hiney, and I had the sudden sensation that Hades had just frozen over.

12

"I'll do it," Agnes said. "I'll go on the show."

That was when Ruth fell off her rocker and landed with a thud on the floor.

"But Agnes . . . " I helped Ruth back to her seat. "I thought you were against the publicity and—"

"I'm not gonna do it for that reason. I think the good Lord's purposes can be served quite nicely over the airwaves—just like Sheila Makefield and the PTL Club."

Ruth straightened herself and regained her composure. "But, Agnes, that Rassie Harper—he just wants to poke fun at you. And that miserable sister-in-law of mine too. They aren't believers. They're just out to make fun and laugh at your—"

"My size?" Agnes said. "Call me a shyster? A fraud miracle worker?"

"Well, I'm sorry, Agnes, but it's the truth."

"I know what they want. And name-calling never troubled me. I was listening to you in the kitchen, and what's more I was listening to Rassie's show Wednesday." She looked at me. "I'm not exactly living in a cave, Griselda. I know what's what."

"How come you didn't say anything?"

"No need . . . till now."

Agnes took a breath that struggled to get into her lungs. "You tell Vera to tell Rassie to set it up and I'll be here."

Ruth looked scared. "It's by remote. I don't know what that means exactly. I mean we aren't gonna have to put wires on our heads like they did with Bubba?"

Bubba was Ruth's dead husband—inoperable brain tumor. He started falling down for no good reason and then went completely deaf in one ear before he saw the doctor. By then it was too late. Agnes prayed but God needed Bubba in heaven, and Ruth took much comfort in knowing her Bubby Hubby, as she called him, was there, helping out wherever he could. That's how Bubba was—a helpful man, a carpenter by trade, and Ruth figured God needed help building all those mansions.

I was always amazed at the human brain's capacity for turning tragedy into a comfortable resting place.

"Wires on our heads?" Agnes laughed. "Of course not, Ruth. They'll probably put an antenna outside and run wires into the house."

"Kind of like a makeshift radio station in the house," I said, "with microphones and dials and stuff."

"Well, I don't like it," Ruth said. "I just wanted to get the Pearly Gates Singers to town."

"And you did," Agnes said. "They'll be here next month. Just think. The Pearly Gates Singers . . . here in Bright's Pond . . . April, 1972. Something to tell the grandkids about, don't you think?" Agnes's countenance dropped when she said it.

"Maybe we can find a way for you to see them." I patted my sister's hand.

"That's okay, Griselda. Just knowing they're here will be fine."

Ruth left a little while later with the funniest look on her face. "I'm sorry, Griselda, I didn't expect all this, but if Agnes is happy about it, then I guess we should be too."

"I don't know if happy is the word for it, but at least she isn't jumping mad, you know?"

Agnes had been eating M&Ms and washing them down with orange juice—a combination that made me sick to think about.

"I don't get it, Agnes," I said. I started pulling the sheets off her bed.

"What? I like M&Ms and orange juice."

"No, not that. You were dead set against the sign and now that doesn't trouble you anymore and now this radio show."

Agnes reached for her inhaler. "I decided to give the people what they want, Griselda. It's just easier that way."

"Easier doesn't make it right."

I carried the bedclothes into the laundry and put fresh ones on Agnes's bed: blue and yellow striped ones. "There you go. Let's get you back to bed. You've been on that sofa all day."

"I am getting tired. What time is it, anyway?"

I looked at the clock on the mantle. "My goodness, Agnes, it's nearly five-thirty."

"I thought I was ready for dinner."

I put a tray of fish sticks into the oven and unwrapped a macaroni and cheese Janeen brought by. I was just cutting the stalks off of a bouquet of broccoli when the doorbell rang.

"Cora," I said, "what brings you by?"

"I just heard all about the Pearly Gates Singers and Agnes going on Rassie Harper's radio show. It's all the talk down at the Full Moon. I had to come by. I want to be on the show too." She pushed past me. "Agnes," she said, "I want to be on the radio with you. I got to tell everyone about my miraculous heart healing."

The next thing I knew, Zeb, Janeen Sturgis, and Edie Tompkins were in the viewing room, shouting reasons why they should be on the radio show too. Five minutes after they arrived Boris Lender, Ivy Slocum, and Hazel Flatbush came with their own reasons for being on the show. Forty minutes later I remembered the fish. It was burnt to a crisp. You should never over bake Mrs. Paul's.

I could believe it of the others, wanting to horn in on the radio show, but Zeb? He didn't seem the type to me, but ever since the Jesus pie incident he had been acting a little bit weird and flighty like he had been given some special notoriety that entitled him.

Agnes did a good job of quelling the crowd and pretty much told them that under no circumstances would she have them on the radio show. But I had a sneaking suspicion they were going to try.

"The idea isn't to proclaim our glory," she said. "I don't want nooooo boasting over healed bodies or paid-up mortgages or even Jesus pie. I just want to tell people whatever the Lord sees fit to proceed from my mouth that day. My mouth—not yours. And not Rassie Harper's, either."

Disappointed, but eager to hear Agnes on the radio, the folks left. Agnes and I ate spaghetti with sauce. We had plenty of desserts, seeing as how everyone who stopped by brought something, including a cherry cobbler that went down tart, but landed sweet in my stomach. Arthur didn't seem to mind that the fish was burnt.

The next day, Monday morning, Hezekiah showed up for work—oblivious to any of the preceding day's activities or surprises.

"Morning, Griselda," he said, coming in the back door with an arm full of wood as usual. "Should I make a fire for Agnes? I'll be here most of the day to tend it."

It was another cold Pocono Mountains morning, and a fire would be cozy, but I was still concerned about Agnes's breathing.

"I'm not sure it's a good idea with her breathing and all."

"I heard that," called Agnes, "I'd like a fire. I'm breathing just fine. Morning, Hezekiah."

"Good morning," he called.

I went back to stirring oatmeal. "You heard her. Just keep an eye out today and make sure she uses that nebulizer."

"I will, Griselda." I deliberately avoided asking him where he was the day before. It really wasn't any of my business.

He brushed by me just barely touching my shoulder with one of the logs. A splintered piece snagged my sweater.

"I'm sorry, Griselda. Did I get you with a piece of wood?"

"Yeah, just a second, you caught my sweater."

I unstuck the wood as he stood close enough to me that I could smell his toothpaste.

"Did I ruin your pretty sweater?"

"No. I'll just pull the thread through the back."

He looked right into my eyes for a second, and I felt my heart beat. "I'm sorry," he said. "I can be all feet sometimes." He smiled and headed for the viewing room. That was when I noticed Hezekiah was wearing a brand new pair of black shoes and white socks. Looked like the Society had paid him a visit.

I heard the dried oak he was carrying fall to the floor.

"A fire would be pleasant," Agnes said.

"I'll have her going in just a few minutes."

Then I heard him balling up newspaper, and before I could get breakfast to Agnes he had a fire roaring. I will admit it felt nice on my face. Arthur found a spot on the hearth.

We all ate breakfast together, and Agnes, although I think she was champing at the bit, waited until I cleaned up the dishes before mentioning the Pearly Gates Singers to Hezekiah. He wasn't all that impressed.

"I never heard of 'em," he said. "Any good?"

Agnes chuckled. "I think they're the best gospel singers around. I hear them on the radio and occasionally on Sheila Makefield."

"I'm glad for you, then," Hezekiah said. "I hope they put on a good concert, except how—"

"How will I get there?" Agnes beat him to the punch. "I won't get there, but I'm sure the men will rig up a speaker and pipe it into the house. That's what they did that time the evangelist Billy Bray came by. You remember that Griselda, although I'm sure I'll enjoy the Pearly Gates more."

I did remember. It was about three years ago and it worked out kind of nice for Agnes. Pastor Speedwell and Studebaker connected a wire from the church microphone to a speaker they set up just inside our front door. Pastor measured too short and the wire was cut wrong but it didn't matter. Agnes said later that Billy Bray screamed so much she probably didn't even need the speaker. She might have been right. The church rafters shook that night, and Fred Haskell got saved, baptized, and made a member of the church all in one fell swoop. Agnes had been praying for his salvation, and Fred ran right over after the service, leaping and jumping up a storm on account of getting "his ticket to paradise," as he called it, thanks to Agnes.

Hezekiah excused himself. "I better get on down the basement. I'm starting on that little room today."

Agnes screwed up her face. "Now remember, I'm pretty sure most of what you'll find in there is just a bunch of stained rags and trash. You can just burn it all."

"No problem, Agnes. I'll have it clean as a whistle in no time."

Hezekiah headed for the basement.

"I was dying to ask him where he was all day yesterday," Agnes said. "Weren't you?"

An image of Hezekiah with Olivia flashed in my brain. "No, not really."

Agnes grabbed her notebook and pens and Bible. "I'm expecting Cora and Janeen today. I think Cora just needs some reassurance, and I can't figure out what Janeen wants. She called me Saturday and said it was of vital importance."

"Hard to tell with her. Could be a hangnail or a misplaced bobby pin."

"Sometimes folks just need a sounding board," Agnes said.

"I forgot there was something I wanted to tell Hezekiah. That leak upstairs is back; maybe he can help Fred fix it once and for all."

"Okay, I got to get to my notebook. I'm gonna add the Pearly Gates Singers."

"Good idea." But before I could get to the cellar the doorbell chimed. Thinking it was either Janeen or Cora I opened the door. It was Filby Pruett.

"Morning, Griselda. I need a couple more shots of Agnes. Close-ups. I want to get her face just right."

I heard Agnes grumble.

"Let me see if she wants to have you in."

"Tell her it's important if I'm going get the statue finished by Memorial Day."

"Memorial Day?"

"Yes, that's what Studebaker said. He wants to unveil it at the Memorial Day celebration."

I watched the little twerp contain a snicker. I got the distinct impression that Filby was not in the project for love of Agnes.

"Just a minute," I said.

Agnes was already shaking her head no when I went inside.

"What should I tell him?"

"Just tell him to use what he's got. I don't want my picture taken anymore."

It didn't matter. Filby was standing behind me with his camera poised and ready to flash.

"Please, Agnes, just two pictures. One head-on and one profile. Then I'll be gone."

"Make it quick," she said.

"Well, I am sorry, Agnes," Filby said, "it's a lot of face, and I can't seem to get some of them neck folds exactly right."

"Filby," I said, sounding like a scolding mother.

"Ah, it's all right," Agnes said. Then she burped.

I pushed some stray hairs behind her ears and wiped the sweat from her forehead. Filby snapped his pictures and left without saying another word. *Or taking a breath.*

"Now I got to go, Agnes. Hezekiah will get your lunches today. I'm expecting the high schoolers again later, but I'll be home for dinner—fried chicken tonight, I think."

Agnes dug her hand into her candy jar. "That's fine." She opened her notebook, and I watched her write Pearly Gates Singers and the date they were coming.

After I pushed the logs back in the fireplace and added two more I put my hat and coat on and had my hand on the door when Hezekiah sneaked up behind me. I turned around with a start. "You scared me, Hezekiah."

He held a bundle of fabric. It looked like an old faded baby blue sweater with mother-of-pearl buttons, covered with some kind of large dark stain.

"What's that?" I asked, still examining his puzzled look.

"I can't say with any certainty, although I'm pretty sure it's a lady's sweater. I found it in that old World War II ammunition box in that little room down there."

"So?"

"Well, look at it, Griselda. That ain't chocolate sauce all over it, and someone went to a lot of trouble to hide it down there."

"Then what is it?"

"Looks like dried up blood to me. Especially if I turn it over and look under here. It's still discolored but look—" he pushed it toward me— "it sure looks like blood."

"What? Well maybe it belonged to my father and—"

"Nah, your father kept his stuff too neat, and I don't think corpses bleed all that much."

"Then my mother."

"Could be, but it still doesn't make sense to hide it."

"Then just burn it with everything else. I'm sure it's nothing."

"It's a lot of blood, Griselda, and that ain't all. I found shoes down there with the same stain—girl's shoes."

My heart started to pound. "Maybe my father had to work on an accident victim and that was what she was wearing."

Hezekiah looked past me a second. "That sounds logical. But like I said, your father wouldn't have gone to the trouble of hiding this stuff."

I grabbed the sweater from Hezekiah. "Maybe Agnes knows something, even though I think you're making a big deal out of nothing."

Agnes had her eyes closed and her hands on her opened King James. "Agnes," I said, "Hezekiah found this downstairs. Do you know anything about it?"

She opened her eyes. For the briefest second I thought I saw horror cross her face.

13

"Is that what you two were discussing just now? Agnes said. "I never saw it before."

I shook my head. "Me neither. I think Daddy must have left it there—used it for a rag or something."

"Probably." Agnes squirmed like she did when her legs ached. "Just burn it with the other garbage. And the shoes too."

Hezekiah looked at the sweater. "Seems to me a sweater this bloody should have a reason, a good reason. And those shoes . . . someone, a little girl, I think, was walking in blood. They ain't no bigger than this—" he held out his fingers about six inches apart— "and they got buckles, stretched out buckles, and the heels are all crushed."

Agnes took a rattled breath. "Just get rid of it, Hezekiah. There ain't no use in standing here second guessing who, what, or why."

"Don't get so excited, Agnes," I said, "or you'll get into a coughing jag."

"I'm not excited. There is just no reason on God's green earth to stand here discussing some old, stained sweater. This was a funeral home after all, and you're liable to find anything down there."

"Okay, okay, Agnes. Please." I watched her face turn pink, starting at her neck.

Hezekiah shook his head. "I'll do as you say, Agnes, but I think—"

"Well it don't matter what you think," Agnes said.

He carried the bundle back to the basement.

"Make sure he burns that stuff, Griselda."

Our basement was never a pleasant place because that was where our father prepared bodies for burial. My mother had no trouble going up and down, even bringing Daddy a sandwich or cups of coffee and sitting awhile to chat while he did his job.

"After you seen so many dead, naked bodies," she had said, "it stops being a problem. It's like they aren't there anymore."

The basement smell hit me like a freight train. It was a strange mixture of dust, chemicals, mold, and dampness—if damp had a smell. I had to knock back some cobwebs as I made my way through the maze of rooms. I found Hezekiah in the little room at the south end of the basement. The sweater was laid out over a metal box with the little shoes by it on the floor.

"Make sure you burn that stuff," I said.

Hezekiah was on his knees rooting through some other boxes. "Griselda, look at these." He showed me the shoes.

For a second I thought I might have seen them somewhere before but I couldn't be sure. "Sad, aren't they? I still think they must have belonged to a child our father buried."

Hezekiah shook his head. "Why would he have stuffed them in this box?" His foot tapped a small, green, metal box with the word Ammunition stenciled in white.

For the first time since Hezekiah's arrival to Bright's Pond I heard softness in his voice, but also uneasiness, almost like the items he found made him nervous.

"He must have had his reasons. Please just burn them and forget about it."

When I got back to the viewing room I found Agnes straining to get out of bed. "Oh, good, you're still here. Help me out of this bed. I got to move."

"Come on." I grabbed Agnes by her two arms and pulled. She lurched as far forward as she could and tried to throw her legs over the side of the bed. The thick folds of skin were like waves as they rolled off. Once she got to her feet I grabbed her walker and placed it in front of her. Then I grabbed a handle of nightgown behind her and led my sister down the hall.

"So what do you think about it?" I asked.

"What?"

"That sweater."

Agnes stopped moving and huffed. "I don't think anything about it. Just an old sweater that got left behind."

When we reached the kitchen Agnes grabbed a couple of lemon squares off a pretty pink plate on the table. "I do love Cora's lemon squares."

I waited until she swallowed them. "Let's get you back to bed. You could stand a change of clothes too." So I arranged Agnes's blankets and helped her into a fresh nightgown—a frilly one with tiny flowers all over it. When she lay down she looked like an acre of tea roses.

"Now I should get to the library."

"Okay, Griselda. I'm expecting Cora any minute. Or Janeen. Hope they both don't come at once. I hate it when I have a waiting line."

I met Janeen on the porch.

"Morning, Griselda," she said. A gust of wind blew up and knocked her hat to the ground. She bent down. "I'm sure looking forward to seeing Agnes this morning. I got some terrible news, terrible news."

"Oh, no, what's the matter, Janeen? Is it your health?"

"Not about me at all. It's my sister, and you know about sisters—how special they are."

I smiled. "Yep, they can be special."

"Anyway, you know I have a sister, Francine, lives in North Carolina since that no-count husband of hers went there six years ago to raise alpacas or camels or some such nonsense with some guy named Maurice."

"Yes, I remember you were awful upset when she left."

"Anyway, it turns out that crumb bum and his—" she made the sign for imaginary quotes "—business partner got into hot water and now they're both sitting in jail. Seems they were—" she leaned close and whispered "—growing that mari-joo-wana down there."

"Well, I don't see what Agnes can do about that."

"She can pray that Francine comes to the good senses the Lord gave her and come back home where she's loved."

I nodded and opened the front door. "I think she's waiting for you."

"Agnes," Janeen called, "you are not gonna believe . . ."

That was all I heard. All I wanted to hear.

"Good bye," I called from the front door.

I parked on top of Hector Street and tuned into the Rassie Harper Show.

". . . loyal listeners, two weeks from today, March 27, we are heading to Bright's Pond to bring you an exclusive interview with Agnes Sparrow."

"That's right, Rassie, and all you folks out there in radio land." Vera chimed in. "We're going by remote to the home of Agnes Sparrow, miracle worker and the fattest woman in the Pocono Region."

"Maybe the whole East Coast," Rassie said.

They had a good chuckle, and my stomach ached. Why in heaven's name would Agnes have agreed to such a stunt?

"Now on to other news," said Vera. "I am proud to announce that our own Rassie Harper has arranged for . . . now I hope some of you are sitting down for this. I know how excited you can get . . . . Rassie has arranged for the Pearly Gates Singers to appear in Bright's Pond next month, April 12, the Wednesday after Easter."

She paused a moment, and it sounded like she might have sipped coffee. "So even if you don't live in Bright's Pond, and I know that's most of you God-fearin' listeners, you might want to drive on up there and take in the show. Tickets will be sold at the door, first come, first served, so get there early. And stay tuned to this station, WQRT, for more info."

Then she took a deep breath and moved on to gossiping about some woman named Trina Lovelace who got caught at the Lamplighter Motel with Grant Fingerhut, the owner of the largest Buick dealership in the region.

I dropped the truck into gear and drove the mile and a quarter to the library. It was cold for the middle of March, so I had the heat going full blast. My feet still felt cold. I hit a bump and the glove box fell open spilling most its contents on the floor, including a baggie filled with green stuff.

I pulled over and examined it more closely. It had a pungent, sweet smell but looked a lot like oregano. There was no mistaking it. I was holding a small quantity of grass, weed, reefer, pot. Whatever you called it, it was still illegal.

Now, I know, what a coincidence that Janeen's husband had just gotten nabbed for growing the weed, but it's the truth. Things happened like that sometimes.

My first thought was to take it to Mildred Blessing, but I thought twice on that, what with the upcoming publicity on the Rassie Harper Show. I decided the last thing we needed was some scuttlebutt about us having pot in our possession.

So, I tucked it into my coat pocket, thinking that the only person it could belong to was Hezekiah. I took another whiff. Why in the world would anyone want to smoke it? Zeb tried it in high school and even offered me some out back of the football field while we were cutting Social Studies. I will admit, I took a hit, but I couldn't hold it in my lungs very long and just blew it out. Ten minutes later I was admiring the fancy buttons on Zeb's shirt.

I stuffed the bag into my pocket, dropped the truck into drive, and headed down the hill toward the library. Headlines flashed in my brain, "Local Librarian Arrested for Possession of Mari-Joo-Wana."

Nothing eventful happened at the library that day. Mildred Blessing stopped by to peruse the hard-boiled detective novels in the stacks. She loved them, especially Mickey Spillane, and Sam Spade. I wondered if she might have smelled the pot and came snooping. But I was just being paranoid. She checked out two books.

"How's the dog case coming?" I asked as I stamped her books. "Catch him yet?"

"Nah." She looked pensive. "I had him three days ago, though, sitting in the back of my cruiser, ready to go to the big house, when he lammed on me."

"You mean he opened the door and escaped?"

A slightly embarrassed look crossed her face. "I stopped at Personal's to check on a disturbance that turned out to be nothing but a trip for biscuits, and when I got back, the mutt was gone."

"No kidding."

"If I'm lyin', I'm dyin'. Last I heard he was seen tromping through Cora Nebbish's backyard. Took her good linen tablecloth, the one with the tiny eyelets all around it, with him. She put in a report for theft, that's how I know about the eyelets. I'm thinking that canine perp's got an accomplice."

I smiled with my head down. "Enjoy your books, Mildred."

She saluted with two fingers and left. "See ya in the funny papers."

I didn't have the heart to tell her I had just seen the daring dog in back of the library . . . or that I had a bag of pot in my pocket.

Five o'clock rolled around, and after the last of the high school kids finished his research, I closed up the library. I stopped at the café on my way home to pick up meals for Agnes and me. I didn't feel like frying chicken anymore. It looked like a lot of folks had made the same choice. Monday was meatloaf night, and some of the older folks like Jasper York and Harriett Nurse stopped in for a plate. I walked in and the smell of onions and brown gravy hit me. Zeb had been cooking meatloaf all day.

Studebaker and Boris sat at a booth deep in conversation as usual. Sometimes I think those two had designs to take over the world. It was like watching Harry Truman and Dwight D. Eisenhower.

"Hi, Stu. Hi Boris," I said.

Boris stood like he always did. "Griselda. Nice to see you."

Studebaker smiled, but I think he was still feeling a little embarrassed about the sign catastrophe. He could hardly look at me.

"Stu was down in Scranton making certain they got the name right this time," Boris said.

"I heard that," I said. "You were gone for a quite a little while. Kind of missed you around here."

"I have family in Wilkes-Barre so I spent some time there— got a sister and two nieces."

"I'm glad you were able to visit with family, Stu, but please don't give that sign thing another thought."

I said hello to Jasper on my way to the back end of the counter. He and Harriett were sitting together waiting for their specials. Lately, Jasper had been getting even more confused and forgetful than usual. He stood when he saw me and saluted like he was still in the army.

"Evening, Colonel," he said.

I saluted back and moved to the end of the counter where Cora was standing.

"Poor old guy," she said. "Harriett told me he's been slipping his gears. Thinks the war is still on and he's somewhere in Belgium."

"Ah, that's really sad." I shook my head. "I guess we should play along."

"That's what Doc says. He's trying to get Jasper to go to Greenbrier."

"Oh, I don't know if that's the best thing. Harriett'll take care of him, don't you think?"

"She isn't much better. I mean the lights are on, but I don't think anyone's home. Just a little while ago it took about eight minutes for her to order the meatloaf. Kept forgetting where she was."

Cora smiled and looked out the diner window a second. "Got to count my blessings. I'm headed down that same road, I suppose."

"You? You're still one of the brightest lights in town."

She grabbed my hand and squeezed. "Thanks to Agnes."

"Make me up two meatloaf specials to go, will you? I'll be right back. Need to visit the little girl's room."

"Sure, I'll put extra mashed on for Agnes."

That was when Olivia sashayed past. We were both headed for the ladies room. She was wearing a tight, lime-green sweater and even tighter black pants, cropped at the ankles, and platform shoes with chunky heels that looked like they were made from cork. She threw her hair back as she passed.

"Yo, Griselda," she said.

"Yo."

I followed her into the small two-stall restroom. She adjusted her pants and then her sweater. I watched. She put her hands on her waist and examined herself in the small mirror by standing on tiptoes.

"Does this sweater make my breasts look big?"

"Yes." They were like two large cantaloupes.

"Good."

She checked her lipstick and fixed her hair so that it lay on her shoulders with just the right amount of natural swoop, all while I watched. Something stirred in the pit of my stomach as she adjusted her sweater, and I caught a glimpse of myself in the mirror. Some women were just born with beauty and good taste. That gene skipped me entirely. No wonder Hezekiah liked her.

"You know what you need, Griselda? A man. A man to work out some of those kinks in your face. You always look like you're about to throw up."

She dropped her lipstick into her purse. "See ya. Hezekiah is meeting me here in a few."

I washed my hands in the rust-stained sink. The sweater Hezekiah found flashed through my mind. How could he be sure it was blood? Could be anything, including rust from a leaking pipe. Could be that Agnes spilled fudge all over it and didn't want to tell our mother and she just forgot.

I waited at the counter until Zeb brought me the meatloaf specials. "Hey, Griselda," he said. "I gave Agnes extra everything."

"Thanks, Zeb. Business looks good tonight."

"Meatloaf night. The old folks love their meatloaf." He wiped his hands on his apron. "So, when we getting together?"

Olivia, who was sitting close enough to hear, slurped her soda loud enough to draw my attention. She winked.

"I don't know, Zeb. Got something in mind?"

"They got *Dirty Harry* showing down at The Crown. Supposed to be a good movie. Clint Eastwood."

"Go on," said Olivia, "go see a movie. Do ya some good, Griselda, like I said." She winked again and then pulled her straw across her lips. "You know you wanna."

"How about it, Grizzy? You. Me. A movie? Have you home by ten."

"Not if you get lucky," Olivia said.

I gave her a glare. "All right, Friday."

"Great. I'll pick you up at seven."

I paid Cora for the dinners and left feeling just a little lighter then when I entered, but a little shaky at the knees.

Agnes enjoyed the meatloaf special, eating most of mine as well. I couldn't eat a bite.

"What's the matter, Griselda, you sick?"

"Nah, just not hungry."

"How come? You got to eat. You'll get skinny. Not that you ain't skinny already."

I took a bite of the meatloaf. "It's good tonight."

"Yeah, that Zeb can sure cook. Gonna make some gal a good husband someday."

"Now why did you say that?"

"What? I'm just saying."

I swallowed potatoes and poked at my peas. "He asked me out for Friday."

"You gonna go?"

"Yes."

Agnes sucked in air and then finished off her meatloaf. "I don't like being alone at night."

I felt a sigh rise up in my chest like a wave. It was always about what Agnes wanted, and I wondered if the day would ever come when she'd see that. But I didn't let on that I was feeling the least bit frustrated.

"I'll see if Hezekiah can stay with you or maybe Vidalia will come by. You can play Scrabble."

"Well, okay, Griselda, just so I'm not by myself."

"I heard Rassie Harper today," I said, desperate to change the subject. "He's advertising your radio show."

"No kidding. Guess we'll have a lot of listeners. I've been praying about it, and I still don't know what I'm gonna say."

Agnes poked at her dessert. "Did Hezekiah burn that stuff?"

"Said he was going to. Why are you so interested? If he said he did, I see no reason to question him."

"Now there you go getting testy. I just want things cleaned up."

"I'm not testy, Agnes, but you never had me check on him before."

She swallowed some ice cream. "You're right. It's just . . . those things he found gave me the willies, you know?"

"I know. It's weird. Why would Daddy save those terrible things, if it is what Hezekiah says—blood?"

Agnes dropped the spoon in her bowl. "So Rassie is making a big deal out of the show."

"Yep, he sure is. And Vera Krug mentioned the Pearly Gates Singers."

That made her smile. "Oh, good. I'm looking forward to that."

After I cleaned up the kitchen and called Arthur in for the night I managed to do three loads of laundry. I must have been moving on adrenaline that night. I could hardly think about anything more than Zeb, although it wasn't entirely pleasant thoughts. I didn't even know if I liked him like a woman is supposed to like a man.

14

Hezekiah came by early the next morning. He entered the back door as usual while I was making breakfast.

"Did you burn that sweater and shoes?" I asked right off, not giving him a chance to say hello or start another subject.

"Um, sure. Burned to a crisp, Griselda, just like you said. He smiled at me in a way that sent a chill down my spine. "No more evidence."

"Evidence? What are you claiming?"

"Ah, nothing. I'm just making a joke."

I heard a long, desperate meow at the door. "Oh, there he is. That cat's been out all night. Would you let him in, Hezekiah?"

Arthur strolled in with a bloody mouse hanging out of his mouth by the tail. Small droplets of blood dotted the linoleum as he walked close to me and dropped it at my feet.

"Look at that," I said, "It's a wonder there are any mice left in this entire town."

Hezekiah stared at the blood droplets. His eyes darted to the still squirming rodent.

"Hezekiah," I said, "it's just a mouse. You've seen Arthur's little gifts before. Would you clean it up for me?"

He grabbed a role of paper towels and wrapped a couple around his hand and cleaned the mess. He tossed the mouse out the door.

"Do you want breakfast?" I flipped a slice of French toast.

"Sure. It smells good. I could eat a few pieces. You put cinnamon in there with the eggs?"

"And vanilla."

He took a breath through his nose. "Just like my Mama used to make it on Saturday mornings."

"You don't talk much about your family."

"Ah, I never knew my old man, and my Mama's been dead going on six years."

"I'm sorry to hear that."

"Don't worry about it, Griselda. I don't."

I wanted to ask him the question that had been on my mind since the day I met him. I wanted to ask him how come he ended up on the streets. But I didn't. I can't explain why, really. It just seemed like something you shouldn't ask a grown man.

We finished breakfast. Everyone was quieter than usual like we all had things on our minds. Hezekiah helped me with the dishes.

"Does that library of yours have old newspapers?" he asked.

"Some. Why?"

"Just something I want to look up. Something that happened, I figure, maybe twenty or twenty-five years ago."

"Oh, well, for that you'll need to look through the microfiche files. Most of the papers are on file, but a lot are missing."

"Can you show me how?"

"Sure. Just come by later."

I opened the curtains for Agnes, revealing a bright, blue day. Not a cloud in the sky and you could see clear to the mountains.

"They sure look nice this morning," I said.

"They sure do," Agnes said. "I can see spring making its way here."

She was right. It wouldn't be long before the trees would bud and bloom. The crocuses always popped up first and then the daffodils.

"I saw a tree full of robins the other day," I said.

"Oh, it must have been a sight. I thought I heard them singing this morning."

"Spring is coming, but it's still cold, so you keep your socks on."

"It was only twenty-one degrees this morning," Agnes said.

I pulled on my coat and slipped my hand into the pocket looking for gloves when I remembered the bag I found in the truck.

"Did I hear Hezekiah go out back?" I asked.

"Yeah, I think he said something about having some more stuff to burn—old magazines—and I told him to go ahead and chop up a couple of old stools he found yesterday."

I found him tossing wood on to a pile inside a large, black, scorched area in the yard. "Stand back," he said, "I was just about to throw some gasoline on there."

"Thought you burned all this stuff yesterday."

He twisted the lid on the gas can. "I burned the sweater and shoes yesterday. This here is leftovers, stuff I wasn't sure about until I asked Agnes."

I pulled the baggie from my pocket. "What do you know about this? I found it my truck."

Hezekiah snorted a laugh. "Ah, come on, Griselda, it's just a little pot."

"So it's yours then."

He dumped gasoline on the pile. "It's no big deal. I picked it up when I went into Shoops with all them clothes. No big deal. Hardly ever use it."

He tossed a match onto the pile, and flames ignited with a whoosh. I stepped back from the sudden heat. "Then take it. Don't leave it in my truck or my house, and I better not hear you been keeping it at Vidalia's."

Hezekiah tossed a stack of magazines on the fire. "All right, Griselda." He moved close to me. "Look, I'm sorry. I haven't hardly used it, and I promise you I never came to work high."

I believed him. "Okay, but please be careful. Now, I got to get to work."

"I'll come by later," Hezekiah said. "Check out those papers."

"If you want to tell me what you're looking for I could start researching, maybe find something before you get there."

Hezekiah looked into the roaring fire. "Well, I'm not too sure exactly," he said. "I was just wondering about any unexplained deaths in town, or accidents that might have seemed suspicious at the time."

I felt my eyebrows arch. "I don't know of any right off. Why you so interested?"

"Oh, no reason," He grabbed the garden hose and squirted the high-rising flames. "I like to keep it with me in case the fire gets out of hand. Don't want to burn the trees."

"Come by later, but make sure the fire in the fireplace is down before you leave and don't lock the front door and—"

"I know the routine."

I refilled Agnes's M&Ms jar and made sure she had working pens. "You got visitations today?"

"Sure do. Hazel Flatbush is coming by. She called yesterday and said she needed prayer for her knees again."

Hazel was a good egg—a quiet woman with six incorrigible children she loved to pieces. Her husband Colby and she worked one of the dairy farms nearby and came to town for church occasionally and for baloney sandwiches with Full Moon pie about once a month. Hazel came to town often to stop and visit with Agnes. An active member of the Society of Angelic Philanthropy, Hazel felt a responsibility to keep her finger on the "pulse of the town."

"And, Jack Cooper," Agnes said. "He's coming by."

"Jack?"

"Yeah, he drops in now and again. Doesn't ask for much. Sometimes I think he just needs a check-up."

"I'll be home by four."

The whole way to the library, Hezekiah's interest in looking up accidents in town nagged me. So, after my usual chores, mail and such, I set to work on the microfiche. Hezekiah said he was looking for something that might have happened twenty or twenty-five years ago. I would have been a kid, so nothing obvious popped into my memory.

I pulled out some sheets of microfiche, figuring I'd start at 1952, and fired up the reader, a contraption that didn't get a whole lot of use in Bright's Pond. But, if the truth be known, it was the most interesting task I had been given in quite a long time.

Before I could get through 1952, Vidalia came by to return some books.

"You're hard at work," she said.

"Oh, Vidalia, I didn't even hear you come in."

"Guess not. Look at you all busy like a bee. Researching something?"

Vidalia was always so pleasant. She wore a camel coat with a gray scarf wrapped around her neck. She pulled off her knit hat and set it on the counter.

"Not sure exactly. Hezekiah was asking about unexplained deaths in town.

Her eyes lit up. "Really? Here? In Bright's Pond?"

"Yeah, I was thinking that maybe it has something to do with why he came to town in the first place, you know. Or maybe it has to do with the miracle he needs."

"Um, could be, could be." Vidalia unbuttoned her coat and flopped it over the back of a chair. "Can I help?"

"Not unless you know about some unexplained death in town."

Vidalia picked up a sheet of microfiche and held it to the light. "Amazing what science can do. Just think, a full year's worth of newspapers on these little plastic cards."

"Well, I don't think there is a full year of anything. Just miscellaneous months."

"That don't help if you're shy a few pieces."

"I know, but I thought something might jump out, Hezekiah said he was interested in going clear back to 1948."

"Um." Vidalia shook her head slightly. "I wasn't even in town back then, and you would have only been a little girl— you and Agnes that is."

"Eleven," I said.

I scanned a few more papers while Vidalia looked through the stacks.

"I quit," I said when Vidalia returned with an armful of books.

"Babette Sturgis is doing her research paper on the carpet-baggers. Came by for some information."

"You're a good neighbor, Vi. I don't think anybody in town takes as much interest in those kids as you do."

"Oh, I love them to pieces. Makes missing my own children easier, you know what I mean?"

I had just finished stamping her books when Hezekiah came in. "Hey, Hezekiah," said Vidalia, "you coming home for supper?"

He shoved his hands in his pockets. "Not tonight, Vidalia, I have other plans."

No doubt a date with Olivia.

"Well, good luck with your research," Vidalia said.

I showed Hezekiah the reader and explained how to use it. "You're certainly welcome to look as long as you like, but I didn't see anything, not in 1952 anyway."

"Oh, you were looking."

"Just starting. It could take a while to go through all those years. Just remember you don't have full years. A lot of months are missing."

"I'll take a look anyway."

Hezekiah left two hours later with no more information then he had when he walked in the door. "Still got a few years to get through."

"Why are you so interested?" I put on my coat.

"Ah, I don't know. It might all be for naught."

I ran into Ivy Slocum on the way home that evening. She was standing on her porch holding a bowl of dog food.

"That Mildred sure has her sights set on that dog of mine," she said. "I was hoping to lure him home with this, but he gets tastier meals trampin' through town than I can give him at home."

I laughed. "Yeah, I saw him not too long ago with a steak in his mouth."

"I haven't seen him in a whole day now. Going on three. You don't think Mildred caught him?"

"Nah, she told me she had him once, but he escaped."

"Good old dog," Ivy said. "He's a smart one."

"Must be. He escaped from the back of her cruiser."

We had a good laugh, and I headed toward home by way of the Full Moon. I felt nervous. Friday was only a day away, and I still wasn't sure I really wanted to go out with Zeb even though I had agreed. I thought a moment about running into the café and canceling with him, but Jasper York distracted me.

"I nabbed me seven Nazis, Colonel. I'll be taking them in."

"Good man, Sergeant York." I saluted and kept walking.

Harriett pulled up in her Buick. "There you are, Jasper," she yelled out the window. "I went by to check on you, and you were nowhere to be found."

She stepped out of the car and grabbed Jasper by the elbow, knocking over his walker. "I'm sorry." She picked it up. "Let's go home before you really get into trouble."

"You're a nice lady, Mrs. Lincoln," he said.

"Criminy," said Harriett, "now we're back in the Civil War."

I found Agnes asleep with her Bible open on her chest. I closed it and set it on her table but not before noticing she had been reading the Psalms again. Agnes always went to Psalms when she was feeling a little off.

Her eyelids suddenly popped open like they were on springs. "Griselda. When did you get home?"

"Just a moment ago. You fell asleep reading your King James."

"I'm hungry," she said, sounding annoyed. "Hezekiah left early without giving me my second lunch. I tried to make it myself but I got so dogged tired, Griselda."

"You have been getting more tired lately. You feeling all right? Should I have Doc come take a look at—"

"Oh, for goodness sakes don't call him. I'm fine. Just tired. Not sleeping real well."

"I guess we all have times like that. I'll go get you some supper."

"Ivy brought a beef potpie when she come over today for prayer."

"Oh, I saw her and she didn't say anything."

"Imagine that, asking me to pray for that dumb mutt of hers."

"Did you?"

"Sure did. Prayed for him to be swifter than lightning and to keep clear of that Mildred Blessing."

"That's my sister. Good for you."

After we ate Ivy's delicious stew—she made it with just a few niblets of corn thrown in and the most delicate crust ever—we watched the news. It occurred to me that Agnes had been awful quiet all evening and only ate a few M&Ms.

"The season is turning," I said, hoping to get her talking. "I saw a crocus today—a purple one on Ivy's lawn."

"That's nice."

"And the forsythia out front are turning yellow. You know, they have that early spring look."

My mother loved forsythia. She watched and waited every year for the pretty, little yellow buds to open, a sure sign of spring, renewal, and hope. As long as the forsythia bloomed all seemed right with the world. Once they had been open a day or two, Mama would cut a few branches and bring them into the house to make wonderful, wild sprays of color. I continued the tradition and looked forward to bringing that little bit of sunshine inside for Agnes.

"Agnes," I said, sitting on the rocker, "are you all right? I mean you haven't seemed yourself for a couple of days."

She squirmed, and I watched her leg cramp. "Help me, Griselda, another cramp."

"This is getting silly." I pulled her leg as straight as I could and stopped when her knee popped. "I'm gonna have Doc come take a look at you."

"Don't you dare. I'm a grown woman, and I'll make my own decisions about things."

"Then maybe it would help if you took one of those sedatives he prescribed after your last big asthma attack."

"Okay, I'll do that."

We watched television the rest of the night and went to bed after the eleven o'clock news. The news was never very good in those days—all about the Vietnam War and President Nixon's troubles. I'll tell you, there were days when I thought for sure Jesus was about to split the skies and scoop us all up into heaven. I tucked Agnes in for the night and kissed her cheek like I always did.

"Take your pill?"

"Yes, Griselda."

"Good. I hope you sleep tonight."

Finally, I crawled into bed, and Arthur curled up at my feet. I read for a few minutes but my eyes grew so tired I could barely get through a chapter. As I turned off the light and closed my eyes, my thoughts turned to God and I asked him to watch over Agnes and help her rest. Only the Lord knew why she was troubled.

15

Friday came and Agnes didn't seem much better. She was still quiet and not quite herself. I had made arrangements for Vidalia to stay with her while I was out with Zeb. As I dressed, I wondered if I should cancel.

"What do you think, Arthur?" He was perched on the sill watching the birds.

I chose a pair of tan, corduroy pants that I hadn't worn in a very long time and a brown, cable-knit sweater. Not exactly what Olivia would have worn, but for me it was high fashion. I pulled my hair back in a ponytail and looked in the mirror. I dropped my hair and it fell straight and lifeless like strands of silk. I snapped in a silver barrette with two tiny faux pearls on one side of my head, but it looked out of place. I snapped another barrette on the other side, but that just made it look like I wanted to appear younger than I was. Finally, I fell back on the old reliable ponytail that I secured with a green rubber band.

Arthur mewled and stretched. I patted his head and held him like I always did. He purred in my arms. I glanced out the window in time to see a pheasant strut out from the high grass.

"Look at that, Arthur. Isn't he beautiful?" The bird walked toward the black fire circle but carefully avoided it. "That bird knows where life is. He isn't even touching the scorched ground."

No longer interested in the pheasant or me, Arthur leaped to the bed, leaving orange and white hairs on my sweater.

"Gee, thanks." I brushed them off and headed downstairs where Agnes was watching the six o'clock news and munching cheese doodles.

"Zeb will be here in a few minutes, Agnes. We're going to the 7:40 show. Can I get you something before I leave?"

"No." She barely looked at me and kept watching the TV like something had totally absorbed her attention.

"Really? Nothing? You don't want a sandwich, or some ice cream? Anything?"

"I said no, Griselda. I got my cheese doodles. It's all I want."

"Are you mad at me for going out?"

She shook her head. "No. Go. Have fun. I'll be all right. It will be nice to spend some time with Vidalia."

Still, something didn't set right in my gut. "Okay, I'll set up the Scrabble board for you guys."

Agnes was quite a good Scrabble player. She often rendered her opponent unable to make a decent word unless it left her the triple-word squares.

Vidalia let herself in. "Hey, ya'll. It's Vidalia."

"Hey," Agnes called, "come on in. Griselda is about to leave."

Vidalia dropped her lime-colored coat on the sofa. She looked comfortable in jeans and a dark blue sweatshirt with PENN STATE printed on it.

"There's fresh tuna salad in the fridge," I said, "if she gets hungry, and we always have pie and ice cream."

"That's fine," Vidalia said, "we'll be just fine." Then she smiled at Agnes.

I motioned for Vidalia to follow me into the kitchen. "Let me show you the containers."

Vidalia opened the refrigerator. "I know tuna when I see it, Griselda. And when was the last time you changed your baking soda?"

"No, that's not it. I wanted to speak with you alone."

"Oh, everything okay? You a little nervous about tonight? Afraid he might try to kiss you? There are worse things in life, you know what I mean?"

I felt my eyebrows arch. "No. It's got nothing to do with Zeb. I'm a little worried about Agnes. She hasn't been herself lately—kind of quiet and tired. Says she's not been sleeping well but she won't tell me what's bothering her."

"Oh, is that all. Maybe it's just a mood. Maybe she's starting menopause. Lots of women, even healthy women, start in their forties."

"Nah, I don't think it's that. She hasn't been regular for a long time. Doc said it's because of her weight."

"Don't fret, Griselda. I'll keep a good eye on her. Want me to try and find out what's troubling her?"

"No, it might be better if she just had a peaceful night. No pressure."

We walked back into the viewing room.

"I set up the Scrabble board in case you want to play, Agnes."

"Sounds good," Agnes said. "I haven't had a good game of Scrabble in a while." She pulled the little table over. "Go on now, Vidalia, pick a letter."

The doorbell rang. "That's probably Zeb, so I guess I'll be going." I looked at Agnes. She barely made eye contact. "You gonna be okay, Agnes?"

"Sure she will," Vidalia said. "There's plenty to yak about, food, and Scrabble. What else do we need?"

I felt a smile bubble up in my chest, although I did my best not to make it apparent on my face. "Okay, I'll be home by ten."

"Take your good old time," Agnes said.

A date. I was going out on bona fide date, something I hadn't done since high school when Charlie Parker took me to the drive-in down in Shoops. That was a dreadful evening. Charlie was all hands and mouth and pretty much made me sick to my stomach. He kept trying to kiss me and touch my breasts—the Holy Grail of male adolescence. I don't think I saw five minutes of the movie because after a while he got angry and took me home. He said I wasn't any fun.

I opened the door and saw Zeb standing there holding a bunch of carnations with a single red rose stuck in the middle. His hair was slicked back, and he wore jeans, a striped sport shirt under a green army jacket, no tie, and cowboy boots with pointy toes.

"These are for you, Grizzy." He pushed the flowers toward me.

"Oh, thank you, Zeb. I'll just put them inside. They probably won't last if I take them with us."

As I turned around I thought of a billion other things I could have said that would have been better.

"Vidalia," I called. She came running. "Would you put these in water?

"Oh, how sweet," she said. "Carnations. Look, Agnes, Zeb brought Griselda some flowers."

Zeb offered me his arm, which I took even though I didn't think we were at that stage yet. "I thought we could walk tonight," he said, "if that's okay. It's a little chilly out, but the sky is clear and the stars are bright."

I looked into the dark, purple sky. It was the color of the last Concord grape caught in the corner of the crisper too long. About a million stars shone like specks of broken crystal. "It is a nice night," I said. "Not too chilly and the stars are pretty."

"Just like you."

I think my heart stopped for a second. No one had ever called me pretty. Not even my mother. Not even my father. I wasn't certain how to respond. It just embarrassed me.

We arrived at the theater. "The movie starts at 7:45," Zeb said. "Fred Haskell is running it tonight." He stepped up to the counter to purchase tickets from a tall, blonde kid with his hands in the popcorn machine.

"Hi, Miss Sparrow," he said when he turned around. "I haven't seen you at the movies in a long time."

"Hi, Nelson, it's nice to see you. How are your folks?"

Nelson had come a long way since joyriding through Farmer Higgins's fields. He was working to earn money for college, even though he assumed he would be drafted any day.

"Oh, you know, they're okay, I guess."

Zeb paid for a medium popcorn and two Cokes.

Walking into the theater was like walking into a cave. The only light shone from the tiny bulbs that lined the aisle and a few bulbs in the ceiling. Zeb led me to a row in the middle. After we sat down, I counted nine other people and wondered who was there stag.

"It'll fill up a little more," Zeb said. "It's supposed to be a good movie. Not often we get a cop movie, you know."

"Right." I didn't think I'd ever seen a cop movie. I mostly liked older pictures starring Humphrey Bogart and Lauren Bacall and, of course, Cary Grant and sometimes Doris Day, even though I hated the way men treated women back then, like they were only around for them to have sex with.

Zeb offered me some popcorn, which I took reluctantly. I mean I liked popcorn well enough, but for some reason I always choked on the stuff and bits of kernel got stuck in my teeth. "Thank you," I said with a smile.

I sighed and I actually started to relax as I rested my head back.

"It's supposed to be a good movie," Zeb said.

"Yeah, you told me. I'm sure it will be."

"We can go somewhere else if it gets to be too much. I heard there was some bloody scenes."

"Blood doesn't scare me, Zeb." I washed a kernel down with Coke that stung my throat.

The movie started, and I took a deep breath. I could hardly believe I was out for an evening. It felt nice, almost like a reward. But, I should have known the feeling wasn't going to last. Harry had no sooner pulled out his gun for the first time when Nelson tapped me on the shoulder. "We just got a call, Miss Sparrow. It's Agnes."

"Is she all right?"

"Don't know. Miss Vidalia called and told me to tell you to come home right away."

Zeb took my hand and we hurried back to the house.

"It's probably another asthma attack," I said. "Last time it was a pickle, but sometimes I think it's—what do they call it? Psychosomatic. She brings it on herself when she feels afraid." I caught my breath.

"What's she got to be scared of?"

"She doesn't like it when I leave her at night?"

"I thought you said Vidalia was there?"

"She is."

Zeb and I ran the distance home. I saw Doc's car parked on the lawn as usual. Vidalia was standing on the porch.

"She's okay," Vidalia called, "physically, anyway."

I sprinted up the steps. Vidalia was hugging herself against the chilly air.

"What are you saying?"

Vidalia opened the door and let me go in first. Zeb followed after Vidalia. She stopped me in the entryway. Vidalia pulled my elbow "Before you go in there, I got to tell you I never seen her like this. We were playing Scrabble, and I made the word 'rock' and she burst into tears. About scared me to death."

I pushed past her. "That doesn't make sense. Agnes never cries."

"That's why I got so worried. I called the Doc. Then she started asking for you."

I ran into the viewing room. Doc was hanging over Agnes with his stethoscope in his ears.

"Agnes," I called, "what happened?"

Doc backed away. Agnes looked at me through tiny, scared eyes. Her fat face was like a Beefeater tomato about to burst. I could smell her sweat from where I was standing. I grabbed her hand.

"Agnes? Talk to me."

She just shook her head and sobbed. Dammed up tears flowed in rushing streams down her fat cheeks and into the folds and wrinkles of skin on her neck. She tried to wipe them away but they kept coming like a melting iceberg.

Doc touched my arm. "Let's step over here."

I patted her hand. "I'm not leaving. I'm just gonna talk to Doc. I'll be right back. Vidalia and—" I looked to make sure "—and Zeb are here."

Zeb was standing to the side still holding the box of popcorn. He looked like he just witnessed the destruction of the Hindenburg.

I followed Doc into the kitchen where he washed his hands as he talked. "I never seen her like this. Nothing physical, well not more than usual, but it seems like she had some sort of breakdown."

I finally took a breath and draped my coat over a kitchen chair. "Breakdown? Agnes?"

"Something got her going. And from what Vidalia said, nothing unusual happened tonight, except that Scrabble game."

"And I went out on a date."

"You go out all the time."

"Just to work, church, the café, and usually during the day unless it's a meeting."

Doc sat at the table and folded his hands in front of him. "I don't think that could have gotten her this upset."

"Well, to tell the truth, Doc, she has been acting kind of distant. Said she hadn't been sleeping real well." I leaned against the refrigerator, and Arthur slinked through my ankles. "She hasn't been her usual self."

"Really? Something happen?"

"No, not exactly. Maybe it has something to do with the radio show."

Zeb appeared at the kitchen door. "Uh, excuse me. It looks like she might have fallen asleep."

"Good," Doc said, "the sedative is working. Just let her sleep tonight."

I took a step toward Zeb. "I am so sorry. I don't know what to say. I enjoyed the movie, what I saw of it anyway."

He smiled. "It's all right, Griselda. I guess taking care of Agnes is a bigger job than I thought."

"Sometimes. But this is out of the ordinary." I glanced at Doc. He nodded.

"Sure is," he said, "I don't think I ever saw Agnes Sparrow cry."

I sat at the table. "She hasn't cried for a long time, not since we were kids. I wonder what happened this time to get her so upset."

Zeb put the red and white box of popcorn on the kitchen counter. "Look, Griselda, I think I better be going and leave you to figure this out."

I apologized again and offered to see him out. "No, it's okay," he said. "I can find my way."

I put a pot of coffee on to percolate. "I still have pie, Doc. Want a slice?"

"Sounds good."

Vidalia joined us after a few minutes, and we talked but none of us could come up with anything that might have set her off.

"It happened so fast," Vidalia said, "I put my tiles down and spelled "rock" for a double word score worth twenty points, but that's not such a big deal."

"No, this was more than being a little upset," Doc said. "She was really worked up over something. It's not good for her to get upset."

"It's got to be that dang radio show," I said. I thumped the table with my fist. "I'm gonna cancel it first thing in the morning. What's the matter with her thinking she could go on the radio like some television evangelist? She ain't Kathryn Kuhlman, you know."

Vidalia grabbed my hand. "Now don't you go getting all fired up. We don't know what this is about. She'll tell you in the morning."

I wasn't so sure.

After coffee and pie, we checked on her. She looked calm, sleeping and breathing like usual with tiny whimpers and snores. Doc listened to her chest.

"Sounds clear enough, but that heart murmur has gotten louder. She should sleep through the night. If she wakes up give her another one of these." He handed me a bottle of Seconal. "And then call me. I don't care what time it is."

"Mind if I ride home with you, Doc?" asked Vidalia. "I walked over tonight."

"Sure thing," Doc said.

I walked them both to the door, turned the porch light off, made sure I had unplugged the coffee pot, and headed for bed. I heard Agnes stir as my foot landed on the top step. I paused and waited, expecting to hear her call my name, but not this time.

I switched on the small bedside lamp and changed into sweat pants and an over-sized tee shirt. Sleep did not come easy that night.

16

Finally, after seeing every hour on the hour through the night, the first fingers of morning poked through the curtains, tracing long slivers of light on the wall. I glanced at the clock just as it flipped to 7:12. Saturdays were, as a rule, lazy days. I rarely opened the library on Saturdays unless a student had a research emergency, but the likelihood of that happening was pretty slim.

I found Agnes sitting up and attempting to get her legs over the side of the bed. Her hair was mussed, knotted on the sides and flat in the back, her face still red and blotchy.

"Good morning," I said. "How'd you sleep?"

"I'm fine, I suppose. I guess whatever the doc gave me was pretty powerful. It knocked me out." She blew her nose into a pink tissue. "And that's kind of like putting a whale to sleep."

"Agnes, don't be that way."

"I'm just so embarrassed, Griselda, getting upset like that and causing such a ruckus."

"What happened to get you so agitated?"

Silence. "The heart is deceitful and terribly wicked, Griselda. Who can know it but God Almighty?"

"What is that supposed to mean?"

"Nothing." She let her head sink into her pillow and closed her eyes. "I got a terrible headache, Griselda. Bring me some aspirin."

"Okay, but I'm not surprised. You were pretty upset last night."

I waited a moment hoping she'd tell me what happened but no explanation came. "I'll put on coffee and get you some breakfast too. How about some eggs and scrapple this morning?" It wasn't often we had scrapple, but every so often the Piggly Wiggly down in Shoops stocked it, and one neighbor or another would bring us a couple pounds. Agnes loved scrapple, and I'll admit to eating quite a few slices of it in my life. Our father always said it was made from the scrapings off the floor after they got finished butchering the hogs. That's how it got its name. It wasn't until I was in my twenties that I learned he was right. I stopped eating it for a time, considering hog scraps included mostly livers and brains.

"Sounds good, Griselda." Agnes reached for her notebook. "I got some folks to pray for this morning." She opened to the last page with writing and then closed it again, heaving a great sigh. "Maybe later."

She attempted a deep breath. My heart went out to her. I don't think I had ever seen Agnes close her notebook like that—like she couldn't muster the prayer muscles it took to care for all those people nestled inside like a momma hen with a nest full of constantly peeping chicks.

"Okay, I'll just get started in the kitchen."

I called Doc after I started the scrapple frying.

"She seems okay," I said. "Maybe a little hung over. Still kind of sad or—"

"That's to be expected," Doc said. "I gave her a lot of medicine. Stay close to her today, Griselda, and see if you can find out what she is so upset about. It could help us avoid this in the future."

I hung up thinking that solving this mystery wasn't going to be as simple as figuring out what set off her asthma attacks. This episode wasn't caused by a deli-sized, dill pickle. I let Arthur scramble outside and noticed dark, bottom-heavy clouds hanging over the pond. A storm was brewing.

Agnes managed to eat four slices of scrapple and three eggs followed by a cherry Danish and orange juice. Then she settled back with a second cup of coffee as the rain started pounding against the house.

"You gonna tell me what happened?" I asked.

Agnes shook her head.

"Fine, be that way. I'm just interested in you, that's all."

She opened the very notebook she had just closed. "I wonder how that young Neil Armstrong Haskell is doing. The boy with the stutter."

Agnes was as closed lip as I had ever seen her about what happened. "Is it supposed to rain all day?" I asked.

"Don't know."

"Expecting Hezekiah?"

"Uh, yes. He said he was gonna come by and finally get that faucet upstairs fixed and replace some washers in the kitchen."

"Finally. I'll be glad when that drip stops." I hate drips.

It turned out to be about as uneventful a day as I could remember. Agnes rested on and off, and I puttered around the house, catching up on laundry, vacuuming, and even scrubbing down the bathrooms. Every so often I checked on Agnes, got her something to eat, or changed the television channel. She liked to watch the Tarzan movies that came on in the afternoon.

Hezekiah never did show up that Saturday and, to be honest, I don't think Agnes or I cared all that much. His not showing up was becoming a habit. To be honest, it felt nice to be alone in the house. Vidalia called to check on Agnes and offered to come by but I told her that we were okay.

By evening I had a chicken roasting and potatoes boiling and Agnes started to look like her old self again. She settled into her freshly made bed. I had managed to turn the mattress and replace the cover with a brand new one I had stuffed in the linen closet two months previously and completely forgotten about until that day.

"You're a good sister," Agnes said.

The comment took me by surprise. Agnes so rarely thanked me anymore, and I guess that was to be expected after so many years of caring for her. It would get tiring to say thank you all the time. I figured that when you're in the position of being the one cared for, taking things for granted could be a way of denying it all.

After supper, Vidalia poked her head through the door and called, "Yoo hoo, it's just Vidalia." Actually, it wasn't just Vidalia. She had Ruth Knickerbocker and Cora Nebbish with her. Cora brought a plate of lemon squares, Ruth brought chocolate cake, and Vidalia held a lasagna the size of a pillowcase. "For tomorrow," she said.

"Thank you." I took the lasagna from Vidalia. "You didn't have to do this."

"It's not like we held a meeting and decided to come," Ruth said. "I met Vidalia right out front. I wanted to come see how Agnes was doing, and I thought a double-fudge cake would be welcome."

They shook out their umbrellas and pulled off boots and raincoats that they left in the entryway near the radiator.

"Me, too, I wanted to check on Agnes," Cora said, untying her see-through, plastic headscarf. "Vidalia told me what happened last night—"

"Why'd you go telling them about me getting a little upset?" Agnes called.

"Now, I'm sorry for spilling the beans," Vidalia said walking into the viewing room. "I was at the café this morning and it just came out. I was so worried about you, Agnes."

A smile pudged its way through Agnes's lips. "It's okay."

For those few minutes it seemed like Agnes had true friends.

Ruth pulled up the rocking chair, while Vidalia and Cora sat on the sofa. I went to make tea and divvy out the treats the women had brought.

I chose the pretty dishes our mother recieved as a wedding gift. They were white with tiny, blue flowers. I believe our mother called it the Royal Ascot pattern. I sliced cake and laid out lemon squares on a serving dish and poured tea into the dainty cups with saucers. It was like an impromptu tea party. For the first time that week I felt warm, even though the chilly rain still poured, and the winds whipping through the trees in the backyard sounded like angry ghosts. But as I sat with my friends and Agnes, I thought what a good day it had turned out to be.

When I got to the viewing room with the tray, Ruth was already telling Agnes and Vidalia all about the radio show. She had apparently been so distraught over it she made a trip into town and visited Vera to get as many details as her brain could hold.

". . . and Vera said not to worry one bit over the remote. It ain't nothing but a bunch of wires that will come from the station truck that Rassie will park out front."

I handed Ruth a cup. "Thank you, Griselda. I was just telling Agnes about Monday." She sipped. "Um, could use a bit of sugar, if you don't mind."

I dropped a sugar cube into her cup. It made a gentle plopping sound.

"Anyway, Agnes, like I was saying, Rassie will bring a, well I forget what Vera called it, some contraption or another right inside here."

"Console?" Vidalia asked.

"Yes, yes, that's the word. A console. It will have the microphones and other gizmos he needs to do the show."

Agnes swallowed chocolate cake. "It's good. Fudgy."

"Thank you," Ruth said.

I pulled one of our seldom-used dining room chairs close to Agnes's bed. "So you're feeling better about it being by remote, Ruth?"

"Oh, heavens to Betsy, yes, Griselda. I most certainly am feeling better. Why the way Vera explained it, it won't be much different than an ordinary conversation." She sipped. "Kind of like we're doing right now."

"Say, wouldn't that be a fine idea," Cora said. "We could do our own radio show right from Agnes's room—report on all the miracles and happenings."

"Now, hold on," I said. "Let's not get carried away."

Agnes finished the last bite of cake. "Yes, please, let's get through the Rassie Harper Show."

"That Rassie can be kind of tough on his guests," Vidalia said. "I heard he had the wife of the Mayor of Shoops on one day and somehow got her to tell the whole listening audience that Mayor Rattigan wore a toupee. Imagine that? A toupee."

We all laughed. "I remember that," I said. "It's not like it was some huge surprise. Mayor always did look like someone snuck up behind him and plopped a squirrel on his head."

"I'm not scared of Rassie Harper," Agnes said.

"Goody for you, Agnes," Ruth said. "We'll be here at six o'clock. Rassie told Vera his Monday morning audience is one of the biggest on account of people going back to work after the weekend and needing a few laughs." Ruth grimaced and grabbed Agnes's hand. "I'm sorry, Agnes. I didn't mean to say they'd be laughing at you."

"That's okay, Ruth. I know what you meant. But, why so early?" Agnes adjusted her nightgown.

"Vera said they had to set up and do sound checks and what not." Ruth handed me her cup. "Now, you're both looking sleepy, so we best be going."

Cora, who had gotten rather quiet, stood up. "I still wish I could be here and tell that fellow about how Agnes prayed for me with such unwavering faith and devotion and how the good Lord touched my ailing heart."

Ruth jumped in. "It might not be such a bad idea, Agnes, to have someone here, like a witness to the miracles. Especially if Rassie gets rude."

"It's not about that," Agnes said.

"Well, you might not think so, but Rassie will make it about the miracles. Vera told me he might try to get you to admit to being a fraud, right there, on the radio."

Agnes coughed. "I'll be fine, Ruth. Rassie Harper's got no power over me."

"Well, you just better be on guard. He's a crocodile, he is. Moves real slow and slinky like, hiding under water, and then all of a sudden—" she snapped her skinny fingers right in Agnes's face "—he bites."

"Don't be so dramatic," Agnes said. "Now get on home. I need my beauty rest."

I watched Ruth, Vidalia, and Cora walk part of the way down the block. The rain had stopped, or I would have piled them all in the truck and made the rounds.

It was good to see Agnes smile and even take potshots at herself. She had been surly and distant all week long.

"You feeling better?" I asked just before I turned off the lights. "It was good to see the girls and laugh a little."

"It sure was," Agnes said. "Nothing left to do now, but get ready for Monday. What should I wear?"

I smiled. "Agnes, it's radio, not TV."

"I know that, but there will still be strangers around, and I want to look nice . . . as nice as I can anyway."

We eventually decided Agnes should wear a flowery housecoat, one she could button all the way up, and that she should sit on the couch like a normal person, not lay in bed like an invalid.

"Tomorrow after church I'll go over to Gordon's and buy you some new slippers—pink ones with pretty white bows."

"But don't throw out my old ones. I got them broke in just the way I like."

"I was thinking I'd have Hezekiah burn them."

"Don't you dare! They might be worn, and Lord knows the heels are flat as a penny, but they're comfortable." We both laughed.

I fell asleep that night thinking that maybe, just maybe, the show would be okay, and so would Agnes.

It wasn't until I walked into church and Nettie Barker, one of the teenagers, handed me a palm frond that I realized what day it was. I had been so worried about Agnes and wrapped up with things at home, I hadn't been paying attention to the calendar. Palm Sunday arrived without notice.

As usual, I sat with Vidalia who was looking fine in her Navy dress and hat with a small, white veil covering her eyes and nose.

"Morning," she said, sliding over so I could sit. "I had a nice time last night. It was so good to see Agnes smile." Then she nudged my spleen. "And you, too, Griselda. You too."

"You know, Vidalia, I was thinking. Agnes did relax, so maybe it truly was some kind of menopausal thing that got her so worked up."

"Could be, could be. Those mood swings can be horrendous. One minute you're feeling fine and the next minute tears are pouring down your face, feeling like you just want to die, and you don't know why. Terrible curse that menopause. Don't get me started on those hot flashes."

The church filled quickly, and Sylvia started playing *All Hail the Power of Jesus' Name* as Pastor and the men entered like zombies. By the time Pastor got around to his annual Palm Sunday sermon about Jesus' triumphal entry into Jerusalem, I was feeling as fidgety as the children and wanted to get on over to Gordon's and then back to Agnes. I can't say why for sure, but my heart just wasn't in the right place that Sunday. I must confess I was getting a little starstruck about the next day's radio show.

After the final hymn, *Hosanna, Loud Hosanna*, and the benediction, I took Vidalia's hand. "I got a confession," I whispered. "I'm really excited about Rassie Harper coming to my house."

Vidalia looked me in the eyes. "Why, Griselda Sparrow, you're getting caught up in celebrity. What would Agnes say?"

We made it to the back of the church and stood in line to shake the pastor's hand.

"Nice to see you," Pastor Speedwell said with a cold fish handshake. I hated that. Weak handshakes gave me the creeps. "How's Agnes?"

"She's fine, Pastor, Agnes is fine."

"You tell her I was asking for her."

"I will."

"You tell her I'll be listening tomorrow."

"I will."

Ruth came rushing up to us as we stepped outside. "I plum forgot to put it in the bulletin. Potluck is this Wednesday instead of Friday on account of it being Good Friday. Think folks will realize?"

"Potluck?" I said. "I thought we decided that in months with a holiday we wouldn't have a congregational dinner?"

"That's true," Vidalia said, "but most folks don't consider Palm Sunday the holiday and Easter isn't until next week which is April—"

"And besides that," Ruth said, "some of the older folks without family nearby said the potlucks are the only celebration they get."

I could understand that.

"So what am I gonna do?" Ruth said.

"Well, Ruth," said Vidalia. "Maybe you better start making some phone calls."

"Oh, dear me, I know you're right but I just hate gettin' on the phone with people, takes forever to get back off."

"Would you like me to help?" Vidalia asked.

"Oh, would you, Vi?"

"I am on the committee. What say we split the list and even if we miss one or two, word will get around. You know how news travels in Bright's Pond."

"I'll get right on it. This afternoon," Ruth said. "I don't want to miss the radio show tomorrow."

Vidalia started down the path toward home.

"I think I'll just get in the truck," I said. "I have to go to Gordon's."

"Oh, that's fine," Vidalia said, "I best be getting on home. Winifred and the boys call every Sunday, you know what I mean?"

"Don't hang on the phone too long then, you won't want to miss them. Ruth can make those calls."

"No sir, I don't want to miss my babies."

Gordon's was what we called the five- and ten-cent store, a two-floor variety shop selling just about everything a person could need from rolling pins to Dr. Scholl's arch supports. Shep Gordon and his third wife, Stella, owned and operated the store. Stella, a tiny woman with platinum hair who always wore a cowgirl hat with blue rhinestones, sat behind the candy counter dolling out licorice whips, red buttons, Swedish fish, sen sen, candy cigarettes—ten to a box—and, my all time favorite, caramel pinwheels. I used to love to buy a nickel's worth after school.

I walked into the store. It was open on Sundays from noon to six. Shep was standing at the cash register ringing up a new curtain rod.

"Afternoon, Griselda," he called.

"Hey, Shep." I kept walking to the shoe aisle. They didn't carry many brands, and the variety was slim, but if your kid needed a new pair of Keds, Gordon's was the place. Except sometimes he didn't get Keds in, and you had to settle for something called Pattywinks. I never liked Pattywinks— always got blisters with them.

I located the slippers and chose a pair I thought Agnes would approve—pink with tiny white bows just like I told her.

"I heard about the radio show," Shep said. "I guess Agnes is pretty excited."

I handed him a ten-dollar bill for a three-dollar pair of slippers. "I think she is."

He gave me my change. "We'll be listening. Gonna put Bright's Pond on the map, that sister of yours will."

As I was getting into my truck I sensed an unkind presence behind me. Eugene Shrapnel, fresh from church in his stiff suit, walked out of the drugstore carrying a little, white paper sack.

"Mark my words, Griselda. If she goes through with this atrocity tomorrow, there will be hell to pay."

"Oh, come now, Eugene. Nobody is gonna have trouble because my sister is going on Rassie Harper's silly little radio show."

"She's doing the devil's work. She's recruiting converts to her way over the airwaves—the devil's medium, Griselda, the devil's medium."

"Stuff it, Eugene."

He backed off and lifted a gnarled finger in the air. "Mark my words."

I started the truck and pulled away from the curb, wondering how one small man could have gotten so mean.

Agnes wasn't too happy with the slippers—too tight. So I cut the backs and that made all the difference in the world. "Ah, much better," she said. "But I still like my old ones."

I spent the rest of Sunday getting the house cleaned and ready for the morning's onslaught. I had no idea how many people it took to do a radio show, but I figured on at least ten, including Agnes and me.

Agnes had me make blueberry muffins and an egg casserole in case they were hungry, and I made certain there was enough coffee. Vidalia stopped by in the evening to help where she could and was followed by Ruth and Cora. Even Zeb dropped over with pie.

"Too bad Jack fed the Jesus pie to the birds," he said. "I would get a kick out of Rassie seeing it."

That's pretty much how the evening went. Folks kept showing up at the door with food and offering their help. Most tried to get a shot at being on the show as a witness for Agnes.

By nine the people cleared out, and Agnes started to yawn and get quiet. Then Stu showed up.

"Can I come in, Griselda?"

"Stu, I was wondering when you'd stop by to plead your case."

"My case?"

"Yes, to be on the radio show tomorrow and tell the world how Agnes healed you of your cancer."

"That's not why I'm here, but now that you mention it, maybe—"

"Stu."

"Okay, okay. I really came to apologize." He wiped a knit hat off his head.

"Apologize?"

"For the sign disaster. I've been feeling so terrible over it, and I wanted to tell Agnes."

"Well, I was getting her ready for bed."

"I won't be but a minute. I never apologized and what with the show and all."

"Come on in." I stepped aside and let him walk in front of me.

The radio show had stolen some of Studebaker's thunder about the sign. He leaned down and kissed Agnes's cheek. "I never said I was sorry about the sign mistake."

"It's okay, Stu," Agnes said. "I never cared that much about it. You know that."

"I know, but we all did, and I just wanted to tell you that I tried to get the sign here in time for the radio show. I thought maybe Rassie would unveil it right on the air."

"Oh, Stu," I said. "I thought you were really sorry and maybe gonna stop this nonsense."

"Stop it?" Stu shook his head. "Why would I do that? It's been bought and paid for and will be arriving this Wednesday."

"Wednesday?" Agnes said. "That didn't take too long."

"What do you think about another unveiling celebration? Maybe right before the next potluck. This time I made sure those boys got your name right, Agnes."

Agnes took a shaky breath and reached for her inhaler.

"Maybe now isn't a good time to discuss this, Stu," I said. "Agnes has a big day tomorrow."

"Well, that's just it. I thought maybe Rassie could at least talk about the unveiling. Really play it up, you know?"

I saw that Agnes was getting agitated so I took Stu's hand and led him toward the front door. "We'll have to discuss it at the next town meeting."

"But that ain't until next month, Griselda."

"That'll suit us fine. Good night, Stu."

After he left Agnes and I had a little chuckle. I tucked her into bed. "Maybe you should take a pill tonight," I said.

"No, not tonight. It'll give me a headache in the morning, and I got a big enough one already."

"Still? I'm sorry, Agnes. Guess it was all the late night hoopla."

"You're probably right."

"Have you figured out what you might tell the world about the great Agnes Sparrow?"

"Phooey on that talk, Griselda, you know better than that. I am not the great Agnes Sparrow. I am not Houdini with a Bible doing tricks."

"This town sure thinks you're pretty amazing."

"I know and it pains me. Sometimes I wish I never . . ." She paused. "You know, I think that's most of what I'm gonna say tomorrow, come to think of it. I'm gonna tell folks how God has blessed Bright's Pond, not me."

"They'll still claim it was you. You and your prayers."

"I'm just the intercessor. We all know that, I hope. God works the miracles and that's what I got to say."

17

I rushed down the stairs at quarter after five the next morning. "Agnes, they're gonna be here in less than an hour."

Agnes was propped up with two pillows behind her and one under each arm. She clutched her M&Ms jar. "I ain't doing it, Griselda."

"What?" My forehead wrinkled like a cotton tablecloth.

"That gall darn radio show. I changed my mind."

"You can't change your mind now, Agnes. Those folks are on their way. They planned on this."

"Phooey. Rassie Harper can just make other plans."

"I don't understand. What changed your mind?"

"It just ain't right tooting my own horn and telling the world about the miracles. It shouldn't come from my mouth."

"Didn't I say that? Didn't I say we can't start advertising this all over the place? Isn't that why we tried to stop that whole sign thing? Wish you'd just have listened to me from the beginning."

"That's right. I know and I'm sorry. My prayers are between me and God, nobody else."

I flopped onto the red sofa. "What in tarnation am I gonna tell Rassie Harper?"

"Tell him the truth. Tell him Agnes Sparrow is not for sale. Tell him I got my reasons for praying, and God's got his reasons for answering, and it ain't nobody else's beeswax."

I took about ninety choppy breaths and started to hyperventilate. Agnes pointed to her oxygen. I declined with a wave.

"I'll think about this one. I'll get us some breakfast. Those folks are liable to show up early, now, the way things are going."

I put coffee on and checked the thermostat. A cold front had moved in overnight. I fed Arthur who kept looking at me like he had all the answers. And then I stood like a member of the walking dead and stared out the kitchen window as the coffee pot bubbled. Most days, I loved to look out over the mountains and dream of a day when I would travel past them. But not that morning. That morning those mountains were so wide and so tall and so high I believed there was no force in heaven or earth that could get me to the other side.

Agnes and I ate breakfast. I slathered her toast with raspberry jam and salted her eggs while she drank juice.

"I thought I could do it and give God the glory, but the more I thought about it, the more I knew I couldn't."

I bit the end of a triangle of toast. "That's good jam. Ruth brought it the other day. She said it's made by hippies in Binghamton."

"Best jam I've ever had," Agnes said.

"Well, speaking of jam. I still have to tell Rassie Harper."

Agnes waved her fork. "Ah, phooey. Rassie can go fly a kite. I can't be the first person to cancel at the last second."

"I suppose, but he's going through all that hassle of coming here. Might make it a little tougher."

The doorbell rang.

"Maybe we could just pretend we're not home and he'll go away."

"Agnes. We can't do that."

Fortunately it was not Rassie Harper standing on the other side of the door, but Ruth and Vidalia both in their Sunday clothes.

"Now don't go getting your dander up," Vidalia said before I could even open my mouth. "We tried to stay away, but—" she stopped. "What's the matter, Griselda? You look like someone just kicked you in the stomach."

"Oh, Vi, I just don't know what we'll do. Agnes wants to cancel the radio show."

"Why?" Ruth said, practically jumping over me. "Is something wrong with her—and on the day of the radio show?"

"No, Ruth. Agnes is fine. She just changed her mind is all."

"Oh, good, it's nothing too serious," Ruth said as she squeezed between Vidalia and me. "I thought we were gonna have to kiss the Pearly Gates Singers goodbye."

Agnes was sitting up, and Hezekiah, who must have slipped through the back door, was helping her into the old pair of slippers.

"You go on now and cancel the show," she said. "I really don't want that Rassie to even see me."

Ruth pulled my arm. "You can't let her do this, Griselda. She already agreed."

"What's this all about?" Vidalia said. "I mean I'm pleased that Agnes came to her good senses, but why now?"

"I decided that Griselda was right all along," Agnes said. "It's just not proper for me to go on the radio and toot my own horn like that."

"But, Agnes," Ruth said, "you made a promise. I've never known you to go back on any promise. You can't do it. Rassie'll sue you . . . take you to court or something."

"Nah, I'd never fit in the witness chair, and the jury could never take it serious. He won't sue. I never signed a contract or anything."

"Don't fret, Ruth," I said. "Agnes is right. We can't go advertising the miracles and such."

"You got to understand, Ruth," Agnes said, "my prayers are for the people of Bright's Pond. That's what I told God when I started, and it isn't right for me to draw attention to myself, you know?"

Vidalia coughed. "I agree with Agnes. I never liked this whole radio foolhardiness from the beginning."

"I'm sorry about this, Ruth," I said. "But don't you see what could happen if Agnes went on the air? I'd have more people at my door than I could count."

"That's right," Vidalia said.

Ruth sat in the rocker with a thud. "What in the world are we gonna tell Rassie Harper and that sister-in-law of mine? They'll have a field day with this—whatever a field day is. I never did understand that one. Vidalia, do you know what that means?"

Vidalia shook her head no. "I think we need to figure out what we're gonna tell them and then be done with it—field day or no."

"Well, we certainly can't tell the truth," Ruth said. "Vera will hold it over my head like an albatross for the rest of my life."

Vidalia squeezed Ruth's hand. "No, dear, it's an albatross around your neck and that isn't the situation. I think you mean sword of Damocles, and then I'm not certain that applies either."

Ruth gave Vidalia a quizzical look. "Sword or albatross, it all means the same. She'll never let me live this down."

The doorbell chimed.

"I'm doomed," Ruth said.

"Now, now, it won't be as bad as all that," Vidalia said.

I raced to the door, and sure enough, Rassie Harper, Vera Krug—I just assumed it was her having never met the woman—and three strange men stood on our porch. Rassie was not what I imagined from listening to him over the air-waves. For one thing he was a lot shorter than I expected and nearly bald, except for tufts of dark hair above each ear and hanging down the back. His pot belly probably was the result of drinking too much of the Budweiser he advertised. He smelled like cigarettes and wore a baby blue tee shirt that said something I can't repeat.

Vera, on the other hand, was exactly what I would have pictured, if I had ever taken the time to imagine her. She was wearing tight beige Capris that went smartly with her tight, hatchet face with the long nose and beady eyes that darted around like a lizard's. She wore an orange coat and orange knit hat.

Rassie reached out his hand, and I shook it just to be polite. I closed the door before they could get a foot inside. "I'm sorry," I said, "but Agnes—" my mind raced; what could I say? "—Agnes isn't feeling well and we'll have to cancel the show."

"What?" Vera said. She definitely had a radio voice and a real-life voice. I much preferred the radio voice. "You can't do that. We had an agreement."

"Well, we got no choice. Agnes is sick as a dog. I can't even let you in. You could catch something." I was sliding down that slippery slope of lies. "Doc said she was highly conta-gious, so unless you feel like spending the next twenty-four hours having explosive diarrhea and vomiting—"

Rassie backed off. "Okay, okay. But I have a show to do, Miz Sparrow. I got to be on the air in less than one hour."

Ruth came outside and shut the door behind her. "Hello, Vera."

"Good morning, Ruth. What are you doing here? I thought Agnes was contagious with some kind of intestinal thing."

"Oh, well, ah. . . . Griselda needed help," Ruth said. "You got any idea what it's like to be around a seven-hundred pound woman with dia—"

"All right, all right, I get the picture." Vera grimaced like she had swallowed bile.

"Now, listen to me," Ruth said. She all of a sudden sounded like a woman in charge—more like a woman determined not to spoil the chances of the Pearly Gates Singers coming to Bright's Pond. "I was listening at the window. You could take the show down to the café. Folks there will love to tell you all about the miracles. Just ask for Cora or Zeb."

"Ruth," I said. "We don't want—"

"Now don't you worry, Griselda. Folks can tell all about how they got their prayers answered. It will be fine, just as fine as a spring shower."

"Come on, men," said Rassie without even giving it a second's worth of consideration. "Let's go. We got a show to do."

"Where's this café?" Vera asked like she had never set foot in Bright's Pond. Ruth and I shared a smirk.

"Ah, you remember, Vera, it's just down the road. Look for the big, full moon hanging over a building that looks more like one of them stainless steel campers than a restaurant."

"Oh, this has got to be rich," Rassie said.

"Well, no choice," Vera said, as the entourage headed for the station truck.

"Does this mean we still get the Pearly Gates Singers?" Ruth shouted.

Rassie opened the truck door, "Yeah, yeah. We'll just come back next week and put Agnes on the show."

"Over my dead body," I whispered to Ruth.

"Maybe they'll get enough of a show down at Zeb's."

Now I was really worried. "I better call Zeb and warn him."

Ruth came in as far as the radiator and put on her coat and scarf. "I think I'll go on down there. Maybe I can help."

"Good idea."

I rejoined Agnes and Vidalia. "They left. I told them Agnes was sick and they seemed to buy it. Ruth sent them all down to the café. They're gonna do the show from there."

"Really," Vidalia said. "All those folks will start blabbing on and on about how Agnes saved them from death's door and the like."

"I know, I know. But what can I do? Maybe it will all sound so silly no one will ever believe it."

"Okay," Vidalia said, "but do you think it's a good idea leaving Ruth down there by herself?"

"You're right. I'd better call Zeb and let him know."

Agnes reached for her M&Ms while Hezekiah tended the fire. "Maybe I should go down and keep an eye on Ruth," he said.

"No," I said, hanging up the phone. "I better get dressed and get down there. You and Vidalia stay with Agnes."

"Get that radio tuned in, Hezekiah," I heard Agnes say on my way upstairs. "You might have to put it near the window to get good reception."

I was about a block away from the diner when I saw the WQRT truck with a long antenna sticking up from the roof and what looked like some kind of radar dish.

Shoot, they must be on the air already. I picked up my pace and pulled open the café door. A small crowd, which I knew would grow larger, had already gathered. Everybody was talking at once. Rassie had set up his console on one of the booth tables. It was an odd-looking thing with lights and knobs and microphones. He sat in the booth with a pair of black headphones on his head.

Vera, with her own set of headphones, sat across from him, looking pretty uncomfortable. The Full Moon Café was not known for its spacious booths.

"Here she is now, folks," Rassie said, "the sister of the famous but ailing Agnes Sparrow. I'm sorry, dear, what's your name?"

I felt a slight nudge from the back. It was Zeb of all people pushing me to talk. "Griselda," he said.

"So, Griselda, you mean to tell me that all these folks in this diner claim to be witnesses of some kind of miracle or another?"

"Pretty much," Zeb said. He poked his head around me. "If it wasn't for Agnes we wouldn't be standing here today inside Zeb Sewickey's Full Moon Café, Number 12 Filbert Street, Bright's Pond, Pennsylvania. Just look for the bright full moon. It's always on."

"Zeb," I said, "stop doing commercials."

"That's okay, Griselda," Vera said. "This place will be famous. You'll have folks coming from miles away to see it."

"Too bad Jack Cooper fed the Jesus pie to the birds," Zeb said. He practically yanked the microphone away from Vera before he realized it was connected to the console.

"Wait a minute, wait a minute," Rassie said practically laughing. "Jesus pie?"

"That's right," Cora chimed in. She had managed to get between Vera and Zeb. "Zeb here baked one of his famous Full

Moon pies, and when it come out of the oven, the dewdrops formed the face of Jesus. It was nearly—holy."

Rassie had a quick laugh. "So what you are saying then is Jesus himself came to Bright's Pond."

"That's right," Zeb said. He pulled himself up to his full height. "I was just in the back trying to get another pie to come out the same way, but it ain't working. Just ordinary dewdrops."

"I want to hear more about these so-called miracles," Rassie said into his microphone. "And I'm sure my listeners do too."

Cora raised her hand and waved. "Oh, oh. I got a miracle," Cora said, "Agnes prayed and my heart was healed. Doctor said I didn't have long to live. I was in heart-failure."

"No foolin'," Rassie said. "Just like that—" he snapped his fingers "—and your heart is healthy."

"Well, it took three times, three times of praying, and then I got all tingly like a zillion fire ants were inside my body. The next thing I knew I was skipping up and down steps—good as new."

Rassie laughed. "I think what we got here folks is a town full of liars."

"Now hold on, Mr. Harper," I said.

"Wait, Griselda, speak into the mic."

"It happened just like she said. Cora got the bad news and she went to Agnes for prayer and—I guess it does sound fantastic—but even the doctors couldn't believe it at first."

That was when just about everyone in the café started talking at once. They were shouting out about what Agnes did for them and had gotten so loud and so adamant that Rassie went to commercial break, flipped off his headphones, and stood up.

"Shut up, all of you. I can't do a proper show if you're all going to yak at once. Make a single line down the center of the diner if you want to tell about a miracle."

Five minutes later the line reached out the door. Now it wasn't that all those folks received a miracle. Most of them just wanted a chance to talk on the radio and say they knew Agnes Sparrow.

Ruth Knickerbocker sidled up beside Rassie. I had taken a seat on one of the spinning stools. My heart raced a bit faster when I saw she wanted to talk.

"Do I talk in there?" Ruth said.

"That's right. Now this is a treat. Standing here beside me is none other than—" He looked at Vera.

"Ruth Knickerbocker, my sister-in-law," Vera said.

"Vera's sister-in-law, Ruth," he said into the mic. "You got a miracle to tell us about?"

"I sure do." She wobbled slightly. "Goodness, gracious, I'm all atwitter. Never been on the radio. It's what they call remote."

She was proud of overcoming her fear.

"My miracle is that Agnes asked God to heal my bleeding ulcer. Doctors kept giving me pills, tranquilizers, and that awful tasting antacid, but nothing worked."

"So you decided to see Agnes," Rassie said.

"That's right, Rassie." She put her hand over her mouth and giggled "I'm just so tickled to be here. Anyway, it was while my Bubby Hubby was so darn sick and—"

"Bubby Hubby?" Rassie said.

"Bubba, her late husband, my brother." Vera said. "He died from a tumor on the brain."

"Well, how come Agnes didn't make his tumor go away?"

"She couldn't," Ruth said.

"Hear that folks? Agnes can't heal them all."

"Well, then, there'd be nobody dying, and the town would get so full we wouldn't have room for all those people. Ain't you just so silly, Rassie."

"He refused to go to the doctor," Vera said, "until he went stone deaf, and by then it was just too late."

Rassie's voice softened. "I'm sorry."

"So anyway, Mr. Harper, I grew this bleeding ulcer from all the stress of the brain tumor, and I went to see Agnes. Within three days it was gone. No more pain."

Person after person stepped to the mic and told one story or another about Agnes. Some of the stories got repeated, but it didn't matter. Rassie still poo-pooed the whole thing.

He eventually tired of hearing about the miracles and turned his attention to Agnes. "I hear she weighs nearly a thousand pounds."

"No, she doesn't," I said.

"But she is fat," Rassie said.

"Oh, my yes," Vera said into her mic. "My sister-in-law Ruth Knickerbocker, who just spoke about her bleeding ulcer, says Agnes is as big as a whale. The last time they weighed her they had to load her into a truck and take her down to the granary and have her put on the scale.

Rassie laughed. "That's hysterical. How does a woman get that big? I mean if she has to get weighed at the granary, where does she take a bath? The water tower in Shoops?"

I saw a button on the console that said power off, so I flipped it. "That's enough. Take your show and get out."

"Now, hold on, Griselda," Rassie said. He flipped the dial back to the "on" position. "I still got an hour left and I'm sure all these folks have stuff to say about your sister, and I got an audience listening to this show."

"Leave. Now. You're just making fun and laughing like you were in junior high school."

Rassie sounded no smarter than the kids who used to laugh at Agnes.

"Go on," I told Rassie. "Get out of here and don't say another word about my sister."

"Griselda's right," said Janeen Sturgis, "you can't poke fun at our Agnes, just 'cause she's fat. That's why she prays."

"Wait a second, wait a second," Rassie said. "What do you mean, that's why she prays?"

"Well, that's what we all figured on account of her being so gosh darn huge and all. She can't do nothing else, so God gave her the gift."

"Gift?" Rassie motioned for Janeen to get closer to the mic.

"Sure," hollered Fred Haskell from the back. "Agnes got a gift, and she uses it for us."

Janeen took hold of the microphone like she was Dinah Shore. "God made Agnes fat so she could stay home and pray."

"Ah, come on," Rassie said. "Agnes turned into a blimp 'cause she ate too much."

That was when the manure really hit the fan, and no matter what I did to adjust it, the manure kept blowing in Agnes's direction. That mean old Eugene Shrapnel came limping out of the men's room bringing a stink with him that made everybody rub their noses.

"Sinners!" he yelled. "You're all sinners and partakers of sorcery and witchcraft, I say. Agnes Sparrow is nothing more than the devil's handmaiden."

Well, I don't have to say how that perked up Rassie Harper. I never saw a man smile wider in all my days. I thought his partial plate might pop across the room.

"And who are you, sir?" he asked.

Eugene squirmed closer, taking tiny steps with his crooked cane. "My name is not important. I am God's agent, here to say that you all better stay away from that woman."

"But why?" Rassie asked. "Please, sir, speak into the mic."

"I just said it, young fella. Agnes Sparrow is in league with the devil."

"You mean the miracles never happened?"

Eugene cackled. "I ain't saying that . . . ain't saying that at all. Miracles do happen, wonders do occur, but they ain't from the Lord God Almighty."

Vera looked shaky. "Then who?" she asked.

"The devil. Satan hisself has dominion in this world. Satan hisself, that's who."

Rassie sat back down and started to laugh. "Oh, come now. I don't believe in any of this stuff. Satan is a myth like Santa Claus."

Eugene's shifty eyes burned. "I been telling these folks the sky is gonna fall if they keep up with Agnes Sparrow. You mark my words. The sky will fall."

Then he shook a finger at Rassie. "Leave now, before you get swayed to their side."

The café fell silent, except for Hazel Flatbush, who started to cry. "I just come in for scrambled eggs and toast. I had such a morning with my boys, I only wanted some peace and quiet and eggs I didn't have to scramble myself . . . and . . . and I wasn't expecting this."

Cora comforted Hazel with a raspberry Danish and more coffee with a shot of whipped cream. "There, there, dear, it's all okay."

Ruth moved next to Hazel. "You eat your eggs, honey."

I pulled myself up to my full height and said, "Now you see what this has started? Get on out of here, Eugene."

"The man is entitled to his opinion," Rassie said.

"Maybe so," Zeb hollered from the kitchen, "but he's the only one who believes that bilge water he spews."

Rassie ignored him and said something about a station break and twisted a couple of dials on the console.

"Well, how about this?" Rassie said. "How come Griselda here ain't fat like her sister? And how come she don't have the gift? Does God only give it to fat people? Maybe the weird little man is right. Maybe you are all in league with the devil."

Just then one of the men who came with Rassie twisted some knobs and an eerie, haunted house sound floated through the café.

Zeb pushed through the quieting crowd. "Maybe you better go, Mr. Harper."

Rassie flipped a couple of buttons on the console and whipped off his headphones. "You can't kick me out. I've got a show to do."

Zeb moved a step closer. "But this is my café, and I can pull the plug on your show."

Rassie and Vera exchanged glances. Vera said, "Maybe we better pack up before it gets too ugly."

"I need to call the station before those commercials end. Tell them to put on a Best of Rassie Harper."

"Go on, make your call and then pack up," Zeb said. "You got no right coming here and making fun of Agnes like that."

There was some grumbling from the folks who didn't get a chance to speak into the microphone, but they made way for Rassie and Vera and their crew to leave. I stood to the side and watched Zeb give Rassie a Full Moon pie on the sly. "Be sure to mention it on your show."

18

Ruth and I sat in the truck for a while that morning. I needed to catch my breath. The previous few hours had left me feeling like I'd been taken down to Peevy's sausage factory and run through the grinder. I stared at our front porch: the gray steps leading to the gray, chipped floorboards: the old, broken light fixture suspended from the porch roof, the small, bronze sparrow on the door.

"That was ugly," Ruth said. "How about that Eugene?"

"He's just a pain in the butt. Twisted, deluded, and maybe even a little scared."

"I guess, but he sure is mean. What about that Rassie? I think I might hate him."

"Yeah, but he got the Pearly Gates to come."

"Do you think they'll still come? I mean I wouldn't be surprised if Rassie cancels it on account of what happened."

I chuckled. "Are you kidding? He loved every minute of it. I'm sure the people listening got a big laugh too. It's the kind of stuff that keeps folks tuning into shows like his."

"Really?"

"Yep, the Pearly Gates will appear as scheduled, mark my words, as Eugene would say."

We sat for another minute. The mountains were veiled in an early spring mist so that only the tops could be seen poking through the clouds like funny party hats. It was like they knew that a perfectly silly episode had just been written into the history of Bright's Pond.

I glanced in the rearview mirror in time to see Studebaker pull up in his baby blue Caddy. Boris was with him. After them, the Sturgises parked, and I saw Cora making her way up the street on foot. All of them, no doubt, wanted to see Agnes.

"Here comes trouble," I said.

"Why would they come up here?"

"Probably to check on Agnes and talk about the show. I bet Boris thinks Bright's Pond has just become famous or something."

I jumped out of my truck and stood in their way. "I don't think you should go in just yet," I told Stu and Boris. "She needs to rest."

"Well, is she all right?" said Stu. "I heard she got poisoned—some sort of ptomaine or botulism."

"I heard she fell and broke her hip," Boris said.

"No, no, nothing like that." I was forced to drag the lie out even further. "It's only a stomach thing. Twenty-four hours ought to do it."

Cora caught up with us. She was puffing a little and looked a little red in the face. "I come to see Agnes. I heard she had a stroke." Boris grabbed on to her elbow when she wobbled just a bit.

"Heavens, no, Cora," I said, "but Agnes isn't seeing anyone yet. She's got that virus."

"I'll bring her some chicken soup after while," Janeen said. She and Frank sidled up next to Stu and Boris, forcing us into a circle on the sidewalk.

"Well, as long as it ain't nothing serious," Boris said.

I feigned a smile. "Nothing serious."

Studebaker leaned against his car. "We saw the show. You didn't see us, Griselda, but we saw you. Boris and me were sitting at the last booth."

"Oh, I missed you. I was so caught up in—"

Boris lit a cigar, shook the match, and tossed it in the street. "It was like a butcher's slaughterhouse down there."

"And I didn't even get a chance to tell my miracle." Studebaker crossed his arms against his chest. "You got so angry and kicked him out. Why'd you go and do that?"

"Well, you heard what he was saying about Agnes. And that Eugene—"

"Yeah, we heard," Janeen said, her voice an octave or two above fingers scraping a blackboard. "That Rassie acting all high and mighty like he didn't believe any of us about Agnes and the miracles. He laughed like we were all part of some vaudeville act."

"And called us liars," Frank said.

Boris draped his arm around Frank. "What's worse is he called Agnes a liar. But we know she isn't, don't we." He blew brown smoke past Frank's face.

"Oh, I wish we could go inside," said Janeen. "I feel the need to see her—to tell her we believe."

"No, I can't let you just now."

"I better get inside," Ruth said, "and see how she's doing." She nodded at everyone and kept moving up the steps and went right into the house.

"How come Ruth can go inside?" Janeen puckered her sour mouth.

"She's been here since early this morning helping me."

"Well, I can help," Janeen said. "Maybe Ruth would enjoy a break."

"Vidalia and Hezekiah are inside too. I got all the help I need."

Frank shook his head. "Hear that, Janeen? She don't need you, and besides, you'll catch her virus."

"Will not. I'm strong as an ox."

"You'll still bring it home. You don't want to be a carrier, Janeen."

"I won't get a germ."

I believed her. I couldn't imagine any self-respecting germ managing to thrive in her body. "Now look, I better get inside. I'll see you all tomorrow and let you know how she's coming along. Just go on home and relax."

I waited until they got back in their vehicles and drove off. Cora left with Studebaker and Boris. I reached the top step and took one final look behind me before opening the door. That's when I saw Eugene standing across the street. He shook his rickety old cane at me and cackled like some evil leprechaun. I refused to dignify his presence and went on inside.

Vidalia met me at the radiator. "Griselda," she said with a huff. "We heard the whole thing. We even heard you tell that Rassie Harper to get out and stop talking about your sister."

"You heard that? I thought I turned that fool box off. I didn't know it was going out."

"It sure did, Griselda," Agnes called. "I never been more proud of you."

Agnes was sitting up in bed straighter than I've seen her in a while. She laughed when she saw me.

"And what about Eugene?" she said. "He got his minute of fame, didn't he? What a hoot."

"I thought you'd be mad?"

"Nah, I never let the things people say about me hurt my feelings. I got cast iron sensitivities."

"But he made fun of you?"

"Griselda, I know I'm fat. Fat jokes don't bother me. They haven't for a long time."

"Where's Hezekiah?" I asked.

"He took off about a half hour ago. Said he had some business in Shoops."

"Probably ran off with Olivia."

"Most likely," Vidalia said, coming out of the kitchen with the coffee pot. "I sure don't know what business they could have in Shoops, you know what I mean? Want some fresh coffee?"

"No, thanks. Maybe I'll go open the library after all. I was going to take the day off but Agnes is fine and—"

"You do that," Agnes said. "I'll be all right here. Hezekiah will probably come back in a bit. He can handle things. Just make sure I have my remote and notebooks."

"Will you take care of what Agnes needs, Vidalia? I think I want to get on down there."

"Sure thing, Griselda. You have a good day now."

A good day? It had been anything but. I disliked Agnes's cavalier attitude about the way people spoke about her. But, I suppose when you've endured as many slings and arrows as she has, you're bound to develop a thick hide. I just wished she wasn't so smug about it.

I went to the library and went about my paces as usual. A few people came in looking for one thing or another or to make copies for their tax returns. Even Eugene came by, more to gloat than anything, but he made me work and find him a book about rose diseases.

"It's that mutt," he said. "I know it's his toxic waste that's killing my roses."

I stamped his book and reminded him that his library card should be replaced, but he acted like it would be the hardest thing in the world to fill out a new form and wait thirty seconds while I wrote up a new one.

"It's really raggedy, Eugene. Let me get you a new one."

"It's fine, Griselda. It still works fine."

He tucked his book under his arm and paused. "I'm glad I did what I did this morning. People got to know that Agnes ain't a miracle worker."

"She's not what you claim, either, Eugene. And besides, how can you be so all-fired certain Agnes doesn't have a gift from God?"

He turned without so much as a blink, stopped, and looked back. "Because God don't answer prayer like that."

By the next morning I decided to forget about Rassie Harper as best I could, until Agnes brought it up while I was making breakfast.

"I sure hope people are forgetting about that silly radio show yesterday," Agnes said.

"Oh, I imagine they will. Are you expecting Hezekiah?"

"I believe so. He said something about getting started on the garage roof now that the weather is breaking."

"Oh, that's right. The roof."

After oatmeal and coffee Hezekiah showed up in the kitchen as I was putting dishes in the sink.

"Well, I got to tell you, Griselda," he said. "Agnes is certainly the talk of the town this morning. I was down at Zeb's for his Tuesday special Wake-Up Breakfast—you know the one with sausage and bacon and three silver dollar pancakes."

"Zeb makes a great pancake, light and fluffy."

"I ate six of them. But that's not what I want to say. I wanted to say that the joint was packed out and everyone was talking about the radio show and how terrible Rassie Harper was and that Agnes ought to get a chance to defend herself."

"No way. There will be no more radio shows. We're going to let it all blow over."

"Like a lead balloon," Hezekiah said with a smirk.

"What's that supposed to mean?"

"It means, Griselda, that those people were on fire or something. It won't blow over that easy."

"Oh, great." I shot a squirt of Joy into the dishpan and watched the bubbles swell.

"Agnes is their treasure or something, you know," he said.

I balled up the blue dishcloth I was holding and threw it into the soapy sink water. "Nothing I can do about it. I got to open the library. By the way, what were you doing in Shoops? I don't remember you telling me you had to go."

"I needed to order shingles for the roof. I chose what they call Emerald Isle."

I felt ashamed for a second. "Oh." I dried my hands on a yellow towel.

"Anyway, the shingles will be delivered the day after tomorrow, so I'll need a check for two-hundred and ten dollars."

"Fine, I'll leave it on the mantle."

I opened the drapes. Sunshine burst through, exposing dots of dust and lint in the air.

"A bright morning," Agnes said. "I can feel the warmth already."

"Are you expecting visitors?"

"Oh, I'm expecting a slew of people today, Griselda, after yesterday. I imagine people will want to talk about the radio show and lots more to have their prayers lifted up."

"I suppose so."

I needed to air out my mind so I walked to the library that morning and met Ivy Slocum along the way. She had her dog on a leash.

"Ivy, when did that happen?"

She yanked on the strap and pulled the dog away from a hydrant. "He came home a few days ago. Just sashayed through the front door and fell asleep on my sofa, like he needed a rest."

I laughed.

"So I went right out and bought this . . . this instrument of repression and torture because Mildred Blessing said she had an order to take him to the pound when she caught him."

"Eugene Shrapnel did that."

"I know it. That miserable creep. Anyway, it breaks my heart, Griselda. Look at him. He's pathetic."

I patted his head. There was definitely sadness looking at me through his chocolate eyes. "It's for the best, I suppose."

"But he ain't a dog that's meant to be on a leash. He's a free sprit. Goes with the wind."

"That's the problem, Ivy. The wind has taken him into Eugene's rose garden too many times, you know what I'm saying?"

"I do." She gave the leash another tug. "That's why I asked Hezekiah to put a fence around my yard."

"Hezekiah? He never told me he was building you a fence."

"Yep, he took my truck into Shoops and came back with all the materials he needs. Supposed to start next week."

"I think you made the right choice, Ivy. Your dog will get used to it."

I squatted down and rubbed the pooch behind his ears. "You'll be off this tether in no time, running around your yard." He licked my face. I rubbed it off. "When you going to give him a name?"

"I was thinking about that. Thought I might post a notice down at the café. Make it like a contest. Let the folks decide what we should call him."

"Sounds like fun."

"Yeah, the winner gets free pie for a month."

The dog barked at a squirrel and lunged for it, taking Ivy with him.

"I'll see you, Ivy."

"Oh, I heard the radio show yesterday," she said, as the dog wrapped the leash around her legs.

"I suppose everybody did."

"It wasn't as bad as you probably think."

"Really?"

"Really. Forget about it."

Ivy lifted my spirits. I would tell Hezekiah to start on Ivy's fence before our roof.

19

I switched on the library lights and turned up the heat. The building was cold and silent, and I felt chilled to the bone. Leaving my hat and coat on, I piled up all the mail that had accumulated on the floor by the door, started coffee, and shuffled through papers on my desk.

It turned out to be the kind of day I liked best—only the books and me. After a few chores and phone calls, I picked up a copy of *Wuthering Heights* and read till my heart felt content. The words helped shoo away any lingering chill, as I wandered the English moor with Heathcliff and Catherine, while steam rose from my coffee and an occasional tear trickled down my cheek.

At mid-afternoon I knew I had allowed myself a month's worth of self-indulgence and closed the book and the library.

Mildred was walking up the path to the library as I turned the key in the lock.

"I'm sorry, Mildred, did you need to get in?"

"Oh, I just wanted to return these." She held three books. "They were really good, Griselda."

"I'm glad you enjoyed them. Sure you don't want to choose a couple more?"

"Not right now. My brother—he's a cop in Sarasota, Florida—sent me a box of paperbacks."

"Oh, that's good. Say, I ran into Ivy earlier. She had that dog of hers on a leash."

"I know. Looks like I lost the case."

"Nah. I have a feeling that mutt will find a way to escape. Always does."

Her eyes lit up, and she dropped the books into the blue, metal depository.

"Thanks, Mildred. Always on time. I'm heading down to the café. Want to walk with me?"

"Sure, why not."

We took a few steps, and I mentioned Ivy's dog-naming contest. Mildred looked thoughtful a moment.

"I've got the perfect name for that canine criminal: Al Capone. He wasn't that easy to catch, either."

I smiled. "Make sure you enter."

The café was full as usual with folks stopping by for early supper. Mildred added her choice of name to the shoebox sitting near the cash register.

Studebaker spotted me. "It's here," he said. "The sign. It arrived this afternoon. It's already up on the interstate. Me and a couple of the boys are gonna install it over the weekend."

"What? No fanfare? No unveiling?"

Stu looked downcast a second but he brightened. "Nah, I think the radio show kind of stole the thunder, you know? And that's okay. The sign is all that matters, and I hear tell that Filby has been working steadily on the statue."

My heart skipped a beat—always did at the mention of that silly statue. "Oh, Stu, I hate that idea."

"I know you do, Griselda, but we'll make a big deal of that unveiling for certain. Right on Memorial Day."

I found Cora and asked her to make up two large chocolate milkshakes. After enduring the last couple of days Agnes and I deserved something special, and Cora's milkshakes were something special. Thick and delicious. You had to eat them with a spoon until they melted a bit, and then you wanted to slurp the last tiny of bit of chocolaty goodness from the paper cup through a red and blue striped straw.

Cora was moving a little more slowly than she had been, and her face looked pale and maybe a little drawn like she hadn't been sleeping.

"You feeling all right?" I asked.

She brushed her hair back with the back of her hand. Her fingers were covered with chocolate ice cream clear up to her elbows from dipping in so deep. The container was pretty much empty. "I'm fine, Griselda. Just a skosh tired lately."

"Maybe you should see Doc."

She rang up my shakes. "Yeah, I've been considering it."

I saw the shoebox. Ivy had made up a sign that said,

NAME THE DOG.

WIN PIE FOR A MONTH!

No other explanation was needed.

"Lots of folks have been dropping names in there," Cora said. "I think Ivy is going to have a hard choice."

I was partial to Al Capone but kept it to myself.

The next time I saw Cora was on Good Friday when Cora dropped by to see Agnes. She looked so skinny in her little pink dress. I saw her coming up the street when I opened the drapes for Agnes.

"Looks like Cora's coming to see you, Agnes."

"Good." She adjusted her clothes, and I scrunched the pillow behind her neck.

"Comfy?"

"It's about as good as it gets. Why don't you go let Cora inside?"

I opened the door and Cora was still on the bottom porch step.

"Are you all right?" I asked walking down to her.

"I'm feeling tired, Griselda. Steps have become kind of a nuisance."

I was afraid her heart had started to give out again. I took her hand and helped her up the steps.

"You been to see Doc?"

"Went yesterday. That's why I came to see Agnes. She's my only hope now—once again."

"Oh, Cora, I'm so sorry." I helped her into the house and with her coat and hat.

Agnes took one look at her and started to pray that once again the Almighty Hand of God would reach down and touch Cora and heal her heart. But it wasn't to happen.

Cora Nebbish died later that day. From all accounts she left Agnes, went home, sat down in her living room where she was surrounded by photos of her children and grandchildren, closed her eyes, and went home.

The funeral, one of the saddest I had ever attended, took place down in Wilkes-Barre two days after Easter Sunday. Cora's son, Stanley Junior, had come for her body and drove it to the mortuary in the back of his family's car.

I drove down to the service with Zeb, Vidalia, and Ruth. Studebaker, Boris, and several other members of the Bright's Pond Chapel of Light and Grace, including Pastor Speedwell, who did the graveside ceremony, came in separate cars.

Even Eugene Shrapnel made an appearance at the graveside. He hung back from the assembled guests, but I could feel him glaring at me and I had to wonder why in heaven's name he came.

Zeb fought back tears like a valiant soldier until Pastor mentioned how she loved her work at the café. Then he broke down like a little boy and sobbed in my arms. Vidalia, who looked proper in her black dress, black-veiled hat, and black shoes handed him a white hanky.

"You were my friend," Zeb said, as he laid a pink rose on Cora's casket. "I love you."

I pulled a rose from the large spray and set it next to Zeb's. "I'll miss you," was all I could muster through the ache in my chest.

Eugene stopped me on my way to the car. "I told you. I told you something like this was going to happen if your sister kept playing with the devil."

Ruth stamped her foot. "Eugene. How could you?"

"You make no sense, Eugene. Agnes can't keep people from dying. Never said she could."

"Mark my words. A new page is being written."

"You are the rudest man on the planet." Ruth wiped her tears with an already soaked hanky.

"I just come to warn you, that's all."

When I got to the car and opened the door I took one last look and saw Eugene lay a rose on Cora's casket. "What a mixed-up little man."

Ruth cried and cried from the minute she sat in the car until we got back to the café. Zeb closed it to regular customers but opened it to anyone who wanted to stop by for pie and coffee in Cora's honor.

"I'll never forget when Cora first started working here," Ruth said. "She couldn't keep nothing straight. Got everybody's orders mixed up. She was a mess."

Zeb laughed as he poured my coffee. "She sure was. Remember that time she was carrying four pies—two Full Moon, a pecan, and an apple—to the case, and Herm Detweiler spun around on his stool and stuck one of his big feet out and accidentally tripped her?"

"Yeah, I was there," I said.

"You sure were," Ruth said. "You ended up with Full Moon pie all over yourself."

Zeb smiled and loosened his tie. "I think I'll name a sandwich for her, you know. Something real special."

"Unique," Vidalia said.

It took a while but finally Zeb concocted the Cora Nebbish Special. It was thin-sliced turkey and ham on whole wheat, with a slice of American cheese, or Swiss if you preferred. Then it was battered and deep-fried, and he served it with maple syrup or raspberry preserves. No one had the heart to tell him that the sandwich had already been invented and called a Monte Cristo.

Studebaker was the only one who wondered out loud how come the miracle wore off. But no one had an answer. I simply said, "Stu, let's be thankful that God saw fit to give her a few more weeks."

"Wasn't that nice of him?" Ruth said as she chewed pie.

But Stu appeared thoughtful, worried even, like maybe some miracle reversal had started in town.

"She was old, Stu. She had a bad heart and high blood pressure."

He didn't say a word.

I walked home with Vidalia. The air had turned warm, the sky cloudless. The mountains had grown greener, and an occasional wind gust blew our hair.

"Isn't it kite month?" Vidalia asked.

"No, last month," I said.

"Oh, yeah, March. I loved to fly kites when I was a kid."

"Me, too. I guess all kids liked it. Wonder why?"

Vidalia looked thoughtful. "It's like dreaming while you're awake, you know what I mean? Didn't you want to fly?"

"Sure, still do sometimes."

"That's what flying a kite is like. It's like flying. Holding on to the string, feeling it flap and pull and soar and dip. Remember that, Griselda? Remember that feeling in your arms and legs? It was like you were the kite, soaring to the heavens." Vidalia practically danced. "Let's do it."

"Do what?"

"Fly a kite."

"I'm game. Let's get Ruth and go up on Hector's Hill, like we did when we were kids—that's where we flew them, Vidalia. The winds come up real good there."

That afternoon, Vidalia and I walked into Gordon's and came out with a Hi-Flier kite and enough string to fly it to the sun.

"Remember how to build it?" Vidalia asked.

"Sure. Let's go back to my house. We'll need a tail."

"Right, and let's get Ruth on the way."

Agnes donated one of her old housedresses for the tail. The fabric was light and pretty and pink.

"Like Cora," Vidalia said.

"Make sure it's balanced," Agnes said. "And don't rip the paper or you'll be sunk."

"How long should the tail be?" Ruth asked. "I don't remember."

"Long enough," I said.

After a few minutes I held it up. It was bright green with white stripes."

"It's a real Hi-Flier," Agnes said. "The same we had when we were kids."

"That's right." I looked at Agnes looking at the kite. "I wish you could go with us."

She closed her eyes and laid back. "You go on and enjoy yourselves. Fly it for Cora."

"I will."

The three of us drove to Hector Hills in my truck with the kite safely secured in the bed. It took six tries, but then the kite caught a wind and started to pull. Up. Up and away. I let the string out more and more as it pulled, getting further and further into the sky. I felt the tugs in my shoulder as it swooped.

"Watch it," Vidalia called. "Don't crash."

Finally, our kite settled into a current of air.

"Let me hold it," Ruth said.

We made the switch flawlessly as the kite soared higher above the trees and out over the town.

Vidalia took her turn, and after a few minutes, we stood together—all of us in black—and watched our kite dance, a sparkling emerald against a pale blue sky. I took hold of the string with my hand touching Vidalia's, and then Ruth grabbed on and we sailed it together.

"For Cora," I said.

"For Cora," we all echoed.

20

About a week after Cora's death, a blanket of peace and routine had settled over the town. Cora's family put her house up for sale and moved out any furniture worth keeping, donated nearly all her clothes to the needy, had the electric turned off, stopped mail delivery, and closed her curtains.

The season changed. Spring pushed winter away, quiet at first, with just hints of color—purple and yellow crocuses. The forsythia bloomed in all its yellow best. But something else took hold of Agnes.

It was the end of April. Hezekiah had finished Ivy's fence with some help from Fred Haskell. It was one of those silver chainlink jobs that stretched around her entire backyard. Both Ivy and the newly named Al Capone were getting used to the idea.

Mildred was thrilled to have won the contest. It might have been one of the few times I ever saw the woman smile. The winner was announced at The Full Moon Café the second Monday after Easter. Ivy chose that day because it was after the holiday and most of the folks who entered would be enjoying the Monday meatloaf special.

I arrived about 4:30 after locking up at the library. Ivy got everybody's attention and then made her announcement.

"Now before I announce the winning name, I want to thank all of you for taking part in this little old contest of mine." She cleared her throat. "I owned that dang dog for going on nine years and never bothered to give him a proper handle."

Some of the folks laughed.

"Well I just couldn't come up with a fitting name, and I believe all God's creatures, especially the ones we love and consider family, should have a proper name, you know, one that fits."

Studebaker Kowalski walked in right then, excused the interruption, and sat near me at the counter. He whispered. "Hey Griselda." I smiled and sipped my coffee. Zeb hired two of the high school girls to take the place of Cora. Babette Sturgis was one—a pretty, tall, dark-haired girl with good grades and a pimply complexion. She poured coffee for Stu.

"Anyway," Ivy said, "I made my choice and I think it's a good one."

Zeb walked out of the kitchen and made a drum roll on the counter with two wooden spoons.

"The winner is Mildred Blessing, who suggested the name —" the drumroll grew louder "—Al Capone."

A collective sigh of pleasure swelled up in the little café that night. There wasn't one person who didn't think it was the absolute best name for that troublemaking mutt.

"Hear, hear," Jasper York said a mite louder than he needed.

Eugene, who was sitting by himself at a booth hollered, "First sensible thing this town's done in years, fencing that canine miscreant hoodlum."

Ivy steadied herself. I could see she was holding back from giving Eugene what for, but there was happy business afoot.

Harriett, Jasper's now constant companion, beamed. "Al Capone was that famous bootlegger. My daddy, God rest his soul, actually met him in Chicago back in '21. Lit his cigar for him. Al Capone flipped him two bits, and we ate supper that night, we did. Ate supper on account of Al Capone."

Well, that riled a few of the more straightlaced women in the group, including Darcy Speedwell, who had brought the boys in for meatloaf and milkshakes. She expressed her shame that Harriett's father had anything to do with a criminal.

"My daddy did what he saw fit during the Depression," Harriett said. "He was a good daddy. Fact is, Daddy went to work running gin down Canal Street for Mr. Capone. We ate good after that."

That was when Jasper, in a surprisingly lucid moment, reached out and took her hand. "Sing it, sister."

Darcy was so shocked she bounced out of her seat. "Harriett, my boys are at an impressionable age. What would Jesus say to you?"

Then she marched those boys right outside without paying the check, which was sitting on the table.

Zeb slapped me on the back. "Al Capone, imagine that, having ties to Bright's Pond."

Harriett stood up and sighed. "Jesus weren't there. Not in those days. He was off taking care of others, because I remember before my daddy went to work for Mr. Capone he prayed every day and every night for work. There just wasn't a job to be found."

"Your daddy did what he saw fit," Studebaker said. "Don't you go feeling like you got something to be ashamed about."

Harriett smiled and sat down.

Mildred was on patrol that afternoon and missed the big announcement. She showed up just as I was leaving. A round of applause erupted when she entered.

"Congratulations, Mildred," Ivy called. "You're the winner."

A smile as wide as Wyoming burst across Mildred's otherwise poker face. "Me? I won the dog naming contest?"

"That's right," Ivy said. "Al Capone it is. I'm going to see Boris tomorrow and get him a license and everything."

For a moment Mildred looked sad. The chase was over. "About time that dog got legitimate," she said when Zeb handed her the first of what would be several slices of free pie.

I headed home with two meatloaf specials.

"This town is sure gonna miss Cora," Agnes said staring into her meal. "She always put in extra."

"I know, it's going to take some time to get used to her being gone."

A couple of days later I parked Old Bessie on top of Hector Street and tuned into the Rassie Harper Show. I hadn't dared listen since I kicked him out of the Full Moon, but the urge struck that morning. I figured I was about ready to take any insults he might sling, but I hoped that the whole Agnes ordeal had blown over and he had forgotten all about her.

"Budweiser, the king of beers," Rassie shouted over the airwaves. It's funny how my impression of him changed now that I knew what he looked like.

"Vera Krug will be up in just a few minutes with an exciting announcement about the upcoming Pearly Gates Singers coming to Bright's Pond." I turned up the volume. "That's right, boys and girls, Bright's Pond. You remember them. They tossed me out of The Full Moon Café for calling a fat woman fat. Hey, it's a free country."

Well, I can say this, my timing is impeccable.

"And here she is now, that winsome woman of the air-waves with all your small town news and gossip, Vera Krug."

Vera's lead-off stories were about a farmer named Mike Micklin, who discovered one of his ewes gave birth to a two-headed lamb, and a pitch for the brand-new Dairy Queen opening in Shoops.

"Now the announcement you've all been waiting for," Vera said. "Our own Rassie Harper has made it possible for the Pearly Gates Singers to appear, in person, at the Bright's Pond Chapel of Faith and Grace Wednesday night at seven o'clock p.m. Tickets will be sold at the door, so you better get there early, friends. Those folks down there are expecting a crowd."

I dropped the gearshift into drive and started down the hill to the library where I would spend a relatively peaceful morning among my books.

Lunchtime rolled around, and I made my way home where I found Hezekiah up on the garage roof. He had torn off all the old shingles and some of the wood underneath.

"I've been giving it some thought, and it's probably best to replace the wood," he called. I watched him yank out nails. "That wood is all waterlogged and sagging down so far it makes no sense to keep it."

"You're the boss. I'll go get lunch ready."

"I'm starved, Griselda. Didn't get breakfast this morning."

I threw together ham and cheese sandwiches while I warmed condensed tomato soup.

"Here you go, Agnes," I said, as I carried her tray to her. "I'll go call Hezekiah."

"Griselda, on your way back could you grab a sack of Fritos."

"Don't think we have any."

"Look anyway, and if not, see if there's any chips at all . . . any will do."

Hezekiah sat in the rocker and pulled the TV tray close, and I placed his lunch in front of him. "Thanks, looks good," he said, and then he proceeded to explain his garage findings to Agnes.

"Don't want to put new wine in old skins," Agnes said.

Hezekiah looked at her with a screwed-up face. "I ain't talking about wine, Agnes. I just think it's dumb to put new shingles on old wood."

Agnes smiled. "I was making a Bible reference."

Hezekiah finished his sandwich and chips and went back to work, still chewing on what Agnes said.

"Got many visitors this afternoon, Agnes?" I asked as I gathered dishes and napkins.

"No, not really. It feels so odd too. Seems like since Cora died and Studebaker had that sign trouble and poor old Hezekiah is still waiting on his miracle, folks are coming around less and less."

"Maybe folks haven't got many troubles they need to talk about this month."

"Now you know that can't be true," she said with a swallow. "People are always stewing in troubles. But I got to admit that I've been feeling a little bit on the empty side."

Agnes snagged her last crust of bread just as I pulled her plate away. She had this peculiar habit of ripping the crust from her white bread and eating it after the sandwich. I never asked why.

She looked out the window a second or two. "Do you think maybe God is taking folks away from me?"

"Now why would he do that?"

"Maybe I just don't deserve them. Maybe I never did."

That was the first time I ever heard Agnes doubt herself.

"So, what is the deal with Hezekiah?" I asked. "Are you still praying for him?"

"Everyday . . . until Cora died."

"Why'd you stop?"

"Like I said, I just got this emptiness in my heart. I'm afraid—" She took a shaky breath. "Oh, Griselda, I'm afraid I might be losing my touch or something."

"Cora was an older woman," I said. "It was her time. Even you can't stop time."

"I didn't tell you, but Janeen came by for more prayer for her sister and that scum of a husband of hers. She always leaves feeling lighter, you know, like she has hope, but this last time, she said she was still afraid—afraid for her sister."

"Maybe that's because her sister is the one who has to go to God. You can't be in charge of everybody, Agnes. You can't pray for the entire world."

"Why? Why can't I, Griselda?"

I cleaned up our plates and glasses. "Because the world is not your responsibility."

"But what about Hezekiah? I've been praying for months, and he still says he hasn't received a miracle. He told me a few days ago that whatever problem he brought to town was still hanging on like a piece of gum stuck to his shoe. He just can't shake it."

"Has he ever told you exactly what he needed?"

"Nope. Just says it's like a dull ache behind his eyes."

Agnes reached for her candy. I carried plates to the kitchen.

"The Pearly Gates Singers will be here Wednesday," I said when I got back to the viewing room. "I talked to the pastor and Studebaker. They're planning to pipe the music right inside the house. You won't miss a thing."

"That's nice, Griselda." She sighed deeply and held her breath for a moment. "Looks like spring has sprung for sure." She nodded toward the window. "The mountains are greening up."

"Yep, and you've got the best view from here."

Agnes pushed her blanket off. "Feels warm today. Is it warm outside?"

"Not too warm but not cold either. Hezekiah was working in shirt sleeves up on the roof."

"I think we're gonna have a hot summer. What do you . . . think?" She had to force the word out.

"Oh, I hope not, Agnes. I don't like really hot weather. It's not good for you, either."

I moved her inhalers closer and noticed that her prayer book was on the floor. I picked it up and placed it near her medicine.

Agnes closed her eyes. "I think I might take a nap."

"That sounds like a good idea. I just remembered something I need to tell Hezekiah, anyway."

I waited until Agnes got comfortable. Then I went out the back way. Hezekiah was up on the garage roof and chucked a piece of wilted plywood. It sailed through the air and landed with a bang on a growing pile of withered wood.

"I wanted to let you know I'm heading back to the library, but I need to know something," I said staring up into the sun.

"Could you leave the truck? I've got to drive over to the lumber yard and get some more plywood."

"Yeah, I can walk back. Now, did you get rid of that stuff in the baggie?"

He tossed a small piece of wood and chuckled. "Yes, Griselda. It ain't no place it could be found. Cool your heels about it."

I watched him for a minute. He was a good man . . . in spite of the pot.

Vidalia dropped by the library later that afternoon looking chipper than I'd seen her in a long time.

"You ain't gonna believe this," she said. "I just saw that miserable Eugene Shrapnel pounding a sign into his front yard."

"A sign?"

"Yep. It says, 'THE END IS NEAR!' in big red letters."

"Oh, my goodness. He's a pip. He's got it stuck in his craw that something bad is happening in town because of Agnes."

"Doesn't he always? Anyway—" Vidalia plopped four books on the counter "—I got good news too. My daughter's coming for a visit with three of the six younguns."

"Winifred?" I couldn't keep the excitement out of my voice. My best friend was coming home. Sometimes it felt like we shared a mom, the way Vidalia had come alongside me over the years since my own mother died. So in a way it was like hearing that another sister was coming home—a sister I felt I had more in common with than Agnes. Winifred and I were kindred spirits.

"Yep. Winifred is coming by train this coming Thursday afternoon, says it's easier to travel during the week with little ones. She's going to stay for a few days, Griselda. Boy, I sure have missed her."

"That's wonderful! It sure will be good to see her."

"I remember how close you two were, yakkin' all night on the phone, listening to them Beatles up in her room, smoking cigarettes out back."

"You knew about that?'

"Why sure, baby girl. I knew everything."

A warm sensation filled me at that moment. "And you never stopped us or said anything?"

"Nah, I knew you two couldn't keep it up. And see, neither one of you smokes today."

I pushed my glasses onto the bridge of my nose. "What else did you know?"

"I knew everything I needed to know and the stuff I didn't, well, it took care of itself. Now I got to get back to business here. My baby is coming home with her babies—the three little ones. The others will be in school."

"Six kids all together, right?" I said.

"Six beautiful ones. I wanted to make sure I returned these books because I have a lot of baking to do and I won't have time for much reading."

I placed her books on the cart to be shelved later. "I was wondering if you might stop by and see Agnes. She's feeling a little down, Vidalia."

"I don't believe I ever heard you or anyone say that Agnes was feeling down—ever."

"It is strange, but to use her words, she said she feels empty on the inside. Mostly she's worried that she's lost her praying touch."

Vidalia looked at me with that sideways glance she had a habit of when she was thinking. "Come to think of it, I was at Gordon's the other day buying some lace when I heard Janeen yakking it up with Hazel Flatbush. I didn't think much of it at the time, you understand, or I would have said something."

"What did she say?"

"She was complaining that she went to see your sister and Agnes prayed but Janeen didn't receive a blessing. Then Hazel said she felt the same thing the last time she saw Agnes."

"Really? I don't like that folks are talking about her. She's not a gumball machine spitting out prizes, you know."

"I know, but they seemed awful—what's the word?"

"Awful works for me."

"No, they seemed . . . it's a word that means afraid, but kind of angry at the same time. Maybe there ain't no word for it, but you know what I mean. Like pouting children who didn't get their way."

"Oh, really. That makes me angry because Agnes is not here for folks to count on all the time. Folks got to make their own miracles sometimes."

"I hear that, Griselda. Speaking of the market, I got to go buy some chocolate chips. I'm going to make those Toll House cookies on the back of the bag."

Vidalia opened the door.

"Bye-bye, Vidalia. Have a good day."

She took a step or two, stopped, and turned around. "Sulking," she said. "That's what those two women were doing. They were sulking like disappointed children."

On my way home that day I ran into Studebaker. He was washing his car. The air was warm, but not warm enough to be outside with water in my opinion.

"You don't want to get all wet," I said. "You'll catch a cold."

"I'll be fine. I was just up the road with Fred and Nate Kincaid hanging the sign. Have you seen it?"

"You mean you guys put it up already?"

"Just a few bolts. Tricky part was getting it level. It took two men to hold her and one to tighten the bolts."

"Thanks for letting me know. I'll get out there to see it I'm sure."

"It's a beut. Dabs Lemon took some pictures. Be in tomorrow's news."

"Oh, goody. I'll see it then."

I took a few steps and Studebaker stopped me. "I just want you to know that I don't believe what the others are saying."

"Saying? About what?"

"About Agnes. I heard talk down at the Full Moon that Agnes has lost her powers or something."

"Powers? Agnes never had any powers."

"Lots of folks in town believe she does, and they're saying her prayers aren't getting answered."

"Ever occur to people that sometimes the answer is no."

He dropped his sponge in a yellow bucket of soapy water and picked up the hose. "I'm still just as proud as a peacock of her."

Hezekiah was gone when I got home, probably off with Olivia. Agnes was watching the early news and chewing on pie. I flopped onto the sofa with a thud and a sigh. It had been a long day.

"Mildred stopped by with pie," Agnes said. "Says she can't eat a whole pie every week."

"Don't fill up on pie," I said. "I'll start dinner."

"Don't you want to hear why Mildred stopped in?"

"Not especially." I cracked my neck.

"She said I had to sign a permit to have a speaker set up and wires draped across the street. Something about ordinances and traffic and such."

"So, we'll get a permit. I'll see Boris tomorrow."

"I don't like it. We never needed a permit before."

"Times are changing, Agnes."

"I don't like it, Griselda. Not one bit. Used to be a person could do what they wanted around here without folks looking so close, you know?"

"It's just a permit. It's not like the Gestapo is marching into town."

"And I say it's just a wire stretched across the street. What's the big deal?"

"It's not a big deal. You're making it a big deal, and besides you don't have to do anything, Agnes. I'm the one who has to sign a permit for you."

Agnes's forehead wrinkled. "Why are you so grumpy, Griselda? No need to treat me mean."

"I am not grumpy. I just don't understand the way you've been acting lately. It makes me uneasy."

That whole evening continued to tighten like a rubber band until I thought it might break. Agnes and I watched television for a little while, mostly in silence, until I finally decided to call it a night. "I'm tired. Think I'll get into bed and read a while."

"Don't you want to watch the news?"

"No. Not tonight. Good night, Agnes."

She just grunted and turned back toward the TV.

21

Early Wednesday morning Ruth pounded on the front door as I was just about to fix coffee.

"Oh, Griselda, I am just as tickled plum pink as I can get. Tonight's the night I've been waiting for—oh glory, seems my whole life."

I grabbed her hand and pulled her inside. "I expected you to come by, Ruth, but this early?"

"What time is it?"

"It's not even six-thirty."

"I'm sorry. I hardly slept a wink I'm so excited."

Ruth made her way into the viewing room. "Morning, Agnes."

Agnes yawned and stretched. I could see from her scowl that she was hurting this morning. I helped her straighten both legs and untangle her nightgown. "My knees are telling me it's gonna rain today."

"Don't say that, Agnes." Ruth moved closer and helped tug on Agnes's gown. "It can't rain on the Pearly Gates."

Agnes shot me a glance.

"I was just about to fix breakfast, Ruth. Join us?"

"Oh, glory, yes. I'm starved this morning. I'll help."

"First, I need to get Agnes into a new housedress before I get started."

"That's all right by me, Griselda. What say I get some coffee percolating while you take care of all that?"

Ruth turned toward the kitchen and then doubled back. "Oh, Agnes, I wanted to tell you that I don't believe what folks are saying about you."

"Ruth," I said, "it's not the best time to bring that up."

"Bring what up?" Agnes asked.

We pulled her to her feet. She was stiff that morning—stiff and creaky. It was like moving a hippo through mud with a shoestring for a leash.

"I just wanted her to know," Ruth said.

"Know what?" Agnes asked.

"I didn't want to tell you Agnes," I said, "but you were right about folks feeling like something has started to go wrong."

Ruth helped me steady Agnes and said, "Some people, I'm not saying who, but her initials are Janeen Sturgis, claims you lost your powers."

Agnes plopped back down just when I had a good grip on her and situated her walker.

"I'm sorry, Griselda," she said. "But I just couldn't get steady enough."

"Don't worry about what Ruth said. People are just being dumb, Agnes. Real dumb."

"But they're right. I haven't been able to pray for a week now."

"A week?" Ruth grabbed her left arm while I grabbed under her right. "You just wait until you hear the Pearly Gates. They'll get that praying electric of yours back on. You'll be okay. You just burned out a bulb is all."

Good old, Ruth. She had a way of bringing smiles where frowns had hold.

"One, two, three, lift," I said. "Come on, Agnes, you've got to help too."

I wrestled Agnes into a fresh dress and soon smelled coffee percolating. Ruth, Agnes, and I enjoyed French toast and eggs with sausage before Vidalia came by to check on Agnes. Even with all the excitement of Winifred's visit, Vidalia still made room in her heart for Agnes.

"You're coming to the concert tonight, ain't you, Vidalia?" Ruth asked. She poured coffee.

"Now ain't that a silly question. I wouldn't miss it," she said. Then she took hold of Agnes's hand. "How are you, dear? I heard you were feeling under a bit of a spiritual dark cloud these days."

Agnes sighed. "I guess you could say that, Vidalia. Something doesn't feel right."

Vidalia adjusted her little hat. It wasn't much more than a ring of faded, yellow daffodil petals with a breezy veil covering—perfect for a spring day.

"Your praying spirit will come back," she said. "Wait and see, Agnes. Wait and see what God can do."

By three o'clock Studebaker, Boris, Fred Haskell, and Pastor Speedwell had a speaker system set up with wires strung across the street and a speaker sitting on the floor near our radiator.

"I think that will be close enough," Stu said. "Don't want to blast you out of bed tonight."

"Oh, no danger of that happening, Stu," Agnes said. "It would take a lot more than that to blast me out of anything."

By four the Pearly Gates Singers rolled into town in a big, black bus. "ARE YOU READY FOR THE PEARLY GATES?" was emblazoned on the side of the bus in the biggest gold letters I had ever seen.

Under their name was a picture of heaven's pearly gates, opened partway and surrounded by clouds. It was a sight to behold as that huge, long bus pulled up outside the church.

"Look at that, Griselda," Agnes called. I was in the laundry room shoving sheets into the washer. "The Pearly Gates Singers are here."

Okay, I will confess that my heart went pitty-pat, and I felt a little bit of joy in my heart when she called me. It had been ages since anything that exciting had happened in Bright's Pond, outside of the miracles and our potlucks. I stood at our window as the bus rolled to a jerking stop.

"Look at that, Agnes, the Pearly Gates are right outside our house."

"Go greet them," she said. "Shake their hands. And explain about the wires and all in case they're wondering what the heck is going on."

I was no sooner across the street and standing outside their bus door when Ruth and Studebaker, Pastor and Darcy Speedwell, Boris, and Jasper York gathered. Ruth was jumping up and down trying to get a look through the darkened windows.

She took a huge breath as the doors opened. The driver nodded, and then one by one the four Pearly Gates, dressed in gold suits with white shirts, white shoes, and no ties, walked down the bus steps and stood on Bright's Pond soil.

"My goodness gracious," Ruth said. She grabbed my sleeve. I thought she might faint dead away. "They're—they're all Negroes."

"Black, Ruth. They're black, but you knew that, didn't you?"

She took another breath. "Well no. I just assumed that they were like the rest of us."

"They are like us. Now don't go embarrassing yourself or the town."

I recognized Ezekiel Moses Ramstead right off from a record album. He played piano and guitar.

Boris pushed his way through the growing crowd. He reached out his hand to the biggest of the four men.

"Welcome, welcome to Bright's Pond."

"My name is Marvin Smith," the man said. His voice was low and booming like it had come out of a cave. "And this is Abel Washington."

Abel stepped forward. "Groovy." Then he made the peace sign and stepped back.

Ruth gasped for air. "Are they Communists too?"

"No, now settle down, Ruth. They're musicians."

Marvin put his hand on the drummer's shoulder. "And this is Sticks Monroe. He plays the drums." Sticks didn't say a word, smile, or move.

Marvin introduced the last of the quartet. "Ezekiel Moses Ramstead, our piano player." All Ezekiel said was, "Your town is out of sight, man."

Boris shook all their hands.

"I have a question, man," said Marvin. "Who's this Agnes Sparrow chick? We saw that sign coming over the hill."

Studebaker, who had just arrived, said, "She's our miracle maker. Agnes has made more miracles come true in Bright's Pond than anyone, anywhere?"

"Even Jesus?" Sticks said.

"Well . . . n . . no, of course not," Stu stammered. "But plenty right here."

Janeen moved forward and leaned into the four men. "But it seems that Agnes might be losing her connection."

I thought Marvin was going to bust his shirt buttons he laughed so hard.

"Then why you got a sign out there advertising her?"

Boris and Stu looked like they couldn't figure out if it was more important to defend Agnes and their sign or forget about it and get the singers into the church. They chose the church.

I turned to Ruth, who was still paralyzed by the sight of the Pearly Gates. "Ruth, how come you didn't say hello?"

She reached out a little, leather-bound book. "Autograph?"

But it was too late. Boris and Stu had already shepherded the men away from the fans and into the church.

I helped Ruth across the street into our house. "Now you get a grip on yourself, Ruth. They're just men like any other."

"Glory, no," Ruth said. "They're the Pearly Gates." She took a breath. "I couldn't even say hello."

"You will tonight. Now come on in for tea and a slice of pineapple upside-down cake."

"I saw the whole thing," Agnes said. "That Marvin is a big man now, isn't he?"

"You know about him?" Ruth asked.

Agnes pointed to our HiFi. "Got one of their albums in there. Haven't played it in a long time, but it has their pictures on it. 'Course they were younger when that record came out."

"I never bought any records," Ruth said. "We never had a HiFi so I didn't see the point."

Ruth opened the side of the mahogany-colored cabinet. "Right on top. Yep, that's them." She ran her finger along the side and the album jacket opened revealing more photos of the group. "Look at that. They're black as coal."

"Ruth," I said, "you've got to get over that."

"Well, it ain't like I mind. I mean we got Vidalia, and I love her to pieces. I don't even think about her being colored anymore. I just didn't know it about the Pearly Gates. I mean, wouldn't you think a group with the word *pearl* in their name would be white?"

"Oh, Ruth, come help me make tea."

"Lookie there," Agnes said at about five after six. "A line is forming. Looks like a hundred people already."

"Really?" I looked out our window, and sure enough there was a line that stretched clear down to the Sturgis's house. I recognized most of the people from church or around town but there were some I didn't.

"Looks like Vera Krug's advertising paid off. I do believe I see some out-of-towners."

"Well, it ain't every day a singing group like the Pearly Gates makes it up the mountain. They'd rather play the big places in Wilkes-Barre and Scranton."

"Maybe we better get going," Ruth said. "I want a good seat."

"Okay, but let me get Agnes settled. Hey, has anyone seen Hezekiah?"

"Not since earlier," Agnes said. "Was he planning on going to the concert?"

"Didn't say."

Agnes scratched between the folds of skin on her arm.

"I told you not to do that. Doc said you'll get infections. I'll put some talc in there before I go."

"And the backs of my knees," Agnes said.

The doorbell rang and Ruth went to answer it while I took care of Agnes's itchy spots.

"It's Vidalia," Ruth called.

"I thought we'd sit together," Vidalia said. "I looked for you in line."

"We were here," Ruth said.

"I can see that." Vidalia looked stunning in a yellow pants suit with a baby blue blouse. She chose a funky hat for the occasion—a floppy thing with a wide bill that made her look a little younger.

"You gals ready?" she asked.

"Just a couple more minutes," I said.

Ruth refilled the candy jar while I tucked Agnes in.

"All set," I said. "Let's go."

The doorbell rang again.

It was Pastor Speedwell and his skinny little wife Darcy, who looked like she had just been blown around in a windstorm. She stared at Agnes like she was looking at a sideshow freak. Darcy was one of the few folks in town who had never gotten over Agnes's size.

Pastor, who was carrying his Bible tucked under his arm, said, "I just came by to tell you that we'll miss you at the concert tonight, Sister Agnes."

"It's going to be a real hootenanny," Darcy said, and I knew in that moment Darcy Speedwell was in for a surprise.

"Ever hear them?" Agnes asked, looking at Darcy.

"No, but Milton told me they're real good. They sing all them old-time gospel songs and Nee-gra spirituals. I ain't never heard a Nee-gra spiritual before."

My toes curled. "You're in for a treat, Darcy. A real treat."

Ruth, who had gone to use the second-floor bathroom, came back.

"Well, hello, Pastor," she said. She smiled at Darcy.

"Hello, Ruth. I'm glad you're here," Pastor said. "I wanted to thank you for making it possible for the Pearly Gates Singers to come to our church."

"You're as welcome as a dandelion in winter," she said. "I can hardly believe it myself. That Rassie Harper sure came through for us even if the radio show turned out to be—" she glanced at Agnes and then me "—well, not what we expected."

Pastor took a step closer to Agnes. "Now, how are you? Word around town is that you might be feeling a little . . . off."

Agnes coughed. "I'm fine, Pastor. Just fine."

"Good. Glad to hear it." Pastor nodded to his wife, and she walked to the door like a trained dog.

"Oh, don't you worry about tickets, Griselda." Pastor said. "Just come around the back. I made sure the front row was roped off for you and Ruth."

"And Vidalia," Ruth said. "And Hezekiah, if he's coming."

"Of course." Pastor took Agnes's hand. "God bless you, sister."

"Thank you."

After Pastor Speedwell and Darcy left, I made sure Agnes was comfortable and had everything she wanted and needed for the next hour or so. "You sure it's okay if I go? I know you don't like me leaving you alone."

"I think I'll be fine. It's such a special occasion."

"I'll come home right after."

I scrunched up her favorite pillow and crammed it behind her neck, and then I switched on the speaker the way Studebaker showed me. We could already hear the noise from the crowd gathering at the church.

"Hear that?" Ruth said. "It sounds like a full house."

Vidalia, Ruth, and I entered through the back door and filed through Pastor Speedwell's study. Sure enough the entire front row on the left side was empty. I looked around for Hezekiah, but I didn't see him.

"I wonder where he could be?" I said it out loud even though I didn't mean too.

"Who?" Vidalia asked.

"Hezekiah. I thought he would come."

"Me, too," Ruth said. "I saw him at the Full Moon, and he said he would come if he could."

Hezekiah had been missing just about everything since he started running with Olivia, missing church and leaving work a little early, even though we didn't keep him to a schedule.

I spied Zeb making his way to the front.

"Can I sit with you, ladies?"

"Sure," Ruth said. Then she whispered to me. "I bet he's missing Cora tonight."

Pastor Speedwell looked uncomfortable on the raised platform that night. His podium had been removed to make way for the group and their instruments. It was like watching a man with no arms try to climb a ladder.

But after some stammering and awkward glances he got to the point. "The Bible says we are to make a joyful noise unto the Lord. And from what I hear about these folks about to perform, that's just what we're gonna do. Let's welcome the Pearly Gates Singers."

A long round of applause with some folks on their feet, rang out as the men entered from the side. I glanced at Sheila Spiney who would ordinarily be at the piano. She detested any applause in church, believing that it took the glory away from God. This time was no exception if her puckered, sour puss meant anything.

"Those Gates boys look so nice," Ruth said with a nudge to my spleen.

They wore dark suits, but somehow I could see all the colors of the rainbow shimmering like abalone in the sun.

"Look at them suits," Vidalia said. "Um, um, um. Like oil in a puddle. Reminds me of my Drayton. He wore such pretty colors."

Then without so much as a throat clear, they started playing and singing and shouting. The music bounced and ricocheted all around the sanctuary that night.

They sang *This Little Light of Mine*, but let me tell you, it wasn't the Sunday school version. They were jumping and shouting and pouring sweat over that little ditty of a tune, so much so that Darcy, who was sitting in the front row on the right, looked like a woman with the vapors and had to fan herself with a leftover bulletin. I noticed Pastor snap his fingers once, but he recovered quickly from that display and folded his hands on his lap.

It wasn't until after their third song, *Take Me to Beulah Land*, that Melvin spoke up.

"All God's children got hands and feet. How 'bout usin' them? Come on now, get up, and clap your hands." He started clapping and walking back and forth across the platform as they started the music.

No soap. What the Pearly Gates didn't know was that the congregation of the Bright's Pond Chapel of Faith and Grace was about as animated as a pound of slugs in summer. The only folks who shouted back, or raised their hands, or clapped were the out-of-towners, and even they got embarrassed after a while. Most of the people in Bright's Pond wouldn't dance if they caught fire.

The only person I saw who expressed any emotion that night, besides the Singers, was Ruth. She had stars in her eyes, and every once in a while she swayed—just a bit.

But I got to hand it to the group, they hung in with us and ended the concert with a beautiful rendition of *The Windows of Heaven Are Open,* which brought tears to my eyes and made Ruth grab onto my hand and not let go. Even Vidalia had to take out her hanky. Zeb left early to open the café. He was expecting a large after-concert crowd.

By eight-thirty the sanctuary cleared out. Ruth lingered a moment still dabbing tears and fighting back full-scale blubbers.

"I wish my Bubby Hubby were here tonight. He would have loved them Pearly Gates."

Ezekiel Moses Ramstead was on the platform packing up his keyboard. He was so kind to Ruth and so gentle even though Ruth quivered like she had been stung by bees when he reached out his hand and took hers. He looked into her eyes and smiled, his white teeth bright against his coal dark face.

"That man you're missing was here tonight, dear."

"Who was?" Ruth asked, nearly mesmerized.

"I'm assuming it's a husband you're missing. He was here darlin', looking down on you with such love in his heart—" he practically sang "—missin' his sweet, sweet woman."

Ruth swooned and Ezekiel caught her just before she slipped to the floor. She thrust her autograph book in his face. "Sign it, please."

Ezekiel took the little book and opened to a clean page, not that Ruth had many autographs beside Frank Sinatra's, who had gotten lost once on his way to Jack Frost and stopped in at the Full Moon to ask for directions. Ezekiel signed: "For my friend, Ruth. God Bless. Ezekiel Moses Ramstead."

She clutched it to her breast. "Oh, thank you."

Then the rest of the Singers came out and shook our hands and signed her book. Melvin was still curious about Agnes, but I told him she was home resting and he seemed satisfied.

"How about we head over to Zeb's for coffee?" Vidalia asked.

I felt a yawn coming on and said, "I think I better get back home."

"Me, too," Ruth said. "I'm just all atwitter now, and I think I want to go home and look at my photo album."

"Fine," Vidalia said. "I'm not tired at all, and since Winifred and the children are arriving tomorrow, I best be getting things in order."

In the time it took to watch the concert and walk home I forgot all about the speaker sitting in the entryway and tripped right over it. Fortunately, I was able to grab onto the radiator and stop myself from falling flat on my face.

"That you, Griselda?" Agnes called.

"Yep, just me. I tripped over the speaker."

I rubbed my knee and joined Agnes. Her face was red and blotchy like she had had an asthma attack.

"Are you all right?"

"Yeah, I just had a coughing jag in the middle of *Bound for Canaan Land* right through *Do Lord*.

"Oh, I'm sorry, Agnes. Did you enjoy any of the concert?"

"Oh, sure I did, Griselda. I was sitting here like I was having my own private concert—like they came to town just for me."

"In a way, that's true, you know."

About twenty minutes later I heard the bus pull away from the curb. "There they go."

"Did Hezekiah go to the concert?" Agnes asked after I brought her a snack of cake and tea. I wasn't hungry.

"No. I didn't see him."

"I wonder what's up with him? I thought he'd go for sure."

"Well, if he did, he was sitting in the back or standing out in the lobby with the other latecomers, because I never saw him."

22

Mildred Blessing came knocking on our front door at eight-twenty the next morning.

"Why's someone knocking?" Agnes called. "You forget to unlock it?"

"No, I unlocked it first thing, same as I always do." I dried my hands on a red, terry towel on my way to the door and found Mildred Blessing on the other side.

"Mildred, what are you doing here?"

Mildred was not on my mental list of frequent visitors.

"I better come inside, Griselda," she said.

My heart sank just a bit as in that second my brain flashed on the day the state policeman came and told us about our parents.

"Agnes," I called. I motioned for Mildred's jacket but she refused. "Mildred Blessing is here."

"Well, my goodness. Invite her in."

Mildred and I went to the viewing room. It was a tad dark. I hadn't opened the drapes yet. "What do you say I shed some light on the subject?"

"What can I do for you, Mildred?" Agnes asked. She reached for her candy jar and popped a few.

"Actually, I came to see both of you. Official business."

I swallowed. "Official business? Something happen?"

Mildred held her cop hat in her hands. Her eyes darted around the room like they were looking for a place, any place, to rest as long as it wasn't on one of us.

"Spit it out, Mildred," Agnes said. "You look like—"

"It's Vidalia Whitaker."

My heart jumped into my throat. "What about Vidalia?"

"She was found dead, Griselda. Looks like she was stabbed with a butcher knife, right there in her house, in that big room. You know, the one with that pretty, flowered settee."

I can't remember everything that happened in the couple of minutes that followed, except that my heart stopped beating for a second or two and my knees weakened so much I fell onto Agnes's bed. Agnes reached out and grabbed my hand.

"Stabbed?" Agnes said. "How's that possible? People don't get stabbed in Bright's Pond."

"Well, that's what Doc said. Whoever did it used one of Vidalia's own kitchen knives."

"Wait a second, wait a second," I said. "When?"

"Not too long ago. Sometime late last night, near as Doc can figure."

"How? Who—" I couldn't catch my breath. Agnes continued to hold my hand.

"Ivy Slocum found her."

"Ivy?"

"That's right, Griselda. Ivy was expecting that Hezekiah fellow—" my heart started to pound "—around six to fix her screen door, and when he didn't show, Ivy called over to Vidalia's but there was no answer. So Ivy took Al Capone with her and knocked on Vidalia's door. She thought maybe Hezekiah overslept or something."

I took a huge breath as Agnes squeezed my hand.

"Anyway, Ivy says the door was open slightly. She rang the bell anyway, wanting to be polite and all. But after a minute or two Al Capone went loping through the door like he knew something."

Tears welled up as my whole body started to shake.

"Oh, poor Ivy," Agnes said. "She must be a wreck."

"Ivy said Al Capone went straight to her. I'm thinking Vidalia was one of Al Capone's regular stops for treats."

"How's Ivy?" I asked.

"She went on home after she told her story. She said Al lay down next to Vidalia and kept licking her hand like he was trying to wake her up."

"What about Hezekiah? Did Ivy find him?" I asked.

"No, ma'am, Hezekiah wasn't at the boarding house, so I thought maybe he came over here," Mildred said. "Doc and I figure he might have heard or saw something."

"He was here yesterday working on the garage," Agnes said. "He left around four, but I haven't seen him since then."

"I can't say for sure if he was there or not, but I didn't see him at the concert. Vidalia was—" I couldn't fight the tears. "Vidalia was there, with me and Ruth and Zeb."

"Um." Mildred scribbled notes in a little black book she pulled from her hip pocket. "I am so sorry to have to tell you this." She pushed hair behind her ears.

I stood and then sat right back down. I was so shaky. "Where is she now?"

"Still in the house, I think. Doc will need to do an autopsy."

"Doc?"

"He's also the coroner, Griselda. It's S.O.P. in suspected murder."

I nodded. "How terrible for him. I didn't think Bright's Pond would need a coroner."

Mildred scribbled another note. "Heck, Griselda, even OZ had a coroner. Now, I'll need to contact her next of kin."

"That would be Winifred. She lives out of town. Oh, but wait." I didn't think it could be possible but my heart sank lower. "She's on her way here. She's supposed to arrive by train this afternoon."

"Oh, my goodness," Agnes said. "This is just awful."

I swiped tears away and let out a sigh. "She's coming here with three of her kids."

Mildred looked thoughtful a minute. "Do you know what time her train arrives? I imagine she'll be coming into Shoops."

"No, but maybe you'll find a clue at Vidalia's house," Agnes said. "I'm sure she wrote it down somewhere."

"Wait a second. Are you sure her train has even left?" Mildred asked.

"Winifred probably left yesterday. She's coming from Michigan," I said.

Arthur slinked past my ankles. I picked him up and held him close. "Who would want to hurt Vidalia? She's the kindest woman in Bright's Pond. She opened her house to anyone in need and—"

"Speaking of which," Mildred said, "if Hezekiah comes by, let him know I want to speak with him."

"Sure thing, Mildred."

Crying, I walked her to the door. "I guess you could just call the train station and find out when the train from Detroit will arrive."

"Good idea."

I grabbed her arm. "Mildred, let me go to Shoops and meet her. It will be less traumatic."

She cracked a rare smile. "We'll get the scum bucket that did this."

When I got back to Agnes she was trying to reach a box of Kleenex. I plucked three and wiped tears from her eyes.

"Agnes," I said, "am I dreaming? Wake me up because I don't want to be in this nightmare anymore."

She patted my hand. "I'm so sorry, Griselda, but it's not a dream."

"But why would anyone want to kill Vidalia. I can't believe it. I'm going over there."

"Oh, Griselda, don't go. What if you see her?" She took a breath. "Remember her alive, not . . . like that."

"I've got to go, Agnes. Vidalia was my friend. I need to see for myself."

I pulled a gray sweater over my head and slipped into my sneakers. "Would you call the train station, Agnes? Get the time the train is arriving."

"Sure, but I wish you wouldn't go."

I stepped out on the porch and saw Eugene Shrapnel across the street. "I told you," he hollered, shaking his crooked, old cane. "I told you the sky was gonna fall."

"Go on home now, Eugene, you miserable, old fool. Get away from my house."

He harrumphed and kept walking like he owned the town.

Word had already started to spread. I thought a minute about going over to Ruth's. She would be devastated. But I had to see Vidalia first. I had to see with my own eyes. I had to hear Doc tell me she was gone. The closer I got the faster and harder I walked, until I was running down the sidewalk.

I stopped when I saw a red and white ambulance backed into Vidalia's driveway. Doc met me at the door, and by the time I got to Vidalia, she was zipped tight in a black body bag. Two men in white doctor coats carried her out as a small group gathered.

Tears poured down my face when they closed the ambulance door. I turned to Doc.

"Stabbed? Really?"

Doc nodded. "A detective from Shoops was here. He did some snooping, dusted for fingerprints, but didn't have much to say. Thinks whoever did it, knew her."

"Knew her? Like someone in town?"

"Looks that way."

I fell on Vidalia's flowery sofa. Anger boiled inside. "Who would do this? Why?"

"The detective said it might have been robbery. Her jewelry has been rifled through, and we found her purse open over there." He pointed to the dining room table. "If she had any money, it's gone."

"Doc, this is all too weird. She didn't have any other borders except Hezekiah and—you don't suppose—"

"Hezekiah? Don't know, but he hasn't been seen all morning."

"Sometimes he goes into Shoops for supplies, but he didn't take my truck and didn't say anything to me or Agnes."

I pulled myself up. "I can't believe this has happened. Nobody dies like this in Bright's Pond. Nobody deserves to die this way, especially Vidalia."

"I know, Griselda. This is our first murder."

I cried.

"Come on, Griselda," Doc said. "Let's go. You shouldn't be here."

"No, I want to stay a minute or two."

Mildred came into the room. "Can't let you stay, Griselda. It's a crime scene. I've got to make it off limits now. There might be more detectives coming in to look around."

Doc and I left. He climbed into his Dodge Dart and followed the ambulance—slowly like the funeral procession had already begun. Folks stood in Vidalia's front yard, yakking at each other like chickens, each one sadder than the next.

"Who did it, Griselda?" Frank Sturgis called.

"Yeah, who's the son of a—" Fred Haskell hollered. He was leaning against his plumbing truck.

I shrugged. "They don't know."

I saw Ruth running down the street. "Griselda, Griselda, Zeb just told me."

She ran into my arms and sobbed. "I just saw the ambulance pass by."

"Come on, Ruth. Let's go home." We pushed our way through the group.

Agnes was on the phone. "The train is due in at 2:25 this afternoon," she said, replacing the receiver.

"What train?" Ruth asked.

"Winifred's."

"You mean Vidalia's daughter?" Ruth shook her head and continued crying. "This is the most terrible thing that ever happened—ever."

"Winifred was coming for a visit," I said. "And now—"

"Now she's coming to plan a funeral," Agnes said.

"Does Mildred have any clue who did this?" Ruth asked.

I shook my head no.

"She'll get him," Ruth said. "Say what you will about Mildred but she'll nab the killer. I mean even a blind squirrel finds a nut once in a while."

The ride to Shoops was the longest of my life. Every bump and curve down the mountain stabbed and pulled at my heart. Even in Stu's Caddy, I felt every single one of them. My friend had been murdered, and now I was going to tell her child and grandchildren. It was the worst day of my life since my parents died.

The Shoops' train station, located right within the city limits, was a large white house with a green, shingled roof and pillars out front. I found Winifred's train on the large schedule that hung over the ticket counter.

"On time," it read. "Platform nine."

I only waited ten minutes on the platform before the train pulled into the station. It was a silver and red Amtrak Night Coach. It screeched to a stop, and within minutes, the doors opened and people flowed out.

I searched the sea of faces and found Winifred. I hadn't seen her in years but she looked just like Vidalia, except thinner and prettier. I moved closer to the woman who was holding fast to two little children while a third ran in circles around a pole.

"Winifred," I called and waved. "Winifred."

Our eyes met. "Griselda?" she called. "Where's Mama?"

I stopped moving as the swarm of people circled around me in a blur. "Winifred, I . . . I came instead."

"That's fine." Then she looked into my eyes. "It's so good to see you, Griselda. I'd give you a big hug but I'm afraid to let go of these two. They'd be gone in a flash."

Winifred looked good, happy, standing there with two little boys. She had shortened her hairstyle since I last saw her.

"Maybe we should get the suitcases. I'm so anxious to see Mama. Why didn't she come for us?"

I ignored her question and bent down to introduce myself to her boys.

"This is Chester," Winifred said, lifting her left arm. "And this is Drayton. The child climbing the railing is Tobias. He's six and never stops moving."

"I'll get him," I said.

I pulled the child from the stair railing. He looked at me like I was trying to steal him until I pointed to his mother.

"Come on, Tobias," Winifred called. "I want to get to Nana's."

"Nana," Tobias said, and he wrapped his arms around my legs.

"Oh, no—no honey. I'm Griselda, not . . . Nana." I choked back an urge to cry or scream.

"Winnie," I said, "let's get the bags. I took Studebaker's car."

"Studebaker Kowalski? How is he?"

"Fine. Just fine."

I felt a tear run down my cheek as I moved ahead of her. We retrieved their four suitcases and found the car. Everyone and everything fit nicely in Stu's Caddy. I looked at the boys in the rearview mirror, and all three looked like they could fall asleep any second.

"They had a long trip," I said still looking.

"*They* had a long trip," Winifred said, her voice raised an octave. "Ever travel with three little boys? Let me tell you, I thought I might lose my mind. Tobias disappeared somewhere between Detroit and Cincinnati. I thought I'd go out of my head until the conductor found him hiding in an overhead baggage rack. Said he was playing suitcase."

I laughed.

"Then Chester threw up all over that nice Father Franklin, while Drayton ate a Band-Aid he found in my purse after he emptied it onto the floor. My prescription bottle and two marbles rolled down the aisle."

"Okay, okay, you all had a long trip."

We drove ten minutes before I noticed the boys had finally nodded off.

"Now, you gonna tell me why Mama couldn't come? You'd think she'd want to greet her grandchildren, unless of course she's home baking up a storm. Um, um, um. I am so gonna eat all the sticky buns I can."

"Winifred. I . . . I need to tell you something."

I pulled off the road and stopped the car.

"Your mama—your mama died this morning." I said it fast like it would somehow lessen the blow.

"What? I spoke to her yesterday. She sounded fine. She would have told me if she was sick. I don't understand, Griselda?"

I grabbed both her hands. "Winifred, she wasn't sick, she—she was killed."

"What, a car wreck?"

"No. She was stabbed." I hollered the words that time, hollered them loud. The boys woke up and called for their mother.

Winifred turned to them. "It's all right, boys. Go to sleep. We'll be to Nan—we'll be there soon."

"Griselda," she whispered, "what are you saying?"

It wasn't sinking in. So I told her again. She buried her face in her hands and cried silently until we reached Bright's Pond.

23

Ruth greeted us on the porch and managed not to say a single word about Vidalia until Winifred and I snuggled all three boys into the extra bedroom upstairs.

"They'll sleep for maybe an hour," Winifred said. She lingered a moment at the bedroom door. "How do you tell three little boys their Nana is dead?" She closed her eyes and leaned against the doorjamb. "Oh, Griselda, I can't believe this is happening. It's like my heart's been twisted and wrung like a rag."

I pulled my friend close and let her cry into my shoulder. "I know. I keep thinking I'm about to wake up, but—"

"It's a shock. A shock, but stronger. Isn't there a better word?"

Vidalia's death was a storm of lightning strikes that wouldn't stop.

"Why my mother?" Winifred pulled away after a minute and went back to her boys. She double tucked them, kissed each one on the forehead, and pulled the door closed to a crack.

"Come on," I said. "Let's go downstairs. Agnes is anxious to see you. It's been a lot of years."

"I had a much different image in my mind about seeing you all again," she said.

Agnes clicked off the television and stretched her arms to embrace Winifred. "I'm so sorry. I just don't have words to say."

Ruth, who had busied herself in the kitchen while we settled the boys, poured coffee in all our cups. Then she added cream to each. "It's terrible." She blubbered louder with each cup. "Terrible. First Mabel Sewickey, then Cora, and now Vidalia. Of course it ain't exactly the same seeing as how Cora died from a bad heart and your mama—"

"Ruth," I said. "Mabel died ten years ago."

"I know that, Griselda, but she was still my friend. You don't forget friends just 'cause ten years slips by."

Winifred sat near Arthur on the sofa. He curled close to her as she rubbed his neck. "Maybe if I never left town."

"No, no, you can't take any blame for this tragedy," Agnes said. "This came right out of the blue."

"But maybe if I came last week. Mama wanted us to come early, but I told her I had other plans."

"Winifred," Ruth said. "Don't go stirring them waters, dear. No good can come of it. You decide right now that you had no control in what happened to your mama. You start thinking about what she would want you to do right now."

Winifred sipped coffee. "This is good, thank you. That stuff they called coffee on the train was like dishwater."

"Yuk," Ruth said "You'll always get an honest cup of coffee here."

Ruth had a knack for saying just the right thing to lighten the mood even though I never believed she had any idea of what she was doing.

"Now I remember when my Bubba died," Ruth said, "'course it wasn't exactly the same, although if you ask me, that nasty brain cancer is as much a murderer as the creep who did this."

Winifred touched her stomach like a wave of nausea had rippled through. Funny how folks touched their stomachs when they felt sick. Maybe it reminds us of when our mamas would rub our tummies after we ate too much candy.

"We want you to stay right here with us," Agnes said after a while. "It might be too hard to go home right now."

"That's probably the best idea, Winnie," I said. "They sealed off the place as a crime scene."

"Thank you." She took a deep breath. "I guess I better make plans and . . . should I talk to the police?"

"I imagine we should start at the funeral home," I said. "I'll go with you."

"Thank you, Griselda."

"I still have Stu's car. I'm sure he'll let me keep it so we don't have to take the truck into Shoops."

"And the boys can stay with me," Ruth said. "I'd love to have them."

"You're all being so wonderful." Winifred dabbed away tears. "I better call Toby before I do anything else. He must be worried because I was supposed to call the minute I arrived. He might have even called Mama's house five or six times by now."

We finished our coffee, and Winifred bundled the boys up for the drive to Ruth's. The children were skittish at first, but the second Tobias laid eyes on Russell, Ruth's blue and white parakeet, he was fine, and Chester and Drayton followed right behind.

"Don't you worry a minute, Winnie," Ruth said. "They'll be fine, just fine."

"I'll need to tell them soon," she said.

"Later," I said. "Maybe we should see if Mildred's heard anything before we head into Shoops. Agnes is going to call the funeral home and let them know we're coming."

"Thank you, Griselda. I'm so glad you're here."

She kissed each boy on the nose. "Now you all be good for Ruth, and I mean it Tobias. That bird better be alive when I get back."

Ruth cringed but covered it nicely. She didn't know the first thing about children. She and Bubba never had any.

Mildred had a little office in the town hall. It was really little more than a desk and a telephone. She had WANTED posters hung on a bulletin board on one wall and a portrait of Richard Nixon on the other. She had her head buried in *True Crime* magazine when we interrupted.

"Excuse us, Mildred," I said. "But this is Winifred, Vidalia's daughter."

Mildred shoved the magazine into a drawer and stood up. "I was just taking a quick break from the investigation." She reached out her hand. "I wish we were meeting under better circumstances."

"We came by on our way down to Shoops," I said. "Have you heard anything new?"

"Only this, Griselda, and you aren't going to like it."

"Me? Why?"

"I just got a call from the lead detective in Shoops. He said they're combing the streets for that handyman of yours."

"Hezekiah? Why?"

"He's the prime suspect. No one's seen hide nor hair of him since last night when he and Olivia left Personal's."

I couldn't breathe. "Hezekiah? A suspect?"

"Mama told me about him," Winifred said. "According to her he was a nice fellow—very helpful."

"That's what we thought," I said, "but now . . . now I don't know what to think. Wait till Agnes hears this. She's really going to be upset."

"Why would Agnes be so upset?" Winifred asked.

"It was her idea that Hezekiah move in with your Mama and stay in town while he waited for his miracle," I said.

"Miracle? You mean the man who killed my Mama came to town so Agnes could pray for a miracle?"

"Now hold on," Mildred said. "He hasn't been convicted. They just want to talk to him."

"That's right. We need to wait this out." I said.

The Digman Funeral Home was located on a dead-end street near the Shoops Drive-in Theater. The mortuary was a large white building that looked like it would be better suited for a plantation in South Carolina. Barry Digman, a tall, huge man with bad breath and blonde hair, met us in the lobby dressed in a black suit.

"I'm so sorry for your loss," he said. Then he led us into a small consultation room.

"Mama said she wanted to be cremated, like my father," Winifred said. "I've been hanging onto his ashes for years now. We'll bury them both together back in Detroit."

For a second I felt like Winifred was taking Vidalia away from me and I hated myself for feeling such a thing. After all, Vidalia wasn't my mother. It just felt that way sometimes.

"That's fine," said Mr. Digman. "We are the only mortuary in the three county district who has their own crematory."

Winifred rolled her eyes at the sales pitch. "When can I get her ashes?"

The funeral director's eyes grew wide. "We have to get her here first. I—I understand this was a—murder."

Winifred shot me and Digman a look. I grabbed her hand. "Agnes—remember? She was going to call."

"Yes," Digman said. "Agnes Sparrow, that miracle-worker woman called."

I fake coughed and the man caught on. "Right, right." He took on a solemn look. "We'll bring your mother here once the police release her. And you can pick up the ashes the next day as long as she gets here early enough."

The man's casket-side manner was irritating as he tried to talk Winifred into purchasing an expensive bronze urn with cherubim and ivy inlay.

"Now why am I going to spend all that money on a jar that I'm just going to bury in the ground? Most ridiculous thing I ever heard of. Let me see what else you've got."

She selected a cheaper model while Mr. Digman apologized.

It wasn't until we were about halfway back to Bright's Pond when it struck me that Winifred had grown quiet. That wouldn't be unusual under the circumstances, but she also had a look on her face that I couldn't decipher—almost like she was angry.

"What about a service?" I asked on the way home.

"Service? Oh, I suppose so. We should have a small gathering at her church, not that I ever liked Milton Speedwell and that skinny wife of his."

"I'm sure it can be arranged. You know it will be important to the town, Winnie."

We drove in silence another couple of miles until Winifred's bad mood became so palpable it made my chest hurt.

"Are you all right? I know this is tough but—"

"Why did Agnes invite that man to live at my mother's?"

"Agnes didn't know anything about him. Just that he needed prayer. She was trying to be helpful."

"Prayer? I think he came looking for someone to kill, Griselda."

"We don't even know for sure if it was him. And besides he was here for nearly three months. Why would he wait—"

"Who else? Who else in town would kill my Mama?"

I had no answer.

"It's on account of Agnes and her stupid prayers that my mother is dead. Now please, I want to get my boys and go home."

"But you can't stay there. The police have it sealed off."

"Well, I'm gonna unseal it. Now, please, I ain't mad at you, Griselda. It wasn't your fault."

The next twenty minutes were the longest I've ever spent. I parked outside Ruth's and helped Winifred get the boys. She never said a word to Ruth except, "Thank you and good-bye."

I pulled Ruth aside while Winifred got the boys situated in the car. "She's a little upset. I'll talk to you later."

"Did I do something wrong with the boys? They were just fine, except Tobias tried to flush his GI Joe down the toilet, but I fished it out in time. Boiled it as best I could. And Russell squawked his head off whenever the boys went near, but he's just a dumb old bird."

"No, you didn't do anything. Agnes did, maybe."

"Agnes?"

I glanced at Winifred. She was in the front seat with her arms crossed so tight across her chest I feared she might bust a rib. "Let me get her settled. I'll meet you at the café in about an hour. We need to plan a service for Vidalia, and I'll tell you then."

"Oh, can we fly a kite for her too? I was thinking she would love that, you know. We could go up to Hector's Hill and set it free. You know, let the kite go and sail to heaven."

I smiled for the first time that day.

A police car from Shoops was parked in front of Vidalia's house next to Mildred's.

"Now, what do they want?" Winifred asked.

"Mildred said some officers might come looking for more information."

"Great, they're going to frighten the boys."

"Winifred, I can drive right past, take the boys back to Ruth's, and then bring you back here. It would only take a couple of minutes."

"No. Just park."

The boys climbed out of Stu's big car. Tobias headed straight for the cruiser. "How come there's a cop car here, Mama?"

Winifred grabbed all three of them—two around the necks and one by the elbow. They squirmed but knew who was boss. "Now you boys go on out back of Nana's house and play. Don't mind the cars."

They did what they were told. "And Tobias, you watch Chester for me now. Don't let him run off."

Two large police officers stood in Vidalia's living room with Doc and Mildred.

"Oh, good," Mildred said. She pointed to me. "This is Griselda Sparrow, the woman I told you about."

"Doc?" I said. "What are you doing back here? I thought you had to—to, you know."

Doc took my hand. "You'll understand in a minute."

I took a deep breath and wondered how long the house would smell like Vidalia's—all cinnamon and coffee. Then

I squeezed Winifred's sweaty hand. "And this is Winifred Strange, Vidalia's daughter."

The officers greeted her kindly and introduced themselves.

"Officer McGarrett," said the shorter of the two. "And this is my partner, Officer Lu."

Winifred stood with her arms crossed. "All I want to hear is that you caught that—that maniac."

Officer McGarrett bit his pinky nail and spit it on the floor. "Well, Ma'am, that's why we're here."

He went on to tell us how they had gotten a call about a disturbance at the Busy Bee Motel in Shoops, and when they investigated they found Olivia Janicki stabbed to death and Hezekiah Branch leaning over her bawling like a toddler.

"They both had been drinking and smoking pot," Officer Lu said. "An argument started, and Mr. Branch hit Miss Janicki several times. She scratched his face up real good. Then he stabbed her in the heart and killed her—just like Vidalia."

I swallowed. My stomach churned and my brain flashed on the last couple of times Hezekiah cleaned up one of Arthur's bloody surprises. He seemed transfixed on the blood for a second or two before he was able to get a paper towel and toss the critter outside. "I guess you're certain it's the same Hezekiah?"

"Yes, Ma'am. He had no identification, but when we took him down to the station we discovered he's been wanted for nearly ten months now."

Doc cleared his throat and looked at the floor. "He confessed, Griselda."

Winifred went a little wobbly and Doc steadied her. "Maybe I should prescribe a mild sedative."

"No, I'll be fine," she said. "Confessed?"

"That's right," Officer Lu said. "He was mighty shaken over it. Blubbered like a baby in the interrogation room. He confessed that he'd stabbed Mrs. Whitaker while Miss Janicki stole her jewelry and money."

"But why did he have to kill Vidalia?" I thought my head would explode it pounded so hard.

"Yeah, why?" Winifred said. "She would have given them her money—and her jewelry. If they had asked."

"Well, Hezekiah started yammering stuff about not getting his miracle. Something about a woman named Agnes and—" the officer looked at us and shook his head "—he kept repeating it over and over."

"What?" Winifred asked.

"He didn't get his miracle." The officer shook his head. "Darndest thing. Kept saying it over and over."

Winifred stamped her foot. "Then why didn't he kill Agnes?" She looked at me and turned away.

"I don't know. Maybe he kept hoping his miracle would come and he didn't want to—"

"Kill the miracle worker?" Winifred fell into a chair and cried.

"I don't understand," said McGarrett. "Miracle worker?"

"I think we're done here," Mildred said. She had stepped between Officer Lu and me. "I might be able to help the officers understand out on the porch. No sense in upsetting matters more here."

I nodded to Mildred. "Thank you."

Mildred and the police officers left. Tobias came bounding through the front door. "Mama, Mama, where's Nana?"

Winifred took a deep breath and then she took her son's hand. "Let's go get your brothers. I got something to tell you."

"That's the hardest thing in the world to do," Doc said, as Winifred led Tobias out the back. "How is she going to tell those boys that Nana isn't here?"

"I've known Winnie for a long, long time. She's a lot like Vidalia. She'll find the words."

Doc nodded. "I'm headed back to the office. They released her body so I'll call and have Digman come get her. You stick close to Winifred and call me if she needs anything." I walked him to the porch.

"She blames Agnes," I said.

"Oh, Agnes had nothing to do with this."

"She invited him to live with Vidalia."

Doc shook his head. "It's still not her fault. All this rabble-rousing will pass."

I held my breath for a second and adjusted my glasses. "I hope so, Doc. Does Agnes know?"

"Probably not. I told Mildred it would be best coming from you."

I stayed with Winifred another hour or so. She insisted on staying in the house. "I'll be fine, Griselda. I need to feel close to Mama, and this is the only way I can do that right now."

Winifred called her husband, Toby, while the boys ate macaroni and cheese. She was cool, collected, and in charge as she went about her business.

"No, you don't need to come," she said into the phone. "I'll get her ashes in a day or two and then take the train home as soon as I can."

She hung up and cried for a minute.

"Mama," Tobias called. "I miss Nana."

"I can stay if you want," I said. "Ruth is waiting at the café, but she'll understand. I'll just call and—"

"No, go plan the service and then you go on home. Tell Agnes what her friend did." She turned her back.

I took a step toward her and put my hand on her shoulder. "Is there anything we should be sure to include? In the service, I mean."

"Not that I can think of right now. Maybe that song she was always singing—about the garden."

"Yes, I know the one."

I lingered a moment. Never in my life had I witnessed so much senseless pain inflicted on another person. The closest I came was when my parents died, but their death was accidental. Vidalia was stabbed to death, and for what? A few dollars? There had to be more to it. I watched Winnie lightly brush her fingers on a crystal vase that had been resting on their mantle forever. I was filled with an overwhelming desire to see Hezekiah—to look into the eyes of the man who murdered my friend's Mama.

23

The Shoops Borough police station was nothing more than a square, red-brick building with a small, enclosed porch that looked like it had been tacked on as an afterthought. A flagpole stood on the left and flew the Stars and Stripes, with the Commonwealth of Pennsylvania flag wagging under it. There was a stand of sugar maples nearby and a small row of azaleas on either side of the porch. All in all it didn't look much like a police station. If it wasn't for the sign out front I would have had to ask someone.

Inside, the place smelled old and musty with blue cigarette smoke choking up the air. I was greeted by a man in uniform who had just pulled a candy bar from the machine. I didn't know his rank; I mean, I never learned how you tell the difference between a sergeant and a captain and all. Plus I wasn't interested. I just wanted to see Hezekiah.

"Can I help you?" the officer asked, unwrapping his Baby Ruth.

"I understand you're holding Hezekiah Branch here."

The cop's eyes grew wide for a second, and then he turned stern. "Well, now, I don't know if that's any of your business." He bit off a chunk of candy.

"He killed my friend. He killed my friend's mother."

"I'm sorry about that, Ma'am, but I can't let just anybody back there."

I blew air out my nose in a huff as frustration began to bubble inside my stomach. "Can't he have visitors? I thought prisoners could have visitors."

"A relative maybe, a lawyer for sure, but—"

"He worked for me and my sister, and now he's killed my friend. I think that makes us close enough."

The officer swallowed and shook his head. "I'll catch it for this, but—"

"Thank you. Where—"

"Come on." He carefully tucked what was left of his candy bar in the wrapper and dropped it into his shirt pocket underneath his badge.

The place was small and tight. We walked down a short hallway with alternating yellow and white linoleum tiles to a single cell—a cage really. Bars all around; a toilet with no seat. A bed, which was more like a metal slab, hung from the wall. Hezekiah lay on the bed with his arm draped over his eyes.

The cop banged on the bars. "Hey, you. Wake up. You got a visitor."

Hezekiah didn't move or speak at first and then said, "I ain't taking no visitors."

"It's me—Griselda."

Hezekiah pulled his arm away from his face slowly. "Go home, Griselda. Just go home."

"No, you're going to tell me why you did it."

Hezekiah practically leaped off the metal bed and flung himself toward me. I backed away, scared. His eyes were wide and his face red.

"Come on, lady," the cop said. "He ain't going to be treating you civil. Most wild animals can't."

I moved closer to the cage. Tears threatened and then fell. I was so close to him, I watched one of my tears fall on his shoe and lighten a tiny dot on the leather. "What happened, Hezekiah?"

He moved back a step and rubbed his neck. "I tried to tell you all. I asked for my miracle, Griselda. It never came, and . . . and the feeling, the horrible hungry inside my stomach kept growing and getting stronger everyday until—"

"What miracle, Hezekiah? You never told us. You just kept asking Agnes to pray but—"

"Can't you figure it out by now? I didn't want to kill no more people. I wanted that god of yours, that lying, stinking no-good god of yours, to reach his almighty hand down out of the heavens and reach into my guts and take the blood lust away and bury it in the deepest sea."

I swiped at my tears. "But you never said."

"How could I? How could I tell you and that sideshow freak sister of yours what I needed?" He turned his back to me; it was wet with perspiration. "You would have thrown me out and called the police."

Hezekiah balled his hands into tight fists and rubbed his eyes. "I thought just asking would be enough. Ain't he supposed to read minds, Griselda? Did I have to come out and say it?"

I looked down at my feet. He was right. I would have taken him straight to Mildred.

He turned around and shoved his hands into his back jeans pocket. "Tell me, Miss God-fearing Griselda, would you have been able to find any Christian charity, any mercy, any forgiveness in your heart and let me stay?"

How dare he put that millstone around my neck?

I glared into his eyes and noticed how red and how dark with rage they were. His weak chin jutted out toward me like a knife. His shoulders hunched back like an animal set to pounce.

"Maybe you got your miracle, Hezekiah."

He lunged at the bars again and grabbed them so tight his knuckles turned white. "What are you talking about? I killed Vidalia. I took a knife, her knife and—and—"

"I know what you did." My stomach curdled as a wave of anger washed over me. "You took away my friend. You left her daughter without a mother and six little boys without their Nana—the best Nana, Hezekiah, the best in the whole world. She . . . she still had so many . . . so many trays of sticky buns to bake and books to read and—"

"Shut up. Shut up. Stop telling me this."

I cried. I stood there and cried.

Hezekiah went to the cot and sat on the edge. He pushed his hands through his now long hair. "I didn't get my miracle, Griselda. How can you say that? God ignored Agnes's prayers. He said no. It's like he wanted me to kill Vidalia, right? Ain't that right? Or he would have stopped me."

"Don't blame God for your crime, Hezekiah. He didn't grab your hand and help you plunge that knife into Vidalia's heart. You did it. You did it all by yourself. I think God did answer Agnes's prayers—just not the way you wanted. He stopped you good. You'll never kill again. You got your miracle all right, and it cost my friend her life."

Hezekiah looked up at me. I watched the color drain from his face. His chest rose as he sucked in a breath and then let it out slow.

I returned Stu's car to him before heading to the café. I knew Ruth was probably still waiting for me. She was that kind of friend.

"Thanks, Stu. It made the trip easier."

"You're welcome, Griselda. It seemed to take a mite longer than I expected."

"I hope you don't mind, but I had another errand in Shoops."

"That's fine, Griselda."

Stu invited me inside his house but I declined and we stood on his porch a few minutes.

"I was just down at Zeb's. Word is spreading like wildfire, Griselda."

"About Hezekiah?"

"Yep. Some of them folks like Janeen Sturgis were saying that it's all Agnes's fault. Eugene Shrapnel is a little too happy if you ask me."

"But Agnes couldn't know."

"Maybe she should have, Griselda." Stu looked hard at me. "I'm sorry. It's been a long day." He kissed my cheek. "It's gonna be okay."

"I better get on down to the Full Moon."

The café was nearly packed out. Hezekiah and Agnes had become the talk of the town. I looked for Ruth and spotted her near the back.

"There she is," called Nate Kincaid, "let's ask her." He grabbed my arm. "Hey, Griselda, how come Agnes let that man go live with Vidalia? Didn't God give her a warning?"

I looked into his eyes. "No, Nate. Agnes was just doing what she thought was right. She had no reason to believe Hezekiah was planning to—well, to do what he did."

"It could of been any of us," hollered Dot Handy.

I pushed my way through to Ruth, who looked about as sad as I had ever seen her.

"I'm sorry I'm late, Ruth. I had something to do."

"What? Ain't nothing I can think of more important than planning Vidalia's memorial service."

"I'll have to tell you later."

"What? What are you talking about Griselda? And why do you look so pale?"

I scanned the café. All eyes were set on me. "I didn't expect this," I said. "Maybe we should go back to my house."

"They sure are mad, Griselda, like they want Agnes to confess a crime or something. That Eugene Shrapnel was here saying how he warned us all, warned us about putting faith in Agnes. Said she was the devil."

"Oh, Ruth, you don't believe that."

"No, I don't. Least I don't think I do."

Ruth stirred her coffee, coffee she wasn't really drinking. "Now, Griselda, you know I love you and Agnes, but she did invite the fellow to stay at Vidalia's and you got to admit that she claims to have a connection to God and all."

"Ruth, Agnes never claimed such a thing. That's your idea. Agnes never wanted the glory. I told you all that. God saw fit to grant those miracles, not Agnes."

"Folks still think she should've known better."

Zeb made his way to us. "Hey, Griselda. Can I get you something?"

"No. I just stopped by to help plan Vidalia's service with Ruth but—"

"You might want to do that some place else."

"What? You angry too?"

"Me? Nah, I'm just looking out for you is all. I didn't think you'd like all this talk. Folks sure have changed their feelings about Agnes all of a sudden."

That's when I heard sobs coming from the counter. It was Hazel Flatbush. She turned toward me. "Poor Vidalia. Poor, sweet Vidalia. She never deserved such a fate. Never."

I had to resist an urge to comfort her for fear she might turn on me and spew some nonsense about Agnes.

"Tell Hazel to come to the service Sunday, right after the regular church service, will you, Zeb."

Zeb nodded, and I watched him whisper to Hazel. She nodded her head and glanced at me for a fraction of a second, but in that fraction I knew she shared the town's sentiments. Once again I shared Agnes's notoriety—by proximity.

I grabbed Ruth's hand. "I need to go. We can finish this at my house."

"I think I'll stay. Maybe you just need to go see Pastor and tell him to do a run-of-the-mill memorial service, especially since there's no body to view."

A bodyless funeral was rare in Bright's Pond. Most folks thought cremation went against the biblical example of burial. Some even thought that God wouldn't be able to resurrect them after they were turned to ashes. My daddy only sent out one body that I know of for cremation, and that was only because the family couldn't afford to buy a cemetery plot.

I found Pastor at the church working on his sermon. His study was a stuffy little room with dark furniture and uncomfortable chairs. Bookshelves lined the walls and smelled like dust and old paper. Pastor sat at a cluttered desk, looking like Bob Cratchit.

"Afternoon, Pastor," I said. "I was wondering if we could talk a minute."

"Certainly, Griselda. I imagine you're here about Vidalia Whitaker. Terrible news, just terrible."

"Yes, it is terrible. Hard to believe. I keep expecting her to come walking down the street."

"It takes time, Griselda." That was about as comforting as Pastor Speedwell could get.

"We need to plan something for Vidalia."

"Yes. Will the casket be delivered here?"

I moved some newspapers off a chair and sat down. "No casket. Vidalia's being cremated."

"Cremated? My goodness. Did she want that?"

"Her daughter said that was her wish."

Pastor shook his head. "I find that a little hard to believe."

"Winifred's already made arrangements," I said. "We still need a memorial service."

"What did you have in mind?"

"Winifred is probably leaving Monday with the ashes so I thought we should just have a simple service right after regular church tomorrow."

"That's fine. You want to take care of getting the word out. I'm sure Ruth will help."

"I will, Pastor. I'm sure pretty much the whole town will turn out. Everyone loved her so."

"She was an easy person to love, Griselda."

Tears threatened again but I held them off. "Would you also ask Sheila to play *In the Garden*? It was her favorite hymn."

"Of course."

That was that. No fanfare, no drawn out eulogies. Just a few words and a song.

"Thank you, Pastor." I stood and turned to leave.

"Griselda?" he called after me. "Would you like to say a few words about your friend?"

This time I couldn't stop the tears. "Can I tell you that tomorrow?"

The hymn repeated in my mind as I walked home.

> *And he walks with me and he talks with me*
> *And he tells me I am his own*
> *And the joy we share as we tarry there*
> *None other has ever known.*

"You'll never have to leave the garden now, Vidalia."

It was nearly four o'clock when I got home, and I figured Agnes would be hungrier than a bear after hibernating. But she managed for herself. I found her eating a bowl of leftover stew and bread.

"I think this has been one of the worst days of my life," I said, flopping onto the sofa.

"I've been waiting for you to come home. I thought you'd be back before now. Had to make my own lunch—wore me to a frazzle. Hezekiah hasn't even been by."

She still didn't know.

She barely moved a muscle when I told her.

"Agnes, did you hear me? I just said Hezekiah killed Vidalia."

"I heard."

24

A gully-washer. That's what my father would have called the downpour that Sunday. It rained in slanting sheets all morning long. I stood at my bedroom window and watched as small potholes and divots in the lawn filled with water. It rained so hard, I thought the pond might rise and spill into the yard. Once, many years ago, it came up to our back door—an unwelcome guest. It took three days to get the water out of the kitchen and basement. Our house smelled from mold for months. I hoped this wasn't that kind of storm.

Arthur mewled and batted the glass.

"Sorry, Bub, not today."

Agnes wolfed down three scrambled eggs, four slices of scrapple, and a large apple turnover, before she said a word. "Not the best day for a memorial service. Hope folks turn out."

"They will. Everybody loved Vidalia." I sighed. "Everybody."

I gathered dishes and dropped them into the sink. The rain had no intention of letting up. Looking through the kitchen window was like looking through a waterfall.

"Did you hear anything about this storm?" I asked as I scrunched her big pillow.

"No, you can't trust that weathergirl. I was thinking, Griselda, I'd like to sit on the sofa."

"Okay, 1, 2, 3—up." I pulled on her shoulder and she wobbled to her feet and grabbed onto her walker. "At least you'll look like spring in your bright flowery housedress today, even if the weather won't cooperate."

"It's just a little rain. Good for the trees and flowers. Are the tulips coming up?"

"A couple of inches already, and the crocuses are wild this year. Hundreds of them around town."

"That's nice. I do miss seeing them."

She flopped onto the sofa, and it buckled into a strained smile. "Guess you're going to church and all."

"Of course."

I changed Agnes's sheets and found a clean blanket. The laundry had been piling up for a few days. "I'll wash sheets later after Vidalia's service."

Agnes's breathing was labored. I could see it pained her.

"I'll set up the nebulizer before I go. You can have your treatment while I'm at church. And please, try and stay away from the M&Ms this morning. They only irritate your stomach and then you get heartburn and that makes you cough."

"I'm not a baby."

I buttoned my coat. "I'll be home as soon as I can." She never made eye contact with me that morning. It was as if seeing me, really looking at me, would bring on feelings she didn't want to have. Just as I turned around, she asked, "Griselda, are they sure?"

"About what?"

"Hezekiah. Are they sure he did it?"

I pulled the rocker close to her and sat down. "It looks that way. Like I told you last night, he confessed."

"He really did it then. He took a knife and—"

"Yes, Agnes." I swallowed and watched a shock wave pass through her body like high tide.

"It makes me sick to imagine."

"I know. I never in a million years thought that he was capable of something like that."

"He fooled us. Fooled me."

"I need to get over there and talk to Pastor Speedwell. He asked me to say a eulogy or at least a few words."

"Are you?"

"Maybe I'll just tell folks what she meant to me."

"Say something from me too."

I couldn't tell her that some of the townspeople were blaming her and the worst thing I could do was mention her name and start a ruckus at church. But I wouldn't lie to her. I just nodded my head and said, "I better get going."

Pastor Speedwell delivered a somewhat sedate sermon that Sunday about the Good Samaritan. When he finished he moved away from the podium and stood at floor level. He raised his hands over the congregation.

"And now may the grace and peace of God be yours."

But instead of the usual mad rush to the back of the church, everyone sat stock still like a nuclear explosion had just happened and they were waiting for instructions.

Winifred and the boys sat between Ruth and me. Winifred kept her mother's ashes on her lap throughout the entire service and had to keep slapping Tobias's hand because he kept wanting to open the urn.

"Don't be disrespectful," Winifred said in quiet tones. "That's your Nana in there, and we're here to say a proper good-bye."

"But how did they get Nana inside that jar?" Tobias asked.

She slapped his hand again. "Hush up, boy."

After Sylvia played a quiet and restful rendition of *In the Garden* and Hazel Flatbush stood up spontaneously and sang a solo, Pastor motioned to Winifred. I pulled Chester off her arm, and she brought the urn to the front and placed it on the Communion table. She looked out at the congregation. Anyone could easily see that Winifred Strange wanted to be just about anywhere else but there. Pastor stood beside Winifred and prayed, and then she returned to our pew and draped her arms around her boys.

"We come here today," Pastor said, "to say good-bye to our friend and neighbor Vidalia Whitaker so savagely killed by a wolf in sheep's clothing."

Winifred clapped her hands over her sons' ears while others in the congregation stifled sobs.

"Wolf?" Jasper York hollered, "I didn't know it was a wolf."

"No, no, Jasper," Harriett said. "It's just a figure of speech, dear."

Pastor continued, "Yes, my friends, evil was with us. But now that evil is sitting behind bars where he will rot until he is dead and buried in the cold, cold ground or until the day Christ Jesus comes to carry us all home."

Winifred squirmed, and I squirmed along with her.

He talked another five minutes or so until I heard a loud sigh behind me. It was Janeen Sturgis sitting with her head on her husband's shoulder. Frank shrugged her off and stood up.

"All I want to know is how come she did it. How come Agnes let that man into our town? We accepted him like he was a long lost relative on her say so and now Vidalia is gone. It's Agnes Sparrow's fault."

"That's right," Janeen said. "Agnes took him in. She should of known."

"Bone?" Jasper called. "There ain't no bones. She's been cremated."

Harriett whispered to him, and he settled down. "I'm sorry, Colonel," he said with a salute to the pastor.

Eugene lifted his cane toward the ceiling. "I told you all this would happen. I told you she was in league with the devil."

"Calm down, Eugene," Pastor said. He took a step down the aisle. "All of you settle down. This ain't why we're here."

"I'm sorry," Frank said. "I guess we're all so . . . stunned."

Winifred grabbed the boys. "We better get going."

"No, sit." I stood and went to the podium.

"Please," I said. "Vidalia wouldn't want this."

A crash of thunder exploded right over the church, and a flash of lightning burst through the windows.

"Hear that?" Pastor asked. "You all quiet down and let Griselda say a few words about our friend and neighbor."

I heard some low grumbling, but I looked at Winifred with her arms around those three little boys and I looked at Ruth dressed all in black from head to toe and I waited. I waited until I felt something stir in my spirit, something that prodded me on to speak about my friend.

"I loved her," was how I started and I told them why I loved her without a single mention of Hezekiah or the way she died. I told them how she invited me to her house for sticky buns and coffee. How she fibbed and said she just happened to make them when all along I knew she planned on it. I knew she made them expressly for me.

"And she was my best library patron," I said. And that was when Babette Sturgis stood up and said in a nervous little voice, "She always helped me with my reports. I don't see how I'll get a good grade on my report about them carpetbaggers, now."

"That's right," said Nelson Tompkins. If it wasn't for Miz Whitaker I'd never have gotten accepted into Penn State."

There were oohs and ahs after that, because apparently Nelson didn't tell anyone he was accepted, not even his mother who started to bawl like a baby.

Then Ivy stood up. She was a picture in her paisley print dress with her heavy bosom sticking out like two large cantaloupes. She had three gold chains hanging down and had piled her hair on top of head that morning.

"I never told none of you this, but Vidalia loved Al Capone. She always put scraps out for him and even helped me get the skunk out of him that summer, you all remember that. Poor dog."

Then Ivy started to cry. She put her face in her hands and sobbed a second or two. "I'll never get her out of my mind. I keep seeing her—lying there next to the flowery settee in a pool of blood."

Fred Haskell dashed to her and let her rest her head on his chest. "He's a monster. A monster let into this town by Agnes Sparrow."

A collective sigh swelled through the congregation. Little Tobias yanked his Mama's sleeve. "How come Nana was in a pool?"

Winifred pulled him close.

Studebaker and Boris stood at the same time, once again giving credence to the rumor that the two were somehow attached at the hip. "She was a good neighbor," Stu said, while Boris nodded so hard I thought his head would snap off.

After a few more people spoke, Winifred joined me. "I never liked coming home to Bright's Pond. It was the happiest day of my life when Tobias took me to Detroit. I begged Mama to come with us, but she didn't want to leave."

She sighed and swiped away tears. Sylvia started to play *In the Garden* again, pianissimo.

"Well, today, I can see why Mama loved it here. You're all good neighbors."

Then sobbing, she grabbed her mother's ashes and the three boys and fled down the aisle out the back of the church.

Ruth and I found her sitting on Vidalia's porch rocking on the swing. She still clutched the ashes. The rain had stopped and a bright noon sun shone down on our little town, drying the streets.

"Look over there," Ruth said. "A rainbow."

Sure enough God had sent a rainbow that day. "See that," I said. "God planned on it from the early morning. First he had to send the storm because—"

"It's the only way to get a rainbow," Ruth said.

Now, what happened next is—well, I'm not sure if it ever happened before. I mean I don't know if anyone ever did what we did, but we took the kite and Vidalia's ashes up to Hector's Hill. Tobias managed to run the kite real fast and real hard and after a few fitful starts the kite soared over the town.

Ruth pulled a little baggy from her purse with two white aspirins in it. She dropped the pills in her handbag, and then I put a teaspoon or so of the ashes into the bag and tied it on to the kite string. It was a real quiet, solemn occasion. We swiped away our tears as the little bag slowly crept its way up and up and up until you couldn't really tell what it was any longer.

"You go, Vidalia," Ruth called. "You keep going higher and higher because ain't nooooobody who deserves a better spot in heaven."

Winifred gathered her boys around her like a mama hen and she cried so hard it rivaled the rain that morning. Tobias cried even though I wasn't quite certain he understood what happened yet.

I don't know who got the idea first to soar the ashes. It might have come to all three of us at the same time. Ruth said it came direct from Vidalia, but Ruth was like that. In the long run it didn't matter. The important thing is that Vidalia soared with us that afternoon. Vidalia was with us for what was the second of many kite-flying escapades.

We stayed up on the hill until another rack of dark clouds moved in and Ruth said she saw lightning in the distance.

Ruth and I stopped by the café before going home. Winifred wasn't interested and claimed she needed to get the boys to nap and start sorting through her mother's belongings. I offered to help but she turned me down. "Nah, I kind of want the time alone."

The café was packed, but that wasn't unusual for an ordinary Sunday, let alone one as special as that one.

"I looked for you at church," I told Zeb as he poured coffee into my cup.

"Ah, I know, I just couldn't go. I decided to make some extra meatloaf and pie. Figured on a big crowd."

"You were right."

Zeb leaned close. "They're still talking about Agnes. They're saying she's lost her powers. Frank Sturgis even said she might have started praying against us, seeing as how Cora died and that Frank lost his temper and clocked Janeen with a loaf of bread. Even Jasper is worried that the Commies have taken over the town."

"This is preposterous. How could Agnes have caused all this?"

That was when Ruth moaned a little. "I—I didn't want to say anything but my stomach's been hurting."

"Stomachs hurt for lots of reasons, Ruth."

"I know, I know, I just was thinking that maybe my bleeding ulcer is coming back now that Agnes has lost her powers."

"Agnes hasn't lost any powers. She never had any to begin with," I said, but it was no use. Everybody had their minds made up.

I sipped coffee and tried to listen in on conversations, but I didn't hear too much until Studebaker and Boris walked in.

"We're glad you're here, Stu," called Nate Kincaid. "We want to know how you and Boris feel about this."

"About what?" He and Boris took a booth just vacated by the Flatbush family.

"Well, I reckon I'm thinking along the same lines as all of you. It's horrible what happened to Vidalia. Imagine having a killer living right here in Bright's Pond for nearly four months and nobody knowing it."

"That's just it," Nate said. "We never had a killer in town before. Not until that—that Hezekiah fella strode in and started charming his way around. How 'bout that Agnes letting it happen? She started the whole thing."

"Now hold on—" I said, while Zeb poured coffee. "Thank you, Zeb. You can't go blaming Agnes."

"But Agnes is the one we went to," Harriett said. She wiped some lingering lemon pie from Jasper's cheek. "We trusted her with everything, all our most private thoughts and needs."

"Even our lives—" Edie Tompkins said, "—our very lives and now—" She blubbered into a napkin and blew her nose so loud it sounded like a train had pulled into town. "Now Vi . . . Vi . . ."

Fred took her arm. "Come on, honey, let's get home."

"I want to go past her house," Edie said. "There weren't no viewing, so I'd at least like to walk past her house and pay my proper respects."

"Sure, honey, come on now."

Stu spied me and invited me to join him and Boris, who was as tight-lipped that day as I had ever seen him.

"He wants us to sit with them," I told Ruth.

"That's fine, but my stomach is not feeling good at all, not good at all."

"Come on, Ruth, you're fine. You come home with me."

Zeb wrapped Ruth's pie and some for Agnes and then we joined Stu and Boris for a little while. Boris clicked his tongue a few times and grumbled about the cost of the road sign, while Stu told folks to simmer down and stop blaming Agnes.

When I got up to leave, Stu took my hand. "You tell Agnes I ain't angry at her, okay, Griselda?" He looked into my eyes. "She couldn't know that Hezekiah was a—killer. She couldn't. Could she?"

25

I half expected to see an angry mob armed with torches and pitchforks out in front of the house, but it was eerily quiet and dark when Ruth and I got there. The bottom-heavy clouds had gotten darker, and I heard thunder rolling over the mountains. Rain would start soon.

"I hate leaving Agnes alone for so long, Ruth, but I had no choice."

"Well, that's right, Griselda. You had to go to the after-church service, and we had to fly the kite and go to the café. It was only proper."

"I know you're right, but I still feel so bad about leaving her."

Ruth stopped me just as my foot landed on the porch. "Today was Vidalia's day. Agnes knows that."

I brushed the little sparrow on our door, a cold and constant reminder of what she used to represent to so many who grieved as they passed through our door. They knew my daddy would take good care of their loved one. *The Shoops Local* even did a feature story on Daddy and the Sparrow Funeral Home a couple of years before the train wreck. They said people used to talk about how they'd turn the little Sparrow and hear sweet chimes like heaven was behind the doors.

I swallowed hard when I thought of Vidalia's body getting burned to ashes. Winifred said it was her desire, but it didn't sit well with me. I remember from when I was child how folks appreciated being able to touch their loved one or slip a note into their pocket like I did when my daddy died. I put his fishing license and a picture of us in the rowboat into his breast pocket. Viewings certainly never mattered to the deceased but they meant an awful lot to those who mourned.

"I'm home, Agnes," I called from the entryway. "Ruth is with me. We brought pie."

Ruth and I stopped near the radiator and removed our coats and rain boots and Ruth shook out her plastic scarf.

"Is she in there?" Ruth said. "I didn't hear her say anything."

"Of course she's in there, Ruth. What do you think, she got up and went out for the day?"

"Now don't go getting all in a snit, Griselda."

"I'm sorry. You go see her. I want to change my clothes."

"Sure. Maybe I can bring her some pie and tea."

"That's a good idea. Just don't tell her that the people are talking about her like it's her fault that Vidalia—" I took a breath. "I'm gonna wait for it to all blow over."

"Oh, I won't, Griselda, you can count on me."

I started up the steps and felt an odd relief when I heard Agnes's bed springs creak.

Arthur met me in my room. A bloody mouse hung out of his mouth. He dropped it at my feet. I opened the window and tossed it to the crows. They swooped from the trees, and I watched as two fought over the tiny carcass.

"I hate those birds, Arthur. They've got no respect for the dead." Rain started again as I changed out of my Sunday clothes.

"More rain, Artie. The backyard will probably flood." Thunder rumbled directly overhead. It sounded like galvanized trash cans getting blown down the street in a windstorm. "Is there anything left to do? Hezekiah's been caught, and Winifred is getting ready to leave and Vidalia—well, she'll be going to Detroit with Winifred."

I sat on the edge of my bed and pulled on a pair of white sweat socks, the long, tube kind with no seams. Then I cried until my stomach hurt.

By the time I got back downstairs, Ruth had told Agnes all about the kite-flying ceremony.

"And she went up and up and up and—"

"No kidding?" Agnes said.

"She just soared to heaven," Ruth said. "She soared. Oh, that sister-in-law of mine will never believe it when I tell her."

"Why are you gonna tell Vera?" I asked.

"I thought she might mention it on her radio show, seeing as how Vidalia was one of the best neighbors this town has ever known, except you, of course, Agnes. I don't care what folks are saying right now." Ruth waved her hand like she was swatting a fly. "I just don't care."

"What?" Agnes said. "What are folks saying?"

"Ruth, I told you not to say anything," I said.

Ruth patted Agnes's hand. "Oh, those bumpkins down at the café are saying it's all your fault for sending Hezekiah to Vidalia's when he first came to town. They're saying Vidalia would still be alive if it weren't for you. They're saying you lost your powers and God ain't gonna answer your prayers anymore, they're saying—"

I watched a blush start at Agnes's neck and then creep into her cheeks. "My fault?"

"It's not as bad as all that, Agnes," I said. "People are just upset over what happened to Vidalia."

Agnes sent Ruth for more pie.

"But what if they're right, Griselda. What if it is my fault?"

"That's nonsense." The doorbell chimed. "Now who could that be?"

"Only one way to find out," Agnes said.

Studebaker stood on the porch, looking like he had lost his best friend.

"You won't believe this, Griselda," he said. "All those folks down at the café said they don't want the sign anymore, they don't want people coming to town looking for Agnes. They're afraid she might invite another killer in."

"You're right. I don't believe it." My heart sped a little at the thought of so much hatred directed toward my sister.

"Well, you'll have to take the sign down, Stu. Maybe that will stop some of this lunacy."

Studebaker looked at me like I had just sold him to gypsies. "But, Griselda, the sign means everything."

"Oh, Stu, let's just give this some time. I'm sure in a few days things will get back to normal and that silly old sign will still be there and people will still bring their troubles to Agnes."

"Do you really think so?"

"Yes. I really think so. Now go on home and stop worrying."

"I'll tell you this. I'm driving on out there, and I'm going to park right next to it. If anybody tries to take it down—they'll have to go through me."

Stu took off toward the interstate, and he spent the entire night out there guarding that sign even though nobody came along to tear it down.

I told Agnes what Stu said. "I don't care if they take that silly old sign down and smash my statue to a million pieces."

"Smash the statue?" Ruth said. "Don't you think this is getting out of hand?"

"Of course it is," I said. "They're feeling out of sorts over this."

"Like they lost trust," Agnes said. She pushed her pie away.

All of a sudden, Ruth decided she had to get home to Russell. He didn't like being home alone at night and, after all, she "hardly saw him all day."

"I'll see you tomorrow," I said from the porch. "I'll be home all day. I'm closing the library."

"Okay, Griselda, good night now."

I watched until Ruth disappeared around a corner.

The next morning I decided to tune into Rassie Harper's show. I told Ruth not to tell Vera Krug anything. But telling Ruth to keep a secret was like asking Al Capone to stay out of Eugene's roses. I parked up top of Hector Street like I usually did, even though I could have listened at home with Agnes.

"There's sad news out of Bright's Pond," Rassie said, "and here to tell you all about it is that winsome woman of the airwaves, the original newsy neighbor herself, Vera Krug, with your Neighborly News."

Canned applause sounded over the airwaves.

"Good newsy morning, you all," Vera said. "And I do hope it's a good morning. Now, I know you folks down in Bright's Pond are waking up to some sadness after what happened to your own good neighbor Vidalia Whitaker last week."

Rassie broke in, "But before we can get to that, we need to break for a station spot from my good friends at Hal's King of Burgers."

I listened to thirty seconds as the King of Burgers hollered about how tasty his burgers were until Vera came back on.

"For those of you who don't know, Vidalia Whitaker was brutally murdered in her own home—stabbed to death by one Hezekiah Branch. He was that man she took in. Nothing but a street person, a hobo, a murderer."

Canned sounds of shock exploded.

"Now cut that out, Rassie," Vera said. "This is a sad moment for Bright's Pond. No one ever got murdered down there before this, and they're saying it happened on account of that fat woman, Agnes Sparrow."

"The miracle worker?" Rassie said.

"The very same. Folks in town are saying that Agnes invited the murderer to stay at Vidalia Whitaker's boarding house and that she, being a good friend to God and all, should have known. God should have told her he was a bad man."

"Well, that makes sense."

"Sure does, Rassie. Makes lots of sense to me. My sister-in-law Ruth Knickerbocker says the people in town are so upset they're planning on taking that new sign down—the one out on the interstate that says Welcome to Bright's Pond—Home of Agnes Sparrow."

"Oh, right, the one they made such a fuss over. The one that came to town with that great big mistake."

"That's right. Now they're gonna take it down."

"Can't say that I blame them none," Rassie said. "About time those folks learned the truth about that woman. She ain't no better than me and you. She is not a miracle worker."

"So true, Rassie, but maybe we should have a moment of silence for Vidalia Whitaker before moving on to other news."

The airwaves went silent for a minute. I dropped the gearshift into drive and headed to Vidalia's house. A taxicab was parked in the driveway, and the driver was loading suitcases into the trunk.

"I would have driven you to the train station, Winnie," I said.

"I know that, Griselda, but under the circumstances, I think it's best we just go, quiet like. I'll be back in a month or so." She helped the two little ones into the backseat and then grabbed onto Tobias's hand before he could sprint away. "I left the electric on and the phone. We'll probably need it when we come back to—to pack things up."

My friend looked so sad standing there holding a box marked "Mom's pictures." The driver offered to help, but she said, "No, I'll carry them."

I reached out to hug her. "I am sorry, Winnie. Agnes is too."

"Well, she should be, don't you think?"

I pulled away and opened the car door. I waved as they backed down the driveway and waited until the car was out of sight.

The Bright's Pond Savings and Loan sat on the corner of Fifth and Filbert Streets. It was the only bank in town. The chief teller, Mavis Turnbell, had her nose in everybody's finances. She knew how much money everybody in town with an account had, who they wrote checks to, and how much money they made, including me and Agnes. Agnes received a regular check from the government, considering she couldn't work, and we were saving the money in a nice little nest egg.

We had talked on several occasions that the day might come when Agnes would have to go to Greenbrier, especially if her breathing got bad or her heart condition grew worse and she needed round-the-clock help.

I needed to cash a check for groceries. Mavis took it and stuffed a small red and blue envelope with the green bills.

"Well," she said. "I expected Vidalia's daughter this morning to come and close out her account. Vidalia saved up a pretty penny. I'd say her daughter is gonna be mighty pleased—if it all converts to her, you know what I mean."

Mavis was a tall, gangly woman with a face that looked like an axe head when she stood sideways.

"Winifred left already to go back to Detroit. She and her husband will be back in a month or so. I'm sure she'll settle matters then."

"That's good enough, Griselda. I can't imagine what she must be going through. Can you? Imagine your Mama getting stabbed by some hoodlum."

I shoved the envelope in my pants pocket.

"Thank you, Mavis."

"Well, you just tell Agnes I'm sorry for her, too. It must be terrible to have God take away her miracle-working ability like that."

"I'll tell her."

The sentiment at the grocery store was not much better. Every person I bumped into had something to say about Agnes.

Hazel Flatbush was squeezing a head of lettuce. I parked my cart near hers as I picked a bunch of bananas and then eyed the apples.

"Oh, Griselda," she said, "I was supposed to see Agnes today but I can't make it. Would you be a dear and tell her?"

I smiled.

Hazel pushed her cart down the aisle to the loose potatoes. I picked up my pace and snagged three Empire apples, a bag of carrots, and a large stalk of celery even though I only needed a small one.

As I rounded the corner to the cereal aisle I saw Janeen yakking to Sylvia Spiney. I grabbed a box of Rice Krispies, tossed them in the cart, and sailed right by them. "Oh, Griselda," Janeen called, "how are you?"

"I'm fine, Janeen, how are you?" I nodded to Sylvia.

"I suppose I'm all right . . . considering."

"Considering Agnes, I suppose."

She ignored my comment. "My sister called last night. Her rat of a husband has been put in jail and she's decided to stay in North Carolina and not come here."

"I'm sorry to hear that. Maybe she just wants to be near her husband and work things out."

She harrumphed. "No, that can't be it. I asked Agnes to pray that she would come here and now—well now she isn't."

"I'm sorry, but I'm in a bit of a hurry."

I finished my shopping, but I got an earful from several other people, including Stella Gordon at the five-and-ten-cent store.

"I think it's just terrible what folks are saying about your sister." She dropped a pound of butter into her cart. "How can they blame her for what happened? It ain't like she told that Hezekiah fellow to go and kill Vidalia." She checked a box of eggs for cracks. "Now I personally never went to Agnes for prayers or miracles. I don't believe in all that mumbo jumbo, but I got to say, Griselda, if I did, I wouldn't let this keep me away." She examined a tube of Oscar Meyer liverwurst, "My husband loves this stuff. Can't stand it myself but to each his own, you know what I mean?"

"Yes, Stella, yes I do, and thank you for what you said about Agnes."

She tipped her cowgirl hat. "Sure thing, buckaroo. Any old gal can make a mistake—even one with close ties to the Maker." Then she winked and went on her way.

Ruby Fink checked my groceries without saying a single word until I pulled out my money to pay her. "Folks is scared, Griselda, real scared. That Eugene was just in here a while ago. Said the sky was falling. Told us all to repent of ever going to see Agnes."

My heart sank right down into my shoes as she spoke

"Called her a she-devil," Ruby continued. "Folks is scared. It's like they don't even trust each other anymore. Darwin told me not to take any checks for a while, just in case it's true about a curse befalling Bright's Pond."

Darwin Crump owned the Bright's Pond Piggly Wiggly, a satellite of the big one down in Shoops. Crump was a strange little man with crooked teeth, gray hair, bushy black eyebrows, and a chin the size of a piece of toast. He was one of Agnes's most vocal tormentors as a child, and as far as I knew, he never grew out of it.

The drive home felt long and lonely. The town looked lonely. People were out and about as the day had turned bright and warm. Fred Haskell's plumbing truck was parked out front of Studebaker's house, and Grace Harkness was sweeping the street along the front of her property, while the Orkin man sprayed around the foundation. She wasn't taking chances that year. Grace hated those tiny ants that invaded nearly every property in town the minute the temperature rose past fifty. There was nothing out of the ordinary, yet there was something in the air—a sense that life had changed.

26

Four days had passed and not a single soul came to Agnes for prayer, not even Studebaker or Hazel Flatbush, who used to come at least once a week. She always had something to gripe or complain about—a troublesome bunion, ornery child, her husband's bad breath. Hazel brought it all to Agnes.

Stu surprised me with his silence, but I think he was just so worried over the sign coming down he didn't have time for anything else in his brain.

I saw Harriett pass by the window once or twice. She would stop and stare, like she was trying to make a decision. but then she'd walk off.

Janeen Sturgis and Sheila Spiney behaved the same way. They would pass by, stop, stare, and then run off like a swarm of wasps chased them.

"Look at that," Agnes said. "What's wrong with them? They think God went out of business on account of Hezekiah Branch?"

The only real visitor we had all week was Mildred Blessing. She stopped by to tell us that Hezekiah had been sent back to Philadelphia to face even more charges. It seemed Vidalia was not his first victim.

"He'll be in the big house a good long time," Mildred said. "Won't have to worry about him showing his ugly mug in our town ever again."

Agnes squirmed in her bed and said, "I still can't believe it sometimes, though. He seemed like such a nice, quiet man."

"They're the ones you have to watch out for," Mildred said.

By Friday Agnes had grown quiet, and her prayer book hadn't moved from its place on her table.

"You still going to pray for those folks?" I pointed to her book.

"I got to, Griselda. I made a promise. It's real hard right now, though. I feel like a parched desert inside. And every day I don't pray I feel more and more dry. It's a terrible cycle."

"You don't have to stay on that merry-go-round, Agnes. You can stop praying for them—at least like you do, with all the pens and books and people coming around."

Agnes pushed scrambled eggs around on her plate and then just about inhaled a Jimmy Dean sausage patty. "But I got to keep praying." She swallowed. "It's what I do."

I finished the last of my eggs. "They'll come around, Agnes. Try not to worry. The people will come to understand that you didn't cause Vidalia's death."

Agnes started to breathe hard and reached for her inhaler. After two puffs she tossed it across the room. "That's just it, maybe I am responsible."

I retrieved her medicine and set it on her prayer book. I sat down on Agnes's bed. For that second I didn't care that the shift in the mattress always made her wince. "What in tarnation are you saying, Agnes? You couldn't have known what was in Hezekiah's mind. He's a sick man."

Agnes puckered her lips and looked at me—hard. "But I think he knew something about me."

"Yeah, he knew you were the miracle worker. That's all."

"No, it isn't. He knew the day he found that sweater and those bloody shoes." I moved to the rocking chair. "They were mine, Griselda, and I think he knew it."

"Yours?" My heart sped like a trip hammer.

"He was right. It wasn't chocolate sauce all over that sweater."

My brain reeled. "Hold on. I can't hear this now. I'm going to make us coffee, and then we'll discuss whatever is on your mind."

"Suit yourself, Griselda, but coffee won't change the truth."

I stood in the kitchen while the coffee brewed, actually a veiled ploy to get away and collect myself. I certainly didn't need coffee. But I made it anyway and set a pot and two cups on a metal tray decorated with an old Pepsi Cola advertisement.

"Now, tell me about the sweater and what it has to do with Vidalia or Hezekiah." I placed the tray on Agnes's table like I normally did when we were having ordinary conversations.

"The sweater—like I already told you. It's stained with blood. Clarence Pepper's blood." Her usually high voice squeaked like a mouse had gotten caught in her throat.

"Clarence Pepper?" The name meant nothing to me. "Who is he?"

"A boy." Agnes's hand shook as she brought the coffee to her lips. "A boy I—I—"

"You what?"

Agnes dropped her cup onto the bedside table. "Killed, Griselda! I killed Clarence Pepper." She started coughing and a bright blush filled her cheeks.

"Oh, come on," I said, "don't say things like that."

"It's the truth. I just never told anyone—not one breathing, living soul. No one."

I grabbed a towel and sopped up the coffee as best I could. "You'll have to get out so I can change the sheets. It splashed all over."

"Griselda, you aren't listening. I just told you I killed that boy." She sucked in air. "We were just kids, you know? I was on my way home from school and went across Hector's Hill. Clarence was there. He started making fun of me, calling me names."

"I tried to run, Griselda, but you know how hard it was for me. He ran next to me and kept saying, 'Look at me, I'm a cowboy leading the cows across the prairie.'"

"Oh, Agnes, that's awful." Tears welled in my eyes as I listened to her voice rising higher and higher, her face getting redder and redder. All I could do was sit there and let her talk. It was like a two-ton truck was parked on my chest. I couldn't move, and I could hardly breathe.

"All of a sudden," she said. "I stopped running and—and I pushed him and he tripped and fell forward and hit his head on a jagged rock."

She covered her eyes with her hands like she wanted to blot out the image. "There was blood, Griselda, so much blood. I took off my sweater and tried to stop it but I couldn't. I got scared—"

My breathing was ragged.

"I didn't mean to kill him, Griselda. It was an accident. The boy died, but I didn't know until they brought him to Daddy."

"He was here?"

"Yes. His father brought him in the back of his station wagon. Found him up on Hector's Hill. I was up at my window—" she struggled for air "—when his daddy came to the door."

I put her oxygen mask over her mouth and nose. "Breathe. Just breathe a little."

Agnes grabbed my arm, and I slipped the clear mask off her face.

"I was up at my window, and I saw Mr. Pepper pull up. I wanted to tell him, but I couldn't."

I replaced the mask and watched it fog over as she breathed.

"Close your eyes. Just breathe." I patted her arm. But she ripped the mask off. "I got to tell you now, Griselda. I got to tell you the whole story, right now, before I lose my gumption."

I sat back in the rocker and white-knuckled the arms like I was clinging to a roller coaster.

"On the way home I saw the blood on my shoes, so I took them off and carried them, wrapped up in my sweater. I went straight to Daddy's workroom, and for a second or two, I wanted him to be there to catch me but . . . he wasn't."

"So you hid the clothes in that box."

"That's right. I saw the little box sitting there, and it was empty, so I stuffed everything inside, closed the lid, and hid it in that tiny room—been there ever since—well, until Hezekiah found it."

"Why didn't you tell anyone later that day when Daddy got home?"

"I couldn't. The more I thought about it, the more my stomach churned, and then I was too scared of what would happen to me."

"To you? You killed a boy, accident or not."

She choked back sobs.

"Maybe I should call Doc," I said.

Agnes grabbed my arm and squeezed me so tight I thought she might break my wrist.

"Stop it, Agnes, you're hurting me."

"I'm sorry, Griselda. Please don't call Doc. I'll be all right."

"You need to take one of those sedatives. You're about to give yourself a heart attack."

"That's why I was crying that day you ran out of church, Griselda, remember? I was crying because I . . . I killed another human being and for no good reason except that I'm fat and he called me a name."

I felt like a hundred bees had stung me, paralyzing my heart as I reached back to that day. Pastor Spahr had just prayed over the cracker and popped it in my mouth and swallowed when I looked at Agnes. Tears streamed down her fat face as she chewed and chewed.

"What are you doing?" I had asked. "Just swallow it."

I thought I might have to bang her on the back because she was having a dickens of a time getting that itty bitty piece of unsalted Premium cracker down her throat.

She just kept crying, and I saw Fred Haskell and Edie Tompkins who was, at that time, Edie Mattigan, covering their mouths and laughing at her. I thought I was about to cry myself they got me so riled. I thought I was going to cry or leap over the pews and pound them into a fine powder.

The elders passed the Concord grape juice, and I held mine waiting for the signal to drink, while Agnes continued to cry. I couldn't stand it another second. I put my tiny glass cup on the pew and climbed right over Agnes who was still sobbing, snorting back the tears and noises so as not to be noticed. I figured the whole church saw her. But interrupting Communion was just not done, it being a holy sacrament and all. Tears were just tears, even though I read in the Bible that God saved them.

Anyway, I ran out of the church. I ran down the parking lot and squatted behind a big boulder and got so angry at God and people I shoved my index finger down my throat and up came the cracker and two slices of scrapple and some oatmeal. My hands balled into fists and I pounded on that rock, cutting my skin and getting so bruised my mother made me see the Doc. I pounded and pounded and told God right then and there that he shouldn't have made my sister so fat. I told him he was a terrible God and since he didn't care about her, I would have to be the one who cared. That was the day I decided to spend my whole life taking care of my sister.

"I remember that day," I said. "I thought you were crying on account of all the teasing that went on." The doorbell rang. "Oh, great. Perfect timing, whoever it is."

"You better get it. Nobody'll believe we aren't at home."

It was Ruth. She stood on the porch wearing a thin, cotton coat over a dress the color of light brown sugar and the saddest frown I had ever seen.

"Ruth? What's the matter?" I took a step outside and closed the door behind me trying not to show how shaken I was.

"Griselda, I am just so sad over the way this town is treating Agnes. I was sitting at my house watching Russell swing on his tiny bird swing, you know the one, it's pink—"

"Ruth, I've seen Russell's swing."

"Anyway, watching Russell swing back and forth in his cage made me think about Agnes, and I had to come see her. It can't be her fault, can it? It just can't."

"No, of course not. Things are happening because they are. Agnes has no control over this town—for good or for bad."

"Then how come Vidalia got killed and the Sturgises are having so many fights? Babette is crying over at the café right this very minute, and Cora went and died. Some folks are even saying it was Agnes's fault the dang fool sign was made wrong to begin with."

"We're just going through a bad patch right now. We all are—the whole town. Even Agnes."

Ruth pulled her coat tight around her neck as a light gust of wind whipped across the porch. "Can we go inside, Griselda? It's a little chilly, and I feel like I need to see Agnes."

"Maybe now isn't the right time. Agnes is resting."

"Please? I'll wait. I'll make coffee and Cora's lemon squares while we wait for her to wake up."

At that moment I had the urge to tell Ruth what Agnes had done, but I couldn't betray her. I forced my tears deep inside before they spilled over.

"What's the matter, Griselda? You look a fright. Still upset over Vidalia?"

"No, it's . . . it's something else."

"Then what you need is lemon squares. Let me in, and I'll whip up a batch."

"Okay, if we sneak into the kitchen without going to her room. I don't want to disturb her."

I opened the door as quietly as possible and closed it with a slight click. Ruth hung her coat on the hook near the radiator. "I'll tiptoe," she whispered.

We took one step. "Who is it?" Agnes called.

"Oh, Agnes, it's me, Ruth. I've been so worried about you, dear. How are you?"

Ruth rushed into the viewing room and took hold of Agnes's hand faster than a hungry trout bites on a cool Spring morning. "I just hate the way everyone in town is saying you lost the gift, that God stopped answering your prayers, and we're all doomed like sitting ducks."

"Ruth, Ruth. Nobody is doomed. Well, except maybe me."

"You? Oh, Agnes don't say such a thing."

"Yes, Agnes," I said. "Stop talking nonsense." I shook my head and widened my eyes, hoping she'd get the thought I was desperate to convey: *Don't tell Ruth about Clarence Pepper!* But sometimes, Agnes could be tenacious as a snapping turtle. Once she got hold of something she never let go.

"Ruth, why don't you show me how to make Cora's lemon squares?" I asked. "I didn't know she gave the recipe to anyone. Thought is was an old family secret."

"All right, Griselda. Agnes, you do look a mite tired. We'll have a long visit just as soon as we put the lemon squares into the oven."

Ruth and I assembled the necessary ingredients except the main one—lemons.

"That's weird," I said. "There's always a loose lemon in the fridge."

"Guess you'll need to go to the store and buy one or two and maybe some more half and half. This carton is about empty."

Telling Ruth I had to fetch my purse, I whispered to Agnes not to tell Ruth about Clarence while I was gone. "Please? Ruth doesn't need to know this. It will only make her sadder."

"You might be right." She sighed and popped a few M&Ms into her mouth.

The market was empty, except for Eugene Shrapnel, who was busy squeezing the life out of the tomatoes. From a distance and maybe because he didn't see me, Eugene looked different. Oh, he was still ugly with that bulbous nose and hunched back. But for a moment he was like any other human being.

I pushed my cart past him and the illusion burst.

"Griselda," he said. "I told you this would happen if folks kept thinking your sister is God. I told you and now Vidalia, probably the only truly kind and generous person in this town, is dead on account of Agnes inviting that monster into our midst."

I ignored him and pushed on even though I could have used some bananas.

"It's only the beginning. Only the beginning," Eugene called. "Repent while you still can." Muttering, he slipped three tomatoes into a brown paper bag.

I picked out two lemons and hurried through the rest of my shopping. The longer I took the more stuff I thought I should buy: shampoo and toilet paper, laundry soap and corn flakes.

Ruby didn't say a word to me as she checked my groceries. She carried on an insipid conversation about what was happening in the make-believe world of Pine Valley on the soap opera with her check-out neighbor, Sadie Fromme.

When I got back to the house it was no surprise that I found Ruth and Agnes deep in conversation about Clarence Pepper and what Agnes did all those years ago.

"Well, it seems to me," Ruth said, "the worst thing you done was keep it a secret. I mean how could you do that?"

"I was just a kid and I was mighty scared of going to jail."

I hurried into the kitchen and plopped the grocery bags on the table before I joined them. "Agnes, I thought we weren't going to tell anyone."

"Now, how can you expect that, Griselda?" Ruth said. "I'm amazed she's sat on it this long. My goodness gracious, that must of been tough."

The idea of making lemon squares had long passed, and the three of us spent a good part of the day discussing what Agnes did to Clarence Pepper. I was able to get them to agree that no one else needed to know; it would bring even more unwanted attention to Bright's Pond and Agnes.

All of a sudden, Ruth looked like she had an idea. "I hate to say this, but I think I might have said that Hezekiah was going to stir up trouble."

"You said nothing of the sort," Agnes said.

"I might have thought it."

"Should you contact the boy's parents?" I asked. "I mean, I'd want to know." I felt my forehead wrinkle. "At least I think I would."

"Heavens, no," Ruth said. "Those folks think their son's death was the result of a simple boyhood accident. You want them to know he died because he made fun of Agnes?"

"That's right," Agnes said. "They shouldn't have to live with that. They're older now, anyway. It wouldn't be a good idea."

Ruth swallowed a piece of cookie she plucked from Agnes's table. "I remember that day now. You never saw a more broken-up mother than Lily Pepper. But I have to say, now that I think about it, that boy was one mean child. I remember the way he taunted you, Agnes."

I didn't remember, not then. I kept trying to picture Clarence Pepper, but I guess he was older than me so I didn't see him much. I watched Agnes, while Ruth did her best to put a bright polish on what happened so many years ago. It was like watching someone receive unwanted news. Agnes played with her hands, locking and unlocking her fingers, averting her eyes until she couldn't hear anymore.

"But I killed him—accident or no." She knocked over an empty, plastic tumbler. It bounced on the floor and stopped when it rolled against her slipper. "He died because I pushed him."

"Well now, you didn't mean to, did you Agnes?" Ruth could not find her off button that day. "Did you ever once say to yourself, I'm going to kill him?"

"No, but—"

"That's the difference in my book. I say we let it go." Ruth smiled and patted Agnes's hand. "Let it fade and let Agnes get back to her normal self. It was good to get it out, though, wasn't it, dear?" She patted Agnes's hand and wiped stray hairs off her pink face. "Let's make a pact like when we were kids."

"Oh, Ruth, don't be silly," I said. "We're not kids."

"I know that, but it'll still work. You'll see. A pact is binding whether you're ten or forty."

Ruth put her hand out and waited. Agnes sighed and placed hers on top and I finally joined them after a few seconds of consideration.

"Now," Ruth said, "repeat after me. I, state your name, solemnly swear to keep this secret for the rest of my life."

It might sound silly for three grown women to make a pledge like that, but you know, there was comfort in the moment and something perhaps even sacred about making a pact. I had to snuff back tears as we lingered a moment with our hands touching, feeling the promise pass between us.

Ruth went ahead and made the lemon squares before she left. "Now let them cool a while. Lemon squares are always better cold. More zing."

She kissed Agnes's cheek. "Don't you worry, dear. No one has to know."

Agnes ate five or six lemon squares before she said another word about what happened to Clarence Pepper. "I just didn't know what to do, Griselda. I've never been so scared in all my life. Can you really blame me for not telling?"

"But, Agnes—"

"But what?"

"Maybe you should have at least told Daddy and let him figure out what to do."

She looked out the window and ignored my question. "I kept telling myself it would look brighter in the morning. And every morning that God gave me was brighter, Griselda. It was like what happened got further and further away, and I started praying harder and harder and that was when things started to happen."

"You mean like miracles and stuff."

"Not exactly. It was small things at first. I figured that was God's way of setting it up so the town got blessed on account of me and what I did. It was a way of paying my debt, I suppose."

My brain reeled as she spoke. I couldn't get past the fact that my sister, provoked or not, was responsible for the death of another human being. "I still think you needed to tell someone. I can't for the life of me figure how you kept it quiet all these years and especially—"

Agnes yanked on her nightgown. "Darn fool thing is always getting caught between my knees. "Maybe I should switch to sweat pants."

"Especially me. I've been taking care of you all these years, day after day, night after night, and you never told me. And I can't find pants big enough, not even in Foster's Big and Tall Shop for Men."

Agnes clicked on the TV. "Maybe I'll watch a little before I turn in."

"Agnes, you can't ignore this or me."

"I'm not doing that. I'm getting tired is all, and Doc doesn't want me overexerting myself."

I stood there for a good three minutes, staring at Agnes while she picked at lemon squares and watched *Columbo*. I wish I could say what I was thinking. It was probably a mixture of disbelief and sadness that my sister had imprisoned herself for her crime. I managed to wash some dirty dishes, but the whole time I was getting angrier and angrier at my sister. After awhile, I thought I would pop. Instead, I told Agnes I was going down to the Full Moon for a while.

"Griselda, don't leave me here all alone. Not at night."

"I won't be that far away. Call the café if something happens."

"You're mad at me."

"Mad? Of course I am, Agnes. You lied to me. You lied to everyone."

Zeb was still inside the café closing up for the night. I rapped on the door and waved when he saw me.

"Griselda, it's a little late."

"I know. I just needed a place to sit for a spell."

"I might have some coffee left, and how about a piece of pie?"

"No, thanks, Zeb. I just want to sit."

"Suit yourself. I need to finish up in the kitchen. They're collecting the grease tomorrow morning."

Zeb swung through the skinny door with the round window, and tears welled up in my eyes.

"Zeb," I called. "Can you come out here?"

"Sure, Grizzy, what is it?" He came through the door wiping his hands on his apron.

"I . . . I need to tell you something that . . . that, ah, I had a good time at the movie and maybe we could do it again."

Zeb smiled into my eyes. "Sure, sure we could."

323

27

Agnes was asleep when I got home that night. I pulled her blanket up, and she stirred a little but never opened her eyes. I confess that I was glad she didn't. The last thing I wanted was to discuss Clarence Pepper. I checked the locks, turned off the lights, and fell into bed with a thud. Arthur leaped from the sill onto my stomach.

I reached for the lamp and noticed the picture of my parents I had kept on the table for years—a picture I saw every day but rarely noticed. They were so young in the picture; it was taken before I was born. My father had just bought the house and started his business.

He would have understood. But Agnes never gave him the chance. Imagine embalming the body of a boy your own daughter killed. I lay there listening to Arthur's gentle purr against my stomach. It was like the soft hum of distant bees. It changed from a low, raspy purr to a high trill, and then it finally wound down as Arthur fell asleep.

I must have fallen asleep with him because the next thing I remembered was Agnes calling out to me.

"Griselda, I got to get to the bathroom. Griselda!"

I tossed Arthur onto the floor. "She needs me." A loud sigh escaped from my chest.

After a quick stop at my own bathroom I helped Agnes, like I always did, one painful, slow step at a time.

When I took her back to bed she said, "I'm glad I told you."

"Me, too, I guess. I just wish you had told me sooner."

"Why?" Agnes wiped her nose with the back of her hand.

My forehead wrinkled. "Why? I don't know. It would have made a difference, that's all. Maybe I could have helped."

Agnes lay back. Arthur leaped onto her stomach and pawed at her nightgown for a second or two and then curled into a puddle.

"I've been thinking," Agnes said, stroking Arthur's neck, "that maybe the reason all this stuff is happening is because I haven't been praying enough. I haven't been praying hard enough for the people all these years."

"What? You pray all the time, more than anyone I know, including Pastor Speedwell. I doubt you can pray any harder."

"But I've been thinking that maybe that's why Hezekiah tricked me. I wasn't praying enough. I had been getting tired before he came. Remember, Griselda?"

"Agnes, it's not your fault."

"Well, I'll tell you this, I am not going to stop my prayers. I'm going to step them up a bit. I swear to you, Griselda, I will pray for each and every member of this community by name, every day, all day if need be. I only wish I could get on my knees."

"Agnes, you don't have to do that."

"I do. That's where you're wrong. I really do."

After breakfast, I left Agnes with her notebooks. She asked for the older, full ones. "I want to go over them again. See how God has blessed the folks, you know? It's good to do that now and again, don't you think? Maybe I forgot about someone I had no business forgetting."

There was something desperate in her voice.

"Should I open the curtains?"

"Of course. It's supposed to be a delightful day full of sunshine, no rain. But you didn't answer me. Don't you think it's a good idea to look at the many ways God has blessed our town and for me to check on folks?"

She winced as I pulled the drapes open and a bright shot of sunlight burst through the glass. The sky was that perfect spring blue—cerulean—just the deepest sky blue imaginable. I stood a moment and caught a glimpse of Pastor Speedwell making his way into the church. I don't think a day has passed since he came to town that he hasn't gone to his office. I smiled when he stopped and touched the forsythia and looked into the dogwood tree where the Jesus pie plate dangled in the breeze. The sun glinted off of it like a searchlight.

"Pastor just went into the church," I said. "Ever think of talking to him?"

"About what?"

I turned around. "Agnes, you know perfectly well."

"I am not going to discuss it. I made my peace."

Even though it was Saturday I made the decision to open the library and took my time walking there. The town was already busy as folks decided to take advantage of the bright, warm morning.

"Hey, Griselda," called Studebaker. He was across the street getting his mail. "Beautiful day."

I waved. "Sure is."

Ivy was pulling weeds away from some shrubs in her front yard. I could hear Al Capone barking his fool head off in the backyard.

"Hello, Ivy. How are you?"

"Oh, hey, Griselda." She wiped hair away from her eyes with the back of her hand. "I hate weeds. They spring up so fast. Will you listen to that dog?"

"I hear him. He doesn't sound happy."

"Not in the least. But he'll be back to his old self once I get that lousy fence down."

"You're taking the fence down?"

"I can't abide it, Griselda. I can't live with a fence built by the man that killed my friend." She tossed a handful of tangled vines onto the pavement.

"You can't do it yourself, can you? That's a big job."

"Of course not. Fred and Stu and even Boris said they'd come by this afternoon."

She made me think about all the work Hezekiah had completed around my home—the pipes, the roof, how he cleaned out the basement so well. His fingerprints were all over the place and there was nothing I could do. Ivy was right to take the fence down. Bright's Pond needed no memorial.

"Good. Well, I better get to the library." I took a few steps and stopped.

"Say, Ivy, maybe Fred Haskell and Studebaker will build you a new one."

Ivy stood and wiped dirt from her red sweatshirt. "Nah, Al Capone was happier on the lam, you know?"

"I think Mildred was happier running after him too."

Ivy smiled and waved her little snippers. "The chase is on."

I switched on the library lights and turned up the heat. The building was cold and silent, and I felt chilled to the bone. Leaving my hat and coat on, I piled up all the mail that had accumulated on the floor by the door, started coffee, and shuffled through papers on my desk.

As I poured a cup, my eye caught sight of the microfiche machine. Two hours and a cup and a half later I pinpointed the day Clarence Pepper died. Well, it made the news the day after. It was just a bitty piece on page two of what was then called *The Bright's Pond Evening Gazette* with a tagline that read, *All you need to know.*

> May 22, 1947—Tragedy struck the Walter Pepper family up on Hector Hill when their boy, Clarence Pepper, was found dead at that location. Apparently, he had been running, tripped, and fell, hitting his head against a large, jagged rock. Doctor Sam Flaherty said the boy might have been saved if help had gotten there in time. The funeral will be Friday at eleven o'clock in the morning out of the Sparrow Funeral Home. All are invited.

The words, "gotten there in time" pounded in my brain. If only Agnes had told the truth, maybe Clarence would have lived.

I scanned a few more records and came across a larger story written the day after the funeral. It told in detail about how the family cried and how Clarence's school chums lined the street while family and friends carried his casket to the cemetery. Walter Pepper, his brother Simon, Doc Flaherty, who at the time was a brand-new doctor fresh from medical school, and a young Frank Sturgis were the pallbearers.

Then I remembered. I stayed with Agnes in her room and didn't attend the funeral. We played *Go to the Head of the Class*. I thought she refused to go to Clarence's funeral because she was worried about the other kids seeing her. They might make fun, or maybe the walk to the cemetery would have been too hard on her, a fat girl following the crowd, lagging behind a casket draped in the colorful quilt his mother made for him.

But all along she was hiding the truth. Maybe she was afraid she would have spilled the beans had she gone to the cemetery and watched his mama cry. My brain reeled as I read the report, and it spun even more when I heard the Doc's words ricochet around my skull, "gotten there in time." Doc's office was closer than our house. Even Agnes could have gotten there quickly.

B y two o'clock the day had grown warm and pleasant. I opened a window to let in fresh and usher out the stale, bookish air of the library. To stay busy I swept up the dust that tended to accumulate in the corners and along the baseboards. At three, Tohilda Best and the rest of the Society ladies rushed in. They were chattering like the finches in the trees outside. Tohilda shushed them.

"Oh, Griselda," she said, "you won't mind if we have an emergency meeting, will you?" She looked a fright, like she hadn't combed her hair in a day or so, but that wasn't unusual. Her dress was wrinkled, and a button was missing. "We just got word that one of the backwoods families is set to have themselves another mouth to feed, and the daddy ain't worked in three months. They've got four other younguns."

"Oh, no, go right ahead and have your meeting. Take your time. I can make coffee, if you'd like."

"That would be mighty kind of you," she said.

The women spread out around the periodical table and pulled out a small map that looked like it had been drawn in crayon on a paper sack in a hurry.

"Now, near as I can figure, the family lives here." Hazel Flatbush pointed to a spot on the map.

I left them to their plans and made coffee. I found a tray of cookies and brought them to the ladies. Hazel pulled one from the plastic tray.

"You have a good meeting now," I said. "I'll be at my desk if you need me."

"Thank you, Griselda," they said in concert.

"And to think, we gave that man new shoes." I heard Hazel say after I walked four steps.

"And socks," added Dot Handy. "We gave that man shoes and socks and then he went and—"

I felt my jaw clench. "Now, look," I said. I turned back to them. "There ain't no reason for you to be talking about Hezekiah and what he did. This town's got to get over it."

"Over it," Dot said. "It ain't easy getting over that big of a mountain, Griselda. That man killed one of our own. People don't forget that easy."

"Then I would appreciate it if you just don't talk about it here."

"Well," Hazel said, "we need to screen our recipients better in the future. I'll tell you that much."

When I got back to my desk I heard someone, not sure who, say, "Maybe Agnes should screen the people she prays for, you know."

There was a hush when I looked up. The ladies finished their plans and left in silence like they always did.

I strolled past Vidalia's house on my way home that afternoon. I lingered a moment and looked up at the tangerine curtains that still hung in Hezekiah's room. Once there slept the man who killed my friend. I imagined him lying on the bed with his hands behind his head, scheming and planning, stoking his courage or maybe his passion to kill. I wondered what finally made him snap.

Before she left, Winifred gave me the house keys in case someone needed to get inside or there was a problem. At the time I couldn't imagine a single reason why anyone would need to get in.

A breath of stale air, not warm cinnamon, hit me as I opened the door and went inside. I left the door ajar to let the fresh breeze clear out the stale.

I missed my friend so much I could hardly stand it. She should still have been there, baking sticky buns and brewing coffee and laughing and sticking up for folks the way she always did, helping the kids with their papers and smiling. No one in town was more willing to give of herself than Vidalia— even her home—which she gave so freely to Hezekiah. My eyes closed at the thought. Why, God?

There was no answer.

I went to the room where Ivy found her and stood over the stained carpet. It was a long, Persian-type runner full of bright colors and designs. The stain formed a large, awkward shape, almost like a silhouette of a fat, fluffy, dark sheep. Tears came. I swiped them away like mosquitoes on a humid night.

"Vidalia," I said. "I'm so sorry. Agnes didn't know what she was doing when she sent him here. She wanted to help."

I rolled up the rug, carried it to the basement, and set it against a paneled wall. Then I filled a bucket with hot water and detergent and scrubbed where Vidalia's blood had soaked through to her polished oak wood floor.

"It's supposed to be a secret, but Ruth, Agnes, and I made a pact. I guess I can tell you," I said as I scrubbed. "Agnes accidentally killed a young boy a long time ago, before you and Drayton even came to Bright's Pond. She didn't know what she was doing then, either. She kept it to herself until just yesterday. Imagine, keeping something like that all locked up inside for so many years."

After the floor sparkled again, I sat in Vidalia's kitchen, in the same place I always did when I visited. What would she say to me?

I stayed a few minutes and basked in the warmth of my friend's memory, and then I took a plate from the counter— the one she always used for sticky buns.

"I hope Winifred doesn't mind, Vidalia, but I'm taking this."

I closed curtains and took a bag of smelly trash outside. Standing at the bottom of the stairs, I contemplated snooping around the room where Hezekiah slept. Perhaps there would be a clue, a sign that he was about to fall off the deep end and kill Vidalia. Instead, I turned the key and heard it lock with a gentle click. I rested my forehead on the doorjamb a moment and listened to the sound of Vidalia's voice inside my head.

"Come on up here, Griselda. I just happened to make some sticky buns."

I clutched the empty plate to my chest and went home to Agnes.

I was late, and Agnes was hungry as usual.

"I've been waiting for you," she said. "I'm famished. Finished all of my M&Ms waiting for you to get home."

"I'm sorry. I made a stop on my way. I'll get your supper."

"What's that?" she pointed to the dish.

"I stopped by Vidalia's and saw it sitting there. It's . . . it's a memory."

"Now why did you go there? You're going to torture yourself doing that. You best remember Vidalia the way she was when she was alive."

"She was my friend, Agnes, and I miss her."

Never in my life had I felt so torn up over Agnes. On the surface she was the same fat sister I always had. But down inside, beneath that self-made prison of hers, was a woman that I didn't know anymore. I wondered if she had other secrets.

I went to the kitchen and surveyed the cabinets for a meal to make and finally settled on quick spaghetti.

"Pasta, okay?"

"I suppose so. Can you help me to the bathroom first?"

"Okay. Did you get there on your own today?"

"Twice. But it was a chore. I had to crawl part of the way and pull myself up onto the toilet."

"Guess we kind of got used to having help," I said.

After she was finished, Agnes pushed one leg after the other as she thrust her walker out in front. "You still mad at me?"

I helped her back to bed.

"Let's not talk about it, Agnes. What's done is done."

I put water on to boil and took care of Arthur. I never knew a cat that appreciated gloppy cat food the way he did. The smell was enough to knock me out sometimes—especially the glop with liver in it.

"How can you eat that?"

He looked at me with one eye while still chomping it down as if to inform me that he was not sharing with anyone.

"And you'll still go looking for a mouse for dessert."

As the water heated I gathered plates and glasses. I thought fruit would be good, but there were no cans in the cupboard. There were probably some Del Monte peaches on the shelf inside the cellar. Agnes liked Del Monte the best. She said the syrup they packed them in was tasty with just the right sweetness. My father built the shelves after an argument with Mama. She had complained that it didn't make sense for such a large house to have so little cabinet space.

Daddy hung three, dark shelves inside the basement door. He used wood from a couple of dilapidated caskets. Mama kept canned goods there and stopped complaining except for the one time when the top shelf came loose and all the cans rolled into the basement like rounds from a machine gun.

"See that," she had called down. "I told you not to use that wormy, old casket wood."

When I opened the door I noticed a light shining in the basement. "Look at that," I told Arthur. "I bet that light's been burning since Hezekiah was here last."

I walked down the stairs and into the tiny room he had been working in. When I reached for the tiny light chain, I saw the sweater and shoes still neatly arranged near the ammo box. The sight took my breath away. I picked up the articles and went tearing up the steps.

"Agnes, Agnes! He never burned this—this stuff."

I shoved the sweater and shoes near her face. "Look at this. He never burned them."

Agnes looked away. "Don't show me that anymore. It isn't my fault. I told you to check on it, didn't I?"

I threw the sweater on her bed and dropped the shoes near it. "Yes, it is Agnes. It's all your fault. If you hadn't lied about Clarence, Hezekiah would never have come to town."

I backed off and looked at her. Anger, the color of over-ripe tomatoes, filled up my chest so I almost couldn't breathe. "You should have told."

"I couldn't. I couldn't tell. I tried but—"

"But nothing. Did you ever read the news report about it?"

"I never knew one existed."

"I did. Today. It said that Clarence Pepper might have lived if help had gotten there in time."

Agnes looked away and struggled for a breath.

"Did you hear me?" I said. "How come you didn't go get Doc?"

Agnes's small eyes grew wide. They were two dark blue-berries. "I never thought to."

I grabbed her prayer book. "And now you're trying to make up for it by saving the town?"

"Not me, God. I never took the glory."

"I think you did, Agnes." Agnes blubbered like a little girl. "And you sentenced yourself for the murder of Clarence Pepper."

"Griselda, he said he burned—"

"You don't get it. He liked seeing them. That's why he kept this stuff and arranged it like a loving mother sets out her child's clothes." I shivered. "What you did made him powerful."

Agnes brought her chubby hands to her face. She hid her eyes, eyes that once only looked out to a world she wanted to save and protect, but now they were windows through which she needed to see the truth. The truth was painful.

After I fixed Agnes her dinner and propped up in bed with the *TV Guide* and her remote, I did the dishes and a couple loads of laundry—whites and towels. A headache crept from my temples into my shoulders and neck as I placed the last of the cups and saucers into the cabinet.

Two aspirins later I went to my room and sat on the edge of my bed feeling lonelier than I did after my parents died. Then I packed a small bag and stood near Agnes and waited for her to open her eyes.

"Griselda, why do you have your coat on?"

"Agnes, I have to leave." I blurted out my words fast and hard. "I can't stay here right now. I'll check in on you and probably get Ruth to drop in and help, but I need to leave, at least for a little while." I took a breath.

Something that resembled horror passed over her face. Her bottom lip trembled as she realized I was serious. "You can't go. How can you leave me? What if I need something?"

"Don't worry, Agnes. You'll get through this night. I might be back in the morning, I don't know. I just need a little space or—something. I need time to think this through."

While she watched with fear, I refilled her water pitcher and brought her two tuna sandwiches on white bread with a tall glass of iced tea. I made certain she had candy and the *TV Guide*.

"I think I'll go to Vidalia's," I said. "It's the only place where I won't have to answer a bunch of nosy questions."

"I can't believe this. You're really going?"

"Agnes, I have to, at least for tonight. Please try and understand."

"I understand I never should have told you about Clarence. I should have understood that you'd take it wrong and get all selfish about it."

Agnes and I had minor skirmishes over the years but they were short-lived. We always found a middle ground. But this time was different. This time I couldn't rise above the situation and move on.

"You have Vidalia's number. But please, Agnes, I need some time. Call Ruth if you need anything."

Then I gathered the blood-stained sweater with the mother-of-pearl buttons and the black shoes with the crushed heels and carried them to the backyard. I placed them gently into the center of the fire ring Hezekiah had made, poured a small amount of gasoline onto the stuff and set it ablaze in the chilly, spring air.

The smoke twirled and danced and disappeared in the star-filled sky while the flames devoured my sister's sweater and shoes. I waited until I was certain there was nothing left but ashes before dumping a bucket of water onto the smoldering pile.

The odor—ash, wool, burned hair—lingered as I walked away.

28

Cuddling Arthur in my arms, I stood on Vidalia's front porch and shook off the idea that I was trespassing. I knew she would understand that I needed to get away from Agnes and sort things out. She and Jesus were probably eating sticky buns and talking about it right about now. Even the Lord had to get away from that sorry, thick-headed bunch of disciples every once in a while. Sometimes he just needed to spend some time with his father.

Yes, that's how I justified leaving Agnes. I needed time, a break, peace. I deserved that much, didn't I?

Finally, I let myself in and passed the room where Vidalia had died.

"I'm glad I came by earlier and cleaned it up." I scratched Arthur's ears and dropped him. He made himself at home and found a comfy spot stretched out across the top of an overstuffed, striped chair.

"Don't get too used to it, Artie, we aren't staying forever, only until I can figure things out. Think of it as our time in the whale, you know?"

The clock on Vidalia's mantle, an ornately carved oak piece from the 19th century, struck nine at the exact moment the telephone rang.

"Agnes. I'm not gone an hour yet and she's calling."

"Hello?" I braced myself to hear Agnes complaining and begging me to come home. But it wasn't her. It was Ruth chirping away on the other end.

"Oh, Griselda, it's you. I saw the light go on at Vidalia's house and I got so scared I about jumped out of my slippers." She snorted a laugh. "Of course, I didn't believe it was Vidalia's ghost or anything. I thought someone might have broken in. You know, what with all that's going on in town."

"Slow down, Ruth. Take a breath or two. There's nothing to worry about."

"Then why are you there so late at night?"

I hesitated. "I just needed a place to stay for a day or so. A quiet place."

"Well, you could of stayed here, you know."

"Thanks, but I needed a place where I could be alone and think things through."

Ruth was silent. I waited and waited and then the doorbell rang. It was Ruth standing on Vidalia's porch in her terry robe and fuzzy slippers. She was panting so hard it made me laugh.

"I didn't know you could run that fast."

She caught her breath. "Now, why in heaven's name are you here?" She had a tone.

"I told you, I needed some peace."

She pushed past me and stood in the entryway, looking around like she had just stumbled into a cemetery. "Creepy, isn't it?"

"No, it doesn't rattle me. I guess growing up in a funeral home helps."

"Well, it rattles me, that's for sure. I haven't been in here since . . . since you know . . . since before Vidalia died." She crossed herself. Ruth occasionally crossed herself even though she wasn't Catholic.

"How come you do that?"

"What?"

"Cross yourself like the Catholics do."

"I always thought it looked comforting. So I gave it a try and you know what? It made me feel better."

"Come on," I said. "I'll make us some tea."

"Sure you should do that? I mean using Vidalia's kettle and cups and tea. It's like robbing a grave or something."

I smiled and felt the corners of my eyes crinkle like wax paper. "Do really think Vidalia would mind?"

Ruth followed me into the kitchen. "You still haven't told me why you're here."

"It's this whole Clarence Pepper thing and the way Agnes handled it. I keep thinking I'm supposed to do something. I just don't know what."

"I was wondering when that was going to happen."

"What?"

"Well, it was a pressure cooker over there, Griselda. Always was, even before all this trouble. You're like two hens in the same coop. Only a matter of time before one of you blew the top off. I'm surprised you made it this long. But then, I figured it was just another one of Agnes's miracles, you being able to live with her, I mean."

The kettle squealed. "Ever wish you could scream like a boiling kettle?" I asked.

"Why don't you?"

"That's all folks need is to hear crazy screams coming from Vidalia Whitaker's house."

Ruth dunked her tea bag. "Oh, right. Well, I know a place you can scream."

"I don't want to scream."

"Yes, you do. It's good to scream sometimes. What do they call it? Therapeutic. But first you have to tell me what broke the camel's back, and I promise I won't tell that sister-in-law of mine because she'll just go blabbing about it over the airwaves."

I sipped my tea and looked around the bright kitchen. Even at night, Vidalia's kitchen was cheery and light with its sunflower walls and lacy white curtains. She had copper-bottom pots hanging from hooks above a counter she had installed to roll out dough and prepare vegetables. The pots twinkled in the overhead light.

"Nothing really happened," I said. "It's not like she said or did anything—well no more than accidentally causing the death of another human being and then choosing to hide the truth."

"Now, Griselda. I think your feelings are hurt."

Ruth sipped her tea and looked at me over the rim of her cup. "Yes, sirree, Bob, you're pouting. You're upset that she didn't tell you and you alone."

I poured cream into my tea and it curdled into something that resembled cottage cheese. "Look at that. I didn't even bother to check the date on that carton of half and half."

Ruth looked at it. "Expired a week ago."

I dumped it into the sink. "She should have told me after all these years. I deserved to know why she holed herself up in the house."

"And in her body." Ruth puckered her lips and her eyes grew wide. "You know what I mean?" It was like she was waiting years to say it. "She built a fine prison. But she had no choice, Griselda. You can understand that."

"When she was a girl, maybe. When it first happened. But after all these years? She should have told me. I might have been able to handle it better, differently. Maybe I could have done something to—"

Ruth clicked her tongue. "Griselda Sparrow, it's time you figured out what's making you so mad. Is it what she did or what she did afterwards? What would you have done? I'll tell you. Nothing more than you're doing right now. This secret's got to stay a secret."

"She lied to me, Ruth. I gave her my life because of a lie. All these years I thought Agnes was hiding from the bullies and hecklers."

Ruth patted my hand. "She was hiding from them too."

I poured more tea and drank it black. "He might have lived. That's what the news report said."

"What report?"

"The newspaper. I looked it up. Doc said the boy might have been saved if help had gotten there in time."

"*Might* have lived, Griselda. How could Doc know for sure?"

"She should have gone straight to Doc's office and told him," I said.

"That's what an adult would have done. Agnes was a kid—a fat, sad child that got bullied every day of her life."

In all my life I had never faced a problem with so many layers. Everybody made sense and yet nothing made sense.

"Let's go scream," Ruth said. "I haven't done it in a while. Very good for the soul. And it gets the old ticker pumping and clears out all that artery-clogging stuff, you know."

"What? Now? It's dark out and cold and—and I don't want to scream."

But we did. Ruth and I went to the edge of town where the train rode high on a black, steel trestle over the river that fed our pond.

"Now we wait," she said when I parked the truck under the bridge.

"Wait?"

"Yep. When the train passes he always toots his horn; you hear it every night, don't you?"

"I guess. Maybe I'm just used to hearing it."

"Every night around ten o'clock that big old freight train from Binghamton crosses the trestle. I know 'cause, you'll no doubt remember, Bubba worked for the railroad as a carpenter."

"I remember."

"Best they had. But anyway, that's neither here nor there. We wait."

We sat for one minute, and I started to feel uncomfortable and silly. I rolled the window down a pinch. The cold air that rushed inside smelled like rust.

"What if Mildred Blessing comes by in her cop car?" I asked.

"She doesn't go out on patrol for an hour yet, and besides we're not doing anything wrong. Ain't no law against two women sitting in a pickup truck screaming, now, is there?"

That was true.

At twelve minutes after ten I heard the train coming— distant at first, but getting louder.

"Right on time. Just a minute now."

I saw the bright headlight coming around the curve.

"Get ready and the second you hear that horn, you start screaming and see if you can scream louder than the train and the whistle. I don't believe it can be done. I tried every night for a year after Bubba died and many a night after. Of course, I don't scream like I used to."

The conductor sounded the horn three times, and Ruth grabbed my hand and we screamed and screamed and screamed until there was no scream left in either one of us.

Ruth laughed while catching her breath. "You know, I think we beat it that time."

I laughed. "You were right. That felt good."

"I think I broke a rib," Ruth said.

I drove her home. "Listen, would you check in on Agnes in the morning? Get her some breakfast and make sure the drapes are open so she can see what's happening in town and—"

"I'll take care of her. Don't worry about that. But what if she asks about you? I'm certain she will."

"Just tell her the truth. I'm fine and I'll be in touch."

"Are you moving out for good?"

I looked at the starry sky. "I don't know. I just need a little time."

I skipped church that Sunday, like a lot of other folks apparently. I saw Pastor Speedwell later in the day, and he said there was only a handful of people in the service. I assured him that it was probably on account of it being a long month and that seemed to satisfy him.

"Thank you, Sister," he said. "I'll expect to see you and the rest of the town next week."

I smiled.

Monday came and I decided to face the music and headed for the café. If I knew Ruth, she had already been there before she went up to the house and told as many folks who would listen that I was staying at Vidalia's.

Sure enough, the usually noisy restaurant went dead silent the second my foot landed inside.

"Griselda," called Stu after a couple of tense seconds. "Join us." He was sitting with Boris and Fred Haskell.

"I just came in for some eggs and toast," I said.

"You can have them with us." Then he got Zeb's attention. "Get Griselda the number three."

I didn't want the number three—two eggs, any style, hash brown potatoes, a slice of ham and a sausage link—but I wasn't in the mood to argue. I squeezed in next to Boris. His cigar smell made my nose itch. He was finishing up the last of what looked like a number five—pancakes and sausage.

Dot Handy appeared wearing a light blue apron and a hairnet. She was holding two pots of coffee. "Regular or decaf, Griselda."

"Dot, what are you doing here? How come you aren't crossing kids?"

"Zeb asked me to work the mornings, and since it pays a little better than watching kids cross the street, I got Harriett Nurse to take over for me—not that I minded the kids. I love the little nippers."

"Harriett? Sure that's a good idea?"

"Yep. She'll do okay. I mean on a busy day, she might have to stop six cars and occasionally a truck—it ain't rocket science, you know. Regular or decaf?"

"Regular."

I looked at Boris.

"Now, I know what you're thinking. We didn't vote on Harriett taking over for Dot but it was an emergency."

That wasn't what I was thinking.

"And besides," Stu said, "we can vote at the meeting tomorrow night."

"Tomorrow?" I said. "We don't have a meeting for a couple of weeks."

"Well, under the circumstances," Fred said. "We think we need to meet and discuss how to handle the situation with Agnes." He bent his head down like the name embarrassed him.

"What situation?"

Dot stood next to me with her pencil poised to take my order.

"Stu already ordered for me."

She walked away slightly disappointed.

"Folks are calling for the sign to come down," Stu said.

I looked around the room. Every head strained in our direction.

"Fine. Take it down. I never liked it, you know that. Neither did Agnes."

"But, Griselda," Stu said, "she still did all that good stuff."

"You have no idea what she did."

I took a sip of coffee and dropped my cup. It spilled. Boris quickly sopped it up with a used napkin.

"What do you mean? You talking about Vidalia? I don't blame Agnes—not directly."

"No. It's nothing."

Fred grabbed my hand. "Lots of folks do, Griselda. They are all kinds of mad at her. Like she should of known or something, what with her having that direct line to God."

I sighed. Dot brought my breakfast, but I had lost my appetite. I slid out of the booth.

"Take the stupid sign down. I don't care and neither does Agnes. And she is not to blame for Vidalia's death." I said that last part loud enough for the entire café to hear.

"Hold on a second," Boris said. "It isn't like we're running her out of town."

"Then why does it feel that way?"

I dropped a quarter on the table for the coffee and walked out.

Ruth dropped by the library later in the day to tell me she had checked on Agnes and she seemed to be doing okay—mostly. I was reorganizing the encyclopedias when she came in. The kids had a bad habit of shelving the volumes any which way, even mixing up *The Britannica* with *The World Book*.

"How is she?"

"Who?" Ruth handed me volume nine of *The World Book*. "It's such a pretty blue."

"What is?"

"The book you just shoved into the shelf."

"I'm talking about Agnes."

"She's sad, Griselda. She said I should tell you she's sorry for creating such a terrible mess."

"Is she taking her medicine?"

"Well, I don't know the answer to that for sure. She says she does and then doesn't sometimes, but you know that."

"Are you going back today?"

"Want me to?"

"Please. I can't just yet."

Ruth and I finished organizing the encyclopedias and then the magazines that were left on tables. I put the periodical indexes back in order while Ruth sat and watched.

"I usually do my shopping with Vidalia," she said. "I need to stop at the Piggly Wiggly, but it's gonna feel real strange going without her."

"I know. The library isn't the same. She came by nearly everyday."

"I still can't believe it, Griselda. Why would Hezekiah want to kill her?"

"He couldn't help himself. I don't believe it had anything to do with her. I mean I cannot for the life of me believe she provoked him in anyway."

"Oh, no, no. It was random. Like hitting the lottery."

"Maybe . . . except Agnes did send him there. She bought the ticket, you know what I mean?" Ruth scrunched up her face and stared at me a second. "She couldn't help it."

"Maybe." My stomach grumbled, and I realized I hadn't had much to eat in a day or so. "I'm starving. You want to drive into Shoops and get some lunch?"

"Well, I did have my shopping—but yeah, let's go."

Ruth and I drove into town like two teenagers on a joy ride. We rolled the windows down and let the warm air rush around us like a healing breeze. I could smell the new grass and flowering buds as we drove down the mountain. My last ride into Shoops was fraught with sadness and questions and fear. But on this ride I felt free, like I could keep driving and driving just to get away.

"You better slow down," Ruth said. "You'll miss the town."

"Would that be so terrible?"

"Griselda, you can't. The town meeting's tonight, and you need to start caring for your sister again. I can't keep doing it."

She was right, but for the first time in a long time—maybe even for the first time ever—I felt like a shooting star streaking down the mountain.

I pulled the truck into a diagonal parking spot in front of The Pink Lady Coffee Shop. We arrived just as a tall, skinny lady rolled out a pink and white striped awning with a scalloped edge.

"Ain't that pretty," Ruth said.

"It is nice. In the warmer weather she puts out little bistro tables and chairs for folks to eat *alfresco*."

"I don't think I ever had *alfresco*," Ruth said. "Is it a salad?"

"No, it's an Italian word that means in the open air."

The Pink Lady was exactly that: pink vinyl booths and gray tables with metal chairs with pink vinyl seat cushions. Curtains, the darker pink color of a Mr. Lincoln rose, hung in each window, and a large pink pearled jukebox with flashing neon lights stood in the back.

We chose a booth next to the window to soak up some sunshine. After a few minutes the skinny woman we saw out front took our order.

"I'll have a burger, fries, and a Pepsi," I said, after scraping off the ketchup from the one-page laminated menu. It covered up the price.

The waitress wrote my order.

"I didn't eat breakfast this morning," I told Ruth who was still studying the menu. The waitress shifted from one foot to another, wiggling like a toddler. "If the weather were warmer, we would have our lunch *alfresco*, but since there's still a bite in the air, we'll stay indoors. What's Italian for indoors?"

The waitress rolled her eyes.

"Anyhoo," Ruth said. "I'd like the chicken salad on just plain old white bread and a cup of coffee. Make sure it's fresh, please."

Our waitress pulled a straw from her pink apron pocket, dropped it on the table, and left with our order.

"Well, she certainly is no Cora Nebbish," Ruth said.

"I'll say, but we can't let a surly waitress spoil our lunch. It feels good to be out of Bright's Pond, doesn't it?"

Ruth looked around at the strange restaurant and unfamiliar faces. "A little. But I much prefer the Full Moon. I know everybody there."

"Ah, they're all yakking about Agnes and what they're going to do at the meeting tonight. I have half a mind not to go."

Miss Surly brought us our beverages.

"Thank you," Ruth said.

"Your orders will be up in a minute," the waitress said.

Ruth dumped cream in her coffee from the little metal pitcher. "Oh, you'll go. You have to."

She was right, of course. "Well, other than taking that ridiculous sign down what can they do? They can't make her leave town."

"Oh, they won't do that. Folks just need a person to blame when the unimaginable happens, you know? Makes it more—"

"Palatable?"

"I was going to say easier to swallow, but I thought that would remind you of the sign mistake and all."

"Ruth, you really are a real good friend."

She touched my hand but pulled it back when the waitress came with her chicken salad sandwich.

"It looks good," Ruth said. "Lots of chicken in there."

"Your burger will be up in a minute," Miss Surly said. "Yo, Hank." She headed for the kitchen. "I need that hockey puck and them frog sticks."

Ruth leaned across the table. "Maybe the Pink Lady is the wrong name for this place."

The afternoon went quickly, and Ruth and I made it back to Bright's Pond before the dinner hour. I dropped her off in front of my house.

"You go on back to Vidalia's," Ruth said. "I'll check on Agnes and see you at the meeting."

"Okay. Make sure she did a treatment. Turn on a light before you leave and tell her . . . tell her I—"

Ruth waited. "Tell her you what?"

"Ah, nothing."

"You sure?"

"Yes. I'll see you at the town hall."

While I waited for Ruth to open the door of the house, a heated debate raged in my spirit. Should I go in? Nope. I could muster up the desire to go inside but not the courage. I still couldn't let it go.

29

I walked the short distance to the town hall from Vidalia's house. The early spring air felt damp like rain was trying to move in. It was having a hard time getting over the mountain, so it sent ahead tiny dewdrop feelers. Twilight was winding down into darkness. No moon was visible through the gray clouds, setting the perfect mood for whatever was about to happen. The air had an ominous feel and so did my heart.

Ruth and I met about halfway there. She had just come from Agnes.

"Try not to worry, too much," she said. "I checked in on Agnes. She's so sad—down in the dumps, you know."

I knew. My heart ached with every thought of her lying in her bed, alone in that crickety old house. Vidalia's words kept echoing in my head: "Ever think Agnes might not be your problem?"

Maybe now I understood what she was trying to say. Maybe my problem was bigger than Agnes.

"Is she getting enough to eat? Getting back and forth to the bathroom, all right?"

Ruth paused and pulled a tissue from her purse. She wiped her nose. "Allergies starting up. Grass and trees. Anything green is poison to my sinuses."

"You were telling me about Agnes."

"Well, I wanted to tell you that when I opened the front door, the—" She signaled for me to bend down so she could whisper even though there wasn't a soul in sight. "—the smell about knocked me off my dang feet it was so—pungent."

"I'm sorry she can't take care of herself, Ruth, but I can't go back. Not yet."

"Then you might want to get a nurse in there. Ever think of hiring one of them visiting nurses? I'm sure Doc Flaherty could make some arrangements."

Ruth had already grown weary of Agnes's care, and I couldn't blame her. "I guess I should check on it."

We had just reached the café, and I could see that a large crowd was gathering for the meeting.

"Did she say anything else?"

"About what?"

"Anything, Ruth. Did she say anything about anything?"

"Just that she's going to keep praying. I found her trying to get off her bed. She said she wanted to get on her knees to pray."

I stopped walking. "Ruth, why do you wait to tell me the most important thing? You didn't let her, did you? She can't do that. Getting on her knees could be dangerous for a woman her size."

"I didn't let her, Griselda. I told her she'd need a lot more help than I could give her to get down there and back up. She got that determined look on her face, like she was going to do it one way or the other, but I think I talked her out of trying."

"I hope so. She'd be like a turtle on its back."

"She came to her senses and went back to bed like a good girl."

Ruth started walking again. "Imagine that, Griselda, she wants to pray on her knees now. She said she has to for some reason I couldn't understand. I told her it was foolishness for a woman her size to be thinking that way."

I stopped again just as we reached the town hall steps. Folks pushed past us to get inside. The town hall was packed to the gills that night.

"It's okay, Ruth. I think I know why she was trying to get on her knees. Now we better get inside if we want a seat. Looks like standing room only tonight."

Ivy stopped me at the door. "Where you sitting, Griselda?"

"Oh, it doesn't matter. Anywhere I can get a seat."

That was when I saw Boris and Stu waving at me from up front. They had saved me a seat. I signaled to them that I would get there. Ivy and Ruth sat in a back row.

"Sorry," I said, "but maybe I should go up front with them."

"You go right ahead," said Ivy. "You should be where everyone can get a good look since you'll probably get called on to say something on behalf of Agnes."

As I made my way to the front I intercepted snippets of conversations and whispers. Janeen was leaning so close to Hazel Flatbush I doubted you could get a slice of raisin toast between them.

"I just don't know what we'll do now that Agnes can't pray." I heard Janeen say. Then Hazel cupped her mouth but I could still hear. "How can we trust her, though?"

Frank Sturgis stood with Fred Haskell and a couple of the other men. "I still think she should have known something." he said. "She should have gotten a feeling about him, a sign."

"Well, I don't know about that," Fred said. "She ain't a mind reader. And just 'cause you and Janeen are fighting again night and day don't mean Agnes failed you."

I paused near the snack table and plucked a raspberry cookie from a tray with a white paper doily.

"All I know is that ever since that Hezekiah came to town things have been going from bad to worse around here," Frank said. "And you got to admit that—"

I had heard enough and found my seat next to Studebaker Kowalski. Stu was wearing one of his better leisure suits—a pale blue one with a white and yellow striped shirt. "Now don't you worry about a thing, Griselda, this is going to turn out just fine."

"I'm sure it will, Stu."

Boris reached his hand around Stu. I took it in a handshake. "Don't you fret," he said. "I won't let Agnes down."

Jasper York and Harriett had front row seats along with Tohilda Best, Sheila Spiney, and most of the ladies from the Society of Angelic Philanthropy. It wasn't often they went to town meetings as a group. Most of the time they sat with their husbands or children.

Dot Handy, still in her crisp waitress uniform, appeared at the front and sat at the table with her trusty steno pad and pencils. She nodded to Boris.

Boris stood and approached the table. Ordinarily, the other council members would be on his left and his right but he ran the show solo that night. He banged his gavel and someone in the back flicked the lights off and on a couple of times. The crowd quieted down in record time.

Jasper York stood, in spite of the fact that Harriett was trying to keep him in his seat. "General, sir," he said, "there is a spy in our midst, a double agent." Then he looked straight at me and sat down. Folks snickered but it didn't last long.

"Now we all know that a terrible tragedy has befallen our community," Boris said.

"Because of that Agnes Sparrow," shouted Janeen Sturgis. I would recognize her voice anywhere. "She invited that—that monster into our town, into our very lives and hearts."

"That's right, that's right," others shouted. "It's Agnes Sparrow's fault that Vidalia Whitaker was killed."

I heard a few sobs and boo hoos from some of the ladies. Hazel even waved her hanky. "Poor, poor, Vidalia." Then she blew her nose.

Boris brought the meeting to order. "Settle down. I won't have any ruckus tonight. We'll follow our ordinary rules of order. Those of you with something to say will raise your hands and wait until the chair recognizes you."

"Recognize." Jasper said, "I—I don't recognize none of these soldiers, General. I seem to have lost my platoon."

Harriett whispered in his ear, and he calmed down. But then she raised her hand and Boris indicated that she had the floor.

"One thing still confuses me. How come they burned her body to ashes and put it all into that little jar like it was nothing more than dust? The Bible says God is going to resurrect the dead first. I can't see no ashes meeting Jesus in the air."

"Jesus is here?" Jasper said. "Is he in a pie this time?"

"No, no, Jasper, Jesus in the air. In the air," Boris said. He banged his gavel.

"Jesus is not here," Harriet said. "Not tonight and there is no Jesus pie."

"Oh. I'm sorry, General, I thought I heard someone mention Jesus pie."

That was when Zeb made his way down the side of the hall and stood near me, his back against the wall while he chewed on fudge.

Sheila fielded Harriett's concern. "Don't fret about how Jesus will resurrect bodies, dearie. God can certainly put all the ashes back in their proper order. I'm sure he's got them all numbered."

Harriett looked incredulous. "I don't see how. So much has gone up in smoke, sheer smoke. And I was so looking forward to being in glory with Vidalia. She was my best friend."

Never had such a lie as that been floated during a town hall meeting. Harriett was never a big fan of Vidalia's. She could never get past the notion of having a black woman in town.

Stu stood and raised his hand like a schoolboy. "We are not here to discuss whether or not God can resurrect ashes or who was Vidalia's best friend. There are more pressing issues to tend too."

Boris recognized Frank Sturgis.

"I demand we take that sign down," Frank said. "We don't need no more drifters coming to town looking for the powerful Agnes Sparrow."

"Hear, hear," echoed some others.

Boris stood and pulled the original sign petition out of his jacket pocket. "You all signed this. You all trusted Agnes. How can you let one mishap turn you against her?"

"Mishap," shouted Dot Handy, even though she was not usually supposed to have an opinion. "That wasn't no mishap. That was murder, and people who commit murder should be dealt with severely."

By that time my blood boiled and started to run right out my ears. I stood and turned so I could face them.

"Agnes did not kill Vidalia," I said, my voice shaking like an aspen tree. "Agnes didn't know what Hezekiah Branch was capable of, and you have no right to say such things."

Studebaker applauded along with a few others.

"Now take the sign down, if you want," I said. "Agnes never wanted that sign to begin with. Now stop blaming her."

"It could have been any of us," Hazel shouted. "Or any of our children. As far as I'm concerned Agnes is as guilty as Hezekiah Branch."

Whistles and applause went out over the crowd. I felt tears pool in my eyes and swiped them away. I willed myself not to break down and cry even though every cell in my body wanted to.

"What do you propose we do?" I said. "Put her in jail?"

"Can't do that," I heard a small, shrill voice in the back utter. "Ain't no jail cell big enough." Laughter drifted through the hall.

I could hardly believe what I was hearing. It seemed the clock had turned, and I was sitting among children again, the same children who taunted and teased Agnes nearly her whole childhood, right through her teen years, and beyond. These people had not changed.

Studebaker rose and shouted. "Hey! Agnes is our hero. Think about all the good she did. She saved my life and Cora's life—at least for a little longer and . . . and . . . " He looked out over the crowd. "I could point to just about every single person in this room, and you could tell me something that Agnes prayed for that touched your life for the good."

"She healed my bleeding ulcer," Ruth said. "It never came back."

"And my car is still running strong." I had to search the crowd to figure out who said that. It was a voice I didn't recognize until my eyes rested on Sheila Spiney's brother, Rueben. He wasn't quite right in the mind but harmless enough. Reuben only drove his beat-up old Rambler back and forth to his job at the meat-packing plant in Shoops.

"Please don't do nothin' to Agnes," he said. "Or my car might not start in the morning."

That was when the door swung open and Eugene Shrapnel made his entrance, dressed in black from his hat to his shoes.

"Look, Eugene's here," someone shouted, and all heads turned to the back, to the miserable little corner were Eugene stood.

"Eugene was right. Agnes is a devil," someone shouted.

A self-satisfied smile smeared across Eugene's disgusting face as he leaned on his cane. "I told you the sky was going to fall. I told you. I told you all."

From where I stood it looked like his ugly nose had gotten even larger. He thrust his cane toward the ceiling. "Repent! Repent now, all of you. Resist the devil and she will flee."

Eugene slinked down the side aisle as every eye watched. When he finally got to the front of the room, he stopped near me and spat on the floor. "Agnes Sparrow brought evil to this town just like I said she would."

"Hey," Dot Handy said. "You can't go spitting on the town hall floor. Someone has to clean that up."

Boris banged his gavel six times until the room quieted down.

Eugene continued to shake his cane over us like he was trying to dispel evil spirits. "Repent! Repent!"

Then Jasper York stood. I could see his legs wobble as Harriett took hold of his elbow.

"I got no more repenting to do. A man my age ain't capable of too much more sinning, not like in my glory days on the front lines. But I will say this much. Agnes is not to blame. We all took a shine to that boy and none of us was able to see him for what he was."

"Hear, hear," Studebaker said.

Jasper sat down with a thud and a rock of his chair. For a second I thought he might topple back into Hazel Flatbush's lap.

Boris raised his hands and shushed everyone. "Now, before we move on to deciding exactly what we are going to do in light of this terrible tragedy, this severe problem, I got to ask if anyone else would like to speak."

Tohilda Best moved to the front of the room and stood by Boris. She wore a pressed and tidy pink dress with white lace trim and a sweet spring hat for the occasion. "Now I can't say for sure that Agnes Sparrow brought evil to this town. All I know is the man she befriended, the man she prayed for, killed our dear friend and neighbor, Vidalia Whitaker."

She paused until more shouts and applause quieted down. Then she continued. "And to think that the Society of Angelic Philanthropy bought that man new shoes and socks. Well, that just fries my cookies. But we ladies of The Society took our own vote and decided that Agnes Sparrow should not be held accountable, although her reputation as a miracle worker should be expunged from any public record and no longer be tolerated."

"Preach it, sister," Jasper shouted.

"So we hereby agree that the Agnes Sparrow welcome sign should be removed—posthaste."

I swallowed and looked at Tohilda. She didn't look at me, and I had the nasty little thought never to let her have meetings in my library again.

Another hour slipped by as folks shouted and spoke about why or why not Agnes should be held accountable. By the end of the evening, after all the goodies had been eaten, the coffee pot drained to the last drop, and the older folks gone home to bed, it was decided that the sign would be taken down and replaced with the old one.

"Then it's decided," Boris said. "We will also tell Filby Pruett to stop work immediately on the statue."

"He'll need to crush it," Janeen said. "Turn it to dust—" She heaved a sigh. "—just like our dear, sweet Vidalia."

Hazel cried into her hanky.

Zeb took my hand. "This will blow over one day."

"I don't care one single iota about the sign, Zeb. It's what they think about Agnes that has me so worried. She'll die if people stop coming to her for prayer."

Boris slammed his trusty gavel three more times and brought the meeting to a close. Folks filed out, still slinging complaints and barbs dipped in fear and venom at Agnes.

I walked back to Vidalia's with Ruth and Ivy. Ivy didn't know I'd left Agnes.

"It's just for a little while," I said. "I needed some peace and quiet to think on a few things."

"What things?" she asked. "You ain't thinking about siding with Eugene and the rest of them loudmouths?"

"No, no. It's not that." I glanced at Ruth who was biting her tongue so hard I thought it would bleed. "I'll go back—soon," I said.

"I've been checking in on her," Ruth said. "But Griselda is going to have a nurse see to Agnes if she stays away much longer."

"I'll be glad to help," Ivy said.

"Thank you, Ivy," I said. "If you could even stop in tonight, I'd appreciate it."

Ruth said something I didn't catch. "What did you say?"

"Oh, all right. I think you should go tell Agnes what happened at the meeting, that's all."

Ivy grabbed Ruth's hand. "Let's both go. Griselda knows what she needs to do."

I watched as they headed off together toward my house, and a thick sadness settled into my chest like a fog off the mountains. I should be the one going home. But I felt like a torn-up rag inside, and I was much too afraid of my own feelings to handle Agnes's.

When I got back to Vidalia's I tried to carry on as usual, but my thoughts continually turned to Agnes. Finally, I gave in. I packed my small bag, tucked Arthur under my arm, and headed home—on foot.

Along the way I paused now and again and let the fresh, spring air wrap around me. Studebaker was sitting on his porch swing, smoking a cigar. The smell mixed with the dewy air and tickled my nose.

"Griselda," he called with a wave. "Come on up here." I carted my stuff up on the porch.

"I can't tell you how sorry I am for what happened tonight. It's like a slap in the face, a slap in the face."

I waved the acrid smoke away. He smiled. "Sorry, Griselda, but sometimes there just ain't nothing like a fine cigar."

"It's okay. I'm just not used to it."

"Yeah, and I will never get used to people being so mean-spirited."

"Fear makes people act in odd ways, Stu. They're just afraid of another Hezekiah coming to town."

"Oh, I can see that." He blew a perfect smoke ring. "I can see that, but they still got no right to shun Agnes the way they have. It's like they forgot all the good she did. Like it doesn't count anymore."

I rubbed Arthur's neck. He kept his nose tilted toward the sky enjoying the crisp air.

"It counts Stu, it will always count."

Stu stubbed the cigar out in a glass ashtray. "Where are you headed? I just noticed your bag."

"I'm going home, Stu. I've left Agnes alone long enough."

"Yeah, I heard about that. How come you left to begin with? I was thinking maybe you were feeling like the rest of the folks in town."

There was no point in telling him about Clarence.

"I just needed a break."

Stu nodded. I said good night and went home.

Arthur leapt from my arms and made a beeline for the backyard. He had his own business to tend to.

I pushed open the door. Ruth and Ivy were still with her.

"Griselda," Ruth said, "I thought you were staying at Vidalia's again tonight. But I got to say I'm glad you came home."

Ivy, who was standing as far from Agnes as she could without being too rude, looked daggers at me. "It's good you came back. Agnes needs you."

"No, no," Agnes said. "Don't be mad at Griselda. She had a right to leave."

Ivy took a step closer. "What right? What right does a sister have for leaving another sister in such—such obvious distress."

"I am not in distress," Agnes said. "I've just had a bit of trouble getting around and sometimes it's just easier to stay in bed."

Ruth took hold of Ivy's hand. "Griselda's leaving has nothing to do with what happened to Vidalia—well, not directly anyway."

I took off my coat and dropped my bag. "How are you, Agnes?"

She looked at me with those tiny eyes of hers that seemed to have gotten even smaller. "I'm glad you're back. You are back?"

"I better get you changed and get some fresh sheets. Are you hungry?"

"Well, sure. Ruth and Ivy already told me about that Donnybrook Fair of a town meeting. I don't care a lick about the sign, Griselda, and nothing they say or do will ever make me stop praying, so it's like nothing ever happened. They don't know what they're doing."

I understood what she was trying to say, but the words still made me angry. Plenty had happened.

After Ruth and Ivy left, I helped Agnes out of bed and changed her sheets and the mattress pad. Then I gave her a sponge bath and got her into fresh underwear and a nice clean nightgown.

"Thank you, Griselda. I feel so much better."

I nodded. "Are you hungry?"

Agnes and I ate cereal and some old ice cream.

"It isn't terrible," she said. "A little freezer burn, but chocolate is chocolate no matter what."

"I'll run to the Piggly Wiggly in the morning."

30

Morning came quickly. I awoke to the sounds of Agnes coughing and gasping for air. I tossed my blanket off and hurried downstairs to her side. She was in the throes of another asthma attack.

"Agnes. Use your inhaler. Did you use your inhaler?"

She shook her head no.

"Here, use it. I'll call Doc."

She gave me no argument; Agnes was in real distress. She gasped and wheezed like an old train desperately trying to make it up a steep hill. Her hand shook as she lifted the tiny inhaler to her mouth and squeezed the canister. She took one sharp, deep inhale and let the vaporous drug remain in her mouth and lungs, and then she took another. I could almost see the medicine race to her bronchial passages as her breaths started to come more in wheezes than gasps. Perspiration dripped down her blushed cheeks.

I heard Doc's car land on the front lawn. He raced through the door lickety-split, still in his robe and slippers with his stethoscope swinging around his neck.

"Okay, Agnes, I'm here," he called from the entryway. He dashed into the viewing room. "You both look in a panic. Now you know that's the worst thing for asthma." He prepared an injection and shot it into her upper arm.

"Dang blubber, Agnes, it's gonna kill you."

"Doc, bedside manner, remember?" I said.

"No time for that, Griselda." He patted Agnes's hand and then listened with his stethoscope.

He fired up the nebulizer. "Too much stress. Too much. Between that sign and Vidalia and the dang fool town meeting, not to mention all that weight on your organs, Agnes, it just isn't good. Just isn't good for your heart or your lungs, not to mention what it's doing to your joints."

Agnes's face went from fear to frustration. She shook her head with the plastic mask, covering her nose and mouth.

"Doc, take it easy," I said.

He poked the ends of the stethoscope into his ears and listened to her chest. He closed his eyes and listened more deeply.

That was when he signaled that he wanted to speak with me on the side. We didn't go far from Agnes, and both Doc and I kept one eye on her as we talked.

"I am so glad you came to your senses and came home, Griselda. She needs someone here—full time or as near as full time as possible. That attack could have been fatal. Full time is how she needs you. Can you stand that?"

I sighed. I didn't know the answer.

Doc went back to Agnes and listened to her chest. "Better. Keep breathing."

"Maybe it's time to start thinking about Greenbrier," he said when he got back to me.

I peered out the front window. Hazel Flatbush and Tohilda Best had stopped out front. It wasn't hard to imagine their conversation.

"That's the Doc's car," Tohilda would say.

"It certainly is. I wonder if Agnes is sick. Well, it just serves her right." That's what I thought Hazel would be saying.

Doc got my attention. "I'm serious, Griselda. She needs care that maybe you can't give."

Tears pooled in my eyes, and Doc took my hand. "You've worked hard, but it might be time now."

Doc hustled back to Agnes, and I stole away to the kitchen and started coffee percolating. Arthur mewled for his breakfast.

"Okay, okay. It's coming." I plopped a can of a seafood banquet in his dish and refreshed his water. "There you go." He purred and slinked in and out of my ankles.

Doc was listening again to Agnes's chest when I got back. The blood pressure cuff, the largest one he had, was wrapped around her forearm.

"Rest and medicine," he said. "And think about Greenbrier, Agnes." He looked at me. Then back at her. "Griselda can't take care of you forever."

Her eyes grew big and her breathing heavier. Doc patted her arm. "Calm down, Agnes. You knew this day was going to come."

Agnes closed her eyes and pushed the back of her head into the pillow. Her breaths came slower after a minute or so.

"Good," Doc said. "I gave her a sedative. She'll rest now."

He pushed his stethoscope into his black bag. "Can you stay with her today?"

"Sure. Yes. I'll be here. All day." I looked at my sister. Her color was better and her breathing calmer, but there was still panic in her eyes.

"Anything I should know?" I asked Doc.

"Keep an eye and an ear out. Call if you need me." He made his way to the door.

"Griselda," he said, "I'm serious. It's time to think about Greenbrier."

He opened the door, stood on the porch, and yawned.

"You might be right, Doc. Maybe now is the best time when people are having their doubts about Agnes."

"That's got nothing to do with it, Griselda. It's her health I'm worried about. I don't give a hang what people at the Full Moon are saying. And I advise you to do the same. All this miracle junk." He practically spat.

I moved past him and sat on the wicker rocker. He sat next to me. "I'm just as guilty as all of them, Doc. I never said this before but I think I might have believed in Agnes—in the miracles, the prayers, the power—and maybe I blamed her to for Vidalia's death and Hezekiah coming to town."

"It's time to let it go. Let her go."

"I don't know if I can, Doc. For so many years she was all I had, all I could care about."

"Even if it means she'll die, Griselda?" He patted my arm. "I used to think Agnes's prayers were a good thing. A hobby of sorts. Frankly, I still have a hard time with the so-called miracles, but dang if I can explain Stu's cancer disappearing or Cora's heart mending or even Ruth Knickerbocker's bleeding ulcer going away; but now, who knows. Maybe God is shutting that door, Griselda. It's time for Agnes to rest from all this. Time her health came first."

I walked with him to his car. He had parked on the lawn so many times there were permanent ruts in the grass and dirt.

"Doc, I feel like I need to tell you something about Agnes. About why she started praying and let herself get so big and— and stopped going outside and all."

Doc opened the car door and tossed his bag inside. "I'm listening."

I took a deep breath. "It happened a real long time ago."

I stopped and looked out over the mountains. The green had come in and the hills sparkled in the sun. I turned back to Doc. "There was an accident." My heart pounded as second thoughts drifted into my brain.

"Yes," Doc said, "an accident?"

Tohilda and Hazel came back the other way, each carrying a brown bag of groceries and yakking up a storm.

"Oh, it's nothing. I think I'm being silly. It's not important."

"Griselda?"

"No, really, Doc. It's nothing. I better get inside."

I hurried back inside before the women could stop and ask any questions. I saw them from the window. Doc took care of it and was on his way home in a few seconds.

Tohilda and Hazel stared at the house. I watched them shake their heads in unison and then walk off.

Agnes was asleep—peaceful and quiet. The wheezes were gone; her chest and belly rose and fell in a more regular rhythm. She looked like a baby, a big, fat baby. I wiped sweat from her forehead with a tissue and adjusted her blanket.

"I'm sorry I left you," I whispered. "I'll never leave you again."

The sign came down the next morning. Fred Haskell and Frank Sturgis tore it down. Stu told me later that day that they destroyed the thing—hacked it to splinters with an axe. Well, so be it.

The early spring day was warm. I opened windows and let the fresh air and oxygen circulate through the house. Doc had been by several times since Agnes's asthma attack and each time he suggested the nursing home. "It's really not a bad place. You could have your own room and plenty of people, day and night, to care for you."

"It'll be like being in the hospital all the time, until the day I die," Agnes said. "They'll treat me like a patient. No, I'd rather die here."

She looked at me and waited as though I was supposed to jump in and defend her.

"We don't need to discuss this now," I said.

Doc shook his head and sighed. "You're both being foolish."

I walked him to the door as usual. "Especially you, Griselda."

"Me? What about me?"

"Being foolish. You've dedicated your whole life to her."

"I had, too, Doc. There was no one else."

"I know, but you're still a young woman."

I snorted a laugh. "Young?"

"Young enough. You deserve some happiness. Maybe this whole thing was necessary. Maybe this whole debacle was a sign. All the time people were looking toward the wrong sign."

I opened the door, and we went outside together.

"I love the spring," Doc said.

"Me too. It's like the whole town has been through something together—the miserable winter—and then all of a sudden, in the course of a day or two or three the sun shines, the air warms, the flowers bloom, the birds sing, and all is right with the world again. A new start." Doc smiled wider than I think I had ever seen him smile. "I'm sorry," I said, "for going on like that."

"Sounds like a prescription to me."

Not a single person came by for two weeks. Not a single bunion, wart, or dead car battery was brought to Agnes's attention. And you know what? The people survived. They got along just like they always did.

I went back to work, and Agnes and I settled into our daily routines. The library was a lonely place without Vidalia. The Society ladies had come in twice, and each time they held their meeting and said precious little to me. Tohilda tried to explain.

"Griselda, I had to say what I did, being the president of the Society of Angelic Philanthropy. There was just no denying that Agnes's prayers had a direct influence on the circumstances that brought that terrible Hezekiah Branch to town."

"That's right," Hazel said. "Why, it's just as plain as the nose on Eugene Shrapnel's face."

She didn't have to be rude, but few people could pass up an opportunity to mention Eugene's nose when they had the opportunity.

I smiled and went about my business, all the time wondering what they would do if they knew about Clarence Pepper. The Society of Angelic Philanthropy probably would call for Agnes to be tarred and feathered.

Agnes missed the visitations, but she never stopped praying. She just prayed differently, not so much for miracles but for peace and calm and for God's will and mercy to cover our town like a smooth, cotton blanket. That's how she said it.

"Lord, will you lay down your peace and mercy upon this town. Lay it down like a warm, cottony blanket fresh from the dryer."

God answered—again. Soon the town was back to its old self. Winifred and Toby came and put Vidalia's house up for sale. It had been a long time since I saw a For Sale sign go up in Bright's Pond, and I must admit it struck me kind of hard. I missed Vidalia all over again. I did what I could to help, loading furniture into a rented moving van, scrubbing down counters, and sweeping out rooms. I managed to take the blood-stained rug and trash it before Winifred or Toby found it. My heart sank when Toby closed the van doors.

"Thank you, Griselda," was all he said. Then he reached out and hugged me close, which was something like getting hugged by a grizzly.

"I'm sorry what I said about Agnes," Winifred said.

"I understand," I said.

Winifred even stopped at the house and said good-bye to Agnes. They both apologized to one another.

Maybe I had gotten too used to the calm, but I let myself believe that the town had made some sort of peace with Agnes and Hezekiah, but as it turned out, I was wrong. Folks still didn't trust her. Around breakfast time one day, I stopped into the Full Moon to say hi to Zeb. I made the mistake of talking out loud about my sister.

"Agnes is still praying," I told Zeb. "Goes through her notebooks all day long."

Hazel walked past just as I said those words. "Still praying? What's she praying for? I hear tell ain't nobody been to see her in weeks. Ain't nobody asking for miracles."

Zeb shook his head and went back to the kitchen. I couldn't help myself and let a small chuckle escape from my throat. "Oh, Hazel, Agnes doesn't need a person sitting in her room to pray, and it isn't always about expecting miracles."

I couldn't tell what she thought about that exactly, but she harrumphed and sashayed out the door, kind of like Eugene Shrapnel did when he couldn't think of anything to say.

Zeb brought me scrambled eggs and toast. "You heading to the library today or going home?"

"Oh, I might open the library. I received a shipment of new books and some magazines I need to catalog. I've been kind of lazy about it though—the library I mean."

"Yeah, I can understand that. Working alone most days and then going home to Agnes must be tough."

"Sometimes. I see Mildred Blessing more than anybody; she reads all those crime and detective books. The library is on the route Al Capone takes when he's on the run, so it's kind of funny to see that dog running past the window while Mildred is checking out crime stories."

Zeb laughed. "I can just picture that mutt with his goofy grin sitting there on the grass and waiting for her to come outside to take off."

We both laughed, and I sipped my coffee. Zeb headed back to the kitchen again. I watched him move around preparing eggs and sausage. Babette had school, so Zeb was working as both cook and waiter.

"Did Dot quit?" I asked.

Zeb dropped a dish with eggs and sausage onto the pickup counter and then came around through the door. "No, she didn't quit. Just had some errands, so I gave her the day

off. Babette will be here later. She's got an early dismissal."
He grabbed a damp rag and wiped down the counter next to
me. "I thought we might go out again sometime. You know,
another movie, if it's all right with Agnes and all."

My heart sped up just a tick or two. "Sure. I'd like that."

I finished my breakfast and walked the long way to the
library. The air was warm and new small leaves were bursting
out on the trees. The maples and oaks and even the birch trees
looked bright in their spring attire. There was a hint of hon-
eysuckle nectar in the air that stirred up melancholy inside
me. I really didn't want to go back to the library. Mildred
had already gotten her week's worth of books, and I wasn't
expecting the society for a few more days. I headed home
thinking about Zeb.

31

"Agnes," I called from the entryway. "I'm taking the day off. So I'll be home for you."

I stopped in my tracks when I heard what I thought was a muffled sob coming from the viewing room. For an instant I thought Agnes had a visitor, and my spirit quickened thinking that people might be coming back.

Not wanting to interrupt I tiptoed down the hall and peeked into the room, expecting to see Dot Handy or even Hazel Flatbush blubbering about their corns and bunions. There was no one there but Agnes. I caught sight of her just as she wiped her eyes with two fists full of Kleenex.

"Agnes, what's wrong? Are you sick?"

She shook her head and burbled at me. "No—not sick. Not like you think."

I sat down next to her and waited for more.

"I can't stop crying. It's like the dam busted, Griselda."

I held her chubby hands in mine and looked into her eyes. "What is it, Agnes? You thinking about Clarence again? Vidalia? Cora?"

She nodded. "All of them. Everybody. It's like my heart has been so full of everyone and now it's busted its seams."

"And it's all just pouring out?" I touched her cheek.

She blubbered into more Kleenex. "Cora and Ruth, Studebaker and Clarence, Mama and Daddy—everybody, Griselda, everybody I ever knew, ever prayed a word for."

She adjusted her nightgown and tried to maneuver into a more comfortable position. "I'm so sorry, Griselda. I'm so sorry for not telling you, for not telling Daddy or Doc, or confessing to the Peppers."

My lower lip quivered. "Now you're making me cry. I'm sorry I got mad at you, Agnes. I should have understood. I should never have left you."

We sobbed in each other's arms for a couple of minutes until we found the courage to pull away and replace the sobs with smiles. "I love you." We both said it at the same time.

Agnes's breathing sounded ragged, and I wanted to help her avoid a full-blown attack. "I think we could both use a cup of tea and maybe a slice of pie." Zeb had been sending me home with pie for days. Agnes said it was his way of courting me. She said he'd probably sink an engagement ring into meringue someday, so I should be careful how I swallowed.

"Nah, he isn't thinking that far down the road. He just asked me to another movie."

After tea and pie Agnes took a short nap while I did laundry and dishes. The kitchen cabinets needed organizing, but I passed on them, excusing myself because I needed to buy new shelf paper anyway.

A few minutes past eleven Agnes called for me.

"Griselda, I've been thinking. There's something I need to say."

I sat on the sofa with a basket of technicolor towels piled next to me. "Okay."

She swallowed and then heaved a tremendous sigh that seemed to come from all the way down near her ankles. "Doc is right. It's time for me to go to Greenbrier."

"Agnes. What? Why?"

"It's time. And that's all I've got to say on the subject. But there's something I need to do first."

"Agnes, this is so sudden, we should talk—"

"I made up my mind, Griselda. Now, like I was saying, there's something I need to do first."

I took my sister's hand and looked into her eyes. She had made her decision.

"Sure, Agnes, what do you need to do?"

"Take me to church. I need to finish something before I go to the . . . nurs . . . nurs . . . nursing home." Those last two words stuck in her throat.

"Finish?"

"I want to finish Communion. I never did after—well after that day. But I can now. I want to have Communion and then I'll be ready to go." Her bottom lip quivered, and her eyes sparkled with the tears of someone who just saw their sin close up and found God's grace.

"I don't know if I can get down the porch steps anymore," she said, "so you might need to call some men over to help."

When I stood my knees went wobbly, not because of the task of moving Agnes, but from an overwhelming realization that my sister was leaving. I knew it was for the best, for *her* best, even possibly for mine. But it stung like bees. "I know. It might take a little while, Agnes, to get you over there."

"It's a journey I got to take."

"I guess I can call Stu and maybe Boris, and I should have Doc here."

"Call Ruth, too. I need to say goodbye to her."

"You mean you want to go right away."

"Right away. I'll tell Doc to call and make the arrangements. Knowing him he probably already has the place on standby alert, waiting for the fat woman to arrive."

I made some quick calls. Everyone was home and everyone wanted to help, although I could hear over the phone that Ruth got a little choked up—something I was trying my best to avoid. But then all of a sudden the two of us started to blubber.

"I'll be right over," Ruth cried. "It's going to be okay, Griselda."

"I'll need something fresh to wear," Agnes said. "Maybe my purple housecoat. I think I'll wear those new slippers you bought me."

I helped Agnes into her soft purple housecoat. It was one her favorites—the color of a plum with shiny, silver buttons that glistened when the sun burst through the window.

It took some doing but we pushed her feet into the new slippers. I wrapped a large paisley scarf around her head. Her hair was a bit greasy, and she wanted to look her best for Communion. Then she sat down on the red velvet sofa with one hand on her walker, waiting.

Ruth arrived first and went straight to Agnes. "What brought this on? Are you sure, Agnes?"

"Yes, I'm sure," Agnes said. "It's been a long time coming, and I finally decided the time was right. Remember how I used to tell folks who came in for prayer that sometimes a miracle had to do with timing—the fullness of time?"

Ruth swiped tears from her eyes and grabbed a fist of Kleenex. "I remember."

"Well, my time can't get much fuller."

The doorbell chimed, and Studebaker and Boris came in followed by Doc carrying his bag with his stethoscope around his neck.

After a few minutes of small talk Doc said, "I guess we should get going. We'll have to put Agnes in the truck."

"Truck?" Stu said. "That's not going to work."

"But why?" Agnes asked. "I always rode in the back before."

"Yeah," Ruth said, "she got cold sometimes in the winter, and once it rained on her but—"

Stu cracked his neck. "No offense Agnes, dear, but you've gotten a bit heavier and wider in the last few years. I just don't see how we're going to get you in Griselda's truck."

Doc said, "Stu's right, Agnes. It could be dangerous."

Agnes laughed. "Yep, could be. Don't want me falling on anyone."

"You laugh, Agnes," Doc said. "But it could happen."

"Well how are we supposed to move her?" I asked.

Ruth chimed in. "Maybe Farmer Higgins will bring that big old cattle ramp." Then she smiled at Agnes. "I'm sorry. I don't mean to make it sound like you're a c—"

"It's all right, Ruth," Agnes said. "Now's not the time for politeness."

"Ramp's too dangerous," Stu said.

"Then how?" Boris asked. "There must be some way."

Stu twisted his mouth. "Well, once we get her outside we could . . . " Then he trailed off. "I haven't got a clue."

"It's going to take a feat of engineering," Doc said.

"Ah, come on, Doc," Agnes said. "I'm big but I'm not the Brooklyn Bridge."

"Maybe Fred would have an idea," I said. "He's smart about these things."

"Good idea," Stu said. "You all wait here. I'll go get Fred."

Agnes looked at me. "Did you tell them?"

"What?" Stu asked.

"Agnes needs to go to the church first and take care of some unfinished business."

All three men opened their mouths to speak, but I believe God closed them.

"Now how are you going to get across the street?" Doc asked.

"On my knees if I have to."

"Look, Agnes," I said. "Let's have Pastor come here. He can administer the sacraments right in the viewing room. No need to go inside the church. Church is wherever God is."

Agnes shook her head and started to turn red. "No. I need to go inside the church, into the sanctuary, and finish my business."

I swallowed hard, thinking this could kill her. "Okay, Stu, you go get Fred. Doc and me and Boris will start Agnes across the street."

Stu took off while we helped Agnes make her way to the front door. It was a tight squeeze through the entryway with her hips banging the walls with each waddling step. When Ruth opened the two front doors Agnes lit up like a birthday cake.

"Oh, my goodness," she said. "I haven't been this close to the outside in so long I forgot the beauty. Look at those mountains, Griselda. Smell that air."

We walked her onto the porch and rested. Doc listened to her chest. "Clear as a bell," he said. "They shouldn't be, but her lungs are clearer than I've heard them in years."

We all exchanged glances.

"Of course they are," Agnes said. "God knows I've got business to tend to."

The steps down were the hardest part. Three times I thought she was going to fall, but each time it was like unseen hands reached down and steadied her.

By the time we reached solid ground again, a full half hour had ticked past since Agnes started her journey. Janeen and

Hazel were walking down the street, clutching their grocery bags and yakking. They stopped when Janeen walked into a tree.

"Let's go," Agnes said.

So off we went, one wobbly step after the other. Janeen and Hazel watched. Soon Stu returned with Fred Haskell, and Dot Handy was there. Sylvia Spiney came out of her house, screamed, and then went running down the street in the opposite direction. I think she went through town like Paul Revere telling the people because within a few minutes a full-scale army had gathered. "Agnes is coming. Agnes is coming."

I heard whispers and remarks. Nothing you wouldn't expect given the circumstances. It was mass confusion. When Tohilda showed up, she asked the obvious question.

"Where's she going?" Tohilda called.

Agnes kept her eyes fixed on the church and kept putting one foot in front of the other. Her breathing was getting a little shallower, but she kept going until about three-quarters of the way there, she had to stop.

Pastor Speedwell appeared at the church door with his Bible clutched to his chest.

"She's on her way to church," Janeen blurted. "Agnes is going to church."

"Yeah," Frank said, "look at her go. I've seen tortoises at the zoo move faster."

Zeb came out from behind a tree and grabbed Frank's arm. "Stop it, you bully!"

For a second I worried Zeb might pop him in the mouth. Frank slinked away and stood next to Janeen.

"Maybe she's going to ask forgiveness for bringing Hezekiah to town," Hazel said.

Agnes signaled she was ready to take some more steps, but before we completed two, Eugene Shrapnel arrived and started slinging his hot, venomous coals at us.

"It's about time she repented. Look away all of you. Look away and be healed of this woman's influence. Turn from the devil."

Janeen stupidly turned her back, followed by her husband and several others. I felt a kind of wrath bubble up inside of me that I couldn't contain. I handed Agnes over to Doc and Ruth, while Stu and Fred worked from the front.

I stood on the church steps. The Jesus pie tin twinkled in the late afternoon sun. Jack Cooper stood near it, silently watching.

"Go home," I hollered. "Go home if you can't show respect. You're no better than you were when we were children. A bunch of bullies. You have no idea what Agnes did for you, how she dedicated her life to you—you bunch of ungrateful, selfish bullies." Some gasps and a few loud protests erupted, but they were short-lived. "When did you care for Agnes? When did you pray for her?"

Pastor touched my shoulder. "It's okay, Griselda. Help your sister."

We took Agnes into the dark church lobby. Pastor flipped on the light as Agnes started to wobble.

"She needs to sit," I said. "Where can she sit?"

Pastor grabbed Stu's elbow. "I know."

"Steady, Agnes," Doc said. "Try and stand still until they get back."

"No," Agnes said. "Can I get to the sanctuary . . . please?"

We exchanged concerned looks but walked Agnes into the sanctuary. That's when we heard a ruckus coming from the church basement steps.

"Here they come," Doc said.

"No, you have to stand it on it's end," I heard Stu say.

"I'm sorry," Pastor said. "I am not a moving man."

Doc was hesitant to leave us at first, but he went and helped them carry a regular-sized bright red sofa into the lobby.

"Look at that," Agnes huffed. "They got a couch."

The men carried it to the front of the church and set it down right behind Agnes so all she had to do was fall back. "It's Brother Jack Cooper's," Pastor said. "He takes his coffee breaks on it."

"I don't mind if Agnes sets on my couch," Jack said. "It's the least I can do. Why I'd give her the moon and the stars if it were in my power." Pastor raised his eyebrows at Jack, and he slinked away into the shadows.

Agnes fell into the grungy sofa with a tremendous thud. It buckled under the weight. "That's better," she said.

Doc listened to her chest. "Still good. A little wheezy but I'm not worried."

Pastor Speedwell crouched in front of Agnes and looked into her eyes. "Are you ready, Sister Agnes?"

"Yes."

Pastor Speedwell gathered the sacraments and led Agnes through Holy Communion. Tears flowed as she chewed and swallowed the cracker. I stood there and cried. Joy returned to her eyes as she drank the juice and made peace with her past.

"Thank you, Jesus," she said with both eyes on the large wooden cross that hung above the baptistery. "Thank you."

The sanctuary doors swung open. A wide swath of sunlight burst through as Janeen, then Zeb and Hazel and Tohilda Best walked inside, followed by Boris and Fred.

"We came to help, Agnes," they said.

Pastor Speedwell prayed a short prayer about nothing much in particular. It was like he didn't know what to say until he got near the end. "And Heavenly Father," he said. "We thank thee for thy mighty hand at work here among us this day, for lifting our dear sweet, sweet sister Agnes up out of her bed and carrying her across the street into this, thy sanctuary."

It was decided that Agnes should rest awhile right there on Jack's couch, before attempting the other half of her journey that day. The town rallied in a way I had never seen them. They brought her a lunch of pork chops, applesauce, mashed potatoes, broccoli, a large glass of chocolate milk, and Full Moon pie for dessert. Ruth even ran home and whipped up a batch of Cora Nebbish's lemon squares for her to eat at the nursing home.

After lunch Stu spoke up. "This is all fine and dandy. But we still haven't figured out how we're going to get her to Greenbrier. It's a nine-mile trip from here."

I turned to Fred. "Have you come up with a plan?" I asked.

He chewed his bottom lip and shook his head. "Nope. Nope, I can't say that I have, Griselda."

All of sudden Ruth piped up and chirped like her parakeet. "Oh! Oh! Oh, my goodness. Nate Kincaid can help us. I mean, how does he move them extra large pumpkins of his around? Don't he carry three or four of them giant pumpkins all the way to Shoops every year for the weigh-in."

"Weigh-off," Pastor Speedwell corrected.

"Don't matter," Ruth said. "Off or in he can still help, don't you think."

"That's right," Stu said, and he and Fred took off like bullets. "We'll go get Nate."

"Now how in tarnation is a pumpkin grower going to get Agnes to Greenbrier?" Doc asked.

"Well, you got to admit he's used to moving big things," Boris said. "Let's give him an opportunity."

Agnes sat quiet the whole time like she didn't have a care in the world, or more likely she knew that the Almighty already had her in his hands. We just had to provide a little support.

Several anxious minutes later Jack Cooper came running into the church. "He's here. Nate's here with his forklift."

Sure enough, there he was sitting in the driver's seat of a yellow Caterpillar forklift.

"Hey, Griselda," he called. "This baby will do the trick."

"Nate," I said. "You just aren't planning on picking her up with that thing, are you?"

"Nah, we'll need to think it through." Then he climbed down and headed into the church with the rest of us.

"Well, how do you move them pumpkins?" Boris asked.

"Simple. We just roll them onto a pallet and then raise the pallet with the fork and off we go to Shoops."

I watched Agnes turn white. "Now how in jumpin' blue heck do you expect to roll me onto a pallet, Nate? I am not a pumpkin."

Nate scratched his head.

"Can you lift her on the couch she's sitting on?" I asked.

The men all looked at each other and then wandered away a few feet to discuss the possibility.

"That I think we can do," Nate said. "'Course we'll have to strap you in there, Agnes. Wouldn't want you falling onto the street or nothing."

"Oh, my goodness gracious," Ruth said. "It sounds too dangerous. Maybe you better just go on back home, dear."

Agnes shook her head. "Nope, can't and won't do that. Now you boys think on it a minute. I'm sure you'll find a way."

"Well," Fred said. "I reckon we could make it work, but we'll have to get Agnes up first, move the couch outside, and then bring Agnes out and let her sit again. Yep, that's the only way."

Agnes heaved a huge sigh. "Oh, my, that sounds like a lot of work."

"Hold on a second," I said. "You mean you want to forklift Agnes all the way to Greenbrier?"

"Yep," Nate said. "It's how I move my pumpkins, about fifteen hundred pounds worth, and Agnes don't weigh near—"

"But she is not a pumpkin."

Nate smiled and rubbed the back of his neck. "She'll be perfectly safe once we figure a way to strap her into the couch."

Doc took another listen to Agnes's heart while the discussion continued. "You're sounding good, Agnes. Keep up the good work. We'll get you settled somehow. I called, and they're waiting for you."

"It would be a lot easier to remove that wall over there," Nate said. "Wouldn't take much. Not much more than some wood and plaster."

"You saying you want to dismantle the house of the Lord?" Pastor said. "Why that can't be right. Not right at all."

"We'll rebuild it," Stu said. "Won't take more than a day with all us working together."

"But it's the house of the Lord," Ruth said. "Don't we need to say some special prayers or anoint something before we can knock it down?"

"What are you asking, Ruth, that the Pastor here should bless our hammers and chainsaws?"

Ruth stood closer to Agnes. "I'm just asking a question. Don't go getting all twitterpated over it."

"I suppose it will be all right," Pastor said after a moment. "If the good Lord can cause the walls of Jericho to fall, then he can cause the walls of this church to crumble."

"Now don't go writing a sermon about it," Stu said. "It's just one wall. There won't be any trumpet blasts."

The next thing we knew the men were outside making a tremendous racket. The church was little more than wood and plaster, which would account for how cold it got in the winter months, so it didn't take long before they had torn a hole big enough for Agnes and the couch to fit through.

On the other side of the hole we could see pretty much everyone in town standing around with the same shocked expressions on their faces. But the men continued working and tied Agnes to the couch with a rope around her body and knotted onto the couch legs.

"That should hold her," Stu said.

Fred agreed.

Agnes said nothing.

"Are you all right?" I asked her.

She nodded, but I wasn't so sure.

That was when we heard Mildred's siren blaring. She pulled up right next to Nate's forklift and came leaping into the church.

"What in tarnation are you people doing?"

"We're moving Agnes to Greenbrier, and this is the only way to do it."

"But how?" she asked. "Are you tied to that sofa, Agnes?"

Agnes smiled and took a breath. "I sure am."

"Come on," Nate called from the forklift, "stand aside so I can lift her."

Mildred about had a heart attack when she heard that. "You're planning to forklift her all the way to Greenbrier?"

"Yep," Stu said. "Now you best be getting out of the way so Nate can manuever that machine."

"Now, I don't know about this. I'm nearly certain you need some kind of permit to be hauling a human being on a fork-lift," Mildred said.

"It's only nine miles, and I'm sure Nate will go nice and slow," I said.

"That isn't the point, Griselda. We got to abide by the law."

"To jumpin' blue heck with the law, Mildred," said Nate. "We're burning daylight. If we're going to get Agnes to the hospital, it has to be on my forklift or we're gonna have to wait until morning. And I don't think Agnes wants to sit up all night in a church with a hole in it."

Agnes looked up at Mildred. "Please, Mildred. Take the uniform off for an hour."

Mildred sighed. "Well, I better call ahead to the Smokies and let them know we'll be out on Route 113 . . . and that I'll be escorting all the way."

She went out to her cruiser and placed the radio call.

I adjusted Agnes's scarf. "You sure about this?"

I watched her eyes glisten with tears. She snuffed but couldn't reach her nose on account of being secured so tightly. A drip of moisture ran from her nostril. I wiped it off with my thumb.

"I'm sure, Griselda."

"Okay, Agnes. I love you."

"I love you, too, Griselda."

Nate powered up his Caterpillar and in he came. It didn't take long for him to maneuver the forklift so he could raise Agnes and the couch off the ground—not too high, but high enough to avoid any obstacles. I held my breath as he backed out.

Mildred stopped Nate for a minute while she attached a blinking red light to the top of the forklift. "For safety sake, you go as slow as you need to," she said. "Griselda, you can ride shotgun if you like."

"No thanks, Mildred," I said. "I'll follow behind in Old Bessie."

"I'll follow too," Doc said.

"Me too," said Stu.

Folks clambered into their cars and trucks, and before you knew it, Mildred was leading Nate and Agnes, while the rest of us followed behind like we were floats in a parade.

Just before we reached Route 113 I couldn't help but take notice of the big blue and gold sign at the town limits:

WELCOME TO BRIGHT'S POND.
HOME OF THE WORLD'S LARGEST BLUEBERRY PIE.

I will confess that my heart sank just a little bit.

32

A little less than an hour after our caravan left town, I watched Nate forklift my sister into the Greenbrier driveway—a long, straight road that led to four, single-floor brick buildings arranged in a square. He stopped at the front doors of the main building where a crowd of nurses, aides, and residents gathered for the festivities.

I parked next to Doc, and we both hurried to Agnes as Nate ever so gently lowered her and the sofa to the ground. Mildred was already clearing the crowd.

"Move along, go back to your rooms. Nothing to see here."

Many of the residents scattered, but a few hung on hoping, I'm certain, to catch a glimpse of the fat woman.

"Are you okay?" I asked my sister. Although her cheeks glistened red with sweat, and she panted for breath, I have to say there was something regal about her in that moment. She had managed to straighten herself as much as possible and held her head high.

After some discussion between Doc, me, Nate, and the hospital director, it was decided that Nate should forklift her the rest of the way through the wide double glass doors and down the hall. Agnes's room was ready and waiting.

She argued. "I can walk myself. Don't need to go riding into my new home on a blasted forklift."

"Your room is all the way at the end of the hall, and you've had a lot of excitement, Agnes," Doc said. "If Nate thinks he can carry you all the way, then I say we let him."

"You sure it's going to fit?" I asked Nate.

"Yep, let's do it."

A shaky breath escaped Agnes's lips. "You're right. I don't even have the energy to argue. Go on. Forklift me the rest of the way."

Ruth and Doc and I walked behind as residents came out of their rooms and looked on with amazed expressions. When we arrived at the end of the hall, Nate let her down nice and slow. Four male attendants immediately rushed to her side.

"Now it ain't going to take more than two of you to get me into my room," Agnes said. "Fact is, Griselda can handle it."

"That's right." I decided to chime up. "I've been leading Agnes back and forth to the bathroom for a long time. She can make it to her bed."

"Sorry," said the nurse, "policy. We can't take the chance of Agnes falling."

Agnes wobbled one step after the other into her room escorted by two attendants, one burly, one skinny. It took a bit of doing but Mutt and Jeff got her into bed. Doc had arranged ahead of time for a special reinforced hospital bed.

Her room was nice and airy with a wide window through which she could see out over the countryside. Acres of flowering trees—magnolias, tulip poplars, dogwoods, and even more maples and oaks behind them stretched clear to the mountains.

"This is a nice room," I said. "I'll bring more clothes later and your TV and radio."

Agnes smiled. "It's the right thing, isn't it, Griselda?"

"Yes, Agnes. It's the right thing."

"Bring me my prayer books. I still have to pray."

Doc listened to her chest. "You did great, Agnes. You'll be in good hands here."

"You aren't going to be my doctor anymore?"

Doc shook his head. "I can't, Agnes. But you can rest assured I will keep tabs on the Greenbrier doctors. That's for sure."

After the folks who followed in the parade all filed by to say goodbye, Ruth hugged and kissed Agnes. "I'm going to miss—oh, oh, I plum forgot," Ruth said. "I baked you these lemon squares." She pulled a tray of the tart treats from a Tupperware container she had carried the whole way.

"Thank you, Ruth. I'll enjoy them a little later."

That was when one of the starchy nurses piped up. "I'm sorry, Agnes, but those lemon squares will not be on your diet."

"Diet," Agnes said. "What diet?"

"Now Agnes," Doc said. "It's their job to keep you healthy."

"But I need my lemon squares," Agnes said. "I just have to have them and my M&Ms. You bring my jar, okay, Griselda?"

I nodded.

Doc took the nurse aside and spoke into her ear. She turned a half step and said, "Just that batch of lemon squares, Agnes. And maybe the staff can help you eat them."

"That will be fine," Agnes said. "That will be fine." Then she winked at Ruth.

I stayed with Agnes after the others left. Doc offered to give Ruth a ride home. She declined at first but then quickly saw that I needed to be alone with Agnes. I stayed through the long process that included taking an extremely unflattering picture of her with a Polaroid camera and asking about a million personal questions. Agnes weathered them like a champ. She teared up when they asked about her bathroom habits, but she made it quite clear that she could get to the toilet with a little help. She teared up again when it was suggested they find a way to get her down to the truck weigh station out on the Turnpike to get an accurate reading of her weight.

I told them that we estimated her weight to be close to seven hundred and six pounds give or take a few. Nate had used a method he had learned to approximate the weight of his largest pumpkins. It involved taking some measurements and then plugging the sums into a fancy mathematical formula. I could never quite understand it, but Nate swore by it.

After a while it was obvious the long day had taken its toll, and Agnes fell asleep while I sat with her. I didn't leave right away. I lingered a bit until I saw that her chest was rising and falling in a slow, peaceful manner. Then I kissed her cheek and headed for home.

I drove back from the Greenbrier Nursing Home that night in rain coming down so fast and so hard I could only see a few feet ahead—or it might have been the tears that were falling just as fast and furiously. I parked on top of Hector Street, got out, and looked at those purple-brown-green mountains with the tiny dots of shimmering lights that had always been so far away and so immovable. For the first time in my life I felt light, like if I lifted my heels I'd float right over the hills and keep going—straight on until morning. I think I might have even grabbed onto the bumper just to keep myself from floating away. Instead, I sailed up a silent prayer for my sister, Agnes Sparrow.

A few weeks later there was a town meeting. No one mentioned Agnes, except Eugene, but no one paid him much attention. Janeen even told him to shut up and sit down in between bites of fudge and Ruth's lemon squares.

"We have the matter of a needed sewer line," Boris said, and five minutes later a motion was passed to replace the water service down the center of town. Other miscellaneous reports and decisions were made, including a new stoplight on the corner of Hector and Filbert, Boris got the okay to repaint the town hall, and a motion was passed to honor the Society of Angelic Philanthropy with a community dinner, even though Tohilda thought that somehow contradicted the secrecy of their work.

Zeb and I sat in the back with Ruth and listened. It had been a while since they held a meeting where I didn't feel like the main attraction. At one point, I think it was right after everyone applauded the S.O.A.P., that Zeb took hold of my hand. It was sweaty, but I was so surprised and shocked and flattered I pretended not to mind. Ruth got my attention and smiled.

The meeting was about over when there was a tremendous noise outside, like a bulldozer had slammed into the flagpole. Everyone jumped up and went outside. It was Filby Pruett standing next to Nate Kincaid on his forklift. Something large, covered by a gray tarp, sat on a pallet lifted about two feet off the ground.

"No one ever told me what to do with the statue," Filby said.

I watched Boris glare at Stu, "I thought I told you to tell him to get rid of that thing."

"Me?" Stu said, "I thought you were gonna tell him."

"Felon," shouted Jasper, "you mean that rat's back in town?" Harriett reassured him.

"Well," said Filby, "nobody told me anything, but seeing how you all got so nasty over the sign, I took it upon myself and destroyed it."

My spirit sank, and Zeb put his arm around me and pulled me close.

"I plum forgot about the statue," Ruth said. "But if he destroyed it, what do you suppose is under that canvas."

"I did," Filby said. "I busted up the statue. But then I remembered something Agnes said to me." He lifted the tarp with no fanfare, no Dixieland band, no Hallelujah chorus, and uncovered a large, gray stone that read:

BRIGHT'S POND
SOLI DEO GLORIA

Dear Reader,

I hope you enjoyed your visit to Bright's Pond. Come back anytime. There's always pie. I try to get up there as often as I can and would love to come and visit with your book club or church group. We can discuss the novel, and I could tell you all the news from Bright's Pond. Believe me, there is always news. So if you would like to arrange a visit with me, either in cyberspace or in person, please feel free to contact me. And be sure to visit the Bright's Pond blog for the latest news and a recipe for Cora Nebbish's lemon squares. They're the best!

Remember: slow down, take a load off, and have a piece of pie.

Joyce Magnin
joycemagnin.blogspot.com

Discussion Questions

1. Griselda is the narrator of *The Prayers of Agnes Sparrow*. But who do you think is the main character? Is there just one? Would you call Griselda a reliable narrator?

2. Griselda says that she feels her prayers are diminished by the magnitude of Agnes's. Have you ever felt that way?

3. Hezekiah keeps saying he is in need of some powerful prayers but never tells Agnes for what exactly? Was this fair of him? What would you do?

4. In what way(s) was Agnes's attitude or treatment of Griselda inconsistent with how she treated the townsfolk? Should Griselda have told her?

5. Is the sisters' relationship a healthy one? Do you have any personal experience with a similar relationship?

6. Eugene Shrapnel claims, among other things, that Agnes is in league with the devil. He later tells Griselda that he believes God doesn't answer prayer like this. Why would he say this?

7. What's up with Mildred Blessing? What is she getting out of all of this besides a paycheck? How would you describe her pursuit of the dog?

8. Food is an overarching character throughout the book. Talk about food. What does it represent in the book and in your own life?

9. Agnes was adamant about the sign, but she eventually acquiesces to the townsfolk's wishes. Why did she give in? Was she really looking out for the town's best interest?

10. Talk about bullying. Could the Bright's Pond tragedy have been prevented? Would that have been a good thing?

11. Which character in Bright's Pond do you most relate to? Which character do you respect most?

12. Did Hezekiah get his miracle? How is God's holy justice revealed?

13. Would you like to visit Bright's Pond and have lunch and Full Moon pie at the café? Who would you talk to first?

14. Griselda often mentions her secret desire to sail over the mountains and see what's going on in the world. Why didn't she just go? Have you ever sacrificed a dream for the good of another?

Want to learn more about author
Joyce Magnin and check out other great
fiction from Abingdon Press?

Sign up for our fiction newsletter at
www.AbingdonPress.com
to read interviews with your favorite authors, find
tips for starting a reading group, and stay posted on what
new titles are on the horizon. It's the place to connect with
other fiction readers or to post a comment about this book.

Be sure to visit Joyce online!

www.joycemagnin.blogspot.com